P9-DHT-902

WARRIOR DREAMS

"Teach me some of your *vého* words," Lance said.

Suzette flushed and smiled hesitantly. "What words would you like to know?"

He raised his head and brushed his tongue against her sweet, enticing lips. *"Vitanov,"* he said.

"Tongue," she replied in a suffocated voice.

Cupping the ivory globe of her breast in his hand, he bent his head and kissed its rosy crest. *"Matan,"* he said.

She shook her head at his audacity. "Now you're just being naughty. If you're not going to take our lessons seriously, we won't continue."

He reached up and took her lovely face in his hands. "Beautiful eyes, I take our lessons more seriously than you would ever know." His voice was hoarse with an ardent, undisguised desire. "And now it's time for me to teach you how a man worships an angel that's fallen to the earth at his feet."

Other Books in
THE AVON ROMANCE Series

ANGEL OF FIRE *by Tanya Anne Crosby*
DEFIANT IMPOSTOR *by Miriam Minger*
THE HAWK AND THE HEATHER *by Robin Leigh*
MIDNIGHT RAIDER *by Shelly Thacker*
MOON DANCER *by Judith E. French*
MY CHERISHED ENEMY *by Samantha James*
PROMISE ME FOREVER *by Cara Miles*

Coming Soon

DESERT ROGUE *by Suzanne Simmons*
CHEROKEE SUNDOWN *by Genell Dellin*

And Don't Miss These
AVON ROMANTIC TREASURES

DANCE OF DECEPTION
by Suzannah Davis

FIRE ON THE WIND
by Barbara Dawson Smith

LADY LEGEND
by Deborah Camp

ONLY IN YOUR ARMS
by Lisa Kleypas

Avon Books are available at special quantity discounts for bulk
purchases for sales promotions, premiums, fund raising or educa-
tional use. Special books, or book excerpts, can also be created to
fit specific needs.

For details write or telephone the office of the Director of Special
Markets, Avon Books, Dept. FP, 1350 Avenue of the Americas,
New York, New York 10019, 1-800-238-0658.

WARRIOR DREAMS

KATHLEEN HARRINGTON

AVON BOOKS ❧ NEW YORK

If you purchased this book without a cover, you should be aware that this book is stolen property. It was reported as "unsold and destroyed" to the publisher, and neither the author nor the publisher has received any payment for this "stripped book."

WARRIOR DREAMS is an original publication of Avon Books. This work has never before appeared in book form. This work is a novel. Any similarity to actual persons or events is purely coincidental.

AVON BOOKS
A division of
The Hearst Corporation
1350 Avenue of the Americas
New York, New York 10019

Copyright © 1992 by Kathleen Harrington
Inside cover author photograph by Roy Daniels
Published by arrangement with the author
Library of Congress Catalog Card Number: 91-92433
ISBN: 0-380-76581-0

All rights reserved, which includes the right to reproduce this book or portions thereof in any form whatsoever except as provided by the U.S. Copyright Law. For information address Avon Books.

First Avon Books Printing: May 1992

AVON TRADEMARK REG. U.S. PAT. OFF. AND IN OTHER COUNTRIES, MARCA REGISTRADA, HECHO EN U.S.A.

Printed in the U.S.A.

RA 10 9 8 7 6 5 4 3 2 1

With love
to
my father and mother,
James and Frances Persinger,
who taught me
the value of hard work,
the love of history,
and the importance of having a dream

I would like to thank two people for their gracious help:

My dear friend and colleague of many years, Bernice Chin Woo, who generously shared the expertise of her master's degree in Kung Fu San Soo. She patiently explained and demonstrated techniques of hand-to-hand combat, enabling me to dispatch my villains with accuracy and realism. Thanks, Bernie!

And a special thanks to Carol Ann Duthoy, who not only had the incredible foresight to study German in school, but was also willing to share her expertise in the field of medicine. I love you, little sister.

"Why do you sigh, fair creature?" whispered he:
"Why do you think?" returned she tenderly:
"You have deserted me;—where am I now?
Not in your heart while care weighs on your brow:
No, no, you have dismissed me; and I go
From your breast houseless: ay, it must be so."
He answered, bending to her open eyes,
Where he was mirrored small in paradise,
"My silver planet, both of eve and morn!
Why will you plead yourself so sad forlorn,
While I am striving how to fill my heart
With deeper crimson, and a double smart?
How to entangle, trammel up and snare
Your soul in mine, and labyrinth you there
Like the hid scent in an unbudded rose?"

—JOHN KEATS

Chapter 1

The Tongue River Indian Reservation
Montana Territory
September 1, 1885

"**I** must have more medical supplies, Mr. Corby. If I'm to fill the role of physician here at Lame Deer, you've got to provide me with more than just a few bottles of quack pills you've ordered out of a catalog."

Undaunted by the agent's continued silence, Suzette Stanwood stepped up to his battered oak desk. She met his skeptical gaze with what she hoped was a look of absolute determination. Handing him the list of items she'd drawn up that morning, she continued. "Here's a few of the things I'll need immediately. Calomel, quinine, ipecac, paregoric, digitalis—"

The scrape of four wooden chair legs against the cabin's rough plank floor interrupted her carefully prepared speech as the stocky, baldheaded man shoved to his feet. Under duress, his receding chin sank further into his thick neck, and the walrus mustache over his pink lips seemed to quiver in agitation. "I don't *got* to provide you with nothin', Miss Stanwood. Let me remind you that I run this agency. If I say you can stay, you stay. And if I say you go, you go. Furthermore, I personally don't expect you to fill any role at all on my reservation. Why

1

the hell those loony missionaries carted you clear out here is more than I can figure. Jacob Graber must be half-batty to think a woman could ever be doctor to this bunch of ignorant savages."

"The point is, sir, that I *am* here. And I *am* a physician." Suzette took a deep breath and strove to keep her voice calm. She folded her hands behind her back to hide her agitation. "But I can't *be* a physician to these people until I have some real medical supplies."

"I'll get you some *real* medicine when I get a *real* medical budget." Corby jammed his hands into his trouser pockets in apparent exasperation. Then, just as suddenly, his voice softened as he appealed for mutual understanding between them. "Hell's bells, whoever heard of a lady doctor? I sure never did."

Suzette leaned forward and gripped the edge of his desk with both hands. "What difference does that make? From what I've seen since I've been here, these natives need someone to treat them. I can do it, I assure you. Just let me try."

"I've been letting you try for the last two weeks, Miss Stanwood." Corby picked up a brass letter opener and tapped it against his palm. His pale green eyes narrowed thoughtfully. "You're right about one thing, though. There're well over a thousand Cheyenne on this reservation, and every one of them is a potential patient. These Indians desperately need a good sawbones. Just how many have you treated in the last couple of weeks?"

Suzette felt a flush burn her cheeks. They both knew the answer to that question. Not one. Not a single person had come to the cabin she shared with Anna and Jacob Graber.

Defensive, she shrugged uncomfortably. "Naturally these unsophisticated people are suspicious of a white doctor. You can't expect them to come knocking on my cabin door, Mr. Corby. They're scattered over a six-hundred-square-mile area. How am I supposed to reach them if you don't provide me with a guide?" She tilted her chin up in defiance. "And by the way, I prefer to be addressed by my correct title. I spent too many years earning it not to insist upon that small formality."

Corby plopped back down in his chair, shook his head, and threw up his hands in a plea for cooperation. "For cripe's sake, Dr. Stanwood, I've tried to get you a guide. Not a single buck has been willing to take on the job. Seems no one, including the Indians themselves, seriously thinks a white woman can be a doctor to this tribe of veteran plains fighters. Why, these people have only been on this reservation a year."

Suzette's head slumped in defeat. Unless she had someone to take her from camp to camp, she'd never make any headway in establishing a practice among the Cheyenne. "You'll try to honor my request for the supplies, at least?" she pleaded. "No matter who fills the position as agency doctor, you're going to need the things on that list."

The agent picked up the sheet of paper, glanced at it distractedly, and set it back down. "I'll see what I can do, Dr. Stanwood. But I'm not making any promises." He rose and escorted her to the door of his office. Pausing in the open entryway, he met her gaze with candor. "I just can't help but wonder what the hell a lovely young woman like you is doing out here in the first place."

Not wanting to launch into a painful explanation, she swallowed her pride and nodded good day. Without another word, she crossed the cabin's outer room and left the building. She had no intention of admitting to Horace Corby that she often wondered exactly the same thing herself.

What was she doing here? What in the world was she doing on an Indian reservation in the middle of this godforsaken wilderness, trying to set up a practice among a tribe of primitives who didn't even have the common sense to make use of her hard-earned medical training? As she marched dejectedly across the agency compound,

Dr. Suzette Stanwood asked herself once again the question she'd posed over and over for the last two weeks.

Had she taken leave of her senses? How else could she explain her decision to accompany two Mennonite missionaries out to the untamed West?

Kicking up a cloud of dust with the pointed toes of her high-button shoes and trying to ignore the thick film that already covered the pale green underskirt of her silk afternoon dress, she hurried away from Agent Corby's office. She could feel the elegant fringed train of her bustled gown dragging in the dirt behind her, and gritted her teeth in annoyance. She didn't belong here. Good gracious, she'd known that before she came. And what was worse, her prospective patients seemed to feel the same way.

On the long, exhausting train journey across the prairies, Frau Graber had warned her that it would take time before the Indians began to trust her. And Anna should know, for she and her husband had worked on the Southern Cheyenne reservation for five years before being assigned to Lame Deer. Both of the missionaries were confident that she'd succeed as a doctor here in Montana Territory, despite the fact that she'd been a miserable failure in her home state of Pennsylvania. They seemed to feel that her mastery of the Cheyenne language, which Jacob had spent the past winter and spring teaching her, would make it possible for her to be the agency physician. But so far, that knowledge hadn't smoothed the way one bit.

Mentally Suzette calculated the sum of coins left from her journey across the country, and sighed. Not nearly enough for a return trip. And the thought of facing her sister and brother-in-law in total defeat after such a short time was unthinkable. She squared her shoulders. If she stayed—and it seemed she must—she had to have more medical supplies. And a guide. She'd spoken to Corby about it when she'd first arrived, but all he'd given her was lame excuses. Eventually he'd have to listen to her demands. She was absolutely determined to succeed as the Tongue River Reservation's first medical practitioner.

In spite of her disheartenment, she paused in her tracks, beguiled by the magnificent scenery. Glancing full circle around the vista spread before her, she sighed with reluctant admiration. Truly it was beautiful here on this vast expanse of prairie. The very sky above her seemed deeper and wider and bluer than any she'd ever seen before. The agency itself was no more than a cluster of rough log cabins set in a wide valley along Lame Deer Creek. Beyond the backdrop of grassy uplands, rocky hills were studded with western yellow pine and mountain balsam. Cottonwoods, following the creek bed, ran through a rolling plain of waving native bluestem grasses. So far, the land was untouched by the homesteader's plow. She wondered how long this unspoiled beauty would remain before the agent and his clerk succeeded in teaching the Cheyenne the rudiments of farming. In some ways she hated to think of the trappings of civilization disturbing the peaceful scene, though she knew it was necessary for the Indians' own good.

In the afternoon quiet, the shrill whistle of a driver signaling his team caught her attention. A blue Studebaker army wagon, its wheels and running gear painted black, rattled and bounced down the dirt road leading to the agency. Intrigued, she watched it enter the sleepy compound, escorted by four mounted soldiers, splendid in their dark blue tunics and sky blue trousers.

A prisoner stood on the high bed of the platform spring wagon, shackled hand and foot with ponderous chains. He was dressed in a worn buckskin breechcloth and leggings, with a frayed broadcloth shirt stretched across his massive shoulders and chest. His glossy ebony hair had been hacked off just below the ears, no doubt by a spiteful prison barber.

As she watched, the troopers dismounted, their brass epaulets and buttons winking in the bright sunshine. The sight of them in their natty uniforms brought a warm feeling of security. The presence of the heroic U.S. Cavalry always made her feel safer.

In only minutes, a dozen or more curious Indian men and women, who'd been sitting in the shade of the tipis clustered beside the creek, brushed past her, heading for the wagon and its occupant. The sergeant in charge motioned for them to keep back.

Above the crowd, the lone prisoner in the wagon watched the proceedings with apparent disinterest. Suzette drew closer in an attempt to get a better view of the man, for she could sense, even from a distance, the aura of pride and restrained ferocity that emanated from him. Head back, feet braced against the lurching stop of the vehicle, he watched without a flicker of concern as two of the soldiers drew pistols from their holsters. She felt a quiver of uneasiness at his belligerent stance. Good Lord, here was a dangerous criminal if she'd ever seen one.

"Stand back," the burly sergeant growled, facing the crowd. "Back off and give us some room."

Either the watching Cheyenne understood the command given in English, or they recognized the menace in the officer's tone, for they came no closer. The continued silence of the group was unsettling; not one Indian so much as murmured a comment. If anyone in the gathering recognized the prisoner, he didn't give the slightest indication by word or gesture. The stoical faces and steadfast demeanor of the people intimidated Suzette more than if they'd been shouting in anger. But her curiosity was high, and in spite of her timid feelings, she joined them beside the wagon.

"Who the hell've you got there, Sergeant Haskell?" Horace Corby shoved his way through the hushed onlookers. Though the thickset agent was a good head shorter than most of the men around him, he elbowed them out of his path with impatience. Trailing behind him was Obadiah Nash, the agency clerk, in his rumpled business suit. Nash was tall and thin, with a skinny neck and a protruding Adam's apple that bobbed up and down whenever he swallowed nervously. Which was exactly what he was doing now.

"Outta the way. Outta the way," he cried with smug self-importance in his high, nasal voice. "Agent Corby's comin' through."

"Got a federal prisoner here, Mr. Corby," the sergeant bawled back at the agent, not the least perturbed by the displeased man or his puffed-up clerk. "After six years in custody, he's been pardoned by the commissioner of Indian Affairs himself."

"Where's the blasted buck been all that time?" The agent looked up at the tall Indian with dismay. It was clear the last thing he wanted was a released, and possibly still dangerous, felon placed under his jurisdiction.

"The Indian Nation. After the breakout from Fort Robinson in seventy-nine, he was sent down to the Southern Cheyenne reservation to cool his heels." Haskell turned to one of the troopers standing guard and jerked his head toward the wagon. "Awright, Gatton. Get 'im down."

Private Gatton jerked on the iron chains and pulled the man, like a leashed dog, to the edge of the wagon bed. In spite of the shackles, the prisoner leaped gracefully to the ground and landed on the balls of his feet as though ready for any threat. Close up, he was as ferocious-looking as a chained grizzly, and those nearby, Indians and cavalrymen alike, took an automatic step back, allowing him a wide berth.

Unable to see what was happening, Suzette slipped through the audience that surrounded the criminal until she stood in the front row. He was taller by far than any man there. And twice as formidable, even fettered. It occurred to her that if he swung those heavy shackles, he could easily strike his captors with devastating effect. For an instant, his eyes met hers, and the ominous clank of his chains grew deathly still. The full force of his black gaze riveted her with its intensity. She expected his eyes to be cold, deadly. Instead, they were warm, almost glowing, as his glance swept from her face down to her toes and back up to meet her eyes again. Though he was the prisoner and she the innocent bystander, it was Suzette who flushed uncomfortably and looked away.

"Don't let them chains scare you," Haskell told the agent. "He's peaceable enough. I just had him shackled on the way up here to keep any civilians we met from gettin' overexcited. Lotta folks lost family to the Northern Cheyenne over the years. Even though they're on the reservation now, there's still a lot of bad blood. No sense invitin' trouble. Those irons can come off any time."

"Why didn't they just keep the buck down in the Oklahoma lands?" Corby complained peevishly. "I don't need any extra problems. I've got enough trouble on my hands as it is."

Haskell shifted the wad of tobacco in his mouth and spat in the dust. "Seems War Lance Striking's family is here. Commissioner Price wanted him returned to them. Thought that'd keep him pacified. More willin' to stay put." The sergeant scratched the gray stubble on his chin, grinned, and winked conspiratorially. "Why, once he found out he was comin' home, he didn't give us a lick of trouble."

Looking up at the prisoner in awe, Obadiah Nash chewed his gum voraciously. "Jaysus. He's a big'n, ain't he?"

Corby snorted in disgust. "We'll cut him down to size quick enough if he tries anything around here."

Suzette turned to gaze once more at the shackled warrior. Ramrod straight, square chin thrust forward, he looked down his slightly hooked nose at the crowd around him. If he understood a word that was spoken, he didn't acknowledge it by so much as a flicker of interest. As though feeling her attention upon him, he swung his gaze back to her. His large, intelligent eyes were coal black, slightly almond-shaped, and framed by thick lashes and brows. High, prominent cheekbones proclaimed his heritage, and for one frightening moment she pictured him unfettered, as wild and savage as a marauding Mongol from the steppes of Asia.

He was definitely not a cowed, defeated enemy.

Suzette didn't realize she'd unconsciously retreated until she bumped into the elderly Cheyenne standing behind her. Embarrassed, she attempted an awkward apology in the man's own tongue, stumbling over the difficult words in her nervousness. As she turned to look at the prisoner once more, she was shocked to see the ghost of a smile flicker across his lips.

Apparently noticing her for the first time, Horace Corby stepped toward her. His voice was filled with resignation. "Well, Dr. Stanwood, looks like you're going to finally get a patient after all—even if he has to be trussed up in chains and hauled to your cabin. After his release papers are checked, I want you to examine the man before he's allowed to join his family. If you find anything wrong with him—anything at all—let me know. We'll ship him right back to the Indian Territory."

Suzette stared blankly at the agent for several long seconds, then swung her attention back to the formidable prisoner. Dear God, no. Not her first patient. Not him. Her mouth went dry, and she was unable to even swallow, let alone speak. She suddenly had the craziest desire to fling herself, sobbing, into Sergeant Haskell's brawny arms and beg him to take her straight to the Custer Station. Instead she forced herself to meet the agent's questioning gaze.

"Send the man to my cabin, Mr. Corby," she said, her voice cracking in the middle of the sentence like an adolescent boy's. Her brave words were more for her own benefit than for those around her. "I'll be happy to examine him. After all, that's what I'm here for."

With her knees practically knocking together beneath her silk gown, she turned and walked down the wide path the crowd of Indians courteously opened up for her.

* * *

War Lance Striking watched her walk away in shocked surprise. A white woman here. Speaking the Cheyenne language. And a doctor to boot. Why hadn't anyone warned him? He'd almost given himself away, staring at her as though she were some vision straight from paradise. Hell, it was no goddamn wonder he'd nearly made an idiot of himself. She didn't look like any doctor he'd ever seen before. For that matter, she wasn't exactly commonplace for a female, either. Too tall for a woman, and too skinny for his standards, she had a mass of unruly red curls piled atop her head. He'd seen women more beautiful—certainly more well endowed with feminine curves, for he liked his females plump and dimpled. But those enormous violet eyes had literally stopped him in his tracks. From under a fringe of long lashes, they'd met his gaze with a look of astonishing innocence. It was like looking into the eyes of an angel. She'd appraised him with open curiosity for several heart-stopping moments before looking away, obviously shaken by what she'd seen. She was more than wary of him. She was truly frightened. As he watched the ridiculous bustle on her fancy eastern dress bob up and down in a tantalizing motion with every step she took away from him, he felt an inexplicable urge to go after her. He wanted to reassure her that she had nothing to be frightened of. That he'd never harm her. That he wasn't the uncivilized savage she took him for.

But he was. At least for now. Until he finished what he'd come to the Tongue River Reservation to do, there'd be no involvement with a woman. Especially not an educated white one. He wasn't about to give his identity away to any white eyes. Shifting the heavy manacles that encircled his wrists, he glanced over again at the agent. Unlike the lady doctor, Horace Corby was exactly what he'd been expecting: a typical government appointee who liked to collect his full pay while expending as little effort as possible to earn it. Yet he certainly didn't look like the blackhearted villain Commissioner Price had painted him out to be.

Lance hoped the scheme that had been hammered out in the East just a short time before would work. But he doubted it. As he followed Sergeant Haskell to the agent's office, dragging his shackles along like a condemned felon, he felt a foreshadowing of disaster. He never should have allowed himself to be talked into this foolhardy scheme in the first place.

Only a month ago, Lance Harden had been in Washington, D.C., about to begin a sixty-day leave from his diplomatic post. He'd presented himself at the office of the secretary of state to make his report as the chief political attaché of the U.S. legation in London. To his surprise, his superior introduced him to Hiram Price, the commissioner of Indian Affairs.

Lance had been astonished when Price proposed that he work for him as a secret agent to uncover an extensive illegal operation to swindle allotment monies from the Indians on the Northern Cheyenne reservation.

"The idea's preposterous," he told the two bureaucrats. "It'll never work." While they waited in strained silence, he rose from his chair and strode restlessly across the high-ceilinged office to look out one of the tall windows. Then he turned to face them. "What idiot came up with such a crackbrained notion anyway?"

Secretary Frelinghuysen hefted his enormous bulk from his swivel chair and braced his pudgy hands across the top of his solid desk. The heavy wheezing brought on by that slight exertion filled the room. "Now, don't get your dander up, Lance. Give Price a chance. I think the plan has merit."

Lance shook his head in disgust. He leaned his shoulder against the window frame and met with casual indifference the pair of blue-eyed stares focused on him.

"You could make it work, Mr. Harden," Hiram Price said. His bright red cheeks and high-pitched squeak told Lance exactly which one of them *had* devised such a cockamamie plan. "Mr. Frelinghuysen has allowed me to discuss this idea with you because he thinks it can work. As commissioner of Indian Affairs, I *know* it can. Of course, you're free to decline, but I wish you'd take more time to think it over before you refuse so categorically."

Lance crossed his arms over his chest and scowled. "I haven't been with the Cheyenne in twenty years. What makes you think they wouldn't give me away to the reservation agent?"

"Why should they?" Price exclaimed, jumping up in excitement. "Even though you've been away a long time, you're still one of them. They'll recognize that fact the minute they lay eyes on you."

Lance ignored the wiry little bureaucrat and turned to his own superior. "Why don't you get a man from the intelligence department, sir? Someone who's trained in espionage. I'm a diplomat, not a spy."

But Price refused to be disregarded. He hurried over to Lance and peered up at him through wire-rimmed spectacles. "We're asking you, Mr. Harden, because you're the only choice we've got. Two of my best agents have been sent out there, and both men are dead now. One accidentally drowned in a river which was all of three feet deep at the time. The other just happened to shoot himself while cleaning his rifle. I can't afford to lose any more men in 'accidents.' "

While Lance digested this information, Frelinghuysen eased around the polished oak desk, walked across the worn rug, and dropped with a soft groan onto the leather-upholstered sofa. He ran a stubby index finger slowly over the gray bristles above his upper lip and spoke with calm detachment. "It seems you're their only hope, Lance. Why wouldn't it work? You look like a goddamned full-blood. And you speak their gibberish, as well. That correct?"

Lance moved away from the window and straightened his stance, feet braced firmly apart. His clipped words came through clenched teeth. "I'm half-Cheyenne, sir, and proud of it. I lived with my father's people until I was thirteen."

Then, realizing he'd reacted with the fierce, inborn pride Frelinghuysen had hoped to provoke, Lance grinned in wry acknowledgment of his superior's successful tactics. He shrugged, shook his head in good-natured defeat, and walked over to lean against the large desk.

"I've also been out of the country for the past five years," he continued in a more subdued manner. "What I know of my father's people now is based on half-baked newspaper reports of the so-called Indian uprisings in the past few years. And those papers were months old when I read them. I'm on a well-earned leave, but when it's up, I intend to return to my work at our legation in London."

"Our minister's reports about you have been downright glowing, Lance," Frelinghuysen admitted readily. "James Lowell's expecting you back in your position as senior attaché after your leave is up, and he'll be disappointed if his chief political adviser doesn't return on schedule. But when Hiram came to me with this scheme, I thought you should be the one to make the decision. After all, the Cheyenne are your people, not mine. But if you don't want to go along with his plan, then that's the end of it."

"I won't do it because it'll never work."

"Surely you'll take some time before you decide," Hiram Price protested. "The well-being of a whole tribe of people depends upon your answer."

"It can't be that serious, Commissioner," Lance said. "Besides, I have no training in espionage. I've spent the last twelve years entertaining society matrons in the ballrooms of Britain's landed gentry, when I wasn't listening to endless political speeches in their Parliament. I'd probably get out there on the reservation and bungle the whole bloody business. Why not just recall the present agent and appoint a new one?"

"Now, don't be so modest," Frelinghuysen interrupted.

"Word of your athletic prowess in boxing and wrestling has preceded you. We do touch on more than grave international issues in our correspondence across the Atlantic, Lance."

Price paced across the office's rose-patterned rug and onto its worn hardwood floor, his spindly arms locked behind his back. He reached the door and turned to face Lance. "If what I suspect is true, Mr. Harden, there's a very clever scheme being put into effect to swindle the Cheyenne out of most of their allotment monies. In addition to the agent at Lame Deer, I believe that at least two, maybe three, other people are involved. Removing Corby would solve only a small part of the problem. I intend to catch everyone who had anything to do with the cold-blooded murder of my special agents and bring them to justice."

"I wish you luck, Mr. Price. If I thought I could actually be of help, it'd be different. But I don't think a half-breed, who not only speaks fluent English, but does so with a British accent, could successfully pass himself off as an innocent passerby who just happened to wander onto the Tongue River Indian Reservation."

The commissioner steepled his wrinkled, blue-veined hands under his chin as if in supplication. His tenor voice cracked in excitement. "That's just it, Mr. Harden! You wouldn't speak English. We'd send you out there as a newly pardoned prisoner. All you'd ever speak is the Cheyenne language. Agent Corby would only be able to talk to you through an Indian interpreter. He'd never guess who you were."

Lance eyed the diminutive man thoughtfully. He couldn't doubt Hiram Price's sincerity; it shone from his myopic eyes. He also knew the commissioner was a retired banker from Iowa, with more knowledge of debits and credits on accounting ledgers than government Indian policies. With his background, he'd be able to spot a swindle faster than most bureaucrats. But the whole idea seemed too farfetched to take seriously. Lance shook his head and sighed deeply. "I'm sorry, Mr. Price. The answer is still no."

Silence had filled the room at the finality of his decision. Without another word, the three men shook hands all round in strained politeness. As he left, Lance had tried to ignore the look of bleak disappointment in Hiram Price's bulging eyes and the dejected slump of his thin shoulders.

But in the end, Lance had agreed to the whole demented scheme. After reading a letter written months before by a complete stranger—and a Jesuit, at that—he'd suddenly discovered he'd had no other choice.

Now, as Lance Harden entered the Tongue River Agency's office, he wished the commissioner of Indian Affairs could have a taste of dragging the heavy chains along with him everywhere *he* went. Hiram Price should try the unique experience of being totally at the mercy of ignorant morons, whose goulish personal philosophy was that the only good Indian was a dead one. Then they'd see if he still thought the plan was so goddamn bloody foolproof.

Forty minutes later, Suzette heard the knocking at the door that signaled the arrival of her first agency patient. She pressed her hand to the bib of the starched white apron tied over her dress, took a deep breath, exhaled, and looked around her small office. Four rough, hand-hewn chairs stood just inside the door for her patients to sit on while they waited to be seen. One corner of the log building's front room had been partitioned off by the placement of a high screen, providing the examination area with the needed privacy. Shiny new medical instruments lay in precise rows on the oak bureau that stood against the roughly chinked outer wall. Behind a glass-front cupboard hastily borrowed from the trading post, small bottles containing bichloride of mercury, acetanilide, belladonna, and spirits of ammonia waited for her, along with cotton, splints, and rolls of homemade bandages. The familiar sight of the few precious items she'd brought with her all the way from Lancaster, Pennsylvania, reassured her.

There was no reason to be nervous. It would be a routine physical examination. Well, goodness, not exactly routine. She'd never examined an Indian before, let alone a dangerous convict. Most of her previous male patients had been derelicts with simple contusions or broken limbs, brought in off the streets around the Women's and Children's Hospital in Philadelphia for emergency treatment.

The sinister clanking of the chains accompanied the staccato stamp of riding boots as the men crossed the packed-earth floor of the dogtrot in front of her door. Like so many pioneer dwellings on the western frontier, the home she shared with the Grabers was really two buildings under a common roof, with a covered hall in the middle. The back of the hall was closed in, to provide protection against the cold Montana winters; rusty tools, including a shovel, scythe, and whipsaw, and an old wrought-iron Betty lamp, hung on the wall.

There was a quick rap, and Anna opened the office door and peeked in. The three visitors stood immediately behind her.

"Your patient is here, Dr. Fräulein," Anna Graber said. Her German accent, thicker than usual, hinted at the uneasiness she felt. In her plain, dark green dress and matching apron, with her graying hair modestly covered by her close-fitting cap, she waited at the threshold. As always, her short, stout frame was unadorned by jewels, ribbons, or even the simple buttons proscribed by her religious beliefs. Not even a wedding band graced her plump fingers.

Next to her, Sergeant Haskell and Private Gatton waited politely. Between them stood the chained prisoner.

"*Ésè-stsehnèstse,*" Suzette said to the man called War Lance Striking, forcing herself to meet his gaze. "Come in," she repeated in Cheyenne, and gestured with her hand for him to enter.

At her invitation, the Indian ducked his head to avoid bumping the top of the doorframe and came into the room. Weighing about two hundred pounds and standing approximately six feet four, he seemed to dwarf her small office. Right behind him came his guards, who remained just inside the doorway. She motioned for the Indian to follow her around the partition and into her makeshift examining room. He complied without a word, his escorts trailing along warily.

"You'll have to take your shirt off," she told him in her most competent manner as she took the stethoscope out of her apron pocket and slipped it around her neck. She'd examined dozens of patients during her years at medical school and her internship at the hospital; she wasn't going to let the fact that he was a dangerous felon throw her off stride.

"That would be difficult," Lance replied. He held up both wrists to display his manacles, and the chain swung slowly to and fro between his iron cuffs. She flinched when he lifted his hands. Her wide-set eyes were huge in her pale face. With a smooth forehead, high cheekbones, and determined little chin, she had the kind of fine bone structure that would remain an asset well into her old age. She had courage, as well, for he'd startled her with his sudden movement, yet she'd held her ground. Her own actions were tight and controlled; she fairly crackled with energy and a fierce resolution.

She turned to Haskell and switched to English. "He's going to have to be unchained, sir, so he can remove his shirt."

The sergeant nodded his agreement. "I'll take 'em off right now, miss. I told the agent they could be removed," he continued as he released the iron cuffs, "but Corby's a buzzard-head, if I ever saw one. I'm sorry now that I ever put the blasted things on the buck."

With the manacles removed, Lance flexed his fingers

and rubbed both wrists. As the shackles around his ankles were slowly pulled away, he swore to himself that he'd never willingly allow anyone to chain him again. Then he unbuttoned the faded blue shirt, slipped it off, and glanced about for a place to lay it.

Despite all her rigorous training to the contrary, Suzette stared in mute captivation, caught up by the sheer beauty of the human being before her. He had the superb body of an athlete: broad shoulders, lean hips, well-defined arms and chest. And she had the schooling in anatomy that allowed her to name each corded muscle, from the pectoralis major to the latissimus dorsi. She'd seen muscular systems as magnificent as his before—but only in the illustrations of her medical books. Until that moment, she'd assumed that such physical perfection existed exclusively in the diagrams wrought by an artist's imagination. Well, good Lord, that theory just went out the window.

He waited politely as she attempted to hide her fascination and failed completely. While her covert gaze roved over him, his black eyes glowed in unconcealed amusement. With a start, she realized that her mouth had dropped open. She shut it with a snap and immediately gathered her wits about her.

"Here, I'll take that," she said, feeling the uncomfortable heat of a blush on her cheeks. She reached for the shirt. "You can sit down on that bench, please."

When the Indian just stared at her uncomprehendingly, she realized her mistake and switched once more to his own language. She spoke loudly and slowly so that he'd be sure to understand her. "Sit down there." She pointed to the narrow examination table for emphasis. With a faint smile, he followed her instruction.

Going over to stand in front of him, Suzette continued to talk in a loud, slow manner, enunciating each word as though speaking to a deaf person. "I'm going to look in your ears first," she said. "I have to use this doctor's tool to do so, and it is important that you hold still."

"I will not move," War Lance Striking assured her. He didn't appear the least bit worried about the strange instrument she held in her hand, and even turned his head to assist her.

"Have you ever been examined by a doctor before?" she asked as she checked each ear with the otoscope.

"By a doctor, yes. Never by a woman." He had a deep, resonant voice that rumbled in his chest. For some strange reason, the rich sound of it seemed to flow directly into her heart and vibrate there like the strings of a bass viol.

"Try not to think of me as a woman," she instructed, annoyed to hear that her own voice was more high-pitched than usual. She placed her fingertips under his strong chin and ignored the heightened awareness of his masculinity brought on by the touch of his warm skin. She lifted his face. "Think of me as a doctor."

"I will try." Beneath incredibly thick lashes, his black eyes flickered up to meet her gaze, the creases at their corners deepening as he grinned mockingly. "And you can try not to think of me as a man, though I doubt you will succeed."

Chapter 2

Shocked at the shrewd insight his words displayed, Suzette glanced quickly at the waiting soldiers to discern their reaction. Sergeant Haskell and Private Gatton stood watching in obvious confusion, clearly unaware of what had been said, and astounded by the sight of a white women who actually spoke the Cheyenne language. Anna, who could have understood, had returned to the building on the other side of the dogtrot.

"That is exactly how I do think of you," she told the Indian with a scowl. She pursed her lips to warn away any further scandalous remarks. "To me you are a patient. No more. No less. You would be foolish to assume otherwise."

She examined his pupils with the ophthalmoscope. Then, placing her thumb and fingers on his neck, she felt his glands and asked him to swallow. When he did, the strong cords of his neck rippled beneath her touch. The contact of her cool skin on his warm flesh brought an instantaneous reaction, sizzling and popping like a splash of cold water thrown suddenly on a hot skillet. Dismayed by the strength of her unconscious response to him, she stubbornly resisted the urge to jerk her fingers away. She was certain he'd uncannily perceive in any such evasive movement just how much she wanted to slide her hands across his massive shoulders and explore their flawless configuration. Maddeningly, he kept his candid gaze on

20

her all the time she worked, moving from her bosom up to stare at her lips in a lingering, provocative manner.

For Lance, her nearness was as beguiling as a lover's tryst in a secluded bower. He could almost hear the trilling of larks as they nested amongst flower-festooned branches overhead. Enchanted, he inhaled the sweet fragrance of violets. She must have tucked the purple blossoms into the folds of her sparkling white apron when she'd laid it in her dresser drawer, for the scent wafted up in intoxicating drifts to tickle his nose as she moved about in front of him. Her firm, small breasts were just beneath his chin. Had he bent his head and leaned forward only a few inches, he could have rested his face between the soft, alluring mounds.

But he knew what hidden snares lay in that seductive haven. The beckoning perfume, the unspoken promise of a woman's gentle embrace, were only a chimera, like an oasis before a thirsty traveler. He could enjoy the vision from afar, but if he made the least attempt to seize it for his own, it would vanish like a mist between his outstretched fingers. Wellborn white ladies were beyond the reach of half-breeds, even educated ones like himself, let alone the illiterate full-blood he pretended to be. He wouldn't become involved with this *vèhoka*—this little white woman—no matter how inviting those enormous violet eyes might seem. He'd never again make the mistake of placing his heart in a pair of dainty hands. Still, that didn't stop him from appreciating what was displayed so enticingly before him.

"Now open your mouth and say 'ahh,' " Suzette said, determined to proceed in a professional manner. Holding his tongue down with a wooden depressor, she tried to ignore the feeling that she was engaging in something more intimate than a medical examination. It was the outrageous sparkle in his eyes that told her he was enjoying the situation immensely.

He had a full set of strong white teeth. There was definitely no sign of poor diet or mistreatment of any kind.

Nor any sign of infection or illness. War Lance Striking couldn't have been stronger or healthier or more vibrantly alive. Horace Corby wasn't going to be happy about that. Wherever this felon had been for the last six years, he'd been well taken care of.

Above both flat nipples were scars that had been purposefully carved by a knife, souvenirs from a pagan ritual that had taken place years ago. She knew, from her long discussions with the missionaries, that the skin of his breast had been slit and pierced by skewers fastened with strings. Tied by a lariat to a tall pole, he'd pulled backward until the skin had broken from the weight of his body alone. Even now, the barbaric ceremony still took place, although the white settlers had tried to show the Indians the foolishness of their benighted customs.

"May I examine your scars?" she murmured, intrigued, and ran her fingers lightly over the old wounds before he'd even responded to her question.

He tensed beneath her touch, drawing in a sudden, sharp breath. Then he slowly exhaled, as though purposely forcing himself to relax. "Reminders of the Medicine Dance," he told her with a faint smile. "A sign of my sacrifice to *Maheo*."

"Yes, I've heard about the Sun Dance," she replied. "How old were you?"

"Thirteen. I have never met a white person who spoke my language," he said, changing the subject with ease, as though he were used to being in charge of any conversation. "Have you spent a long time among my people?"

"I've only been here two weeks. I learned your tongue from a missionary couple who visited my sister's farm in the place where I am from. While I waited for her first child to be born, I spent the winter and spring evenings . . ." She stopped, searching for the correct word.

"Learning Cheyenne?" he suggested.

She flashed him a smile of thanks. "Yes, I studied with Jacob Graber and his wife. After I delivered the baby, they brought me here to Lame Deer. Jacob had been given the task of finding a doctor for the reservation by the commissioner of Indian . . ." Again she paused, at a loss for words.

"Affairs," he said. "Go on."

"You see, Mr. Price is married to a Quaker, and the Grabers are Mennonites—holy people who hold similar beliefs. Anna and Jacob spent the last five years with the Southern Cheyenne in the Indian Nation. Perhaps you met them there?"

"No," he replied, then added with irony, "but I didn't spend any time in the lodges of the holy men."

She lifted the stethoscope and placed it against the solid wall of his hairless chest. His heart boomed loud and strong in her ears. Much faster and stronger than normal, even for such a large, healthy male. Glancing up, she caught a faint smile playing about his lips, and her gaze swept up to meet his black eyes. Wordlessly he told her that it was the intimacy of her nearness that had caused the galloping race of his heart. Appalled at her failure to control her own reactions, she felt her hand tremble, revealing his effect upon her.

"You have a strong heart," she told him as she allowed the stethoscope's diaphragm to fall to her chest. She stepped back, removing herself from the magnetic pull that surrounded him like a wizard's aura.

"That is good," he replied. "A man with a strong heart has strong feelings."

"And is that true for you?"

He smiled. It was a playful, captivating smile that softened his angular face and lit up the depths of his dark eyes. "The Great Medicine's purpose in giving a man his strength was to ensure the survival of the people. Like all Cheyenne warriors, I would gladly give my life to protect the weak and helpless ones from harm."

"I didn't come to harm anyone," she protested, uncertain why she needed to say it. He hadn't accused her of anything. "I came to help your people."

"But will my people allow you to help them?"

"I don't know. Will they?"

"I think not, little white woman," he said, but there was no triumph in his words, only a detached acceptance. "Perhaps it would be best if you returned to your home, where your skills could be used."

She tried to keep the bitterness from her voice. "So you think the Cheyenne will not accept me as a doctor because I am a woman?"

"Not because you are a woman, but because you are white. We have medicine women whom we revere for their knowledge. They are admired for their skill in sewing up a warrior's wounds or making the poultice that will heal an infected cut. But we trust no white eyes, for we have known nothing but treachery and deceit from them."

"It is the Cheyenne who are treacherous and deceitful!" she exclaimed. At his look of astonishment, she bit her lower lip in self-reproach. She swung around to face the bureau and, with eyes suddenly blurred by tears, placed her stethoscope beside the other instruments. "I'm sorry," she said, bending her head in embarrassment at her outburst. Her voice shook. "I should never have said that."

"If you feel that way about us, why did you come?" His words were clipped and harsh. He'd risen from the examining bench and taken a step toward her. She could feel his presence close behind her as surely as if he'd reached out and touched her.

"Here now," Sergeant Haskell interjected. "I don't know what's goin' on, Miss Stanwood, but I sure don't like the way that big buck's actin' around ya."

Suzette turned to face the two soldiers. "My title is 'Dr. Stanwood,' Sergeant," she said in her own language with an exasperated sigh. "And I'm finished with the examination now. You may take the prisoner back to Mr. Corby's office."

She lifted her chin and met War Lance's eyes with determination. She handed him back his shirt and spoke once again in Cheyenne. "I intend to remain at Lame Deer as the agency doctor. With or without anyone's help." She swung back to the glass-front cabinet, opened it, and began rearranging its contents. "Good-bye."

As she heard the cabin door close behind them, Suzette dropped down on the bench in her office and covered her face with her hands. Good Lord, she'd really botched that up. She'd ruined her first chance to work with the Indians. What's more, the proud warrior would probably relate everything she'd said to all his friends and relatives. She crossed her arms and hugged herself to still the trembling. She hadn't meant to lose control and reveal her true feelings, but the man had unnerved her. The intense attraction she'd felt toward him could partially be explained by his stunning physical appearance. Beyond that, there was nothing about him that should have appealed to her. He was an unlettered barbarian. On top of that, he could very well be the murdering savage who had struck down her innocent fiancé.

The image of Captain Jordan Maclure, gallant officer and gentleman, rose before her. Through the years the memory of him had remained vivid and clear. He'd been a man larger than life, filled with pride and ambition, anxious to garner his share of glory in the Indian Wars of the American plains, but noble and committed to honor and duty above all. Her sister claimed that Suzette had idealized him, imparting his memory with all the romantical fantasies a young woman dreams of, and only slowly reliquishes with a wisdom of age. But Suzette knew differently. There would never be another man like Jordan. No one could ever take his place.

Wild rosebushes grew in abundance along the mountain trails and followed the coulees right out onto the open plains. They were thick that year along Rosebud Creek, where War Lance Striking's family was camped, growing in lush profusion amidst the native currants, gooseberries, and hawthorns. Along the stream bank, near a forest of cottonwood, aspen, alders, birches, and willows, the tipis were placed in the familiar horse-shoe pattern that faced the morning sun.

Lance breathed deeply, drawing in the fresh, clear air with joy as he dismounted in front of his grandmother's lodge. Up the valley of the Rosebud he could see the Wolf Mountains on the western horizon, outlined by the orange sunset. He'd camped here many years ago with his mother and father, and hunted the elk and buck deer with his half brothers, Wild Boar, Owl Crooked Beak, and Bear Scalp.

When the news of War Lance Striking's arrival had been carried to his family, Bear Scalp had raced to the agency to meet him. Together they'd galloped on his brother's horse across the high grasses and pulled up with a flourish in front of the tipi decorated with the familiar green stars and red crescent moon.

At the sound of their arrival, Prairie Grass Woman hurried from her lodge. Holding out her hands, she reached up and pulled the tall warrior to her. *"Nixa,"* she said in the soft Cheyenne way. "My grandchild," she repeated. "I prayed to the Wise One Above that you would return to us."

Lance embraced his tiny grandmother. She felt like a fragile bird in his arms. But instead of wearing a dress of finest doeskin decorated with fancy quillwork as he remembered from his childhood, she was engulfed in a white woman's gown of plaid calico that seemed much too large for her diminutive frame.

"Then you know me, *niscehem?"* he asked in joyful surprise. "After twenty years, my grandmother, you still recognize your grandson?"

She stepped back and tilted her head to look up at him. Her hair remained nearly as black as it had been the last time he'd seen her, with only a few threads of gray woven in among the long braids. "You are the very picture of your father when he was your age," she said. "Strong Wolf was as tall and handsome as you." She laughed abruptly and patted his forearm. *"Naaa!* Perhaps not quite so tall or so handsome. Still I could never mistake you." Taking his hand, she turned to the woman who had followed her from the tipi. "This is Blue Crane Flying. She is your brother's wife."

Lance returned his sister-in-law's smile of welcome. Though she was unusually thin and somber, there was an underlying beauty in her expressive brown eyes. "It is good to know that now I have a sister," he said.

A girl of around nine stood beside her. She was easily identifiable as being part white, with light brown eyes and braids the color of freshly perked coffee. From behind Blue Crane Flying, a black-haired boy of about six peeked out. He smiled shyly, his cheek pressed up against his mother's red calico skirt.

"And who are these children?" Lance asked. He squatted down on his haunches and extended both hands to them in encouragement.

Blue Crane Flying placed her palm on the girl's shoulder. "This is my daughter, Yellow Feather."

"Hello, *nàtóna,"* Lance called to her softly, addressing her as though she were his brother's own child. "Come here, my daughter." When she shyly edged toward him, he drew her tenderly into his arms.

At the attention heaped upon his older sister, the little boy bounded forward. "I am Young Wolf," he said with childish pride. "I am named after my grandfather, who was a great chief. Who are you?"

Reaching out and taking the child's hand, War Lance gently pulled him close. "I am your uncle, *nāha.* I have come home to visit you, my son."

Prairie Grass Woman laid her hand on Lance's shoulder. "We shall have a feast and let the children get to know you. And you will tell us all about the strange world of the *vèho."*

While his grandmother and Blue Crane Flying dished up a stew of venison, Lance and Bear Scalp sat crosslegged on the bearskin rugs that covered the floor of the lodge. Young Wolf came to stand beside his father's knee, but the bashful Yellow Feather stayed close to her mother, helping with the food.

"You received the letter I sent to your mother," Prairie Grass Woman said, nodding wisely as she placed the carved wooden bowl in front of him. "The Blackrobe who wrote it insisted that you would never come. He said that I was expecting too much of you. But I knew better." She beamed and then gestured imperatively, her wrinkled face glowing with pride and happiness. "Go on. Eat your food, *nixa*. Then you can tell us everything that has happened since you left us to walk the white man's road."

As Lance enjoyed the first meal he'd shared with his Cheyenne family in over twenty years, he recalled the portentous day he'd met Hiram Price and heard his fantastic proposal. Lily Harden had been waiting for Lance in his hotel room that afternoon, for mother and son had planned to dine together. When he'd told her of Price's scheme, she'd assumed that Lance would leave for Montana Territory at once.

Astounded by the total acceptance in her voice, Lance had stared at the petite, lovely white woman for a long moment before replying. "I told Price I haven't been home in the U.S. in five years. I've been looking forward to this holiday. His lunatic scheme isn't going to interfere with it." Lance shrugged and grinned at her. "The fool actually thinks I could go incognito. Guess to a *vèho*, I look exactly like a Cheyenne buck."

She reached over to him with a slight frown and touched his forearm with a beseeching gesture. "Whatever you do, *nāha*, my son, don't deny your Cheyenne heritage."

He looked at her in astonishment. "I'm not denying it, *nàkohe*," he protested, using the Cheyenne word for "my mother." I just think the idea that I can play secret agent is preposterous." He opened the door and gallantly

waved his hand. "I've heard the hotel's restaurant is excellent. Shall we dine?"

In Washington, D.C., as in cosmopolitan London,
Lance's appearance generally caused no more than an
impolite ripple of conversation, for the populace of both
cities were used to visiting diplomats. It was usually assumed that he was a representative of some exotic foreign government. They would have been flabbergasted to
learn that he was a Cheyenne warrior, and even more stupefied to know that he was their representative to the
Court of St. James.

Lance was aware of the murmurs as he and his mother
followed the maître d'hôtel. Whenever he went to a new
place, he created a stir, so he paid no attention to the
covert stares of the diners or the nervous titters of three
young ladies in the dining room. Lance and Lily were
quickly seated at a table beside a window and had already ordered their meal before she returned to their con
versation.

"If your father hadn't been killed, Lance, I would
never have come back East. I'd have stayed with him.
But Strong Wolf knew that the ways of the Plains Indians
would soon come to an end, though neither of us could
have guessed how quickly things would change out there
on the open prairie." She turned to gaze silently out the
window for a moment, then met his eyes with her worried brown ones. "They say in the papers that the buffalo
are gone. All of them. And with them, the way of life for
an entire people. In less than twenty years. Who would
ever have believed it?"

"I've managed to follow the news over the years. But
it's hard to know what to believe." He stopped for a moment to taste the wine, before nodding to the waiter to
pour it. The high-pitched squeaks of the trio of young ladies nearby continued unabated, and Lance tossed the
cork down on the white tablecloth with an abrupt gesture.

"They're silly young girls, *nāha*," Lily admonished

him, "but they mean no harm. They're just admiring you."

His bitter chuckle surprised her. "They'd have to be young and foolish to admire me, *nàkohe*. To their more sophisticated older sisters, I'm nothing but a barbarian."

Lily reached over and grabbed her son's hand. "Surely you don't believe that, Lance!"

"Why not?" he asked sardonically. "I had it from the most irreproachable source."

"What my mother said was unforgivable. But you have to understand that she was in a state of shock."

"I understand Octavia Harden's feelings about the savage little Indian boy who turned up so unexpectedly on her front porch in Alexandria. But to have screamed that you should have killed yourself before whelping me . . ." He shook his head at the memory, determined not to let the past spoil their evening. The harridan had been dead for years.

Reaching into her reticule, Lily pulled out the folded sheets of a letter. "It's from your grandmother, Prairie Grass Woman. I received it a month ago. A Jesuit missionary visiting Fort Keogh wrote it for her. Read it, *nāha.*"

He took the letter from her outstretched hand and looked at his mother in confusion. "From *niscehem?* Then she's still alive?"

"Yes, but only by a miracle. Go ahead, dearest. But be prepared. It isn't going to be pleasant."

For the next five minutes, Lance was held spellbound. The words of his paternal grandmother were set down on paper in the bold handwriting of an educated man. As he read, his jaw clenched spasmodically. The tragic story of suffering his Cheyenne family had endured in the last six years stunned him.

At the close of the letter, Lance looked up at his mother. He was unable to keep the shock and anger from his voice. "My God, I had no idea. How could my grandmother have survived the flight from the Oklahoma reservation in the wintertime? And my half brothers—dead, except for Bear Scalp. Cut down like mad dogs because they wanted to return to their own country in the north as they'd been promised they could do." He refolded the letter and handed it back to her. "Did you know what was happening at the time?"

Lily shook her head. "Oh, there were reports in all the papers that autumn about how the Northern Cheyenne had fled the Indian Territory and were running wild across three states, murdering every white person they could find. But who can ever believe the irresponsible journalists, whose only interest is selling newspapers? Until this letter came four weeks ago, I was certain I would never hear of Prairie Grass Woman again. Your grandmother is much too proud to beg for help, but if you read between the lines, my son, you know that your people are in desperate straits."

"My people? Mother, I haven't been with the Cheyenne in twenty years! I was educated in England. What do I know of their ways?"

She smiled tenderly. "For the first thirteen years of your life, Lance, the only ways you knew were your father's, the only language you spoke was his. Can you truly return to England without trying to help them? Without trying to see your grandmother and brother?"

Lance shook his head. "You know darn well I can't." He grinned at her. "But something tells me this is going to be one helluva leave."

Chapter 3

As his Cheyenne family ate their meal, Lance glanced around the tipi. The furnishings were sparse and worn. In the back, several sleeping pallets were rolled up and stored on the raised earthen bench that bordered the walls of the lodge. Only one backrest hung from the lodge poles, and that was covered with a tattered buffalo robe. The lodge lining—suspended from the poles, draped down, and turned inward to protect the occupants from any draft—was bedraggled and riddled with holes. He'd never seen his grandmother's home in such a sorry condition. His father and brothers would have been shamed had they lived to see Prairie Grass Woman abiding in such poverty.

He'd tried to keep his observations as cursory as possible; when he turned back to his grandmother, she was watching him with complete understanding in her lucid eyes.

"Much has happened since you left us, my grandchild," she said. "For many years we were able to live according to the old ways, just as when you were young. The people followed the buffalo, stole horses, fought our enemies, and counted coups. But the buffalo herds disappeared, destroyed by the white eyes. And always, more of them came. When we lived on the reservation in the south, we nearly starved to death. The soldiers had wanted us to go there for many years. They promised they would feed us just the way they fed the Arapaho, if we'd only go. But they lied, of course," she added, as though it were a foregone conclusion.

Bear Scalp laid aside his empty wooden dish, a scowl marking his high forehead. "We were forced to stand by and watch the Arapaho and Southern Cheyenne receive their beef allotments while our families went hungry. For the first time in the history of our people, our young women sold their bodies to the Long Knives for food. Like little children, we had to beg the major's permission to go on the buffalo hunt. Even though we were starving, he still refused."

"And so we fled," Blue Crane Flying added, as she put her arm around Yellow Feather and pulled the young girl to her in an unconscious gesture of protection. "We took only what we could pack on our few horses. My father and mother were both killed in the first month of travel. My two younger sisters died at Fort Robinson, hacked to death in the snow."

In sorrow and shame, Lance looked down at his own bronze hands. They were as dark as his half brother's. He knew that in appearance he could easily be mistaken for a full-blooded Indian. But his family was well aware of the white blood that flowed in his veins. How could they help but despise him for it?

"I did not know what was happening," he told them. "In the long years since I left you, I have been far away across the ocean. For many winters I lived in another country. My white grandfather sent me there when I was fourteen to protect me from the hatred of the people in his village."

"*Naaa!*" His grandmother's soft exclamation of sympathy was scarcely audible. She nodded her head in understanding as she gathered the empty dishes and stacked them aside to be cleaned. "The white eyes, like hungry timber wolves, have a deep streak of meanness in them. But Girl Lost on the Prairie told us that her father was a respected old man chief. She was certain that he would take care of you."

"Yes, he is what the *vèho* calls a judge," Lance explained. "He decides who is right and who is wrong when there are disagreements between strangers. In England, *nàkohe* and I lived with my great-uncle, who also studied the laws of the whites. There I learned to read and write my mother's language. I had many wise teachers, who taught me about the world, about all of its peoples and the stories of their past."

The lodge was quiet as each of the family members, in his or her own way, thought about what Lance had told them. The two women quietly cleaned the dishes, and Yellow Feather stored them in their spot on the earthen bench. Then, with a smile, Prairie Grass Woman sat down across from Lance and resumed the threading of a necklace of polished shells she had set aside earlier in the afternoon. Blue Crane Flying opened her sewing case of buffalo calfskin, pulled out an awl and sinew, and began working on a new deerskin shirt while her daughter sat beside her, watching with grave interest. Silently Bear Scalp motioned to his son. Young Wolf scrambled to his feet. The six-year-old, with a look of pride on his round face, lifted an intricately decorated parfleche from its storage space beside the backrest and carried it to his father, who withdrew a long ceremonial pipe. It was decorated with feathers, braided porcupine quills, and horsehair. With an ache of nostalgia, Lance recognized his father's pipe. It had belonged to his grandfather and his great-grandfather before him. Bear Scalp stamped the kinnikinick down into the red catlinite bowl, carved into the shape of a horse's head, and lit it. Then he lifted the pipe heavenward and turned it to each of the four directions in prayer. After a few short puffs, he handed the calumet to War Lance Striking.

As he smoked the familiar pipe, Lance recalled the father he had idolized as a youngster, and all that courageous man had taught him. Strong Wolf was the epitome of what a man should be: brave, trustworthy, willing to sacrifice himself for his wives and children. And he had instilled these qualities in all four of his sons, two of whom had been killed on the flight from the reservation in Indian Territory. Wild Boar and Owl Crooked Beak had been fine warriors. Their loss, as well as the loss of all the valiant men, women, and children on that nightmare journey six years before, had been disastrous for the tribe. Would the Cheyenne ever recover from the white man's purposeful, well-planned, and cunningly executed attempt to exterminate them?

Lance felt Young Wolf plop down beside him on the worn bearskin rug, and regarded the youngster with instantaneous affection. As the boy turned his face upward to watch the pipe smoke rise to the roof hole of the tipi, he slipped his small hand over his newfound uncle's arm in a gesture of trust and admiration. That unearned yet unmistakable sign of faith brought a mist to Lance's eyes, moving him more deeply than even his first glimpse of his grandmother after twenty years. A Cheyenne man did not call the male offspring of his brother "nephew," but *nāha:* my son. And from that moment, Lance knew that was how he's always think of the sturdy youngster who'd been named after Lance's own lion-hearted father. His half brother's son would take the place of the child Lance knew he must never bring into the prejudiced world of the white man.

"I've come for a reason," he said as he returned the pipe to Bear Scalp. "I was sent secretly by a man called Hiram Price, who is in charge of Indian affairs in Washington. He believes that Agent Corby is stealing what belongs to the Cheyenne. Tell all of our people that my white blood must be kept a secret. No whites should know that I can speak their language." He glanced at the three adults in turn. "Do you think this can be done?"

"No Cheyenne, man, woman, or child will give away your identity, *nis'is,*" his half brother promised. "If we have learned anything in these last ten years, it is that no white person can be trusted. The agent sent to run our reservation has not a single Cheyenne friend among us. His interpreter is a Crow who was once married to one of our people. We know that Corby drives to Miles City cattle which have grazed on our land. Since none of us can read or write the language of the white eyes, there is no way we can prove he is selling what belongs to us."

"I'm here to prove just that," Lance said. "Two special agents died on the reservation in the last year. My job is to find out who killed them. Is there any chance it might have been done by a Cheyenne?"

Cradling the pipe in his battle-scarred hands, Bear Scalp spoke without hesitation. "None of us had anything to do with the white men's deaths. I can show you where each incident took place. There were no bands camped near either spot at the time. *Eaaa!* Why would any of us want to kill the men who had come to help us? We'd already guessed that they'd been sent by the Great Father in Washington to check on Hairless Head Corby."

Lance nodded thoughtfully. "You're right. It wouldn't make any sense." With an elbow cocked on each knee, he rested his chin on his folded hands. He spoke quietly, almost to himself. "If I am going to find out who the killers are, I must be able to ride across the countryside without causing suspicion."

Bear Scalp puffed on the pipe. His eyes narrowed as he peered at Lance through the wreath of smoke. "The agent has asked for an Indian to be a guide for the white medicine woman. She needs someone to take her from one camp to the other so she doesn't get lost." He flashed a sudden, lighthearted smile. "What warrior with any pride would agree to a task fit only for young girls or old women?"

"This half-white one would," Lance retorted with a grin of his own. "I couldn't ask for a better excuse. It'll give me a reason to ride back and forth across your land, as well as carry a weapon. If Corby is selling cattle that are part of the reservation allotment, I'll discover it. But I'll have to have a horse."

"There is a herd of mustangs running wild up in the Wolf Mountains," Blue Crane Flying said excitedly. "You could catch one easily."

Prairie Grass Woman chuckled. "It's led by a great red stallion, but he won't be easy to capture. Many have gone up into the mountains and returned empty-handed."

"We could build a surround," Bear Scalp suggested. "The men in camp would be glad to help you and perhaps catch a mount or two themselves."

"All of us will go," Blue Crane Flying said. "The women can help drive the horses into the trap. It will be like the old days, when we used to hunt the buffalo. Then you can go to the white woman doctor and tell her you will take her around our land." She laughed softly, a teasing light in her dark brown eyes. It was obvious she'd seen the agency's new physician. "Since she is a female with two good eyes in her head, she won't refuse you as her guide, *nis'is.*"

Lance returned her smile, but shook his head. "That is one female I'd be wise to keep away from. I have already met her. For a white person, she speaks our language amazingly well. She is as quick and clever as a little red fox."

"She is little only beside you, War Lance Striking," his grandmother told him, looking up from the necklace she was threading. "She is taller than most women and can look down on the top of Agent Corby's hairless head."

Lance laughed at her candid description. "You are right, *niscehem.* But though she is taller than many men, she still only comes up to my chin."

"Then we shall call her 'Little Red Fox,' " Prairie Grass Woman chuckled. She leaned toward her grandson and laid the collar of smooth white shells across his knee. Her black eyes glowed with amusement at her fine joke. "It will remind us of how sly and cunning she can be, just like all the white eyes."

* * *

The agency clerk brought Suzette a message from Horace Corby the next morning, asking her to join him in his office. Obadiah Nash obligingly accompanied her across the dusty compound. As they walked, she noticed that he was limping, and questioned him about it.

"It's my sciatica," he explained with an expression of abject misery. "I oughta be in bed, but that old coot wouldn't give me the day off. Corby's got no sympathy for nobody."

"Would you like me to examine you and perhaps give you something to ease the pain?" she asked kindly.

He stopped in his tracks and stared at her. "Holy moly," he sputtered. Bright red stains spread across his thin cheeks. "I don't rightly think I'd like a female sawbones lookin' at me. No offense," he added sheepishly.

"What does Mr. Corby want to see me about?" she questioned as they resumed walking. She chose to ignore the fact that the limp had disappeared completely.

"Don't rightly know, Miss Stanwood," he mumbled, clearly unwilling to share any more information. He honked his nose on a large yellow handkerchief and shuffled his oversize feet awkwardly.

His obvious embarrassment reinforced her suspicions. She was going to be scolded about the minor contretemps between herself and the Cheyenne prisoner the previous day. She entered the office with her head up and her shoulders back, prepared for an uncomfortable lecture. Expecting to find the agent alone, she stopped short. The bald-headed man was standing in the middle of the room beside the very Indian she had hoped she'd never see again.

He met her glance without a trace of shame, as though she'd never seen him chained like a common felon. There was even a hint of arrogance about him, though he was still dressed in the same decrepit buckskin breechcloth and leggings he'd worn the day before. Instead of yesterday's tattered shirt, however, he was now wearing only a primitive choker of polished shells above his naked chest. An immense hunting knife was strapped to his muscled thigh by a leather string. Goodness, how anyone could be dressed in such a barbaric costume and still radiate the self-confidence of a visiting diplomat was beyond her.

"You wanted to see me?" she asked Corby, moving her gaze away from the indecent display of masculine flesh and over to the agent with a monumental effort. She had no intention of allowing the Indian to see how much he frightened—or fascinated—her.

Horace Corby jerked his thumb toward the man beside him, his words brief and to the point. "You said you needed someone to escort you around the Indian camps. Here he is."

The agent had caught her by complete surprise, and she was unable to hide her horror at his proposal. "Surely you must be joking! This criminal arrived here in shackles only yesterday."

A smile of satisfaction glittered under Corby's huge mustache. "Well now, Miss Stanwood, seems this *pardoned* prisoner's the only one who's offered to take the job. After waiting two weeks without any other response to my offer, I'd say he's probably gonna be the only one who ever will. And I'm not about to let you go traipsing around this reservation without a guide. You'd get lost the first day out and never find your way back to Lame Deer. I'd have a hard time explaining the disappearance of the agency doc to the pencil pushers in Washington."

"I can't believe you're actually proposing that I use this released felon as my guide, Mr. Corby. The idea's too harebrained."

The expression of complacency left Corby's face. "Not any more harebrained than a woman wanting to be a doctor to a bunch of wild Indians, and them well known for their total unpredictability," he told her. "I keep trying to tell you, Miss Stanwood, only a few years ago these savages were on the warpath, rampaging up and down the country, butchering anyone who got in their way."

During this time, the Cheyenne brave waited motionless in the center of the room, staring off into space while they talked. It was obvious from his blank expression that he didn't comprehend a word of their conversation. For several minutes Suzette stood speechless, rooted to her spot on the floor in front of the two waiting men. She realized, with dismay, that the agent's proposition was in earnest. Touching her forehead with a shaky hand, she walked over to his desk and leaned against it for support, staring with unseeing eyes at the paperwork stacked in haphazard piles on its cluttered top. The thought of being in the large warrior's company for days on end was horrifying. It was just such a man who'd killed and mutilated Jordan. She was certain of it. Out on the plains, she'd be at the brute's mercy if he ever turned on her. And in the past ten years the eastern newspapers had hinted in ghoulish innuendoes at the unspeakable atrocities perpetrated on innocent white women by redskinned devils like him.

Corby's tone was one of pure triumph. "Surely you're not going to refuse the buck the job, Dr. Stanwood?"

She realized with a sickening jolt that there was nothing the agent would rather have her do. In fact, from the very beginning, he'd fully expected her to reject the whole idea. She turned to face him, searching for some logical, irrefutable reason for denying employment to this particular Cheyenne brave.

"I . . . I don't know, Mr. Corby. When I asked for a guide, I was thinking of an older person, more like a grandfatherly type. Someone whom I could trust. Does this creature speak any English?"

"Not a word."

From the corner of her eye, Suzette thought she saw the warrior tense, the muscles in his biceps bulging as he clenched two large fists. But when she turned her head to look at him, he was completely relaxed, oblivious of their candid talk. It was impossible that he'd been offended by their remarks, for he hadn't understood a bit of it.

"Perhaps during his years in custody, he picked up some basic phrases," she suggested, stalling for time to come up with a better reason. She couldn't just reject the man outright; she needed a valid excuse to press the agent to continue searching for a more suitable escort. "A couple of the Indians I've met know a little of our language."

"This one doesn't," Corby replied, looking up at the tall, powerful man beside him. The agent cocked his head toward the brave and mugged derisively. "You know the kind. Big and dumb."

Suspiciously Suzette eyed the silent giant. The memory of the intelligence that had sparked in those haunting black eyes, now so cautiously averted, sent a tremor of uneasiness through her. "He doesn't look all that backward to me," she said. "Why would he want to take on this job? Doesn't he have better ways to earn a living?"

"The only work these bucks want to do is steal horses and raid the camps of other Indian tribes. Now that they're not allowed to do that anymore, they just loaf around. They're coffee coolers, lazy by nature. But there's no need to be nervous. The Cheyenne haven't gone on the warpath for quite a while. Once you get them on the reservation, they quiet down real good. Why, it's probably been ten years since this one's lifted the scalp of a helpless female captive." Corby shoved his hands in his pants pockets and grinned at her in sadistic glee. "Don't worry. He'll follow you around like a trained bear on a leash."

Suzette gave a soft, unladylike snort and headed for the door. "I'd have to get a collar on him first."

It was all Lance could do not to swing his gaze back to the infuriating female. He'd never imagined she'd refuse him the job.

She was wearing a yellow satin morning dress draped

up to show a lining of brown and green plaid, with a matching tartan shawl pleated across one shoulder. An oversize plaid bow perched coquettishly on top of her bustle. The ensemble was entirely unsuited for the open country, and absolutely breathtaking. Earlier that morning, her hair had been pulled ruthlessly into a severe chignon, but wispy tendrils had escaped to float enticingly about her temples and the nape of her neck. He wondered what that mass of coppery locks would look like falling freely over her shoulders and down her back. They'd probably reach her waist in a tangle of wild, undisciplined curls.

God, her hair would be beautiful.

It was all he could do to stand there and listen in silence while she dismissed him like some ignorant caveman. He longed to yank her back across the room and give her a sound spanking. After first removing the flirtatious bustle. That would wipe the smug look off her angelic face and put a little fear in those incredible violet eyes. Maybe a little fear of him wouldn't be such a bad thing, after all.

"Well, you wanted an Indian scout to guide you," Corby said with measured disinterest. "Too bad you don't like him." He moved around his desk, sank down on the chair, and propped his intricately scrolled snakeskin boots with their two-inch heels on the desktop. Folding his hands on his ample belly, he continued. "I guess you'll just have to stay within the protection of the agency, Miss Stanwood, and hope the Indians will come to you."

"I didn't say I wouldn't use him." The words were out of her mouth before she'd had time to think. Turning to War Lance Striking, she gulped in a draft of air and spoke in Cheyenne. "Would you like the job of guiding me about the reservation?"

At last he turned to meet her gaze once more. For some strange reason, the coal black eyes seemed to smolder with a barely contained anger. His voice was tight and controlled. "I will make you a fine guide, *vèhoka.*"

Knowing he called her "little white woman," she scowled at him. She had no intention of letting the natives become too familiar. This one, more than anyone else, would have to be kept at a formal distance. She was determined to set the tone of their relationship from the very beginning. "You will address me as 'Dr. Stanwood,' " she snapped, emphasizing the word *doctor.* "And if you work for me, I won't have any impudence from you. Do you understand?"

At her sharp retort, the anger faded from his dark gaze, only to be replaced with mocking derision. Like a tutor with an especially precocious young scholar, he bestowed a dazzling smile of encouragement upon her. "You speak our language beautifully, *náevehoka,*" he said in a patronizing tone. "I understand every word."

Little white woman doctor. The insolent way he'd purred the term at her, rumbling low like a mountain cat about to pounce, made her furious. She longed to withdraw her offer of employment just for the pleasure of watching the cocksure brashness disappear from the wily devil's handsome face. Swallowing her indignation, she clenched her teeth to keep the words from bursting forth.

She needed him.

And somehow, he knew it.

Seeing War Lance's triumphant grin, Corby swung his short legs to the floor and stood in front of his chair. "Well, now, it appears you've got it all settled between you." He looked back and forth at them, unable to hide the consternation in his pale green eyes. She suspected that his next words couldn't have been further from what he really meant. "I'm sure you two will get along just fine."

They left Corby's office together. Side by side, the contentious pair walked across the agency quadrangle toward Suzette's cabin. Lance refused to shorten his long strides to match hers, forcing her to hurry along in her

high-heeled satin shoes as best she could. He didn't
know which of the two he was angriest at: the woman,
with her open dislike for Indians in general and himself
in particular, or the agent, with his sneaky, underhanded
ways. When she'd finally accepted Lance as her guide,
Corby had almost lost his nerve and withdrawn the offer.
If the idiot had had false teeth, he'd have lost them, the
way his mouth flapped open and shut in stupefaction.
Lance wanted to knock the crooked teeth right down the
cretin's throat for the smart remark about his being big
and dumb.

What Lance would like to do to the lady doctor was
something else altogether. She skipped along beside him
like a high-strung filly, all long legs and enormous, velvet eyes. She was afraid of him. He sensed it. Irration-
ally, he felt his wrath dissipate, replaced by the need that
returned each time he recalled the touch of her soft fingertips on his bare chest. He longed to catch her in his
arms and hold her still while he ran his hands over her
trembling limbs, just the way he'd quiet a wild young
mustang. He'd gentle her easy, bringing her along slowly
and patiently, till she trusted him enough to eat out of his
hand. Then he'd nuzzle her softly and gently nip at the
satiny white skin at the nape of her neck.

"I'll be ready to go to the first Indian camp tomorrow
morning," Suzette said in her most businesslike manner
as they reached the small corral near her cabin. "I'd like
to get started early. You can take me in that wagon over
there. Mr. Corby has given me permission to use it on
my rounds."

She pointed to a dilapidated spring wagon alongside
the rail fence. Its green paint was flaked and chipped,
with the words *Moline Wagon Company* barely recogniz-
able on its side. The two-passenger seat slanted at a haphazard angle, indicating at least one broken spring.

Lance looked down at the provocative young woman
in her yellow satin gown, with its modish train dragging
in the dust behind her, and resolutely set aside his lustful

fancies. A logical reason for her presence still eluded him. Why would a lovely, well-educated, and gently bred white woman come to the frontier alone? Though he intended to solve the puzzle eventually, he was determined to keep a better handle on his thoughts. There was going to be absolutely nothing between them except a boss-and-hired-hand relationship. He'd see to it.

At his silence, she pleated her tartan shawl with restless fingers. "We will be able to start tomorrow morning, won't we?"

"I am afraid not, little white woman doctor," he said. "I don't know how to drive a wagon. We will have to ride horses."

He walked over to the corral, where two weary mules stood side by side with their heads hanging over the top railing. He'd had to move away from the spell of those enchanting violet eyes at that last shameless whopper. In England he was known in the best racing circles for his uncanny ability to handle a coach and four at breakneck speed. But it would be highly unusual for a Cheyenne Indian to be competent at it.

Startled, she quickly moved up beside him and gripped the top rail. "We can't, War Lance. I've never learned to ride very well. And all I've got are these two old mules. Besides, Jacob Graber will be happy to show you how to drive a team."

Lance grinned at her. "I'll teach you how to ride like the wind, *hoze zeheszemēnsz.*"

Suzette looked up at the warrior in confusion, for he'd used a term she was unfamiliar with. As she translated it to herself, she frowned suspiciously. "Feathered servant?" she wondered out loud.

"Yes," he told her. "The Wise One Above's feathered servant."

Then the light dawned. "Oh, you mean *angel!*" She said the last word in English with a laugh, delighted that she'd solved the riddle.

46   KATHLEEN HARRINGTON

"Angel," he repeated softly in her language, and the humor in his black eyes fairly sparkled.

"Oh, no! You can't call me that," she warned him, shaking her finger at him like an old maiden aunt. "You pronounced it perfectly, but you can't use that term with me. It's against our . . . our . . ." She sputtered to a stop as she searched for the correct Cheyenne word.

"White arrogance?" he suggested.

"Customs!"

"It's not against mine," he replied with an air of dismissal, as though the strange rules of the *vèho* were not only beyond his understanding but completely unimportant to boot. "I cannot take you to the first camp tomorrow. I will not be ready to begin the job for another week."

It was the second time he'd abruptly changed the subject with her, and she found it irritating. Goodness gracious, she was the one in charge. She had no intention of allowing him to seize control of the situation; she could be as obstinate as any hardheaded Indian. "I want to start tomorrow morning. And since I'm the one who's doing the hiring, you had better plan on doing just that."

"Not tomorrow, angel. I will be gone for a week. When I return, I will take you around the reservation." He turned and started to walk away as though the matter were settled.

"Wait a minute," she called, following after him. "The money for your wages will come out of my salary. And you won't begin earning your pay until the first day you act as my guide."

He turned at that, and the mocking grin was back. "Very well, *náevehoka*, I will wait for my pay. I wouldn't want to cheat you out of any of your government dollars."

She'd been certain he'd change his mind and agree to start immediately. After all, he'd just got out of prison. He should be desperate for money.

Instead he sauntered off, apparently without a care in

the world, leaving her with only two choices. Either she could chase after him, in what she suspected would be a totally useless—and probably mortifying—endeavor, or accept the fact that she wouldn't have a guide for seven more days. She had no intention of giving him the satisfaction of refusing to follow her orders a second time. Anyone thickheaded enough to have the first term he learned in English be a completely unacceptable one, and then have the stubbornness to continue using it despite her warning, could only be expected to be as contrary as a braying jackass.

Exasperated, she whirled about and stalked back to the corral railing. Leaning her elbows on the top bar, she gazed in frustration at the two ancient mules and decided Horace Corby was right after all.

The tall Indian *was* big and dumb and lazy.

Chapter 4

"Goodness, Anna, you're a wonderful cook," Suzette called from her spot at the kitchen table. On her lap rested a dishpan piled high with wild plums. As she sliced and pitted the ripe fruit, then tossed it into a large crockery bowl with purple-stained fingers, she smiled at the middle-aged housewife and sniffed dramatically. "Mmmm, but it's heavenly in here."

The room was filled with wonderful smells. On the back of the cast-iron stove, shiny with the many vigorous polishings it had received in the short time since they'd arrived, bread was rising. On the front burner, Anna was cooking down the first huge kettle of plum preserves.

"*Ja,* you tell me that every morning when I fix you breakfast, Dr. Fräulein, and every evening when I feed you supper." Anna popped more wood into the stove and stirred the bubbling plums. "I think you're just lonesome for your mama's cooking."

Suzette shook her head sadly. "It's been so many years since I tasted my mother's cooking, I can hardly remember it, Anna."

"*Ja, ja,* I know, *Liebchen,*" the plump woman said. In her sympathy, the German accent was more pronounced than usual. It was clear she regretted her words, recalling too late that Suzette had lost her mother when she was only fifteen. Anna left the stove and walked over to the kitchen's heavy stone sink with its bright red pump.

48

Propping her hands on her broad hips, she leaned across the sink counter and pressed her nose to the glass. "Now, where do you suppose that Indian guide of yours is?"

"I wish I knew," Suzette answered with a long, drawn-out sigh.

It had been a full week since she'd last seen her erstwhile scout. Early that morning she'd come to the hopeful conclusion that War Lance Striking might not show up at all.

"Mail's come," Jacob Graber called from the front door as he waved several envelopes high in one hand.

He strode into the open-beamed room, which ran across the front half of the log building and served as parlor and kitchen combined. On the west wall stood a large fireplace to keep the sitting area warm in cold weather; on the opposite side was the cooking stove and sink with the marvelous luxury of an inside pump. That meant that in the bitter Montana winter there could always be a large copper kettle full of hot water waiting on the stove. An old hunting gun rested on its rack above the doorway.

Anna pulled back from her spot of vigilance over the sink and smiled in delight. "Oh, Papa! Letters, at last." She hurried across the room to join her husband. Although the mail was brought on horseback from Birney once a week, it was the first correspondence any of them had received since arriving at Lame Deer.

Standing side by side, the two missionaries were perfect examples of their immigrant background. German-speaking Switzers of hardy farmer stock, Anna was just over five feet, Jacob only a few inches taller. Though the hausfrau was nearly as broad as she was tall, her husband was slightly built. Cleanly shaven around the mouth, with smooth cheeks as well, he wore the heavy fringe of beard along the jawline that was common among the older, more conservative members of his religion. From the cheerful couple's broad faces, two pairs of twinkling

blue eyes shone with a serenity seldom seen outside a
Mennonite community.

"One for you, Mama," Jacob said, handing her an envelope. "From your brother, Jonath." He beamed kind-
heartedly at Suzette. "And one for Dr. Fräulein."

Suzette set the basin of plums on the table, wiped her
stained hands on a wet dishcloth, and took the letter. "It's
from Paulie," she said in excitement as she rose to her
feet. "If you don't mind, I think I'll take it down by the
creek and read it there. I haven't been out of the house
all day."

"*Ja,* go, go," Anna said with a happy smile. She
plopped down in a kitchen chair, pulled out the little pair
of reading glasses she always carried in her apron
pocket, and waved her own mail at Suzette. "I will read
my brother's letter to Papa. Then we can share each other's news when you come back."

In minutes Suzette was seated in the autumn grass beside Lame Deer Creek, under the dappled shade of a
large birch tree. Her fingers trembled as she opened her
sister's letter. She read with relief that the baby girl she'd
delivered in June was healthy and thriving, as were the
Kaufmans' crops, bountiful as a result of excellent summer weather. Joyfully Suzette flung herself back on the
soft ground. She held the missive clutched against her
chest, and gazing in relief and happiness at the bright
blue sky above her, recalled the events that had surrounded the difficult birth of her niece.

Suzette had stayed at her sister and brother-in-law's
Lancaster County farm in the heart of Amish country
during the long months of Pauline's pregnancy. There she
had met Christian Kaufman's missionary cousins and
studied the Cheyenne language with Jacob Graber. On
the day of the birth, the agonizing labor consumed thirty
hours, then forty, as the mother-to-be grew more and
more exhausted. With Anna Graber releasing the chloroform drop by drop just as she'd been instructed to do,

Suzette used forceps to ease the birth. But the little girl she delivered was waxen and limp and silent.

Dropping into an old rocker, Suzette laid the baby on her lap and pressed her mouth against its tiny one. For endless minutes she gently sucked out the air and blew her own breath into the feeble lungs.

"Forget the child. It's already dead," Christian Kaufman shouted in terror as she worked over the still form. "Take care of your sister. It's her we need to save!"

"Wait," Suzette cried. Under her fingers she felt a faint, fluttering heartbeat. With a twitch of the tiny tongue, the baby gasped for air. Suzette continued to work over the little girl as she took another breath, and then another, till the waxy hue slowly changed to a rosy pink.

Despite the tears glistening in his eyes, Christian grinned like a love-struck bridegroom. "Thank you, Dr. Stanwood," he said.

In that simple statement Suzette heard the recognition of her as a physician that her brother-in-law had withheld until that moment.

She had always felt that her young sister was too good for the serious, unsophisticated Mennonite; she'd been gravely disappointed that Pauline had chosen the simple life of a farmer's wife. Her hope that Paulie would go on to a higher education, perhaps even follow in her own footsteps to study medicine, had been destroyed by a man who could do no more than read his worn Bible and calculate practical arithmetic problems. Suzette had realized, months ago, why Christian encouraged her to follow the Grabers across the continent. On the Tongue River Reservation, she'd be safely out of his hair and away from his young, impressionable bride. Though there had been a wall of misunderstanding and prejudice between them, in the end their common love for Pauline bound them together.

With the birth of her niece, Suzette also knew that practicing medicine was her whole life. It was what she was meant to do. More than anything, she wanted to be a doctor.

Lying now in the thick Montana grass, Suzette rolled over on her stomach and reread the cherished letter once again. She ignored the tears of homesickness that plopped in helter-skelter splotches on the pages. At last, with a sigh, she folded the letter, only to notice for the first time a postscript scribbled on the back of the last sheet.

You remember, Suzie, that I told you I believed there was a higher reason for fate to take you to the very people who killed your fiancé and so irrevocably altered the course of your life. I still believe this is so.

Unlike you, I never regarded Jordan Maclure as a swashbuckling military hero, but rather a mercenary who lived and died by the sword. My dearest sister, I don't tell you this to cause you more pain. You've suffered enough already. My hope is that, there on the reservation, you may gain a new insight into the terrible tragedy that nearly destroyed your will to live. I pray that someday you will come to ask the forgiveness of the Cheyenne people.

Suzette clutched the folded letter in one hand and buried her face in her arms. Shocked and hurt by Pauline's words, she fought back the sobs. It wasn't she who needed to ask for forgiveness. Her life had been nearly destroyed by these benighted heathens.

She'd been a starry-eyed young woman of seventeen when Jordan Maclure had come into her father's Lancaster pharmacy on an errand for his mother. In his dark blue and gold uniform, with a long saber belted over an orange sash swinging at his side, the blond cavalry officer was the most astonishingly handsome man she'd ever seen. Urbane, witty, and outrageously bold, he'd enchanted her from the moment they met. Like a child fascinated with a glorious, brightly colored butterfly, she'd followed his every movement. What he saw in a Pennsylvania shopkeeper's serious, redheaded daughter, too tall and skinny ever to be considered pretty, she didn't even try to understand. Jordan courted her with flowers and poetry and pretty speeches of undying devotion. She fell head over heels in love with him. The four short weeks of his leave from the army flew by, and in the last few days of it, they became engaged.

Suzette rested her head on her folded arms and smiled to herself as she recalled their heedless impetuosity in those long-ago, golden days. They'd wanted to marry immediately, before Jordan left for his tour of duty out West. It'd been only at the adamant insistence of her father that she'd finally agreed to postpone the marriage until Jordan returned. For until Pauline was older, Suzette knew she must stay and help their father. It had been a heart-wrenching farewell for the betrothed pair on that last day.

In the years that followed, she came to bitterly regret her decision to wait. For when, at last, Jordan returned to Lancaster, Pennsylvania, there'd been no joyous wedding, but a somber memorial service for a fallen hero. He'd been slain, with over two hundred comrades, by the Sioux and Cheyenne Indians at the Battle of the Little Big Horn. In the long, lonely years that followed, no man had come close to measuring up to Captain Jordan Maclure. She'd had many male friends during her years of medical training—all bookish, soft-spoken students like herself, or older, scholarly professors who peered at her fondly over the tops of their round, wire-framed spectacles. But how her heart had ached for that gallant swain who'd swept into her life for such a brief time, only to leave her alone and despondent, with the certainty that no man alive could ever take his place.

With Jordan's death, she'd lost the best, the bravest, the most honorable of men. He should have been her husband and the father of her children. Instead she was a twenty-eight-year-old spinster with nothing more to hold in her hands than a sheet of parchment with a medical degree spelled out in Latin. And that certificate was nearly useless, for no one, white or red, accepted her as a qualified physician.

Suzette swallowed back tears and propped herself up on her elbows. Despite her bitter feelings, she'd been forced to accept the position at the reservation. For only here would she have the opportunity to build an independent medical practice. She inhaled the fresh smell of virgin earth, bluestem grass, and prairie primrose in one deep draft, as though she could willingly breathe into her lungs the untamed ferocity of the land on which she sprawled. With the unswerving determination characteristic of her since early childhood, she would set aside her bitterness and live up to the words of her Hippocratic oath. Here she was, and here she would stay.

"I thought you wanted to ride to the first Cheyenne camp today, *náevehoka*," a deep baritone rumbled above her.

Startled, she rolled over on her side and propped herself up on one elbow. Silhouetted against the limitless Montana sky was the outline of an Indian warrior towering over her. She recognized those broad shoulders and powerful arms. It was War Lance Striking.

"I did. I do! But I thought you couldn't drive a team and wagon."

Scrambling to her feet, she hastily wiped away the tears. She shaded her eyes with one hand and shifted her position to reduce the sun's glare behind him. He'd fastened two white eagle feathers in his thick ebony hair, and the contrast of downy softness against dark sheen was startling and beautiful.

"We will not be going in the wagon, angel." He took a step closer and lifted his large hand, as though to touch a curl at her temple that had broken free from the combs she'd fastened in her chignon.

Instinctively she ducked her head and moved backward toward the sheltering birch tree.

Her reaction etched the deep crease of a scowl between his straight, black brows. When he spoke again, she suspected he was forcing himself to be coolly polite. "Come back to the cabin with me. I have a gift for you."

"For me?" She couldn't keep the astonishment from her voice. "Why would you bring me a present? And don't call me 'angel.' What is it?"

A smile played around his mouth at her open curiosity, but his voice was solemn. He turned and started back for the agency compound, calling his answer over his shoulder. "I brought you something you will need if you are going to be the agent's medicine woman."

"I'm not that agent's *anything*," she corrected as she bounded after him.

"You were crying," he said in his abrupt way, the minute she'd caught up with him. Goodness, it seemed he never stayed on one topic for long.

"No, I wasn't," she lied. "A bug flew in my eye and it was watering." She vigorously rubbed one eyelid for effect.

He wasn't the least impressed by her histrionics. "It was watering all over the paper," he pointed out with a matter-of-fact gruffness. "The lines and circles on it were running across the page like a storm across the prairie."

"Just how long were you standing there?" she demanded. "I didn't even hear you come up."

"You were too busy crying."

She ignored his candid refusal to believe her little white lie, then halted in surprise. They had rounded the corner of her cabin, and there, tied to the corral railing, was a roan stallion and a painted mare.

Lance watched Suzette from the corner of his eye, hoping she would be pleased with his choice, especially after having found her with her head buried in her arms and the letter clutched in her fist. The sight of her crying had stirred a chord of tenderness deep within him—a feeling never brought on before by a woman's tears.

These tears, he knew, were caused by an aching loneliness for the loved ones she'd left behind in the East.

He'd known the anguish of homesickness when he was thirteen, a pain so deep, it had seemed to carve out a hollow spot in the center of his heart. He'd longed to return to his Indian family, to hunt the buffalo and pronghorn deer, to look up into a star-filled night sky uncluttered by smokestacks and clouds of soot. The yearning to live, once more free and unfettered, among a people who knew that the earth, the streams, the rocks, the trees, and the animals were all sacred haunted him long after he'd mastered the language and customs of the so-called civilized white man.

The estrangement he'd felt as an adolescent still manifested itself in his frequent need to withdraw from society and be alone in the natural world. He was never so happy as when he was out in the woods, hunting or fishing. In London his British friends would complain that, even in a crowded room, he frequently seemed distant and unapproachable. Teasing him for being moody and remote, they made no attempt to understand that some part of him would always be an outsider. It was no wonder that, seeing Suzette's desolation, he'd forgotten his resolution and almost touched her.

With the help of his family's band, Lance had succeeded in trapping the entire wild herd of mustangs in a box canyon nearly a week before. The great red stallion was a giant of a horse, glistening like flame in the morning sunlight, with a darker red mane and tail. He was, no doubt, the offspring of some runaway Thoroughbred, for he had a fine, delicate head with a dished profile, long, slender neck, sloping shoulders, broad chest, and strong legs and knees. He was all muscle, power, and grace.

The piebald mare had been picked for her combination of perfect symmetry and gentle nature. She was white with great splashes of black; her heavy black mane flowed down below her neck, and the black tail nearly dragged on the ground. Lance knew that, in time, she would make a perfect mount for a nervous, unskilled rider. The mare stamped her hoofs and nickered a welcome as they approached.

"The agency must have visitors," Suzette said in awe. She seemed unable to take her eyes away from the unfamiliar stud as she walked slowly toward the fence. "Did you ever see such a magnificent animal?"

"He is beautiful," Lance conceded. "But his manners could be improved."

"Why do you say that?" she demanded in puzzlement as they came up beside the horses. "He's just standing there."

"What about the painted mustang?" he asked her, feeling a flicker of disappointment that she'd not even mentioned the mare he'd worked so hard to gentle for her. He'd put his own mount in Bear Scalp's care while he worked on hers, and the stallion wasn't, as yet, completely broken. "She's a pretty little horse. I thought you would like her."

Suzette's violet eyes glowed with appreciation as she turned to the mare. She patted its velvety nose. "Oh, she's a living doll."

"I am glad that the gift pleases you," he said, astonished at the intense satisfaction her delight brought him.

Confused, Suzette looked from him to the painted mustang and back again. "This is my gift? You're giving me this pony?"

"How else will you be able to ride to my family's camp?" He stepped up to the mare and stroked her silky neck. "I have worked with her all week. She will make you a fine mount, spirited but gentle."

"I don't ride very well," she warned him. "I haven't been on a horse since I was sixteen."

"So long ago," he said. "This will be more difficult than I thought."

"I won't fall off or anything," she assured him, anxious that he not change his mind and switch the mare for another mount. "We'll just have to take it slow and easy."

He'd been looking at the piebald mare. At Suzette's words, he turned toward her. The light of merriment in his dark eyes was dazzling.

"That is always the best way," he said. His even white teeth flashed in a wry grin.

She returned the smile, suddenly self-conscious as she followed his train of thought. "Thank you for the horse, War Lance Striking. Now, why don't you come into the cabin and meet the Grabers. You can talk to them while I change into my riding clothes."

Lance followed her toward the two log buildings joined by the common roof, enjoying the way she moved with unconscious grace. Her walk was nearly as light and fluid as an Indian girl's.

"Have you been in a white person's home often?" she questioned. She led him through the dogtrot and opened the kitchen door. Then, with a look that told him he must surely be astounded by the superlative houses and civilized furnishings of the *vèho,* she gestured for him to enter. Clearly she thought the ugly, drafty cabin was far superior to the graceful lodges of the Cheyenne.

He recalled the splendid town homes in Mayfair and Marylebone, where he'd often stayed as a welcomed guest, and smothered the chuckle that welled up inside him. Glancing around the spartan building with its rough, handmade furniture, he attempted a look of proper admiration as he gave his cryptic response.

"A few times. But none so wonderful as this."

She cocked her head and looked up at him, a smile of pleased superiority lighting her face. Lance turned, presenting his back to her, and with a diplomat's instinct for self-preservation, he bit his cheek to keep from laughing out loud.

Chapter 5

Suzette resolutely brushed away an infinitesimal speck of dust from her jacket sleeve and straightened her shoulders. With the same unflagging determination that had propelled her into her first class in materia medica to study the use of drugs and other remedial substances, she left the sanctuary of her small office. She walked across the dogtrot and into the cabin's main living area, where War Lance Striking waited beside Jacob in front of the minister's rolltop desk. The men were discussing the sermon Jacob had written in Cheyenne, which he was preparing to give to his first tiny gathering on Sunday morning. It was clear that he'd taken the opportunity provided while Suzette was changing into her riding clothes to involve War Lance in the task of translating his talk. They were both so deeply engrossed in their conversation, they hadn't noticed her entering the room.

"Well, I'm all ready to go," she called with forced nonchalance. She carried a small satchel containing a change of clothing in one hand; in the other, she held her medical bag.

The two men glanced her way, whirled about to face her straight on, and stared in silence. In front of the black iron stove at the far end of the kitchen, Anna covered her mouth with one hand. She'd managed to muffle her exclamation of surprise, but her blue eyes were enormous in mute dismay.

Suzette forced a smile of false confidence and stubbornly refused to glance downward. She didn't need to. She'd chosen the ensemble with careful consideration. Beneath a short jacket of dark blue broadcloth, trimmed in military fashion with yellow braid and a double row of brass eagle buttons, she wore a pair of matching tailored trousers. The buttons had belonged to Jordan and carried a *C* for cavalry across the shield proudly displayed on each eagle's breast. They'd been given to her by her dead fiancé's parents. Along with her own mother's book of poetry, the keepsakes were Suzette's most cherished possessions.

The outfit, made specially to her instructions, was unconventional to ordinary folk. To Jacob and Anna it was, no doubt, shocking. Being evangelical missionaries, they were not nearly as conservative as Old Order Mennonites such as Christian Kaufman. Still, they practiced extreme modesty and plainness in dress.

It was Jacob who broke the awkward silence. "I see our young lady is ready at last." His tone was mild, patient, even accepting. He ignored her outrageous apparel and turned to the Indian beside him. "Are you planning on taking Dr. Stanwood to one of the camps today?"

"I am," War Lance replied, his eyes never leaving Suzette. The amusement that had at first flickered across his rugged features at the sight of her trousers was now replaced by somber reflection as he looked more closely at the U.S. Calvary buttons parading down her chest.

"You must come out and see the horse War Lance Striking brought for me, Herr Graber," Suzette interjected, thankful that neither had spoken a word about the scandalous breeches. "She's a beautiful piebald mare. He's worked with the animal all week, breaking her so that I can ride."

"She's not ready for you quite yet," War Lance cautioned. "First I want to get her used to you. Go get an article of clothing and bring it outside. Something that you have worn close to your body."

Suzette flushed at his words. He could only mean one thing. An undergarment. "Is that really necessary?" she protested. "Why don't I just let her get acquainted with me before I mount?"

War Lance scowled at her, apparently unused to a balking female who openly questioned his directions. "That won't work. I'm going to ride her first. I'll settle her down and convince her that you are in charge before you get on. Now get that piece of clothing. We'll meet you outside."

All three of them, Anna, Jacob, and War Lance, were waiting for her beside the corral fence when she left the cabin. Clutched in her hand was a white cotton petticoat. Her face was burning with embarrassment as she handed her hired guide the garment, rolled up into a soft ball.

Without a word, he took the petticoat and shook it out. It was trimmed with rows of lace, pale blue ribbons, and tiny satin bows. In his large bronze hands, it looked as gossamer and out of place as an ostrich feather fan. He turned and draped the underskirt over the mare's neck, sliding it down and across her shoulders, then up over the quivering velvet nose. All the while, he murmured coaxing Cheyenne words to the newly captured mustang. Untying the lead rope at last, he led the mare away from the fence.

Lance kept his eyes studiously averted from the young woman standing in stricken silence beside the rail fence. He was afraid that if he met her horrified gaze, he'd burst into howls of laughter. From her acute embarrassment, it was clear no male had seen her underclothes since she was a small child. She'd be even more mortified if she knew that he had a practical, intimate knowledge of every aspect of ladies' lingerie. And it didn't come from sacking wild mustangs.

With a leap, he was up on the animal's back, the long petticoat draped across his legs. The mare reared and bucked once, then just as quickly settled into a dainty canter. Effortlessly Lance rode the little mustang around the corral and back to Suzette and the Grabers.

Satisfied with the horse's intrinsically gentle nature, he reached down and patted her neck. He'd used a rubber snaffle bit so he wouldn't damage the young horse's tender mouth, and the mare responded willingly now to his lightest touch. Pulling her to a halt beside the threesome who stood watching in rapt admiration, he slid to the ground.

"She's all ready for you," he told Suzette with satisfaction. "What will you call her?" As he spoke, he held out the reins with one hand and the white undergarment with the other.

"Painted Doll," she answered without hesitation. "Because that's just what she is." She snatched the lacy petticoat out of his hand, folded it up, and gave it to Anna without meeting his gaze. Her chin tilted upward, daring him to make any remark at all about his absurd, unorthodox methods of horse training.

At the telltale flush on her smooth cheeks, Lance smothered the hoot of laughter welling up inside him and answered with measured gravity. "A good name. It suits her well. And now we should be going."

"Before you leave, there is something I wish to give you, War Lance Striking," Jacob called. He turned and picked up an old rifle leaning against a fence post. "I want you to take this. Although I am a man of peace, I know that you will react to any threat to Dr. Stanwood in the warlike manner you have been taught since childhood. Since anyone you might meet on your journey from camp to camp may do likewise, I think it would be best if you have some means to protect her besides that wicked-looking blade you carry strapped to your thigh."

Surprised, Lance took the outdated single-shot muzzleloader from the Mennonite. It was a Springfield Model 1863, with a forty-inch barrel and a huge musket hammer on its right side. He ran his hand in admiration over the stock, worn as smooth as the grenadine silk dress he'd bought his mistress the day before he'd left England. The antiquated firearm would have been a marvelous addition to his gun collection at home in London. In Montana territory, it might prove more of a liability than a help.

"I have used it for hunting only," Jacob explained. "When we were young, my cousin and I would hunt deer and smaller game on our grandfather's farm. Do you know how to use the percussion lock?"

"Yes," Lance replied. Hanging the rifle over his shoulder by the leather sling strap, he took the cartridge pouch the minister offered. "Thank you for such a fine gift, Jacob. I will return it to you when I am no longer in need of it."

"Don't forget your things, Dr. Fräulein," Jacob said, turning to Suzette. He pointed to the medical case and canvas satchel that had been set down in the grass beside the fence. "You wouldn't want to leave without them."

Lance lifted the two bags and strapped them behind the mare's saddle. Then he turned to the missionary. "We will be back in seven days. We'll go to my family's camp first. Little Red Fox can sleep in my grandmother's lodge, where she will be well taken care of." He met Jacob's probing gaze with unflinching candor. "After that, we shall spend each night in one camp or another where she will have a safe shelter. She will come to no harm under my protection."

"Fine, fine," the minister answered, not needing to ask to whom Lance was referring. Only one person there had a mop of bright curls that gleamed like the fox's coppery pelt in the sunshine.

Suzette refused to give the warrior the satisfaction of even mentioning the new sobriquet. She'd been warned the Indians would probably attach a nickname to her that had some special meaning to them. And this title wasn't nearly as bad as she'd feared, though why they were referring to her as "little" was beyond her imagination.

What did surprise her was Herr Graber's calm acceptance of the fact that she was going to embark on a journey of a week's duration in the sole company of a Cheyenne warrior. A stranger, and a newly pardoned criminal at that. Jacob had been visiting an Indian camp the day War Lance Striking had arrived on the reservation. When the missionary had returned to their cabin several days later, he knew all about her having hired the prisoner as her guide. Jacob had seemed completely satisfied with the arrangement, to Suzette's astonishment. Although the preacher had told her that he'd never met War Lance on the southern reservation, she suspected that he'd known the brave's family when they were in the Oklahoma lands and was fond of them.

Moving closer to the mare, she noticed for the first time the fancy saddle on Painted Doll's back. She inhaled the wonderful smell of brand-new hand-tooled leather.

"Where did this beautiful saddle come from?"

Lance watched her carefully, wondering how she would take the news of her unexpected purchase—a purchase she wasn't even aware she'd made. "I got it at the traders' store," he told her. "I knew you wouldn't be able to ride with only a blanket pad on your horse."

He ran his fingers lightly over the crafted leather in renewed admiration of its fine workmanship. It was a California stock saddle, with a single cinch, double, rounded skirts, deep-dished cantle, and slim, high horn. The tapaderos that hooded the stirrups were long and intricately decorated with carved conches.

Tentatively she touched the fender's row of ornately tooled shells with one slim finger. "It must have been terribly expensive. How could you have paid for it?"

"I did not give the trader any of the white man's pieces of paper. I just told him to put your name down on his list." Impatiently Lance gestured with his hand. "Go ahead. Get on."

She hopped up and down, trying unsuccessfully to place one booted foot in the stirrup. "But I don't have an arrangement with the trader," she protested as she struggled to mount.

"You have one now."

The breeches grew enticingly snug around her hips with each jerky movement. As he admired the sight, Lance realized the polite thing to do would be to bend and cup his fingers for her foot. But hell, he wasn't playing the role of the sophisticated London gentleman now. He placed one hand on her tiny waist and cupped her round little butt with the other. Without a moment's hesitation, he hoisted her up onto the painted mustang by her curvaceous backside.

Behind him, he could hear Anna Graber's indrawn breath hissing through her tightly clenched teeth as her husband called out, "Wait, I'll help Dr. Fräulein up!" Jacob was so rattled, he'd spoken in German.

But it was too late anyway.

She was already safely ensconced in the fancy saddle.

Even with the initial touch of his large hand on her derriere, Suzette had refused to believe the creature's intent until it was too late. She sat astride the mustang and stared in incredulous astonishment at the tall warrior who stood looking up at her with an air of blank innocence. She met the raven eyes and was only faintly reassured by the unblinking gaze of naïveté riveted upon her. Clearly he had no idea of the unforgivable social error he'd just committed.

"It's all right, Dr. Fräulein," Jacob told her in English with a gurgle that sounded suspiciously like a swallowed chuckle. "He's rough and uncivilized, but with a little patience on your part, he'll learn more of our rules of etiquette and eventually make you a fine guide."

"I sincerely doubt that, Herr Graber," she snapped, unconsciously yanking back on the reins. "You can't make a silk purse out of a sow's ear."

At the poor treatment, the piebald mare snorted and stamped her feet. Lifting her head up and down, she shuffled and swished her long tail, and Suzette clutched both the reins and the saddle horn in tense fingers.

War Lance grabbed the bridle and stroked the mare's neck in a soothing gesture. His eyes remained on Suzette. "That's it, little doll," he said encouragingly. "You're doing just fine."

Suzette ignored the fact that he was probably talking to her and not the mare. "How much money was I charged for this saddle?" she demanded as she switched once more to the Cheyenne language.

He grinned up at her with the insouciance of a born rake. "The trader said it was a fine purchase at one hundred dollars."

"One hundred dollars!" she cried. "Why, that's far too much. I'll never be able to pay it off." She looked at him suspiciously through narrowed eyes. "Why did you get me a man's saddle, anyway? What made you think I'd ride the horse astride?"

"I did not think about how you would ride," he replied, lifting his black eyebrows in honest bafflement. "The trader said he did not have a white woman's saddle. He said you would have to hook one leg over the horn and ride sideways. I guess he did not know you owned a fine pair of leggings." He flashed her a look of admiration, running his glance boldly down her thigh and calf and up again to meet her gaze with eyes that sparkled like jets. "But I have never seen white men's trousers look so nice."

She gritted her teeth and leaned toward him. "We were not discussing my riding clothes, War Lance Striking. We were talking about this costly saddle, which I cannot possibly pay for on my salary."

"But I am giving you the horse," War Lance said in an unruffled tone of dismissal, as though the white man's incomprehensible system of finances weren't worth a moment's worry. He jabbed his forefinger in the air. "Now start riding up that road."

"Aren't you coming with me?" The strain in her voice betrayed her sudden panic.

"I am going to gallop right on by you. I will have to ride the wildness out of Red Wind. But I will come back for you, so keep following the road until you see me."

She adjusted the reins in her stiff fingers and stalled for more time. "Is that what you named him? Red Wind?"

"His name is Red Wind Blowing over the Prairie," War Lance explained patiently. "But sometimes I shorten it." He untied the stallion and led it a safe distance away. "As are all Cheyenne," he called to her over the stud's back, "I am very partial to red hair."

Before she had a chance to comment, he leaped up on the great horse. With a shrill whinny, the animal jumped into the air, kicked out its back legs before it ever touched the ground, and streaked down the road, its long mane and tail flying behind.

Painted Doll, seeing the red stallion disappear into a stand of cottonwoods, took off. Unable to even wave good-bye to the Grabers, Suzette clutched the reins and saddle horn in two tight fists and held on for dear life.

Suzette watched the natives of the North American plains come out of their tipis as she rode toward the busy camp beside War Lance Striking. With every yard that they drew closer to the circle of cone-shaped lodges, she grew more uneasy.

These were the fierce, fighting Cheyenne, known for the reckless bravery of their war charges. With Sitting Bull's Sioux warriors, they had ridden across the battlefield at the Little Big Horn River, wiping out five companies of the Seventh Cavalry. Now they stood in front of their painted lodges, watching the white woman doctor's approach with stone-faced detachment.

An unnatural quiet had settled on the camp the moment she and War Lance had appeared in sight. No one called out a greeting. No exuberant young braves galloped to meet them. A few women rose slowly from their places in front of their tanning skins, scrapers in hand. Old men sat together in groups, their work on pipes or whetstones interrupted. Even a cluster of small boys, who'd been racing wildly about on stick horses, stopped their play and stared in wonderment at the paleface woman dressed in the clothes of a white man.

"I guess they know we're here," Suzette said with a shaky voice. Determined to control her terror, she leaned over and stroked Painted Doll's thick black mane in an attempt to occupy her trembling hands while she regained her composure.

War Lance looked over at her, a faint smile skipping about the corners of his wide mouth. "My people have known of our approach since the middle of the day." He nodded toward the horizon. "The sun is now about to set."

He'd been true to his promise at the start and had circled back to meet her. But as soon as he'd ascertained that she was safe and riding with a modicum of skill, if not with expertise, he'd immediately pulled out well in front of her and maintained that position for what seemed like endless miles. All she'd seen for hours was the broad expanse of his muscular back. Even when he'd stopped to allow a short rest for her and the horses, he'd remained too far away for conversation, except at an undignified shout. However, for a bareback rider, his choice of a saddle had been astoundingly lucky. The padded seat fit both her and Painted Doll extremely well and was amazingly comfortable to sit on. But after the long hours of riding, she still ached all over.

Now he pulled his great stallion up beside an old woman who'd been scraping a green deerskin hide staked out in the grass, and dismounted.

"*Niscehem,*" he called, his sharp features softened by his tender regard for the elderly lady. "I have brought the white medicine woman to meet you."

Too frightened and sore to move, Suzette sat on the little painted mustang and stared about in alarm. Around her were Indians of all ages. Many of the men were half-naked in the early autumn warmth, dressed only in breechcloths. Their scarred breasts were adorned with necklaces of wild animals' teeth and intricately beaded leather pouches. In their long, braided hair were ornaments of feathers, beads, and shells. The women wore plaid calico dresses or loose blouses over fringed deerskin skirts.

"Get down from your pony, Little Red Fox," the old woman called, her dark eyes sparkling with a lively curiosity. Impatiently she waved her hand for Suzette to come and stand beside her.

But Suzette found it impossible to dismount, certain that her stiff, trembling legs would buckle beneath her. She felt suddenly breathless, and her heart pounded.

Shaking his head at her dazed bewilderment, War Lance reached up and lifted Suzette off her horse. He swung her to the ground effortlessly, then pressed his strong hand on the small of her back and gently pushed her forward in the tall grass. There was suppressed laughter in his voice when he spoke. "My grandmother is anxious to meet you, *náevehoka*. Now show your nicest paleface manners and greet Prairie Grass Woman properly."

The tiny woman looked up at Suzette and nodded her head. "Yes, little white woman doctor," she said chuckling, "you do look very clever."

"I am happy to meet War Lance Striking's grandmother," Suzette said with formality. She spoke in a strong voice, anxious that the old woman hear her clearly and understand her badly accented Cheyenne.

At her boldly spoken greeting, Prairie Grass Woman raised her dark eyebrows in surprise. She met her grandson's gaze with a look of astonishment, then turned back to Suzette. Laughter danced in the elderly woman's alert black eyes. "You are a medicine woman," she said, confusing Suzette still further, for she'd been certain the old woman would make some flattering comment about her knowledge of their language.

"Yes, I am the agency doctor." She refused to show her disappointment. "I have come to your camp to help anyone who is sick or injured."

"No one here is sick," Prairie Grass Woman replied, waving her hand in abrupt dismissal.

"But there is someone who is injured," added a young woman who'd come to stand beside War Lance.

At her arrival there was a faint, musical tinkling, and Suzette, fascinated by the unexpected sound, glanced down to see a band of tiny bells fastened around the woman's moccasins at each ankle.

"This is Blue Crane Flying, my brother's wife," War Lance said. He turned and smiled a welcome at the woman.

Though she looked to be somewhat younger than Suzette, perhaps closer to twenty-three, the newcomer had the calm serenity of an ancient monk. An ageless wisdom and tempered sadness glowed in her deep-set, luminous eyes. She was thin, the shadowed hollows at her collarbone pronounced above the plain neckline of her blue calico dress. Her satiny black hair, fastened in two thick braids tied with fur, fell to her waist.

"Do you speak of Yellow Feather?" Prairie Grass Woman asked in surprise.

Blue Crane Flying stepped toward Suzette, worry etched on her angular features. "My daughter has just cut her hand, *náevehoka*. I can put herbs on the wound, but it is deep and ugly and will take long to heal." She looked at Suzette with a frown of concern and continued, "Will you look at her?"

"Of course," Suzette answered without hesitation. She glanced at War Lance and then back to his sister-in-law. "I'll look at the cut immediately."

"Come then," Blue Crane Flying said. "I will show you the way."

Suzette turned toward her horse. "I'll need to get my bag."

But War Lance had already untied the straps and held the black case in his hand. "I will go with you," he told her. "You may need my help when you doctor the little girl. She's bound to be frightened of a *vèhoka*."

Together the group walked across the open meadow to a large lodge and entered. The tipi was pleasantly cool and dim, a refuge from the glaring sunshine. The lodge-skin had been raised to allow the afternoon breeze to flow through the interior. On the earthen bench that encircled the home, a girl of about nine lay on a pallet of woven bulrushes, over which had been thrown a tattered buffalo robe. She looked up, startled, when they entered.

"This is the white medicine woman we have all heard about," Prairie Grass Woman said kindly to the child. She sat down on the floor of the tipi beside her.

"I am here to help you," Suzette told Yellow Feather, speaking loudly and slowly in an attempt to compensate for her faulty pronunciation of their difficult language.

At her words, the girl sat up on the buffalo robe, cradling her injured hand in her lap. She watched Suzette with frightened eyes that suddenly filled with silent tears.

Shocked, Suzette realized that the child was undoubtedly a half-breed. Enormous light brown eyes stared at her from a round face that was much lighter in complexion than that of the family surrounding her. The long braids were a warm coffee color. Suzette glanced quickly at War Lance, who met her unspoken question with an unreadable look on his strong features.

Blue Crane Flying, seeing her daughter's obvious distress, touched her cheek in a comforting gesture.

Before the old grandmother could deny permission to examine the girl, Suzette knelt beside the sleeping pallet and held out her hand, palm up.

"Let the white woman see your hand, *nàtóna*," Blue Crane Flying urged in a soothing voice. "We want her to look at your cut. She has strong medicine and can heal it."

Suzette smiled encouragingly at the terrified child. "What happened to you?" she whispered softly in an attempt to reassure her.

"I cut my hand on my mother's root digger," Yellow Feather answered, her voice breaking in her fright. Hesitantly she placed her fingers in Suzette's open palm.

The small hand was bound with a strip of flannel, soaked with blood. With all the gentleness she could show, Suzette lightly touched the girl's forearm and temple with her free hand. Her skin was cool and dry. "When did this happen?"

"Late this afternoon," her mother answered.

"May I see the cut?"

Blue Crane Flying looked at the stranger and then back to her suffering daughter. In the dim light the young mother's fine, regular features were shadowed with worry and fear. Suzette realized with sharp disappointment that the woman might still refuse to allow her to treat the child.

"Let the *náevehoka* see the injury," War Lance said in a tone of absolute and unquestioned authority. His strong male voice reverberated in the confines of the lodge.

Suzette looked up and met his gaze in silent thanks. He stood with his feet braced apart and his arms folded across his wide chest. He watched her from his great height with a quiet scrutiny, his doubt and misgiving evident in the tenseness of his stance. Still, he was willing to give her a chance to prove herself, and she was grateful for that small measure of trust.

As Blue Crane Flying dropped her eyes in assent, Suzette carefully removed the soiled dressing. The swollen, angry cut was still oozing blood. Suzette resisted the urge to shake her head in dismay at the streaks of dirt encrusted on the small palm.

The cut would most likely become infected if left untended. And if gangrene should set in, the girl would risk losing her fingers, her hand, or even her life.

"I was about to make a poultice of *mahetseiyo,* the red bloodroot medicine," Blue Crane Flying whispered softly. "But I knew that first we must stitch the wound."

"My grandson's wife has great medicine," Prairie Grass Woman said to War Lance Striking. "If her remedy does not work, no puny white woman's medicine will be any better."

"Still, let's allow the *náevehoka* to try," War Lance suggested. "Perhaps the Great Powers will reward her for coming to help our people."

Suzette rose and turned to face him, her hands clasped together as if in prayer. "I know how hard it is for you to trust me. My ways of healing are strange and must seem impossible to understand. But I promise you, War Lance, that I have been trained to treat wounds such as this. I've done it many times before. No harm will come to the child through me. Please believe me."

"Why else would you have come to our reservation, except to bring your powerful medicine?" He looked down at her through narrowed eyes and seemed to search her soul. "Yet no one such as you has ever come before."

Prairie Grass Woman folded her hands in her lap, closed her eyes briefly in quiet contemplation, then opened them to stare up thoughtfully at Suzette. *"Naaa!* What my grandson says is true. The number of white eyes who have come to help the people is fewer than the fingers on one hand. With only one exception, I do not remember a *vèhoka* ever doing something kind for a Cheyenne. It may be that Little Red Fox was sent here by the Wise One Above. We must consider this before we refuse to allow her to work her medicine."

"Yes," Blue Crane Flying said at last, her lovely dark brown eyes tortured with the anguish of her decision. "If I can stay near Yellow Feather and sing my medicine songs, Little Red Fox, you may treat my child."

Suzette turned to War Lance's sister-in-law. "We can

work our healing remedies together, Blue Crane Flying. You have my promise."

At the young woman's quavery smile of agreement, Suzette knelt and snapped opened her medical bag. "Let's get started."

Chapter 6

Suzette pushed aside the splints, sponges, and rolls of bandages in her black leather bag and, with a quick yank, pulled out a large piece of rubber sheeting. "Let's take the child outdoors where there's better light. We can lay her down on this special blanket. And I'll need a kettle of clean, fresh water brought to a boil."

"I will see to the water," Blue Crane Flying offered. With Prairie Grass Woman right behind her, she hurried outside carrying a large iron pot.

Tenderly War Lance lifted Yellow Feather in his arms and ducked through the doorway of the lodge with Suzette following close behind, the rubber sheet over one arm and her medical bag under the other. With a snap, she spread the sheet on the grass in full sunlight, and War Lance carefully deposited the girl in the center. Suzette knelt beside her, first placing her black bag to one side. Next she removed her small, brown, boxlike case with its tiny bottles of calomel, acetanilide, arnica, paregoric, digitalis, belladonna, bichloride of mercury, and spirits of ammonia.

"Now let's see that cut again," she whispered to the frightened child. She smoothed the wisps of brown hair back from the girl's flushed cheeks and smiled reassuringly.

Taking the small hand in both of her own, Suzette inspected the wound one more time. It was a raw, jagged, ugly cut. Pieces of the flannel's red lint had stuck to the edge of it. Dirt from the root digger was encrusted across the length of the entire palm. She glanced up at War Lance, who crouched, waiting, beside the rubber sheet, the child's worried mother next to him.

"I have to clean the wound and soak her hand first," Suzette explained. "It's going to hurt. Can you keep her still and quiet?"

War Lance answered for both of them. "Yes, náevehoka. I will hold Yellow Feather. You do whatever is necessary to help the child."

Suzette heard his forthright answer with amazement. She'd been prepared for suspicion and ignorance on his part, if not downright antagonism. Instead, she encountered a gaze of complete acceptance of her as a physician. Well, as a medicine woman, at least.

By now, the iron kettle was hanging on a tripod over an open fire. While she waited for the water to boil, Suzette pulled out the biniodide of mercury soap and the two bottles of an alcoholic solution of bichloride, containing the sterile catgut sutures and the wet dressings of gauze. She washed her hands and arms up to her elbows, using the soap and the hot water Blue Crane Flying ladled from the steaming pot.

"I'm going to have to sew the cut," she told the watching Indians. "Do you know what that means?"

"We understand, Little Red Fox," Prairie Grass Woman replied. She and Blue Crane Flying stood at the edge of the sheeting, ready to help. "Our medicine men have sewn torn flesh from battle wounds many times. Do not worry about the young one. My great-granddaughter is a Cheyenne, for our children belong to their mother's people. She will not thrash out against the pain. Her mother and I will sing a strong-heart song for her while you are using your best medicine."

Sitting in the grass at the edge of the rubber sheet, the two Indian women, one ancient, the other ageless, melded their soprano voices and sang softly, encouraging the young girl to show the Great Powers how brave a Cheyenne child could be. In return for her self-sacrifice, they asked the Spirit Above to send his healing power to the white woman doctor.

"I can lessen the pain a little," Suzette explained quietly to War Lance. She could feel his dubious gaze watching every move she made, as if he were ready to reach out and stop her at any moment. "I am going to use some of my medicine to soothe her and ease her suffering." Gingerly she tapped out a quarter grain of morphia and placed it under the girl's tongue, where it could be rapidly absorbed. "Now I want you to hold her very still, War Lance. She mustn't move her hand at all. Can you do that for me?"

A smile tugged at the corners of his wide mouth. "I think my strength is greater than that of a young girl of nine summers."

"Your strength is probably greater than ten men," she muttered to herself in English as she replaced the dark brown vial. She looked up to discover his eyes alight with amusement at his own joke.

He moved to the rubber blanket, sat down cross-legged beside it, and lifted a corner of the sheeting over his knees. Then he placed the child gently in his lap and held the fragile, injured hand in his own large one. Softly he crooned Yellow Feather's name, whispering in the child's ear that she would be safe in his arms, that he wouldn't let any harm come to her, that the beautiful red-haired medicine woman, who looked just like one of the Wise One Above's feathered servants, was going to make her hand all better again. At his whispered words of nonsense and encouragement, a faint smile curled the corners of their small patient's lips.

Suzette knelt beside them and bent over the cut. Swiftly and deftly she washed out the wound with the bichloride solution, removing all trace of dirt and bits of flannel. In a wooden bowl scoured with the bichloride of mercury soap, she soaked Yellow Feather's hand in boiled water and disinfectant. Then, while War Lance held the small hand propped on his knee absolutely still, she sewed together the ragged edges of the lesion with the sterile catgut and placed a wet dressing of gauze over it.

As she worked, Suzette listened to the soft Cheyenne murmurings in War Lance's deep bass voice, accompanied in the background by the women's healing song, and realized that, whether he intended to or not, he was soothing the doctor as well as the patient. Although the girl stiffened in pain, she remained calm and still in his arms, barely whimpering as Suzette pulled the needle through the lacerated skin. Finally she secured the dressing in place with a bandage of torn unbleached muslin strips.

She glanced up with relief that the minor surgery was successfully completed and found the warrior's eyes fixed upon her. Their ebony depths seemed fathomless, watching her with an unreadable scrutiny. She was suddenly, overwhelmingly, aware of his closeness. Aware of the way the bronzed muscles of his bare upper torso flexed and rippled like polished copper beneath a fine sheen of perspiration in the bright afternoon sunshine. Of the thick brows that slashed a straight line above his slightly hooked, aristocratic nose. Of the long lashes that framed his intelligent eyes and cast shadows on the angular planes of his proud face. Of the way he radiated male strength and self-confidence.

Good Lord, if any man could be called beautiful, it was he. She could barely keep her eyes off him.

"Will my daughter's wound heal quickly now?" Blue Crane Flying asked, taking the child, drowsy now under the effects of the morphine, in her lap. The woman's dark eyebrows arched expressively over her worried eyes. Suzette looked closely at the young mother and recognized the underlying beauty in her gaunt features. Graceful, small-boned, soft-spoken, she resembled a careworn Madonna.

"Yes . . . yes, I believe so," she told her. "Put Yellow Feather in your lodge and let her sleep. Then feed her some broth. I will look at the cut later this evening and again in the morning before I go."

"Now, Little Red Fox, you must meet the people of our camp," Prairie Grass Woman said. She rose from her place on the ground as smoothly and gracefully as her granddaughter-in-law. Deep crinkles framed her black eyes as she beamed at Suzette. "We will have a feast."

A crier went through the village, inviting people to come to the celebration. The circle of lodges formed a giant horseshoe more than a half mile across, as far as three arrows shot from a strong hunter's best bow. The camp herald called out the invitation at the opening of the circle, which faced the rising sun, then rode around its center, repeating his announcement again and again for all to hear. Suzette caught the faint sound of his voice from the distant tipis and saw the women stepping out of their lodges to question Village Crier and share the information with their neighbors. Deer and elk meat, brought in by a party of hunters, was quickly prepared for roasting over the open cooking fires, the meat deftly skewered on long sticks.

One of the braves dropped an elk carcass in the tall grass in front of Blue Crane Flying's lodge and joined the small group clustered around the camp's special visitor. He studied Suzette with cautious eyes.

"This is my brother, Bear Scalp," War Lance said, standing so close to Suzette that his arm brushed hers. Since the moment they'd been surrounded by the others in the village, War Lance had remained protectively at her side. She was enveloped in an aura of male strength and possessiveness as surely as if he'd drawn a circle around the two of them in the grass at their feet.

The approaching hunter was so similar in features and physique to War Lance Striking, it was obvious they were closely related. Except for the pitted scars of smallpox that marred Bear Scalp's strong features, and the fact that he was several inches shorter, the two men were almost identical, even to the scars that marked their bare chests.

"The white woman doctor used her medicine to heal your daughter's injured hand," Prairie Grass Woman told her eldest grandson.

"That is good," Bear Scalp replied, then added with a deprecating gesture of his hand, "but perhaps it was my woman's strong medicine that healed her cut."

"Perhaps it was both our strong medicines," Suzette interjected. She knew the man was skeptical of her ability and realized, with irritation, that much of the credit for Yellow Feather's recovery would probably go to the Indians' strong-heart song.

Bear Scalp's mouth dropped open in astonishment at her plainspoken words. Momentarily speechless, he stared at her, then turned to his brother with an ear-to-ear grin. "The *náevehoka* really does speak our language."

"And so loudly and clearly, too," War Lance added, his dark eyes sparkling with laughter as he met his brother's look of irony.

Suzette felt a flush warm her cheeks. It was all too apparent they were sniggering at her. "If my Cheyenne is so funny," she snapped, louder still, "maybe it would be better if you tried to speak my language."

The brothers sobered at once and eyed each other warily.

"No, Little Red Fox," War Lance said. He stepped closer, bent his head, and spoke coaxingly in a blatant attempt to soothe her injured feelings. "Neither of us understands any of the *vèho* words. You must forgive our bad manners, angel. You are our guest. Come now, everyone in the village wants to meet you."

"I told you not to call me 'angel,' " she warned him, angry at her own reaction to his scandalous ways. When he wished, he had the charm of a practiced flirt. "Even

if you say the word in my tongue, so only I can understand, it's still not proper."

He took her wrist in his large hand, ignoring the fact
that she managed to jerk away from him twice before he
succeeded in clamping his long fingers around her. "I'll
try to remember," he promised as he strode across the
grass, dragging her along like a reluctant captive. His
voice was gruff and edged with sarcasm. "But the white
man's ways are so strange, it is not very likely I will succeed."

By the time the meal was over, Suzette was certain
she'd met every person in the camp. People of all ages
came over in family groups, smiling and laughing,
warmly welcoming her to their village. The women were
bashful, speaking barely above whispers, and Suzette had
to lean forward to catch their soft words. But in spite of
their shyness, they offered her gifts: intricately beaded
moccasins, a carved wooden bowl, and a fine quilled
shawl. She was humbled by their openhearted generosity,
for she knew how poor in material possessions they
were. Several of the old men chiefs, wearing their blankets folded formally over their arms, spoke to her at
length of her status as an honored guest. One elderly man
hobbled up to her on tree-limb crutches, his leg sewed up
tightly in a green horsehide.

"What is wrong with your leg?" Suzette questioned
with professional curiosity.

Snow Bear grinned toothlessly. "I slipped on some
loose rocks and broke it. It was a careless accident. But
the bone is healing well, for our chief medicine man
wrapped it tightly and shook his healing rattle over it."

"Would you like me to look at it?" she asked, ignoring
the scowl of disapproval on War Lance's face at her unwarranted persistence. She knew what the old man's answer would be before he even responded.

"*Eaaa!* That is not necessary, Little Red Fox. Only
this morning Standing Antelope probed it. He said the

leg is growing together again, and I will soon be able to walk on it."

Suzette saw several older women who looked ill, their blankets pulled up over their heads in spite of the heat. She tried not to show her disappointment when these, too, refused her services, but she heeded War Lance's gesture of warning. She didn't want to offend these friendly people by being too insistent. Patience and acceptance of their ways would mean more in the long run.

At last the bustle of the village grew quieter as families returned to their homes in the evening darkness. In a far-off lodge, a dance was being held by one of the men's societies, and the sound of the drums and the singing hung on the still air. The faint echo of youthful laughter, male and female together, drifted across the open camp circle. But she had not been invited. She wondered if War Lance, who sat next to her outside his family's lodge, wished he could slip away and join them.

"Do you belong to the group that is having the dance?" she asked at last, unable to contain her curiosity.

"No, they are members of the Fox society. The men in my family have always been Dog soldiers."

"Is there a special reason? Or is it just family tradition?"

A shadow of a smiled flitted across his lips as he met her questioning gaze. "Both, I guess. The Dog soldiers have always brought up the rear in any attack on my people's camps. They are the ones who remain behind until all the women and children are safely away." He looked out across the open meadow to the creek, his voice suddenly faraway and tinged with sadness. "That was how my father died."

"I'm so sorry," she whispered. "I didn't mean to bring up unhappy memories."

"It's been many, many years." He stood, and gestured for her to rise as well. "You wanted to see Yellow Feather's hand this evening. If we do not hurry, she will have already gone to sleep."

Together they entered the lodge, where they found Blue Crane Flying unfolding the family's sleeping pallets.

"The pain is gone," she told them joyfully. "My daughter is happy again. When she woke up, she ate some soup and played with her doll." Blue Crane Flying smiled at Suzette. "She has a gift for you."

Awake now, Yellow Feather sat on a robe by the small cooking fire and smiled shyly up at them. A tiny replica of an Indian child lay on the lap of her plaid calico skirt. War Lance and Blue Crane Flying sank down on a nearby rug.

Suzette knelt beside the child and lightly touched her forearm and temple. Her skin was cool and dry. Her eyes were clear. From beneath the dressing, no ominous red streaks spread across her wrist. There was no sign of infection, despite the dirt that had once covered the wound.

"You are feeling better, aren't you?" she exclaimed, delighted to see that the surgery had been so successful.

Yellow Feather lowered her lashes and stared down at the white bandage. Like most nine-year olds, her bashful smile was all the more endearing for the missing teeth.

Withdrawing a package from behind a backrest, Blue Crane Flying gave it to her daughter, who immediately laid it in Suzette's lap.

"This is for you, Little Red Fox," the child piped in her high, sweet voice. "My mother said I might give you a present. I want you to have this."

Curious, Suzette looked down at the worn beaded parfleche, then at the child who waited expectantly beside her. "You don't need to give me a gift, Yellow Feather. I am paid by the Great Father in Washington to be a doctor here at Lame Deer."

"She wants you to have it," her mother interposed. "Do not refuse her. Gracious acceptance of a gift is the Cheyenne way. Please, look inside the bundle."

"Go ahead, angel," War Lance Striking urged. "Open it."

With a shrug of acceptance, Suzette lifted the flap and withdrew the child's gift.

It was a pair of men's gloves.

"Oh, dear God," she gasped, speaking instinctively in English.

There on her lap lay a pair of fawn-colored buckskin gauntlets, made with their large, flared cuffs partially opened at the sides to accommodate the wide uniform cuff of a U.S. Cavalry officer. They were an exact replica of the gloves Jordan had worn the last time she saw him. She looked up to find War Lance staring at her, a harsh scowl hardening his chiseled features.

Mindlessly she started to rise, her gaze once more locked on the gauntlets, then felt the pressure of his strong fingers on her elbow as she was ruthlessly held in her place on the old buffalo robe.

"They belonged to my father," Yellow Feather explained with a tremulous quiver of her lower lip, uncertain of the emotional turmoil that suddenly swirled around them like a morning fog on the spring prairie. "Since you dress like a little soldier chief, *náevehoka,* I thought you would like to wear them."

Suzette's heart gradually resumed its rhythmic, steady beat. She tore her tear-blinded gaze away from the gloves and looked at the girl, meeting her innocent smile with a choked sob. "How very good of you, Yellow Feather. I shall treasure them always."

As Lance accompanied Suzette back to his family's lodge, he glanced down at the young woman's fine-boned face, chalky white in the moonlight. He had walked her down to the stream, giving her some private time to care for her needs and regain her composure. Trancelike, she carried the cavalry gloves clutched to her breast, stumbling once on a clump of thick bunchgrass. He reached out to steady her and realized, at her mute acceptance of his grasp and her failure to acknowledge his comment on Yellow Feather's quick recovery, that she was nearly unconscious of his presence, her disturbed thoughts miles, perhaps years, away.

From the moment she had seen the unexpected gift, she'd hovered on the verge of tears, seemingly unable to gain control of her shattered emotions. She must have thought, at first, that the army gauntlets had been stripped from a dead soldier by some murdering, scalp-collecting redskin. It would have been a logical conclusion, he had to admit, given the past years of brutal fighting and the notoriety of the so-called Indian massacres. He'd come to expect prejudice and suspicion from educated, supposedly righteous, and tenderhearted white females. Even Cecily hadn't been able to withstand the insidious effects of the white man's bigotry.

Cecily.

He hadn't consciously thought of her in years, so successful had he been in blocking out the pain and despair. God, what a shortsighted, rambunctious fool he'd been. He should have known from the beginning that a gently bred young lady could never withstand the cruel recriminations of what the British labeled "genteel" society. Even her own parents had stood resolutely against her. It had been all his fault for ever daring to expose a delicately nurtured girl to the vicious insults and sly innuendos of gossips and louts. Never again would he be the cause of such agonizing vulnerability.

In the center of the Cheyenne village, the meadow of fringed sagebrush and buffalo grass was deserted now. Lance looked down, perplexed, at the troubled lady doctor beside him. Unlike so many white women he'd met, Suzette Stanwood wasn't filled with an unreasoning hatred of the red man. He'd watched in wonder as she'd taken expert care of Yellow Feather's injury earlier that afternoon. The gentle compassion in the physician's skilled, delicate fingers was genuine; no one could have simulated such natural tenderness. And that humane and accomplished skill was badly needed by his father's people. Though it was only a conjecture based on his limited knowledge of medicine, she appeared to have had a fine training at a qualified medical college—wherever the bloody hell it was that females were actually allowed to attend.

"You have seen Yellow Feather this evening?" Prairie Grass Woman called from the doorway of her home as they approached. She'd been visiting friends in another tipi and had just returned.

"Yes, the child is much better, *niscehem*. Little Red Fox will look at her hand again before we leave in the morning."

"Ahhh, that is good." His grandmother smiled broadly and turned to Suzette, her long braids swinging around her tiny shoulders. "You will sleep near me in our lodge, young woman. Blue Crane Flying has already laid out your mattress."

"That is very kind of you, Prairie Grass Woman," Suzette murmured, coming out of her daze. She glanced at Lance as though looking for his guidance in the matter of her sleeping place, but he kept his eyes purposefully averted. That area was strictly his grandmother's domain. And she'd rule it with an iron hand, if he remembered anything at all about her.

"And you, *nixa*," the old woman continued, turning the full force of her pitch-black gaze on Lance, "will find a blanket in the unmarried men's lodge. Since that is what you are." She looked at him with an unspoken message in her twinkling eyes. *And be sure you do not forget it.*

Before Lance could answer, Young Wolf bolted out of the tipi and threw his arms around one of Lance's legs. "Stay here with us," he pleaded.

"I can't, *nāha*," Lance said. He scooped the child up and held him under one arm like a sack of flour. "But in the morning, I will let you ride on Red Wind." Without warning, he pretended to drop the boy, who squealed in delight.

Suzette watched War Lance whirl the six-year-old, tucked safely under his crooked elbow, in a wide circle. During the feasting, as groups of chattering, noisy children had come and gone, Young Wolf had been pointed out to her by his great-grandmother as Bear Scalp's only son. Suzette watched an indulgent War Lance roughhouse with his young nephew and recalled his tender assistance with Yellow Feather. The illiterate savage's open love for his family, even his compassionate treatment of the wild horses he'd captured and broken, was at odds with her original perception of him as a dangerous felon. She knew she should still be wary of him, but seeing War Lance with his own people had thrown her off balance. As he tossed Young Wolf high in the air and caught him with an exaggerated "ooof," she felt an inexplicable yearning for the child she had never borne.

And the husband she had never wed.

It was the twelfth of September, and the prairie shimmered golden under the afternoon sun as Dr. Suzette Stanwood followed her Indian guide across the arid fringe of the Big Horn Mountains. The dry, warm wind of a Chinook had descended the eastern slopes, blowing steadily across the plains, and the temperature had risen at least twenty degrees in the last fifteen minutes. Far away, the mountain peaks were dark and cloudy, a sure sign that rain was falling at the summits. But over the rolling, grassy hills, the sky was crystal-clear, and visibility nearly limitless.

Suzette dragged on the reins, bringing her mount to a halt. She tried to ignore the fact that her hired scout continued to pull well ahead of her in the distance. Her piebald mare snorted and pranced sideways in an agitated dance of disapproval as the great red stallion moved away from them.

"Stop that, Painted Doll," Suzette demanded. She

jerked back on the reins once again, determined to control the mustang, only to have the horse bob her head and
fidget nervously. Suzette frantically clutched the saddle
horn and clamped her trousered legs against the animal's
sides.

Blast the man! It was his responsibility to check on
her to be sure she was keeping up with him. For the last
week, she'd constantly reminded him of that. But did he
pay the least attention? No!

Little by little, she thought she'd begun to understand
the Cheyenne brave, only to come up against his intrac-
tability when she least expected it. And his insistence on
setting the pace and choosing the rest periods seemed to
be one of his most obstinate demands. He always succeeded in reaching the next camp the same day they left
the last, even if it meant arriving late in the evening, long
after most people had gone to bed.

Tired, dusty, and crabby, Suzette lifted her flat-
crowned planter's hat and used the wide brim as a fan.

"War Lance!" she screamed, her voice raw with irritation. "War Lance Striking!"

But by now he was probably well beyond hearing
distance. He was supposed to be protecting her, for goodness' sake. That's what he was going to be paid for. If
they ever got back to the agency.

Then, just as suddenly, he was on his way back, galloping at breakneck speed. Red Wind thundered up and
skidded to a stop, throwing up clumps of dirt and the
broken white blossoms of bear grass.

"What is wrong?" War Lance demanded, a scowl
creasing his forehead. "Did you see something?" He
swiveled on his saddle pad of antelope hair, scouring the
horizon in all directions, then turned back to her with a
look of puzzlement.

"I'm tired," she said lamely, embarrassed to hear the
peevishness in her voice. But it was true, she was exhausted from the heat.

"We'll rest up ahead," he replied. He wheeled his horse around.

"No, I want to rest now," she demanded. "I'm not going any further until I'm ready."

He didn't bother to reply. He simply caught Painted Doll's reins in his hand and pulled her along behind him. "We will rest a little way ahead, angel," he called over his shoulder. "There is a stand of trees and a swift-running stream just over the next hill." Not waiting for her acquiescence, he urged Red Wind into a brisk trot.

The broad-shouldered warrior drew up beside a creek, under the dappled shade of alders and river birches. Sliding off the stallion, he walked to the clear, bubbling stream and bent down on one knee. Cupping his hands, he lifted the water and drank deeply. Then he turned to find her still mounted, watching him.

"Do you need some help?" he asked. Uncertain, he started to move toward her.

She slid off the mare. "No, I can take care of myself." Before he could draw nearer, she scurried to the creek, tossed her light gray hat on the grassy bank, and began splashing cool water on her face.

Soundlessly he came up to stand beside her, so close she could see the toes of his worn moccasins from the corner of her eye. She rose and edged cautiously away in one sliding movement.

"I am not going to scalp you," he said with a mocking grin, his hands propped on his lean hips. "I don't do that anymore."

"I know that!" she snapped, feeling like an empty-headed fool. She turned and walked up the bank toward the trees. Looking back over her shoulder, she pursed her lips. "I'm sorry. I guess I'm just . . . just . . ." She floundered, unable to find the correct Cheyenne word for "overtired."

"A bad-mannered little girl," he offered.

Shocked, she whirled and met his teasing gaze. In

spite of herself, she felt a smile tug at her lips. She shook her head. "No! Yes. Sometimes."

"I won't hurt you, little white woman doctor," he said, his deep voice suddenly thick and raspy.

At the sound of it, she felt an involuntary shudder of fear and anticipation go through her. "I know."

"Then prove it."

"How?"

He stepped toward her, a wry smile turning up the corners of his sensual mouth. "How do white people show they trust each other?"

Breathless, she fingered the top button of her cotton blouse. "They shake hands."

"Then shake mine."

Except for the medical examination on the first day, Suzette hadn't touched him in the nearly two weeks they'd known each other. Not even a careless brush against his clothing. Not once had she so much as accidentally grazed his arm with her elbow.

They met each other's gaze, and both knew it hadn't been mere happenstance. She had purposefully, carefully, painstakingly, refrained from touching him.

Without a word, he held out his hand. His coal black eyes challenged her. Taunted her. Dared her to touch the thieving, no-account, murdering redskin who'd been delivered to the reservation trussed up in chains like a mad dog.

She moved toward him. She lifted one hand and slowly extended it, almost, but not quite, touching his. In the mottled light, her skin looked incredibly pale and smooth next to his bronzed, rugged palm, her oval fingertips startingly feminine and delicate beside his blunt-cut nails. For a long moment they stood only inches apart, their gazes locked. And then the strength of his long fingers encompassed hers. As their hands met, a jolt went through her, as though the Chinook wind had surged around them and wrapped them in a charge of lightning.

"You see," he said, his voice deep and reassuring. "I am totally harmless."

As a wounded grizzly. Or a gun-shot mountain lion.

"Yes, I see that now," she said. She turned her head aside and drew in a deep draft of air, inwardly cursing the shakiness of her voice. She tried to pull her hand away, but he held it securely in his own.

Lance could feel the trembling of the cool, graceful fingers, and longed to lift them to his lips. Under the rustling leaves, the shifting light traced shadows across the curve of her delicate cheekbone, where the skin was as taut and smooth as the finest Staffordshire porcelain. Every night for the last week he'd imagined touching that silken flesh with his fingertips, stroking it with his tongue.

Now he yearned to turn his dreams into reality.

Why had she come into his life, bringing a taunting vision of the one thing he could never have? He cursed whatever powers above had played such an ironic trick. To dangle her in front of him like a shimmering glimpse of a fairy child, when he knew full well that in the end it would prove to be only an illusion.

He pulled her to him. Even to his own ears, his voice was rough and hoarse. "Why did you come to Lame Deer?"

"I came because Jacob Graber asked me to."

"The holy man? Then you were moved by his desire to bring the religion of the white eyes to the Indians?" She had the grace to flush beneath his stare. "No, it wasn't your great love for the Cheyenne people that brought you here, little white woman doctor. But you can save your lies for now. Sooner or later, I'm going to find out what you came for."

Chapter 7

"I don't know what you're talking about," Suzette answered breathlessly. She pushed against his muscled chest with her free hand to no avail, her fingertips grazing the barbaric scars that were his rites of passage to manhood. "I . . . I came here to be the agency doctor. What other reason could there be?"

The touch of her skin on his bare flesh seemed to shock him into a riveting awareness of her vulnerability. And his own power. He tensed, his body rock-hard beneath her softness, his clenched jaw so taut a muscle jumped in his bronzed cheek. His gaze dropped to her lips. She stared up at him, mesmerized, caught in the struggle between self-will and self-restraint that played across his sharp features, and knowing she would be helpless to fend off his attack. From the branches above them came the excited twittering of a warbler, breaking the silence.

He expelled a harsh, unsteady breath, released his grip on her hand, and stepped back.

Shaken by the shrewd incisiveness of his gaze and guilty about her own hidden motives, she scowled at him ferociously. Why she'd come to the Tongue River Reservation was her own affair. She owed no one an explanation, least of all an uneducated creature like him. Clamping her lips together, she thrust out her chin, determined not to betray any more of the painful events that had brought her here. She had no intention of telling him that she'd been forced by circumstances to come to the very tribe that was responsible for the death of the only man she'd ever loved. The bitter irony of it all was like a twisted knot inside her. She wondered, once again, as she had during the long months of her sister's pregnancy, about the wisdom of accepting the position at Lame Deer as agency physician.

The air between them seemed to crackle. He stared at her as though trying to read her secret thoughts, and under his searing gaze, she flushed and looked away.

"Let's go," he said at last. He walked past her and mounted Red Wind, but this time, instead of tearing off across the valley ahead of her, he waited while she climbed awkwardly onto her mare.

She hated it when he watched her mount in her clumsy, unschooled fashion, and she hated it when he left her behind to do it alone. Well, goodness, she couldn't have it both ways.

"You've been hired to protect me," she reminded him, once she was on Painted Doll's back. She was certain he was about to gallop off again. "How can you do that when you ride so far ahead?"

"I would hear a white man coming from miles away," he answered. He looked at her in honest surprise. "The birds and small creatures would signal the clumsy approach of a *vèho* long before he came close to us."

She wasn't that easily placated. "What about an Indian?"

"By now, every Cheyenne on the reservation knows you are a medicine woman who has come to help us. No one— not even the most hot-blooded young brave— would harm you. You are our guest, Little Red Fox. You have the complete protection of the Cheyenne people. You're as safe from harm on our lands as one of our own children."

"I find that hard to believe," she scoffed. Her opinions of the warlike tribe hadn't changed so drastically.

At her outright skepticism, he glowered at her, wheeled his horse about, and galloped out of the shady glen.

They rode at a brisk trot side by side for nearly an hour, neither speaking. Finally he broached the invisible wall between them to suggest that they dismount and walk the horses for a while.

"How did you meet Jacob and Anna Graber?" he asked as they strode through the autumn grass beside each other.

She cocked her head and looked up at him with a sideways glance. He'd spoken with an unblinking familiarity, as though he were suddenly one of her closest confidants, and nothing untoward had ever passed between them. When he wished, he could flit from topic to topic like a slack-jawed gossipmonger. Now she was learning, firsthand, that when he pursued a subject he was interested in, he was unswervingly tenacious. He'd make a good foreign diplomat, she decided, because of his verbal adroitness alone.

"I met them at my sister's farm," she answered at once, unwilling to get him riled up again. "Jacob is her husband's cousin. He and Anna were on a visit after having worked on the Southern Cheyenne reservation. It was in the Oklahoma lands that they learned to speak your language."

"And so Jacob taught you?"

"Yes. He'd been entrusted by the head of Indian affairs to find a doctor for the Lame Deer agency. From the moment we met, Jacob was convinced that I was the one to fill the job." She smiled feebly, hoping her self-doubt wouldn't be as evident as she felt. "He still believes it."

Absently War Lance reached up and rubbed Red Wind's nose. His brow furrowed into a puzzled frown. "And your parents didn't forbid you to travel so far away from their camp?"

"My parents are dead," she replied with quiet gravity. "My mother died in my fifteenth winter, my father just last summer. I have only my sister, Pauline, now. When she married, I went to stay on her farm, to be with her until her baby came."

His voice was filled with sympathetic understanding. "And now you feel you are not welcomed by your sister's man. That you do not belong in their lodge."

Uneasy, she ran the reins back and forth through her gloved fingers. For hired help, he was amazingly perceptive. She tipped her chin up and met his dark eyes with bravado. "No, it wasn't that at all. It was just time to return to the practice of my medicine."

Whether he believed her fabrications or not, he moved to another arena. "Are there many medicine women in the white man's world?"

She smiled to herself at his apparent lack of male prejudice. "Not many. I am one of the few females who have been allowed to study it."

"And did you learn your secrets from an old medicine woman?"

At the sincerity of his question, she laughed out loud. His eyes lit up in puzzled amusement at her reaction.

"No, I went to school to learn to be a doctor," she explained, then looked up at him thoughtfully. "You could go to school," she blurted out.

Goodness gracious, where had that idea come from? She was startled at the depth of her contradictory feelings toward him. Despite his lack of education, she suspected he was highly intelligent. Doggedly she continued. "You could learn anything you wanted to, War Lance. I know you could. But first you'd have to speak the white man's language."

He didn't respond immediately, but bent and picked up the yellow and black feather of a golden plover that had snagged on a clump of small cacti bear. He twirled it between his fingers as he admired the brilliant color, then reached over and stroked it along her jawline, letting her feel its satiny smoothness. "I do not speak the white man's language," he stated at last with gruff finality.

Annoyed by his lack of interest, she pushed the feather away. "I could teach you."

"I do not think so, *náevehoka*. I have never been able to say the *vèho* words. It is too hard to push my tongue into the shape of a spoon."

She chuckled. "Is that what it feels like to pronounce our words?" With further thought, she added, "But you say 'angel' perfectly."

Flashing her a devastating grin, he reached over and stuck the feather into the band of her flat-crowned hat. "For some reason, it is the only word I can remember."

She ignored the teasing light in his eyes and continued seriously. "If you can learn one word, War Lance Striking, you can learn others. I'd be happy to teach you."

"No, Little Red Fox," he said, his dark eyes bright with a wry humor. "It is no use. I spent six years in the white man's iron house and do not remember a single word I heard there. Besides, why should I try to learn the white man's talk when you speak my tongue so well?"

"Do I?" she demanded. She came to a complete halt and turned to face the tall warrior. With the unexpected stop, Painted Doll's shoulder bumped into her back, and she absently pushed the mare away as she regained her footing. She eyed War Lance suspiciously. "Do I really? Sometimes I feel as though people are laughing at me. Even when they appear to know exactly what I mean."

A wicked smile flickered across his expressive mouth before he answered with measured solemnity. "I can understand every word you say, angel."

Two days later, they left the band of Chief White Elk and followed the Tongue River north. At the Elk's camp, as at every other village along the way, no Indian had allowed Suzette to treat him. Her solitary chance to practice medicine, aside from the mandatory examination she'd been ordered to give War Lance, had been the treatment of little Yellow Feather's cut hand.

The temperature had risen steadily, and the Chinook

wind still blew, draining her energy. By the time War Lance Striking pulled into a sheltered draw with a running stream, Suzette was wilted from the stifling heat and the blistering pace he'd set all that morning. Exhausted, she slid down from Painted Doll, stumbled, and nearly toppled headlong into the grass.

He caught her elbow and steadied her. "We will take a long rest this afternoon, Little Red Fox." His voice was edged with regret. "I should have known better. You cannot keep up this fast speed when it is so hot. I'll unsaddle your mare and let the horses graze while you catch your breath."

But they both knew it wasn't just the heat or the frenetic pace that had exhausted her.

She was angry at him.

Downright boiling mad.

For the past two days she had tried to teach him a few simple nouns in her language. Each time she'd pointed at something and pronounced its English name slowly and clearly, he'd repeated the item's label just as slowly, just as clearly, in Cheyenne.

"Hackberry," she said, pointing at a tree with its small, cherrylike fruit.

"*Kokoemen,*" he replied with irritating complacency.

"Ear," she drilled at him, touching her own.

"*Matovōxz,*" he said with a smirk as he reached over and lightly traced the curve of her ear with his fingertip.

The one-sided lessons had progressed to the point where she was completely exasperated with his stubbornness; she was certain he wasn't even trying to learn. Teaching the handsome warrior her own language now became an irresistible challenge.

Finally, during the meal in White Elk's lodge earlier that morning, she'd pointed to the cooking pot and pronounced "kettle" in English.

"Kettle," Broadnosed Woman, the chief's first wife, had repeated in the *vèho* language.

"Kettle," Elk's second wife exclaimed, picking up the new game.

"Kettle," the old man chief parroted, his leathered face creased in a proud grin.

"Maxevetō," War Lance said with a smug look, like a little boy clowning in front of his schoolmates, and the family burst into laughter at his wonderful joke.

"Dunce," Suzette retorted in English, shoving her index finger against his broad chest.

His eyes opened wide and his jaw tensed. Though he couldn't possibly understand what the word meant, she knew he could tell from her caustic inflection that it was anything but flattering.

"That's right," she retaliated in Cheyenne, refusing to back down despite the presence of the fascinated listeners. She put her hands on her hips and leaned toward him, so he wouldn't miss a word she said. "Do you want to know what *dunce* means? It means you're an empty-headed fool. It means you have no brains, understand?" She pointed to her head. "All that's between your ears is a block of wood."

Their audience roared at her explanation. White Elk had to hold his sides as he toppled backward in his blanket and rolled on the floor of the lodge, while Broadnosed Woman laughed until the tears streamed down her wrinkled cheeks. Abashed, War Lance Striking looked at their hosts and smiled sheepishly.

"That's it, grin!" Suzette exclaimed. ''Grin like the simpleminded idiot you are." She darted out of the lodge and stalked toward their horses.

She'd refused to talk to him after that, though he'd followed her over to Painted Doll and tried to help her with the bridle and saddle.

"I can do it," she'd snapped. She'd grabbed the bit out of his hand. "Let's just get going."

"Little Red Fox is like the angry hornet," he said in a taunting voice, as he tossed the blanket and saddle on the piebald mare. "She whizzes around my head, *zzt, zzt, zzt,* and stings when I am not looking." His forced smile never quite reached the dark eyes that sparked with unconcealed annoyance.

But she'd resolutely ignored him as she tightened the cinch, mounted, and rode off. It had made her even angrier still when she'd had to sit and wait until he'd caught up with her, because she hadn't the faintest idea which direction was home. After that, he'd set a breakneck pace, not even looking back to see if she was behind him. It was all she could do to hold on tight and try to catch up.

Now with a reprieve at last, she stood beside Painted Doll in the shade of a cottonwood, removed her dusty gray hat with its brightly colored feather, and ran her hand over her warm brow. Under her blouse, her camisole stuck to her moist, overheated skin. When she started to loosen the mare's flank girth, War Lance pushed her hand aside and motioned for her to sit down in the grass. Gratefully she sank to the ground and pulled off her boots.

"Your face is nearly as red as your hair, *náevehoka*." He smiled teasingly, but she could hear the underlying concern in his voice. He removed the saddle, blanket pads, and packs, hobbling Red Wind only, for Painted Doll would not wander far from the stallion. Then he walked over to Suzette's spot in the shade.

He looked down from his great height and spoke in a detached voice. "I am going to cool off in the stream. It would be a good idea if you did the same."

"I can't go swimming with you," she exclaimed, refusing to admit to herself how pleasurable the idea sounded. She detested the ignorant lout. Let him poke fun at her for trying to help him. She was the one with the education and training. He was the bumpkin.

Lance looked at the flushed young woman with an uncomfortable mixture of remorse, irritation, and irrepressible amusement. He'd purposefully ridden at a hellfor-leather speed that morning in retaliation for her name calling. He'd been furious at her mockery of him. Furious that she believed him such a blockhead when it came to learning a new language. And furious that he had no choice but to continue his performance as the village idiot. No matter that it was the role he purposely played for her benefit, not daring to let anyone suspect he understood a word of English. She rightly considered him an ignoramus, and it rankled like a thistle caught inside a new moccasin.

Now she was literally steaming—from the heat and her own rage. Her face was a bright crimson, her hair matted against her perspiring head, her slender shoulders drooping with exhaustion. The best thing for both of them would be a cooling dip in the stream and a little quiet time to relax.

"You could take your stockings off and wade in up to your knees," he suggested with a dispassion he wasn't feeling. He sat down on the bank and pulled off his moccasins, then rose and stripped off his leggings. He stood attired in only a breechclout and realized that a splash in the water with her would be more than invigorating. It would be intoxicating.

With exaggerated aloofness, she reached over and retrieved a book from her saddlebag. Her tone was brittle with resentment. "I think I'd better just sit here for a while. Thank you."

Lance knew he should turn and walk away, leaving her to calm down alone. But he couldn't resist the chance to let her know he'd understood exactly what she'd called him that morning. "You should cool off, *mashavèhoka*," he said. "Refusing to go into the stream is not very wise."

"Crazy little white woman?" she sputtered. She tossed the slim volume on top of her bedroll and jumped to her stockinged feet. Her violet eyes glittered with indignation. "You dare call me a crazed woman?" Her pert nose tilted skyward. She sat back down on the grass with a plop and folded her arms, plainly determined to do exactly the opposite of anything he suggested. "If you think I would go into the water with you, you're the one who's feebleminded."

He eyed her with growing exasperation. Maybe it was time for *him* to administer a lesson or two. Her full bottom lip thrust forward in the tiniest hint of a pout, making her look like a spoiled schoolgirl who, just once, hadn't been given her own way—petulant and cross and adorable. Except no proper young miss would allow herself to be seen wearing those outrageous trousers. It was no wonder he'd dreamed of her every night, the way the blue broadcloth revealed the provocative outline of her little tail end with her slightest movement. Hell, a man could take just so much temptation.

Before she could even suspect the train of his thoughts, he bent over, scooped her up in his arms, and headed for the creek.

"Put me down!" she screeched. She pounded on his chest. When that didn't work, she tried to box his ears.

Ignoring the punishment she meted out so ineffectively, he waded into the cold water up to his hips. When she demanded once more that he set her free, he opened his arms and let go.

As she felt herself start to drop, she screamed in panic. Grabbing hold of his hair, she hung on with the tenacity of a woman being pushed off a second-story balcony. For an instant, he thought she was going to scalp him, then decided, what the hell. Over on top of her he went. They rolled beneath the water in a giant somersault. He came up first, grabbed the neck of her blouse, and dragged her to the surface. She bobbed up, spitting water and gurgling with laughter.

He stopped, arrested by her sudden change of mood, and waited for her attack—ready to dodge if she made a move toward him.

"You should have see— seen the look on your fa— face just before y— you went under," she cried between gulps of air. She wiped the water from her eyes. Her red-gold hair had come loose from its pins and streamed over her shoulders in soggy disarray. Even soaking wet, it was a glorious sight.

"I was frightened," he confessed. "I don't know how to swim." At that moment he slipped awkwardly on the rocky bottom, staggered, and went under.

"You do, too," she called loudly.

But he didn't come back up.

For a minute there was total silence.

"War Lance!" she shrieked in sudden terror. "Oh, my God, War Lance!" She half jumped, half dove toward him. Just as her fingertips touched his shoulder, he sprang out of the water, soaring up in the air like a dolphin, roaring like a demented fiend.

She screamed again in terrified confusion, then pounded on his chest with her small fists. "You're the one who's crazy!" she cried, laughing at the same time. "You're just plain crazy!"

He caught her behind the knees, flipped her backward, and followed her into the water. This time they came up together in each other's arms. Her cold cheek grazed his bare shoulder as she rose from the stream. She froze, their lips only inches apart. Poker-straight, she leaned carefully away from him.

"Let me go," she ordered in a strangled voice.

Lance released her, as startled by the outcome of his frolicking as she was.

Suzette moved through the water toward the gently sloping bank in total confusion. Although the man's physique was reminiscent of some war god in Greek mythology, he was emotionally just a child, ready to roughhouse and sport at a moment's notice. What had just happened wasn't his fault. He'd never heard of the rules of proper etiquette. For his culture and background, he was behaving just as he ought. He didn't know any better.

But there was no excuse for her. The fact that she'd spent long years on a grueling schedule—kept on duty at the hospital for hours on end until she was nearing exhaustion—was no reason to dismiss her hoydenish behavior as a mere need to kick over the traces. Where their relationship was concerned, she, as the educated, more sophisticated one, was the person responsible to set the tone. Cavorting in the water like some amoral South Sea islander was definitely not establishing the employer-employee relationship she'd originally intended.

When she reached the grass, she turned to look back at him. He was standing hip-deep in the stream, the sunlight bouncing off his ink black hair. Drops of water glistened on his magnificent torso. He watched her with a gaze of sensuality that swept hungrily over the curves revealed so clearly by her soaking wet blouse and trousers. A slow, undulating ache washed over her, an ache she'd never felt before, not even when Jordan had courted her. For the first time in her life, she experienced the physical longing romanticized by poets and bards. Aghast, she whirled and hurried over to her pack, her water-soaked stockings squelching with each step. She yanked them off, then untied her bedroll and pulled out a blanket. Bewildered, she looked about for the means to strip off her wet garments under the protection of the woolen cover.

"I will walk downstream for a little way," War Lance Striking said quietly.

She jumped, realizing that he had left the water and walked soundlessly up the bank to stand beside her.

"I am going to fish for a while," he continued, "while your clothes dry out. You can rest, even sleep a little, if you like. I will remain within the sound of your call, should you need me."

She kept her eyelids lowered, afraid he would see the longing in her eyes. "Yes," she answered, mortified to hear the husky quality of her own voice. "I'll sit here and read."

Monique De Moivre Stanwood had admired the romantic poets of Great Britain. She'd read the works of Wordsworth, Byron, and Shelley aloud to her daughters when they were still quite young, infusing into the rich, descriptive rhymes her own joy in the natural world and its beauty, her delight in heroic themes, and her disposition to escape from society's staid conventions. But most of all, she'd loved the lyrical poetry of John Keats. Two days before she died, she gave her eldest daughter her own treasured volume of his work.

Suzette had read the tender inscription, written in her parent's perfect copperplate, with the certainty that her beloved mother would never recover from the influenza that had struck down so many people in the large cities of the East that terrible year.

Later, the gold-embossed memento had traveled with Suzette to medical school and then on to the hospital in Philadelphia where she'd spent her internship. It was the only keepsake of her mother's that she'd been able to bring on the long journey west. The lines of sensuous beauty in Keat's poetry, underscored with its high intellectual quality, never failed to remind her of her brilliant mother's passionate love of life.

Now Suzette, wrapped in a Navajo blanket with huge red tassels at the corners, sat propped against a tree trunk studying the oft-read passages once again. She wore only a fresh camisole and drawers beneath the cover. In the sunshine, her drying clothes were spread across the branches of a nearby kinnikinick shrub. She was so deeply involved in her reading, she missed War Lance's silent approach until he crouched down on one knee and laid a speckled trout, flopping wildly about, on the grass beside her.

"Tell me what you are reading, Little Red Fox."

She looked up, startled at his sudden appearance. "You wouldn't understand," she replied, not attempting to hide her air of condescension.

"You told me I could learn anything," he reminded her. A smile hovered enticingly at the corners of his mouth. "I would understand the words if you explained their *vèho* meaning to me."

She shook her head and closed the book with a snap, pulling the blanket closer about her bare shoulders. "No, these pages are for people who have gone to the white man's school. For those who can read and write in my language. You wouldn't understand the thoughts the writer tries to express."

His raven brows lifted in skepticism. "Thoughts are the same, no matter what the language."

"You would never understand these particular ideas, War Lance," she insisted as she gripped the slim volume in her lap with one hand and held the blanket close about her with the other.

He ran his fingertips lightly across her knuckles. His deep baritone rumbled softly. "Teach me, angel."

She recognized the muleheaded stubbornness hidden just beneath the dulcet request. With an exaggerated sigh, Suzette opened the pages again. "Very well. I was reading about a man named Lycius, who is deeply, completely, even blindly, in love with a beautiful woman."

War Lance grinned in triumph. "I understand that."

She glanced up to find his dark eyes twinkling with merriment and then looked back down at the printed page. "Lycius has been worried over cares of the world, and the lady, Lamia, accuses him of deserting her, at least in his thoughts."

"She is jealous," he interrupted like an ancient philosopher. "I understand that, too."

Suzette burst out laughing and shook her head. "I can see you are very wise in the ways of the world."

He rewarded her perspicacity with a disarming flash of his even white teeth. "This is easy so far. Go on," he urged.

"The young man praises her beauty, calling her his 'silver star'—"

"Women are all alike," War Lance Striking declared with a smug look. "They want to be told again and again how pretty they are."

"If you are going to keep interrupting me, I'll never

finish the story," she scolded. She felt the heat of a flush warm her cheeks. The unexplainable need for him to consider *her* pretty ignited inside her like dry paper laid over a bed of hot coals.

"I won't say another word," he promised at once, amusement dancing across his angular features.

She lifted her brows sceptically, but continued. "Lycius asks his beloved how she can possibly feel sad, for his greatest desire is to fill his heart with her deep love. He seeks to entangle and ensnare her spirit in his, to hold her there, caught in a maze, like the sweet, hidden scent in an unbudded rose."

"He should offer her father many ponies, if he is so much in love," War Lance suggested prosaically.

Looking down at the book, Suzette bit her lip to keep from giggling. "He does ask her to marry him. But at the wedding feast, his friend sees in the bride what Lycius has been blinded to all along. Lamia is no real woman, but a sorceress who has enchanted him. With this revelation of truth, she disappears before his eyes."

At the bleak stillness that followed, Suzette slowly lifted her lashes.

War Lance was watching her with a burning intensity, as though he half expected *her* to disappear. "I think I understand more than you know, *náevehoka*," he said, so softly she could barely catch the words. Then he stood and walked away.

He cooked the cutthroat trout over an open fire while she pulled on her dry clothes under the protection of the striped blanket. They ate the midday meal in companionable silence, after which Suzette cleaned up the eating utensils while War Lance readied their mounts.

"I have been thinking about your wish to teach me the white man's language," he said when it was time to go. He stood in front of the ground-tied horses, blocking her approach to Painted Doll. "Although I am not really interested in learning the *vèho* words, there is one of your customs I would like to know more about."

Delighted at this unexpected change of attitude, she stepped closer.

"Yes, what is it?"

"I have seen the way a white man and woman press their lips against each other's. This is something adult Cheyenne never do. But I am curious to learn about it. Perhaps you could teach me this custom."

Suzette peered at him suspiciously. The expression on his rugged features was one of naive detachment. When she answered, she found she was nearly breathless, as though she'd just run up four flights of stairs, late for her chemistry class again. "No, I couldn't teach you to kiss, War Lance Striking. It is against my personal code of behavior."

He looked down his aristocratic nose at her, his face a mask of haughty aloofness. "You have many rules, Little Red Fox. If your language is as difficult as your numerous laws of conduct, I would never be able to learn it anyway."

He turned to mount, then faced her again and added in an offhand manner, "But if you teach me to kiss, I promise to try harder to remember your paleface words."

A thrill went through Suzette at the offer. The thought of giving such a lesson was shocking. And fascinating.

She could never do such a scandalous thing.

Or could she?

She stared up at him, trying to discover the hidden motives behind his facade of indifference. But there wasn't a glimmer of lascivious intentions in those commanding black eyes. Nervously she fingered the narrow band of white lace at her throat.

"I'm no expert on kissing, War Lance," she warned him in her most discouraging manner. "For the past eight years I have done nothing but study to become a doctor. There has been no time—nor anyone to practice with."

He held his large hands out in a gesture of uncritical acceptance. "I won't complain about your lack of skill,

angel. After all, I am only a beginner myself. How could
I possibly judge your ability in this unusual custom?"

Suzette bit her lower lip in agonizing uncertainty.
Aside from her practice of medicine, her primary goal
since leaving the agency had become to teach him English. At least it had been, up until this astounding proposal. Surely it could be considered altruistic—this
education of the backward savage.

She folded her hands in front of her, as though praying
for the strength to resist the temptation she was about to
meet face-to-face.

"Very well," she said, drawing a shaky breath. "I'll do
it."

Chapter 8

As Lance watched the play of conflicting emotions on Suzette's delicate features, his heart began to hammer against his ribs with a dull thud. She gazed up at him with the astounded innocence of a red-haired angel who'd accidentally slipped off her cloud and landed with an ungraceful plop at his feet. A flicker of sensual awareness lit her enormous violet eyes when she comprehended, at last, the full meaning of his shocking proposal.

At her look of curious anticipation, it was all he could do to keep from dragging her into his arms and gliding his hands over her slender body. He knew full well that under no circumstances should he have struck such a perilous bargain. Till that moment, he had successfully kept his rampaging desires under rigid control. Now, with utmost effort, he attempted to batter down the instinctive male drive that threatened to destroy his cool composure. There could never be anything between a genteel white lady doctor and an Indian half-breed, no matter what his status or education.

Fleetingly a picture of the voluptuous blond mistress he'd left behind in London rose before him. Even now, Melissa Montgomery was probably entertaining some handsome rake in the very rooms he'd rented for her in Knightsbridge. The thought didn't upset him, however.

He knew she'd be there waiting for him when he returned. If she wasn't, she'd be easily replaced.

But though the British women, including those of the upper class, were intrigued by the idea of bedding the noble savage, it was altogether a different matter with their middle-class sisters on this side of the Atlantic. The two hundred years of unremitting Indian wars, spent wresting the land from its native inhabitants at any cost, had taught the Yanks, including their womenfolk, a hatred and fear of the red man that was as unreasoning as it was irrevocable. Over and over again, tales of Indian atrocities against the encroaching settlers had been exaggerated in the retelling in order to justify the breaking of treaties and forced movements of entire tribes. Wholesale slaughter of men, women, and children was excused in the eastern newspapers in the name of progress as the frontier was pushed ever westward. The festering animosity between the clashing cultures insured that no white woman would be allowed by American society to consort with a despised and degenerate half-breed. The price of such an alliance would be far higher than any member of the weaker sex could ever pay.

Besides protecting Suzette from the danger surrounding his mission as a secret agent, Lance was determined not to become sexually involved with her for her own sake. He could survive, with his world-weary cynicism and bitter personal experience, the emotional havoc such a liaison would wreak. She could not. She was a highstrung, high-minded spinster. He had a hunch she'd never lain with a man in all her twenty-eight years. What right did he have to seduce her? To use the extensive amorous skills he's acquired during his clandestine dallyings with the jaded married ladies of the British aristocracy, knowing there was no future for the two of them? No honorable Cheyenne warrior would seduce an innocent maiden without the intention of staying beside her, to care for and protect her.

Under his steady gaze, her russet lashes swept down to shadow her blushing cheeks. A half smile turned up the trembling corners of her softly molded lips. She seemed unable or unwilling to break the charged silence between them.

"I will not insist that you keep the bargain," he rasped, forcing himself to say the noble, upright thing. "Perhaps you spoke before you'd given the idea enough thought."

"Oh, no!" she exclaimed irrepressibly. She stepped toward him, directly meeting his gaze with wide, expressive eyes, and the sweet perfume of violets drifted about him. "I'm willing to do it. I . . . I want to do it." Her hand flew to her mouth, covering her lips in dismay at her unplanned confession.

At the triumphant grin he was unable to hide, she corrected herself with a shaky laugh. "That is, I want to teach you to speak my language. You do promise to try as hard as possible to learn it?"

"I will try as hard as I can," he lied, ruthlessly shoving aside the twinge of guilt that needled his sense of decency and fair play. He breathed in the enticing female smell of her and felt the blood pound in his veins. A surge of carnal desire flooded his body. With all the self-restraint he could muster, he kept his voice calm and controlled. "And now, what should I do?"

Her smooth brow furrowed in puzzlement as she gazed up at him thoughtfully. She tapped her upper lip in adorable concentration. "Hmm, let me see. I've never instructed anyone on how to kiss. It will be a little bit like taking the lead in teaching you to dance, I suppose. One problem is that you're so tall."

"Being tall is a problem in kissing?" he asked in amazement, fascinated at the trajectory of her thoughts.

Suzette smiled in relief at his obvious naïveté. For a moment she had debated the wisdom of what she was doing, but he was so completely at a loss in the matter, his inexperience soothed her fears. "Don't worry," she told him. "Your great height isn't something we can't overcome."

She glanced around and spotted the fallen cottonwood she'd sat on during their meal. She grabbed his hand and tugged impatiently. "Come on, let's move over by that tree."

Having pulled him after her, she hopped up on the log and turned to face him on his own level. "This is much better," she said as she placed her hands on his bare shoulders. His skin was warm and firm beneath her touch. She could feel the muscles bunch reflexively under her fingertips. "But you need to move closer."

He advanced a tiny step. "Like this?"

"Even closer," she instructed from her perch. When he was directly in front of her, only inches away, she leaned forward and slid her arms about his neck until she stood nearly nose to nose with him. She inhaled the masculine scent of his fresh, clean hair and skin, mingled with the comfortable aroma of buckskin and woodsmoke, and caught her breath as her heart skidded to a halt.

He was prodigiously, marvelously, heartbreakingly handsome. His hawklike features seemed chiseled by some idealistic Renaissance sculptor, the planes of his bronzed face rugged, the slightly hooked nose aristocratic and proud, the brows and lashes thick, shiny, and ebony black. He watched her with inquisitive eyes as though wondering what on earth she'd do next.

"Now I'm going to kiss you," she informed him in a breathy voice, ignoring the pleasurable rush of heat through her limbs. Without further warning, she leaned forward and pressed her tightly closed mouth against his. There was no response as he remained stock-still, apparently waiting for something more to happen. His lips were slightly parted, but he exerted no pressure or made any move in return. With his arms hanging loosely at his sides, he stood perfectly straight, not even bending forward in response to her embrace. Determined to garner some reaction on his part, she gripped him tighter, smashing her lips against his. He remained calm and impassive, allowing her to kiss him with unseemly forwardness without returning any pressure of his own accord.

Disappointment at his wooden response enveloped her. She was put forcefully in mind of a large cigar store Indian she'd seen at a Northern Pacific whistle stop on her way west that summer. It had stood outside a mercantile emporium in Bismarck, staring across the prairie with unseeing eyes.

She released War Lance and pulled back to study him in mute frustration.

He smiled faintly, a look of bewilderment in his eyes. "It is a strange custom, *náevehoka*. I do not understand why one should bother to do it."

She sighed in exasperation. "You are going to have to give me a little help, War Lance. I can't do this all by myself. Don't just stand there and let me kiss you," she scolded him like a flustered schoolmarm to a big, lumbering farm boy who'd failed to learn his times tables. "Kiss me back."

"I thought I was," he said apologetically. "What more should I do?"

"First, put your arms around me. That's it," she said as he followed her instructions and obediently wrapped his arms loosely about her. "Next, you need to return my kiss by pushing your lips against mine."

"Let's try it again," he suggested.

Once more, Suzette slid her arms about his neck and drew close. "This time, do exactly as I do," she directed. Her lips almost touched his as she spoke. "Press your mouth against mine."

She tilted her head, slanting her mouth across his. As she felt his lips beneath her own, an unexpected shock of vibrant urgency jolted through her. But his arms still encircled her limply. He tipped his head in imitation of her movement and lightly returned her buss, the pressure weightless . . . innocent.

Clearly he still wasn't getting the idea.

She increased the force of the kiss, clinging to him with all her strength. Her breasts were crushed against the hard wall of his chest, and she sensed, rather than felt, a faint, involuntary response in the muscles of his powerful torso and shoulders as he drew her infinitesimally closer. The feel of his sinewy arms enclosing her, no matter how gently, sent the blood rushing to her brain, and she was suddenly light-headed. Unwilling to stop until she felt an equal reaction on his part, she prolonged the kiss, drawing in deep drafts of air, as an unfamiliar longing sprang up inside her, coiling its way through the center of her body. She slipped her fingers into the thick hair at the nape of his neck and pulled his head closer, trying to force him to respond to the kiss.

But it was no use.

He simply didn't understand what she wanted him to do. She yearned for him to take the lead, to become the aggressor, to sweep her off her feet in a passionate, romantic embrace. Instead, he was merely allowing her to kiss him while he remained unmoved, his shallow, even breathing scarcely affected. Reluctantly she withdrew from his arms and met his unperturbed gaze with disillusionment.

"Maybe I'm not a very good teacher, War Lance," she said, her heart pounding, her breathing shaky and erratic. "No better with kissing than with words."

"It is not your fault, Little Red Fox," he said. He moved his hands to her waist and gave her a squeeze of consolation. His rich baritone was steady and even. "I had thought there was more to it. I was wrong."

She placed her hands on his broad shoulders, thrilling to the feel of his athletic frame beneath her fingertips.

It was too soon to give up.

She slid her fingers around the base of his neck and rested her thumbs on his collarbone, unable to stop touching him. "There is something we haven't tried," she admitted cautiously as she traced tiny circles on his bronzed skin with the pads of her thumbs. She drew a steadying breath and rushed on. "I've heard that sometimes a man and woman touch each other's tongues when they kiss."

"I am willing to try," War Lance declared without hesitation.

"I'm not!" she gasped, horrified at his immediate acceptance, though what else she'd expected, she couldn't guess. "In the first place, I've never done it before, so I'm not even sure I can do it correctly. In the second place . . . in the second place," she continued distractedly, looking with fascination at his generous mouth, "I don't think it would be a good idea."

"I think it would," he contradicted her with open enthusiasm. "The more I learn of the white man's ways, the more I begin to understand him. Perhaps if I practice this strange kind of kissing, it might help me pronounce the *vèho* words better. How will we know unless we try?"

She met his forthright gaze with fluttery confusion. At the moment, there was nothing she would rather do than help him further his studies. She felt his strong hands encircling her waist, and longed to feel his arms about her once again. She knew darn well there was nothing altruistic about it. And there wasn't a chance in a million it would help him pronounce the words in English any better. Still, he was so totally unskilled in the arts of seduction, there was hardly any danger of things getting out of control.

"All right," she said at last. "I'm willing to give it a chance."

Once more she slipped her arms around his neck and pressed her body against the supporting wall of his chest. Tilting her head, she slanted her lips against his. This time his mouth was open, ready for her. Timidly she touched her tongue to his, and he met her in a sensual, erotic welcome, sliding his tongue around hers, encouraging her to enter and learn the taste and feel of him. Desire leaped up within her, destroying all common sense, driving her over the brink of sexual awakening. Her hands roamed over his bare shoulders and back, exploring the bulging muscles that tensed beneath her touch. She wanted to devour him, to learn on a personal and intimate basis all there was to know between a man and a woman.

With a low growl, he lifted her off the log, pressing her against his hard frame. One powerful hand cupped her bottom as he brought her up against his lean hips, letting her feel through the blue broadcloth of her trousers the full extent of his male arousal. When she thought they could reach no higher plane of intimacy, he turned the tables and thrust his tongue inside her mouth, probing and exploring and stroking every soft crevice and fold. Hungrily he ran his tongue across her teeth and then coaxed her to reenter his mouth. From deep in her throat came an unbidden whimper of surrender as she melted against him and felt his consuming sensuality engulf her.

Her tiny cry of submission seemed to bring him back to reality. He broke off the kiss and pulled away, allowing her to slide down the length of him in slow, agonizing contact till her toes touched the ground. With a soft murmur, he released her and the lesson was over. But whether she was the tutor or the student was no longer clear.

In blushing confusion she averted her eyes and walked toward Painted Doll on shaky legs. Unable to believe her own pagan reaction to his kiss, and mortified at the utter wantonness of her behavior, she mounted her horse, relieved to see that he'd already leaped astride the great red stallion. She followed War Lance out of the shady draw, still unable to meet his gaze.

He took off at a lope, and she realized with a shock the words he'd murmured in her ear as he released her. War Lance Striking had spoken, at last, his first complete sentence in English: *Little woman doctor heap good teacher.*

He might be a slow learner when it came to the white

man's language, but good Lord, he was a quick study in kissing.

Suzette lay on the feather mattress of her brass bed and stared up at the darkened clapboard ceiling above her with discouragement. She wondered bleakly if she would fail even here on the reservation, where a doctor was needed so desperately. After seven days of riding from camp to camp, she hadn't treated a single patient other than Yellow Feather. She'd returned to the cabin she shared with the Grabers only the day before, exhausted, downhearted, and dumbfounded by her own shameless behavior. Neither she nor her paid companion had mentioned the kissing lesson after leaving the stream beside the sheltering cottonwoods. He'd seemed to understand her confusion and avoided the topic completely as he led her across the rolling hills and back to the compound at Lame Deer. Even when they'd said good-bye, she was so humiliated and ashamed of herself, she could barely stand to look at him. How could she have stooped so low? Dear God, he was nothing but a heathen savage.

It was late evening now, and though the entire agency was silent and still, she had tossed and turned for what seemed like hours, unable to fall asleep. Each time she thought about the high-principled man she'd once planned to marry, she had to fight back tears of self-recrimination. Finally giving up the fruitless attempt to sleep, she struck a match and lit the kerosene lamp that sat on the narrow bureau beside her bed. Its round street-light shade was made of ruby glass, decorated with a floral design. It cast a warm, rosy glow about the tiny room. She carried it into her office and chose a thick medical volume from her limited library shelf in the hopes that such serious reading would lull her to sleep.

A soft knock sounded at the office door, and Suzette opened it to find Anna standing in the covered dogtrot, a lantern in her hand. She was dressed in a plain blue flannel wrapper with a white linen nightcap tied snugly over her gray hair.

"I saw the light under your door," she said with concern. "Is everything all right?"

"Come in," Suzette invited, pleased to have company. "I was restless. Couldn't you sleep either?" She led her visitor through the office and into the bedroom, where she replaced the lamp on the bureau. She perched on the edge of the soft mattress.

Anna's blue eyes twinkled. "*Ja*, when Jacob is away, I don't sleep so good," she confessed. She rested one hand on her ample bosom and nodded with patient acceptance. "He'll be back from his trip to Miles City for supplies soon. Now tell me what is bothering you, *Liebchen*, that you can't get to sleep."

"I was wondering what Pauline was doing at this very moment. Is she sound asleep or nursing her tiny daughter? I still feel a sense of responsibility for her even though she's thousands of miles away."

"You were only fifteen when your mother died," Anna said with sympathy as she came over and placed her lantern beside Suzette's lamp. She sat down on the edge of the bed beside her young friend. "And your sister was just eight. It was only natural that you would feel responsible for her care."

With a sigh, Suzette slipped off the bed and padded across the plank floorboards in her bare feet. She pushed aside the chintz curtains and opened the window, allowing the evening breeze to flow into the room. The stars shone like tiny golden lights in the night sky, and she scanned the heavens until she found the Big Dipper.

"With such a heavy burden to bear," Anna asked, "how did you ever come to be a doctor?"

Suzette looked back over her shoulder with a smile. "I've been fascinated with medicine since I was a child. I took over my mother's place in the family drugstore when she died at thirty-five. It was a sudden death that left all of us stunned and bewildered." She turned to face the room and leaned back against the windowsill. "After school each day, when I wasn't waiting on my father's customers or helping him fill prescriptions, I studied his pharmaceutical journals."

Suzette's gaze sought out the photograph on the birch bureau. She walked across the room and lifted the frame for a closer look at the army captain who smiled so jauntily back at her. For an instant a strong, chiseled face with straight, dark brows above shrewd black eyes rose before her, and suddenly Jordan Maclure's perfect features seemed soft and weak, even effeminate, in comparison.

"He was very handsome, your young man," Anna said. She knew only the barest details—the soldier's name, and that he'd been engaged to Suzette years ago—for back in Pennsylvania, neither of the Stanwood sisters had been willing to talk about his untimely death.

Suzette nodded in thoughtful agreement. "Even though we were raised in the same town, I'd only known him for a month at the time of our betrothal. But my, oh, my, he was everything that I'd ever dreamed about, as bold and reckless as any Lochinvar. Blond, blue-eyed, and so terribly good-looking, he came charging into my life on a white steed and literally swept me off my feet. Pauline used to tease me, calling him my knight in shining armor."

Anna clucked her tongue sympathetically as Suzette continued. "I guess my sister was right. I was convinced he was an answer to a maiden's prayers. In the grief and despair that followed Jordan's death, I was certain that no one could ever replace the courageous military hero I'd lost. Looking back now, I realize that I idolized him. I never gave any other man a chance to compete with the romanticized Sir Galahad of my memory. Despite the fact that I barely knew him—or perhaps because of it— Jordan remained a swashbuckling hero in his blue and gold cavalry uniform, with his long saber and shiny black boots, long after my girlish fancies should have been set aside."

She looked at Anna and smiled forlornly. "Is it any wonder I believed him irreplaceable? After he was killed in battle, I searched for something to give meaning to my life. My dear father remembered how, four years before, I'd pored endlessly over his reference books for a drug that could have prevented my mother's death. So he encouraged me to go to medical school. With the assistance of a Quaker physician and personal friend, he enrolled me at the Women's Medical College in Philadelphia. I'm not sure he really believed I'd ever become a doctor. He was just frantically seeking for something that would give his eldest daughter a reason to go on living."

"And you found it," Anna said as she folded her hands serenely in her lap.

Since she'd met them, the peacefulness that surrounded the Mennonite couple had been like a soothing balm to Suzette's tormented soul; she felt that serenity reach out to comfort her now.

"Yes. After earning my degree, I completed my internship at the Women's and Children's Hospital. And then, because of my father's failing health, I refused a residency in New York and returned to Lancaster to open a practice above our family drugstore."

She replaced the picture on the dresser and went to sit beside Anna. Clasping one knee in her cupped hands, she stared thoughtfully at the roughly chinked wall. "I remember the thrill of hanging my own small shingle beneath my father's large storefront sign. But my initial excitement slowly changed to humiliation as I waited in vain for my first case. Not one person climbed the narrow stairs to the second floor and presented himself as a patient."

Anna patted her arm with infinite kindness. *"Ach, du lieber,"* she uttered quietly. "What did you do then?"

"Once again I filled the long hours waiting on my father's customers. Trying to remain cheerful, smiling bravely for Daddy, who watched with silent compassion as the weeks turned into months. A year later, he died of a massive heart attack. That very month, Pauline informed me that she was pregnant with Christian's child and they planned to marry immediately."

When Suzette's voice broke at the mention of her father's death, Anna put her plump arm about her. "So you felt there was nothing to do but sell the pharmacy and go with your sister to live on my cousin's farm?"

"Yes. By that time, I'd abandoned all hope of a private practice." She looked at Anna through unshed tears. "Until I met you and Jacob."

Anna hugged her. Her round face dimpled as she smiled. "I tell you what, dear. I'm going to fix you some warm milk. That should help you sleep."

"No, no, Anna. You go on back to bed. I'm finally feeling drowsy. I'll be asleep in no time."

As the stocky hausfrau was about to close the door, Suzette called to her. "Thank you, Anna. I guess I just needed someone to talk to."

"We all need that," she replied. "Sweet dreams, *Liebchen*."

Suzette's dreams were sweet indeed, for she succeeded, at last, in pushing aside the troubling memories and dreaming instead of splashing about in a fresh, clear stream with a very tall, very naked Cheyenne warrior.

A loud noise brought Suzette reluctantly awake. It was still quite dark, perhaps only a little after midnight. The sound of someone banging persistently on the outer door of her office came from the hallway between the two log buildings. Shoving the coverlet aside, she rose and pulled on a robe over her nightgown, then hurriedly lit her lamp and left the bedchamber. As she crossed the small room that served as her office, she could hear Anna calling to their unexpected visitor from the other side of the dogtrot.

"*Ja, ja!* Who is it? What do you want?"

When there was no response except for the continued banging, Suzette repeated the questions in Cheyenne.

"It's me," War Lance Striking shouted through the wooded barrior. "I need to see you, *náevhoka.*"

Simultaneously Suzette and Anna swung their doors open. The tall scout stood on the dirt floor of the covered dogtrot. In his arms he carried a small Indian boy, curled up into a tight ball of obvious misery.

"It's my son," War Lance said in hurried Cheyenne. "Something's wrong with him. He was in great pain when I arrived at the camp yesterday. His mother says he's been like this for over two days."

"Your son?" Suzette repeated in dazed confusion. She held the ruby-colored lantern higher to see the child as Anna moved closer as well.

"My brother's son, Young Wolf," he amended hastily. He stepped past her and entered the office. His words were clipped and strained. "Bear Scalp is out on a hunting trip. He won't be home for several days. Will you look at the boy?"

"Of course," she said, coming to her senses. She'd forgotten that a Cheyenne man referred to his brother's male child as his own. In the darkness she hadn't recognized the six-year-old she'd met at the lodge of Blue Crane Flying. For some unexplainable reason, relief swept over her when she realized her mistake. "Take him into my office."

Quickly Anna and Suzette spread a clean sheet on the narrow wooden bench that stood against one wall and served as an examining table, then moved their lanterns closer. War Lance laid the suffering child down with open tenderness. His nephew immediately turned to his side, his knees drawn up to his abdomen, his round face contorted in pain.

"How long has he been like this?" Suzette asked as she shook down the mercury in her thermometer.

"Two days. Blue Crane Flying tried to cure him with her strongest medicine and healing songs, but nothing

worked. She has remained at the camp with my grandmother and Yellow Feather. They will come tomorrow
morning rather than attempt the ride in the dark."

"I need to put this glass stick in Young Wolf's mouth,"
she quickly explained, holding up the thermometer for
the boy's uncle to see. "You must tell him not to bite on
it, just keep it still under his tongue."

War Lance held out his large hand. "I will do that,
náevehoka. He will listen and follow my instructions."

As the Cheyenne brave guided the frightened Young
Wolf through his first experience with a thermometer, she
slipped her stethoscope in place and listened to the
child's strong, steady heartbeat, then checked his eyes
and ears, while Anna brought the lantern light closer.

"He's been throwing up his food?" she asked War
Lance with near certainty, noting the signs of dehydra-
tion.

He looked at her with worried eyes, clearly disturbed
that she'd guessed the symptoms so quickly. "Yes. Since
early this morning, although he hasn't eaten all day."

"His temperature is one hundred degrees, Dr.
Fräulein," Anna said, holding the thermometer up to the
light and peering at it through the round little reading
glasses she'd extracted from her pocket.

Suzette nodded abstractedly. The pain and abdominal
tenderness characteristic of appendicitis was often accompanied by a slight fever.

She gently shoved the child's shirt aside, loosened his
breechcloth string, and removed the loin covering. "I'm
going to have to push on your belly," she warned Young
Wolf in her softest Cheyenne. "It may hurt a little."

She palpated the area of his lower right abdomen, and
her sudden release of pressure caused the young boy to
rebound in pain with a spasmodic jerk. He whimpered at
the sudden, unexpected agony, then clenched his jaw, refusing to make another sound. She rewarded his youthful
bravery with a smile of reassurance that she was far from
feeling. In small children an attack of appendicitis was

usually suppurative from the start, and comparatively few cases would subside without surgical intervention.

She didn't have the option of waiting until the next morning for the child's mother to arrive. Not only was Young Wolf suffering from acute appendicitis, but there was also a definite danger of peritonitis should she put off the operation. The appendix might rupture later during the night. The fact that War Lance had transported the boy in an upright position in front of him on Red Wind was a blessing, for any infectious material would have naturally gravitated to the pelvic area, where there was less danger of doing serious damage. But there was no way of knowing for sure until she opened the abdomen.

She stroked the child's long hair back from his forehead. "I know you hurt badly, Young Wolf," she whispered. "Just lie still for a minute longer while I talk to *èho*."

With an inclination of her head, she motioned for War Lance to follow her around the screen that separated the examining table from the rest of her office area, leaving Anna to stay with the child.

"Young Wolf has a serious, possibly fatal, illness," she explained briefly and succinctly. "Unless I cut his belly open immediately and remove the bad part, he will probably die."

Tortured with indecision, Lance gazed down at the slim young woman standing in front of him. She was dressed in a morning wrapper of deep blue cashmere, with a high mandarin collar and gold braided frogs that marched all the way down its front to the floor-length hem. Her coppery hair fell down her back in one long, thick braid, while escaping wisps of it curled about her temples. In the rosy glow of the lantern light, with her schoolgirl braid and her bare toes peeping out from under her dressing gown, she looked all of seventeen. Not nearly old enough to do what she was suggesting.

"You are certain this must be done?" he countered,

scrutinizing her lovely features with harried intensity. He was torn by doubt. What did he really know of her skill as a physician? When he'd questioned her about her past, she'd held back, as though trying to keep her reasons for coming to the reservation a secret. Had she failed as a doctor in the East due to gross incompetence or lack of proper training? There was no way he could be sure of her ability to operate on his nephew successfully.

"As certain as I can possibly be," she replied. She met his gaze with unflinching candor. "Even if I do this, I cannot promise you that Young Wolf will survive. I can only guarantee this: We can't wait for Blue Crane Flying to arrive in the morning. I must do it now. Will you give me your permission?"

"Yes," he said, making the final, irrevocable decision. The determination, courage, and tenacity of purpose he saw in her intelligent eyes convinced him that she had the training and knowledge to perform the surgery. As a diplomat, he'd learned to read a person's character with uncanny success. "Will you make your healing medicine on Young Wolf where he is now?"

"No, my office is too small, and I'll need a better table to work on," she replied. She led him back to re-join Anna and the child behind the screen. "The best area is the kitchen, where all three of us can work together. I'm going to ask both of you to help me."

While Suzette talked, she pulled out the clean, old tablecloths she'd brought with her to use as surgical sheets and handed them to Anna, who'd been holding Young Wolf's hand and comforting him in soothing Cheyenne. Then she opened the glass cabinet and selected the instruments, drugs, and other supplies she would need.

"I'll put on some water to boil, Dr. Fräulein," Anna said. "You just tell us what to do and we'll do it."

"We need to spread these cloths on the kitchen table. But first let's remove the boy's clothing and wrap him in one of these sheets. Then War Lance can carry him over to the other side of the cabin."

They sprang to do as she'd ordered, working over the child with quick, efficient movements, easing off his moccasins, shirt, and leggings, and wrapping him loosely in the linen tablecloth.

"Ach, du lieber Himmel!" Anna clucked. She glanced over at War Lance and frowned in disapproval. "You'd think," she continued in a low tone of censure as she switched to English, "the boy's uncle would at least have put a few more clothes on himself before he came."

Suzette looked up, startled, at the powerful Cheyenne brave who stood beside her. For the first time that night, she realized that War Lance wore only a skimpy breech-cloth. Not only had he left behind his shirt, he'd also not bothered to put on his leggings, moccasins, or even his shell necklace. Unwilling to admit to Anna that it wasn't the first time she'd seen him similarly unclothed, Suzette merely shrugged her shoulders in a noncommittal reply.

Then War Lance lifted Young Wolf and carried him across the dogtrot and into the kitchen area. Anna immediately lit the fire under the kettle of water on the stove, while Suzette readied the big trestle table. Atop the first linen tablecloth, she spread a second, which had been cut to a convenient size, soaked in bichloride solution colored pink with eosin, and wrapped in oiled muslin. When the surgical sheeting was in place, War Lance carefully laid the boy down in the center of it.

"Why, the big heathen's nearly naked," Anna continued to grumble under her breath in English as she dropped the clamps, scalpels, and retractors Suzette had handed her into the large pot on the stove. She lifted her eyebrows and peered over her glasses at the bold display of male flesh. "Perhaps we should send him outside to wait."

"No, I'm going to need his help," Suzette responded with a low chuckle. "And if either of us had a body as sinfully beautiful as his, we'd probably run around without any clothes on, too."

"Mein Gott! You are shameless!" Anna cried with a

mock shriek. But Suzette could tell from her smothered laughter that the little Mennonite missionary was not nearly as scandalized as she pretended to be.

When Suzette looked up to give War Lance further directions, she fought the ridiculous notion that there was a corresponding twinkle of amusement in his eyes as well. But there couldn't be. She was absolutely certain he hadn't understood a word they'd said.

Chapter 9

Mortality rates associated with an appendectomy were extremely low; conversely, the incidence of death after rupture of the appendix was alarmingly high. Suzette knew from her years of training that, even if her diagnosis was less than certain, it would be safer to operate and remove a normal appendix from Young Wolf then wait overnight and risk the chance of finding it had ruptured and an inflammation of the peritoneum had set in. There was no time to waste. She'd been taught that surgery should take place as soon as her patient's condition permitted.

While the surgical instruments were being sterilized, she removed her dressing robe and covered her smocked nightdress with a full, bibbed apron, gathered at the waistband and tied in back. Rolling up the embroidered sleeves of her cotton gown, she ordered Anna and War Lance to also put on one of the many spotless floor-length aprons she'd brought from Lancaster for just such an occasion. The sight of the broad-shouldered warrior outfitted in nothing more than a breechcloth and a long white apron that reached to his bare calves brought a smile to both of the women. Their gazes met and they giggled in nervous release from the tension and dread. As Anna tied the wide bow behind his back, War Lance scowled at the lady doctor in a halfhearted attempt to squelch her unseemly laughter and retain his masculine dignity. But his twinkling eyes gave him away. He, too, seemed to be grateful for the momentary distraction.

Together War Lance and Anna pulled down the Rochester brass lamp that hung by a chain over the trestle table and lit the round Argand wick which would produce considerably more illumination than the other coal oil lanterns. Then it was time to scrub their hands and arms up to their shoulders with a biniodide of mercury soap, followed by an immersion in bichloride solution.

Suzette prepared the child's abdomen for surgery in the same way, explaining to him that he must be very, very clean before she could remove the bad part that was hurting him.

"I'm going to have to put Young Wolf to sleep," Suzette told War Lance. "I will show you just what to do. Then Anna can assist me with my tools while I make my strongest medicine."

Though War Lance looked worried and uneasy at her words, his voice was calm. "I will do everything exactly as you tell me, *núevehoka.*"

Seeing the furrow between his black brows, Suzette heard herself repeating the words of her surgical mentor, Dr. Enoch Crowder: "Now, don't be rabbit-hearted. The sleeping liquid should be given smoothly, with the maximum effect attained as soon as possible. You needn't worry, I won't let you give more than the right amount. We want Young Wolf to go under immediately and stay that way the whole time I am working my medicine on him."

Her doubt about his courage seemed to amuse him, and he chuckled deep in his chest. "No one has suspected me of being cowardly, Little Red Fox. Not until now. I will strive to watch your example. And I won't bound away like a frightened rabbit unless you do."

An answering smile sprang to her lips. Whatever journalist had written the stories in the eastern papers about the stoical Indian brave was certainly unacquainted with this one. She hadn't been teased so unmercifully in her life till she'd met War Lance. And it had been years since she'd felt so lighthearted in someone's presence, reacting to his buoyant sense of humor with a gaiety she'd lost somewhere in those grueling years of schooling and internship.

She pursed her mouth and shook her head in wry amusement at the ridiculous thought of him bolting out of the cabin in wild-eyed fear. Then she turned to the boy who lay on her surgery table, watching her with huge eyes, and the enormity of what she was about to do hit her with the force of an Atlantic gale. She'd been well trained, she reminded herself; she wasn't attempting anything she hadn't done before. But from deep inside, a lingering doubt rose insidiously. What if the unexpected happened? Even the most minor surgery could turn into a nightmare. With no skilled professional to back her up, would she be able to handle any emergency that might arise?

"Am I going to have to fall asleep, *náevehoka?*" Young Wolf asked in a shrill voice that betrayed his anxiety. "I don't think I can. It hurts too much. Three times my mother shook her sleeping rattle over me, but it did not work."

"Do not be alarmed, Young Wolf," Suzette told the frightened child as she bent over him. "You will fall asleep at once when you breathe in my sleeping medicine. And when you wake up again, the pain will be gone."

She showed War Lance how to hold the gauze-covered mask over Young Wolf's nose and pour the chloroform drop by drop while she kept a watchful eye and checked the child's reaction. She preferred ether as an anesthetic and had used it almost exclusively at the hospital in Philadelphia. Chloroform, though agreeable to take and its administration simple, had a narrower margin of safety between the anesthetic and the lethal dose, especially with a child this age. But because of ether's flammable nature, it was unsafe to use with the open flame of the lamp.

Suzette took a deep, steadying breath and fought back the fear that threatened to overwhelm her. Although this was her first surgery outside a hospital setting, she knew she had the ability to remove the appendix and bring her young patient through safely—if only it did not rupture. Dr. Crowder, one of her most talented professors of surgery, had been a country doctor for forty years before accepting a position at the Women's Medical College upon his retirement from private practice. He'd taught Suzette that it wasn't necessary to have a colleague or even a trained nurse in attendance. The enterprising physician could make do in emergencies with a levelheaded layman who would listen to directions and not panic— provided the surgeon herself remained calm.

From the steadiness of War Lance's hands as he dripped the chloroform slowly and steadily onto the mask that covered his nephew's mouth and nose, she realized she could count on him. And Anna had already proven her cool composure under fire during the birth of Pauline's daughter. Suzette knew the missionary could be depended upon to use the large, flat elephant-ear sponges, which had been disinfected and bleached with chlorine, with near-professional precision and dexterity.

With Anna across from her and War Lance standing at the end of the table by Young Wolf's head, Suzette felt the steadying influence of the years of rigorous training take over. She was now fully prepared to make the incision and open the abdomen. Using a shiny steel bistoury, she cut swiftly and surely through the layers of skin, fascia, muscle, and peritoneum. Relief and a feeling of near-euphoria swept over her as she examined the abdominal cavity. She wouldn't know for certain until after a closer examination, but it appeared that her diagnosis of acute appendicitis had been correct. And there wasn't a sign of peritonitis.

"I think it's going to be all right," she told her tense,

apprehensive assistants. "It looks as if we are in time and the bad part hasn't spread."

"*Gott sei Dank,*" Anna murmured with heartfelt thankfulness.

Suzette sent her own father a prayer of silent thanks, as well, for his gift of self-retaining retractors, with their locking devices to keep them in position without support. They enabled her to hold the incision open and the surrounding tissue back without the assistance of another trained professional. Carefully and gently she brought the appendix to the surface, clamped it, tied it at the base, and cut it off. She tied the stump and tucked it into the cecum using silk sutures that had been boiled with the instruments and then immersed in bichloride solution. In less than twenty minutes after the initial incision, she had Young Wolf's abdomen stitched up and a dressing of wet bichloride gauze in place.

It had been like a case out of her textbooks. Although Young Wolf wasn't completely out of the woods, for it was too soon to preclude a surgical infection, the worst of the danger was definitely over.

Looking up, she met War Lance's intent gaze with a grin of triumph. A fine sheen of perspiration covered his brow, and he scowled at her slightly in his fierce concentration.

"Young Wolf's going to be just fine," she told him as she washed her hands in a basin of clean water.

Lance stared in incredulous wonder at the naive, inexperienced young woman who had so ineptly tried to teach him how to kiss only two days before. She now stood beside her operating table, braided and barefoot, dressed in a childishly smocked nightgown and bloodstained apron and smiling up at him with the complete sangfroid of a duchess at teatime. Any doubt of her ability as a physician he might have harbored before the surgery had been blown away like dandelion fluff on a summer breeze.

Unlike most educated white men, he had never

adopted the belief that members of the opposite sex were incapable of rational thinking. He knew that many knowledgeable, supposedly learned, men believed that a heavy regimen of scientific studies was too exacting for the weak female brain. It had long been a common assumption—and was still held by more than a few—that young women should not attempt the rigors of higher education for fear they would sicken and die of brain fever.

But even his Cheyenne childhood, in which women were treated as valued, intelligent partners in the everyday decisions of living, had not prepared him for the sight he'd just beheld in that cabin kitchen.

"Little Red Fox has strong medicine," he said simply, unable to put his torrent of confused thoughts into words.

She flushed with pride at his honest praise. "No, I just had good teachers," she replied. "Now I want you to carry Young Wolf into my sleeping room and put him in bed. He can remain there until he's completely well."

"I will stay with him tonight," Lance told her. He lifted his nephew tenderly in his arms.

"That won't be necessary," she answered, jumping ahead of him to lead the way across the dogtrot, through her office, and into her bedroom. She pulled back the coverlet on her brass bed and fluffed up the pillow for her unconscious patient. "He will sleep deeply for the rest of the night. There will be no chance to even speak with him. You can return to your camp and come back with his mother in the morning."

"I will stay here with Young Wolf," Lance repeated. He carefully laid the child down on Suzette's white sheets. As he bent over the six-year-old, he breathed in the delicate scent of wood violets that drifted up from the bedding, and tried, unsuccessfully, to brush aside the memories it stirred. "His mother entrusted *nāha* to my care. I will not leave him until she arrives to look after him."

Suzette tipped her head in resigned acquiescence. She pulled the coverlet up and gently tucked it about the shoulders of the sleeping youngster. "You may stay in the bedroom with him then. I plan to sleep on the braided rug in the living area."

"You can sleep with me, *Liebchen*," Anna offered generously. She'd followed them into the room with a pitcher of fresh water and a red-striped crockery basin, which she placed on the narrow bureau. "It would be much more comfortable on my feather mattress than that worn-out rug in front of an unlit, sooty-smelling hearth."

Adamantly Suzette shook her head. "No, I will be going in to check on Young Wolf several times during the night. There's no point in disturbing you, Anna." She turned to Lance and eyed him doubtfully. "Don't be alarmed when I come into this room. I will just be looking at Young Wolf to see that everything is going well."

Lance repressed a grin at the look of seriousness in her expressive eyes. It was clear she didn't want to take any chance on jarring awake a drowsy, confused, and therefore dangerous Indian.

"You will not startle me, Little Red Fox," he reassured her. "I am a very light sleeper."

"I'll get you an extra blanket," Anna added in her helpful, matter-of-fact way. "And we'd better close the window."

"I won't need a sleeping robe," he told the missionary. "Young Wolf and I are both used to the fresh air. It is a warm night. Leave the window open so neither of us will smother in the close confines of your wooden lodge."

"Then we'll leave you to watch over Young Wolf," Suzette replied with a soft smile, "while we clean up the kitchen."

Several hours later, Suzette entered her darkened bedchamber. The stars twinkled faintly through the rectangle of predawn sky framed by the opened window, their glow slowly fading in the advent of the morning sun. Placing the ruby lamp she carried on the bureau beside her bed, she bent over Young Wolf's still form. She took his pulse, then pulled back the quilted coverlet and listened to his steady heartbeat with her stethoscope. All life signs were normal. There was no fever. The pupils were not dilated. Tenderly she pushed back the ebony hair from his cherubic face and watched him sleeping peacefully in the soft glow of the kerosene lantern. A faint smile touched his mouth, as though he were dreaming of youthful exploits of astounding skill and bravery. An answering smile sprang to her own lips. The thrill of accomplishment, the certain knowledge that she had saved the small boy's life, filled her with joy. Surely this made the years of rigorous training and the long, heartbreaking months she'd waited in vain for a patient all worthwhile.

From his spot on the plank floor beneath the window, Lance watched in silence—for the third time that night— the soul-stirring scene being played out before him. Her profile, pure and clear and sweet, was silhouetted by the light behind her. A rosy glow from the lantern's etched glass shade surrounded the two figures, woman and child, casting its ruby hues and floral shapes on the bed's white sheets and pillowcases. A halo of light shimmered around her red-gold hair. She leaned over the sleeping boy like a ministering angel, robed in lavender blue.

Lance's battered, world-weary heart skidded to a halt. It was as though he were looking into a genie's magic bottle containing all his heart's desires, everything he'd ever dreamed of in a woman, knowing all the while that it was as illusory and unobtainable as Alladin's storied lamp.

His gaze moved to the photograph on the bureau behind her, illuminated now by the same rose-colored light. He'd seen the picture of the blond army officer the moment they'd entered the room. The young pretty-boy face, with its well-trimmed mustache, shone with all the cocky brashness of a West Point graduate. He was a captain in the Seventh U.S. Cavalry, the same unit that had gone down to such infamous defeat under Colonel George Armstrong Custer. Had the soldier, like his commander, been killed at the Battle of the Little Big Horn? Watching Suzette's tender care of the Cheyenne child, Lance wondered what possible connection she had to the man in the gold frame.

Lance hadn't realized he'd risen to his feet. Or that he'd crossed the room. But as she straightened and was about to turn around, he found himself standing directly behind her. Slipping his arms about her waist, he eased her away from the bed and the unconscious boy. When she tried to turn and face him, he thwarted her intentions effortlessly and pulled her tight instead, to bring her tempting backside securely against his covetous body. He wondered if she could feel his hunger for her through the folds of the soft wool robe.

"War Lance," she protested in a harsh whisper. She lifted her chin and tried to turn her head to see him. "War Lance, don't."

Ignoring her objections, he bent and kissed the exposed skin of her silken neck. His hand found the ribbon that fastened her hair and tugged it off. Gently, surely, he released the coppery strands that had been bound in the long braid. Combing his fingers through the satiny tresses that fell in waves to her waist, he buried his face in the glorious bounty and inhaled the light, sweet scent that surrounded her. Of course, it would be violets, he thought with aching clarity, as he sought to drown his senses in the fragile, feminine beauty of her. Purple violets to match her incredible eyes.

Held captive in his overpowering arms, Suzette felt her limbs tremble beneath the unyielding strength of him. She attempted, once again, to turn toward him. But one strong hand was clamped firmly against her waist, while the other was buried in the loose waves spilling across her shoulders and down her back. He was murmuring wonderful Cheyenne words to her, though she couldn't quite understand his meaning. Something about a spell and an enchanted bottle.

"You mustn't do this," she warned in a suffocated

whisper as she tried to break free of his hold. "The child . . ."

"The child sleeps soundly," he replied, his voice deep and rough with passion. "Only moments ago I called his name to see if he would wake. He didn't stir."

Instead of freeing her, War Lance pulled her even tighter against his muscular frame. She could feel his hardened arousal through her nightclothes. His fingers released her hair and came around to seek the gold braided frogs that fastened the front of her cashmere robe. One by one he freed them as his hand moved slowly, insistently downward from the mandarin collar, across her breasts, to her waist. He slipped his hand inside the soft, lavender blue robe and cupped her breast, shielded only by the embroidered cotton of her nightdress. She gasped at the shock of pleasure and instinctively arched against him.

"War Lance, we mustn't," she said, her voice almost a sob.

But he held her imprisoned with ease.

"You smell like a spring morning in paradise," he murmured in her ear, as he traced its shell with his tongue. His voice was thick with desire. "You are a sorceress come to bewitch me. And should I once believe I could keep you, you'd disappear like some conjurer's magical illusion."

Under his touch, her breast became heavy and taut. He slid his hand across to fondle the other, and she moaned in sweet, sensual enjoyment as his fingers skimmed back and forth across the cloth-covered peak.

All the while, he relentlessly continued to release the fastenings on her dressing gown with his other hand, traveling steadily toward its hem in a slow, hypnotic movement. When the robe was opened to her hips, he slid his hand beneath the soft wool and cupped her woman's mound with his strong fingers. A jolt of carnal delight knifed through her body. She leaned back against him in languorous surrender, allowing him to support her.

She yielded to the rush of vibrant sensations that crashed in upon her. All thoughts of denying him were forgotten. Every nerve ending in her body sang with desire and the tantalizing need for fulfillment. Changing her stance, she opened her thighs to his skilled fingers, driven by a longing for him to touch her intimately. She wanted him to explore her as she discovered, in tandem, all the marvelous feelings she had never experienced before.

His fingers sought and found the very core of her femininity. He stroked her through the thin cotton barrier, touching off a spiraling heat inside her like a torch set to autumn leaves. She relinquished any thought of breaking free and yielded her body to his stronger will, allowing herself to be guided along the unknown path of eroticism he so boldly set.

This, then, was what it was like to be touched by a man.

Intimately.

Passionately.

Seductively.

The throbbing sensations consumed her consciousness, shoving aside all awareness of the outside world. There was only the two of them, and he alone knew the way to release her from this unfamiliar urgency, this irresistible drive for completion. Now, suddenly, she was afraid that he would stop before she learned the mystery of it. That he would draw back, leaving her on the brink of—she knew not what—bewildered, frustrated, and alone. She curled her fingers over his bare forearms, as though to press herself closer to him.

In some uncanny way, he seemed to sense her doubt and confusion. He bent his head and pressed his lips to her temple. "Don't be frightened, angel," he murmured. "Think only about my fingers touching you. Give in to the pleasure I can bring. Push every other thought aside. All I want to do is caress your beautiful female body."

The sound of his deep, masculine voice in her ear, the

erotic images his sensual words conveyed, the feel of his rugged hands as he touched her so familiarly, brought fulfillment at last, in wave after wave of pulsating pleasure. A low moan escaped before she bit her lips to end the verbal proof of her release. In her passion-drugged state, she'd whispered his name.

As the feeling of culmination slowly ebbed, her lashes fluttered and lifted. She opened her eyes to see the breathtaking image of a dark-haired man and a redheaded woman, caught in amorous embrace, reflected in the mirror above the bureau. Her pale face was soft and dreamy, her head tilted back to rest in satiated languor on his bronzed shoulder. In the dark glass, she met his intense, compelling gaze, and was startled by the depth of longing in his hooded eyes. His head was bent over hers, and a lock of his straight hair fell over his brow. His sinewy arms enfolded her, the bulging muscles of his biceps and forearms glistening in the lamplight. Buried deep inside her robe, his hands still held her intimately.

Realizing that he'd pressed and rocked her backside against his hardened manhood as he'd brought her to completion, she flushed and looked down to see the photograph of Jordan Maclure staring back at her in silent condemnation.

She stiffened in the warrior's arms.

"Let me go," she demanded in shock and indignation at her own behavior. She pulled on his arms with frantic, clutching fingers. "Release me, *now*."

He loosened his hold and she jerked free. Turning her back on the picture of the army captain, she faced the man who'd brought her to such shameful disgrace.

"This cannot happen again," she said more calmly, aware that she couldn't, in truth, place all the blame on him. Even if he was a savage, she'd admired him for weeks. She ignored the sudden look of wrath on his proud face and refastened the gold frogs on her robe with implacable deliberation. "Nothing like this must ever take place between us again."

Chapter 10

"**W**hy not?" War Lance demanded harshly. He caught her by the shoulders as she started to slip around him to the door. "Why shouldn't I touch you again? You wanted it as much as I did." .

His steely fingers slid down to clamp her upper arms in a painful hold. His words were sharp with a frosty sarcasm. "Is it because I am red and you are white? Or because I am unlearned in your ways of speaking, and you have been educated in your doctor's schools?" Ruthlessly he dragged her to the bureau and lifted the picture in its shiny brass frame. He held the face of the young officer up to the lamplight for both of them to see. His hoarse voice was filled with a cold, suppressed rage. "Or is it because of him?"

"Put it down," Suzette said, seeking in vain to control her overwrought emotions. She tried to shove him away, but it was like pushing against a solid wall of rock. Outraged fury that he would dare to question her about Jordan's photograph pushed aside all initial thoughts of appeasing the brave's injured male pride. Her fiancé had been everything War Lance was not: sophisticated, charming, elegant, refined, trustworthy, and honorable. The Cheyenne was nothing more than a murdering redskin. She rasped her impotent warning through clenched teeth. "Don't you touch his picture with your bloody hands."

"Who is he?" War Lance demanded, his deep voice raw with a throbbing bitterness, and something more. He shook her impatiently, like an exasperated parent with a foulmouthed child. "Who is this little soldier chief that's so much better than me that I can't even touch his picture?"

"No one," Suzette whispered vehemently. She lifted her chin in stubborn defiance, unwilling to bare her soul to the enraged warrior. "He's no one to the likes of you."

"No one?" War Lance drew back and searched her face with an expression of chilling skepticism. "When you first met my glance in the mirror, little white woman, the longing for my touch was reflected in your eyes. Your lips were soft and parted with a lover's desire. Then you saw the picture of the *vèho*, and your hunger for me changed to disgust. Why?"

He tossed the frame on the dresser and quickly turned to look at the small child in the bed nearby. Young Wolf had stirred in his drugged sleep, flinging one hand up above his head and uttering a soft, muted sound. But his heavy eyelids never lifted.

With his fingers clasped securely around her arm, War Lance guided her away from the bed and over beside the open window. Its flowered chintz curtains rustled slightly in the cool dawn air. He bent over her and lowered his voice to a near whisper. "Did you break your promise to the horse soldier when you let me touch you? Is that what has upset you so badly? Did you and the *vèho* exchange promises to love only each other?"

Suzette closed her eyes and blinked back the scalding tears of self-reproach brought on by his astute, razor-sharp questions. "Yes," she said at last, her lips trembling as she fought the inescapable feelings of humiliation and defeat. "Yes, there were vows between the soldier and me. We were promised together in marriage."

He released his hold on her and turned. Leaning his hands high above his shoulders on either side of the narrow window, he looked out at the hillsides, studded with fir and pine. His head dropped forward. His words were muffled and stilted, devoid of all emotion. "You are promised in marriage to this little soldier chief?"

She covered her face with her hands and leaned back against the rough-chinked wall of the cabin, fighting to regain her composure. Then she lowered her fingers and stared across the small room with tear-blinded eyes. "I was. Once. Jordan was killed in battle." There was resentment and a sharply honed derision in her voice. "But he fell a highly decorated military hero."

War Lance whirled in astonishment to look at her. "The white man is dead?"

She nodded and continued without meeting his gaze. "Jordan Maclure was on leave in my village when he started courting me. He'd just been promoted to captain and was being transferred to the Seventh Cavalry. He was to return West, to the Indian campaigns, in less than a month." She moved pensively to the bed and ran her fingers across the curving top of the brass footboard, the glossy metal cool and soothing beneath her touch. "My mother had died two years before, and I was responsible for the care of my little sister. So we decided to wait to be married till after he returned."

There was a hint of mockery in his voice as War Lance leaned his shoulder against the window frame, folded his arms across his chest, and continued his interrogation. "You agreed to marry, having only known the man such a short time?"

"I felt as if I'd known Jordan all my life." She glanced up to meet his questioning gaze, then looked away. "It was what the white people call a 'whirlwind courtship.' He was older than me and knew so much more about the world. I was flattered by his attention and thrilled to think someone so wonderful could actually want me." Absently she traced the pressed floral decoration on the brass bed's tall leg. "Despite the brief time we had together, we were certain of our love. It was only at my father's insistence that I agreed to wait." She smiled feebly at the quilted coverlet. "After Jordan left for his tour of duty, I never saw him again."

"Which battle was he killed in?" War Lance asked in a voice of such implacable calm, it demanded an honest answer.

Drawing a deep breath, she turned and meet his imperious glance. She gripped the brass rail with stiff fingers. "Captain Maclure fell at the Battle of Little Big Horn."

"Why did you come here, *náevehoka?*" he demanded, his whisper irate and incredulous. "Here of all places?" He moved toward her with the supple, long-limbed grace of a mountain cat, but stopped short, his bare feet only inches from the hem of her cashmere robe. His accusing words were a warning rumble in the quiet room. "Why come to the very people who killed the man you planned to marry?"

Avoiding the look of condemnation on his face, she wrapped her fingers around the footboard's curved rail and stared with unseeing eyes at the small form on the bed. She could never bring herself to admit to the obstinate warrior that there'd been no choice. That no one in Lancaster had deigned to accept her as their physician. She didn't want him, or any of the Cheyenne, to realize that she'd been unable to set up a medical practice among her own people. If they knew, it would ensure that no one on the Tongue River Reservation would ever become her patient.

Her eyes averted from his probing gaze, she tapped her fingernails on the brass frame with nervous energy. "I came to Lame Deer because Jacob and Anna Graber asked me to," she said. She glanced quickly up at him before turning to face the log wall above the ornately scrolled headboard. Halfheartedly she made a carefree gesture with one hand and finished lamely, "And I thought it would be exciting to come out to the wild West."

Lance watched her turn from him, avoiding his eyes, and his heart sank. Her long, russet lashes were lowered against her ivory skin, and her cheeks were pale, even in the rosy light, as though she were stricken with guilt and deeply ill at ease under his scrutiny. With a diplomat's instinct, he knew she'd told him only part of the story. But what was she trying to hide?

"Did you come to Lame Deer to find the Cheyenne warrior who killed your promised one?" he asked tautly, with the swift, practiced attack of a trained statesman.

Shocked, she whirled to face him. But whether her indignation was from the unfairness of his accusation or the accuracy of it, he couldn't tell.

"No!" she exclaimed. Her delicate features were pinched and white. She looked up at him with loathing and self-righteous anger. "How dare you question me? You are the one who wears a knife strapped to his thigh. How many innocent whites have you scalped with it?"

He grinned mirthlessly. "We rarely boast of white scalps around our lodge fires, *náevehoka*. They are too easy to acquire and hardly worth the notice. It is only Indian scalps that bring a warrior honor and respect among my people."

"Honor! What do you know of honor?"

He read the prejudice and hatred in her eyes. Remembering the tender care she'd shown for Young Wolf, and the way she had soothed and reassured the boy's older half sister, he felt a sharp wrench of disappointment and defeat. The thought that the lady doctor's gentle ways had been merely an act to disguise the very real motivation of revenge filled his empty heart with a deep, gnawing sorrow. Without a word, he turned and moved silently across the floor.

Like an avenging angel, she followed him. He heard the soft padding of her bare feet on the plank floor behind him. "Don't be so modest about your accomplishments in battle, War Lance Striking. Surely you'd like to brag about your many coups. Were you there beside the Little Big Horn River the day Jordan was murdered?"

As he was about to cross the threshold, she grabbed

his elbow in a futile effort to hold him there. "Were you the one who brutally scalped and mutilated his body?"

Heartsick at her bitter words, he shook off her hand and left the room. Quickly he crossed her office to the front door. The knowledge that he had allowed himself to be manipulated by the beauty of a small-minded, bigoted white woman filled him with self-disgust. He should have known better. In her educated eyes, the Cheyenne were no better than bloodthirsty savages. What more proof than in the twisted, one-sided accusation she'd just uttered?

He looked back in desolation, seeing her as if for the first time: an entrancing captivating, spellbinding witch. She stood, heart-wrenchingly beautiful, in the bedroom's entryway, holding on to the doorjamb for support. Her marvelous coppery curls spilled across the shoulders of her plush blue dressing gown. Her violet eyes were blurred; tears for her beloved Jordan streamed down her porcelain cheeks. As he left the cabin, he heard her anguished cry pierce the cool morning air.

"Were you there?"

With her tragic words echoing in his heart, he moved to the corral in the deserted compound. After throwing a blanket pad on Red Wind, he mounted the great stallion and turned toward his family's camp, the challenging struggle that was always necessary for control over his capricious, half-wild mount now a welcome diversion. He would meet his grandmother and his sister-in-law on their way to the agency and give them the news that, thanks to the fantastic skill of the white medicine woman, Young Wolf was safe and well. Then he would go up into the Wolf Mountains to find his brother, Bear Scalp.

Morning light was spreading across the shallow valley that followed the meandering curves of Lame Deer Creek. The lovely September day to come would be warm and ripe and golden. Lance galloped across the rolling hills of short grasses and sagebrush, with sand and gumbo lilies, prairie primroses, and clusters of the small, shrubby, scarlet mallow dotting the countryside. It was the land of his childhood, and the awakening autumn day brought back happy memories of his first pony, his first bow, and his first hunting expedition with his older half brothers. It was his people's way to educate a boy through advice and admonition, leading him by example to understand the importance of honesty, truthfulness, courage, and fair play.

Nothing in his early years had prepared War Lance Striking for the harsh treatment he had received at the age of thirteen, when he had entered the world of the white man. After his father's death from a battle injury, he'd accompanied his mother across the tall grass prairie to the *vèho* camp of Omaha, where they had boarded a Union Pacific railroad car for the long journey to her family's home in Virginia. His appearance, in buckskin breechclout and leggings, had so frightened the lady passengers that he'd chosen to ride on the outside platform, insisting, for his upset mother's sake, that it was where he preferred to be. But the bigotry of strangers had been mild and easily deflected compared to the reception he'd received from his own grandmother.

From the minute she'd laid eyes on her Indian grandson, Octavia Harden had treated him with open contempt. She was scandalized that her widowed daughter, who'd run off to marry an irresponsible dreamer heading for the gold fields, had returned to Alexandria with an illegitimate half-breed son. Though Judge Harden had urged his wife to give the youth a chance to learn their ways, she had ignored her husband's plea for patience and understanding. She had openly scorned the tall thirteen-year-old's ignorance, his illiteracy, his halting English, and his pagan beliefs. As a proud young warrior who'd already experienced the Great Medicine Dance and suffered his first wound in battle, where he'd earned

his adult name, War Lance Striking had felt justified in
ignoring his white grandmother with total indifference.

Then one afternoon a neighborhood girl had taunted
him with his supposedly bastard heritage. By then, Lance
had learned enough *vého* words to know that she was accusing his mother of whoring with heathens. He could
readily ignore any abuse heaped upon his own head, but
the virulent epithets hurled against his innocent mother
were intolerable. His Cheyenne uncles had taught him
never to strike a helpless female, and so he had expressed
his anger and bruised pride, unfairly, on her older
brother. Though the nasty, ill-bred girl had been to
blame, Octavia had lashed out viciously at her own
daughter and grandson.

"If you didn't have the nerve to kill yourself before
spreading your legs to the filthy vermin who captured
you," she had screamed at Lily, "you should at least have
had the sense to drown the snotty little beggar when you
whelped him."

"Mother, you don't know what you're saying," Lily
had cried in horror. She took a step forward, as though
trying to shield War Lance from his white grandmother's
ugly temper. "I love my son. And one day, when you
come to know your grandson better, you will, too."

At her daughter's words, Octavia struck her a ringing
blow across the cheek, and Lance sprang upon the old
harridan. Only Lily's quick intervention had prevented
him from strangling his own grandmother.

It was then that William Harden had decided to send
his beloved daughter and her half-Indian son to his bachelor brother, a barrister and representative of the British
Foreign Office. For the two exiles of the Great American
Plains, the cosmopolitan city of London was to become
a safe haven.

The adolescent Lance had learned his lesson well. The
only white woman from whom he could expect genuine
love and a heartfelt tenderness was his mother—and she
was really a Cheyenne at heart. Time and again in Lon-

don, he'd seen the proof of this, from the lures thrown out by married women seeking the thrill of an amorous affair with a forbidden male to the tragic and needless death of an innocent debutante. Was it any wonder that, despite his many friends and his personal achievements, he'd always felt like an outsider, apart and alone?

Now, twenty-one years later, he reminded himself that it was still a basic truth: He stood between two worlds, belonging to neither. Though he sometimes yearned to return to the ways he'd learned at a tender age, he knew that was impossible. The staggering jealousy he'd felt over the dead cavalry officer had rocked him in a way he'd never expected. He'd foolishly allowed the red-haired *vèhoka* to trick him into thinking she considered him a man, not some hulking, primitive creature. Despite all his good intentions, he had become emotionally involved in a relationship that he knew was doomed from the start.

On that point, Dr. Suzette Stanwood had been right. The intimate scene between them must never happen again. Not just because of the danger to his secret mission, but because he refused to allow her to ensnare his heart like some helpless prairie jackrabbit caught in a trap. Relations with the gently bred lady doctor must be kept strictly platonic. He'd learned firsthand from his white grandmother exactly what the likes of her thought about the likes of him.

Blue Crane Flying was at the Grabers' cabin early that morning, accompanied by her grandmother-in-law, Prairie Grass Woman, and her daughter, Yellow Feather. The three females had met War Lance on the road to the agency, and he'd shared with them the wondrous tale of the white doctor's strong medicine.

"I thank you for my son's life, *náevehoka*," said Blue Crane Flying in her soft, gracious Cheyenne as she entered the cabin's sitting area. Dressed in a plaid calico blouse and skirt, she carried her worn blanket folded gracefully over one arm. The tiny bells on her moccasins tinkled musically as she walked. "War Lance Striking told me that my son would have died if you had not worked your healing medicine on him."

With an answering smile, Suzette accepted the gift of two skinned and drawn rabbits from the child's mother and carried them into the kitchen end of the room, where Anna was stirring a large soup kettle on the cast-iron stove.

"Thank you for your gift, Blue Crane Flying," Suzette said. She placed the fresh meat on the sink counter beside the shiny red pump.

Beaming cheerfully, Anna left the stove and wiped her hands on her spotless white apron. "We'll cook those rabbits for supper. Jacob will be home today, and fried rabbit is one of his favorites."

"Let's go see if Young Wolf is ready for something to eat," Suzette suggested.

At her invitation, Blue Crane Flying and Prairie Grass Woman followed her and the little girl to the bedroom. They found Young Wolf wide-awake and propped up on the goose down pillow.

"Mother!" he called as they entered. "Grandmother! *Nihoe* put me to sleep, and while I was asleep, Little Red Fox took the bad part out. I don't remember anything. But I still hurt," he added, his eyes shining with excitement and the need to be completely honest.

Blue Crane Flying hurried to the bed and took her son's small hand. "Where do you hurt, my son?" she asked tenderly. Her narrow features were etched with worry, her solemn brown eyes shadowed with concern.

Responding to the alarm in the younger woman's voice, Suzette went to stand on the other side of the brass bed. "He will be in pain for a little while longer," she explained in a reassuring tone. "But there is no danger anymore. It will just take time for the cut to heal." Gently she lifted back the floral coverlet, exposing Young Wolf's bandaged incision.

"Naaa!" Prairie Grass Woman exclaimed in amazement, standing beside her granddaughter. "Little Red Fox truly did open up the child's belly." Like a little bird, she turned her head to look at Suzette with bright, incredulous black eyes.

"Will my son get well, *náevehoka?*" Blue Crane Flying asked, nearly as dumbfounded as the old woman.

"In two weeks he will be running about with his playmates," Suzette predicted as she carefully replaced the cover. "All he'll have is a scar on his stomach to show for his bravery." At her words of praise for his courage, Young Wolf beamed proudly.

Just then Anna came in carrying a tray with a bowl of steaming broth. The wonderful smell of chicken soup filled the room. "Would you like to feed your son, Blue Crane Flying?" she asked, flashing her dimpled smile.

There was no response to the missionary's kindhearted question, and Suzette glanced over at the two Indian women in surprise. Instead of answering Anna, they were both staring in blank silence at the photograph beside the wooden tray.

"Would you like to help Young Wolf eat?" Suzette repeated with sympathy to the child's mother. Belatedly Suzette realized that a picture of a U.S. Cavalry officer might be upsetting to the Cheyenne women after the many tragic years of warfare between their peoples.

Blue Crane Flying turned to her with dark, serious eyes. "Yes," she answered, and immediately lifted the spoon and the bowl of hot broth from the tray. "I will feed my son the soup."

Yellow Feather came to stand beside Suzette. She leaned across the bed, her elbows propped on the coverlet, and rested her chin on her interlaced fingers. "Did you sew my brother's cut like you did mine, *náevehoka?*" she asked bashfully.

"Yes," Suzette replied. "And today I am going to take the stitches of thread I put in your hand back out again."

Dubious, Yellow Feather frowned at the unexpected

news. She tipped her head to one side and lifted her eyebrows in a gesture of worried anticipation that was faintly reminiscent of someone Suzette had known in the past. But the memory of just who else had had such a similar habit eluded her.

As she glanced back up, Suzette found Prairie Grass Woman and Blue Crane Flying staring at each other in intense, silent communication. Clearly they were astounded by the white woman's strong medicine.

Then Young Wolf's mother turned and began to spoon the warm chicken broth into his mouth.

When Jacob returned from his trip to Miles City later that morning, he was driving an old, high-sprung calash buggy, its worn canvas top folded down, and a milk cow tied to the back. He was also accompanied by several Indians who'd joined him on the road into the agency. A family from White Elk's band wanted to learn more about the white man's religion. It was Sunday, and after the supplies had been unloaded, the curious Cheyenne gathered in the cabin's large open room and listened to the Mennonite speak in their own tongue about the Wise Spirit Above.

Through the open door of her office, Suzette could hear murmurs of interest as the missionary gave his sermon, punctuated by the *Hous* of understanding and agreement from his fascinated audience. Earlier in the morning, Prairie Grass Woman had left with Yellow Feather to return to the family's lodge and care for the men who'd soon be coming back from their hunting in the mountains. But Blue Crane Flying had remained at the agency to care for her son.

While Young Wolf was being nursed by his mother, Suzette used her time to inventory her limited medical stock once again. She'd been appalled at the lack of necessary drugs, bandages, and instruments when she first came to Lame Deer. Before she'd left Pennsylvania, she'd been assured in a letter from the Bureau of Indian

Affairs that all needed supplies would be waiting for her when she arrived. The emergency appendectomy of the night before had brought home to her all the more strongly the need to procure more chloroform, morphia, digitalis, belladonna, and quinine immediately.

She listed the items with painstaking care, choosing the most important first. For financial as well as logistical reasons, she'd been able to bring only small amounts of each with her. Not nearly enough should she succeed in acquiring some patients. She would make another attempt to get Horace Corby to budget the necessary funds as soon as possible. And that wouldn't be easy. She'd already sized him up as an inveterate skinflint. And the knowledge he had of medicine would fit in a small petri dish.

With a sigh of frustration, Suzette sat down on the bench she hoped to use for examining patients and stared absently at the glass-front cabinet containing her meager supplies. The image of her handsome guide as he'd left the cabin at daybreak rose before her once again. He hadn't said a single word in response to her ugly accusations. But the cold, implacable look in his eyes had told her one thing: He despised her. His scathing stare of contempt had left her devastated.

She folded and refolded the list with stiff fingers. Why should she care, anyway? How could a woman, refined, educated—one could even say *genteel*—be attracted to a man who she knew was an uncivilized barbarian? The only thing about him that could possibly intrigue her was his prodigious physical beauty. Good Lord, that was undeniable. But though the aura of sheer male primal force that surrounded him bordered on the irresistible, it was not enough to override the practical horse sense she'd inherited from her shopkeeper father. The fierce, unquenchable ache War Lance had aroused inside her must be conquered. There could never be anything between an illiterate savage and an educated female doctor.

* * *

"Agent Corby wants ta see ya," Obadiah Nash said apologetically. The gangly clerk stood in front of the un-lit fireplace and twisted his black bowler hat in his skinny fingers. At his polite knock, Anna had invited him into the cabin, and now he stood shuffling his huge feet nervously on the room's braided rag rug. "Sorry to bother you so early in the morning, Dr. Stanwood, but he says for you to come at once."

"I'll be right there," Suzette called from the kitchen sink, where she'd been washing the breakfast dishes. It had been five days since the emergency appendectomy, with no sign of infection. Her young patient was well out of danger and on the road to a quick recovery. She slipped off her apron and headed for her office door. "First I have to get the list of medical supplies I need." Before Nash could answer, she dashed across to her of-fice and returned to the parlor with her list.

Suzette matched her strides to the storklike legs of the agency's clerk, and they crossed the open quadrangle to-gether. Flinging the door to the agent's office open wide, Nash announced in his squeaky voice, "Here she is, boss." The moment Suzette walked into the room, the clerk slammed the door shut behind her.

To her astonishment, War Lance Striking stood in front of the agent's oversize desk. He turned to look at her as she came in. Instead of leggings and breechcloth, the tall Indian was dressed in worn Levis and a faded blue shirt. But he still wore the moccasins and primitive shell-core necklace. His straight, shiny black hair came down well past his collar.

Wondering why Horace Corby had summoned the two of them, she went to stand beside her employee, who welcomed her with hooded eyes. She met her guide's un-readable gaze before turning to the portly agent sitting behind his desk.

"Miss Stanwood, come in, come in," Corby said. He pushed back his chair and rose to his feet. Hooking his thumbs into his wide belt, he sauntered around and sat down on the edge of the desktop. "I wanted to see how your hired man was working out." He leaned forward and grinned at her in feigned good humor, his crooked teeth partially hidden beneath his huge handlebar mustache. "Course, seein's how he can't talk a word of our lingo, I guess it's up to you to speak for the both of you."

"The title is 'Dr. Stanwood,'" she told Corby patiently. With the long list of medical supplies clutched tightly in her hand, she couldn't afford to alienate the one person who could procure them for her.

Peeking up at War Lance from the corner of her eye, she wondered what he would tell the agent if he could speak to him. Did he want to quit as her paid escort after the way she'd screamed at him five days ago?

Decency and a sense of fair play demanded that she give him the opportunity to back out of the job if he wished. Even if it meant that she'd be unable to travel about the reservation. With her shoulders thrown back and her head high, she turned to the tall warrior and spoke in Cheyenne. To her dismay, her soprano voice was close to cracking. "Agent Corby wants to know if you'd like to continue as my guide. What should I tell him?"

"Tell him that I wish to continue, *náevehoka.*" His words were restrained and impersonal. The rugged features of his face were stern and forbidding as he met her gaze.

Relief flooded through her, despite his aloof formality. She told herself that it was only because she could now continue to travel about the countryside. After all, despite their differences, he was an excellent guide. The swift surge of happiness that bubbled up inside her had nothing at all to do with the fact that she'd also continue to be in his company.

She looked at Corby and, with a delighted smugness she couldn't quite conceal, returned to her native language. "The man says he hasn't had so much fun since he raided a Crow camp and stole twenty horses."

Beside her, the large warrior seemed to stiffen imperceptibly, but when she turned her head in silent question, he met her gaze with a deadpan expression. At the thought that she was pulling the wool over the eyes of both her male adversaries, she bit the inside of her cheek to keep from laughing out loud.

Corby jumped to his feet and glared at the brave. "Oh, he does, does he?"

"Yes, he says this is almost as good as the time he raided a bull train in the Black Hills and got away with five new rifles and twenty boxes of ammunition."

"I get the idea," Corby replied with a snarl, realizing too late that the Indian couldn't possibly have told her all that in one short sentence. He scowled at her attempt to poke fun at him. "I take it you're happy with the arrangement, as well?"

"Perfectly happy," she replied, unfolding the paper in her hands. "But there is something we need to discuss."

"Oh, and what's that, Miss Stanwood?" he asked warily, suspicion written all over his coarse features. His chin descended into his jowls as he folded his arms across his thick chest and glared at her.

She held out the list she'd written with such painstaking precision. "I need these items, Mr. Corby. Each and every one of them. And I need them desperately."

"Cripes almighty, not that again," he complained. He walked around to his chair, sat down, and ran his hand across his hairless scalp in agitation.

Undaunted, she followed him around his desk. "I'm frighteningly low on chloroform . . . on bichloride of mercury . . . on things that will cost people their lives if I don't have them. Please, Mr. Corby, I'm begging you to budget some money for these medical supplies."

Corby reached into a desk drawer and pulled out a ledger. He smacked it on the desktop in front of him with a bang. Opening the pages, he leafed through the accounts book till he came to the place he wanted and jabbed a pudgy finger at the long column of numbers.

"See this, Miss Stanwood?" he said. "See this zero right here? That's what's left of my allotment for the agency doctor, right there. In the few short weeks you've been here, you've managed to use up the entire year's allowance."

Suzette barely glanced at the ledger page with its scribbled, indecipherable figures. "I couldn't have!" she protested. "I haven't spent any money yet."

"Oh, no? The furnishings in that cabin you're living in cost good, hard greenbacks, missy. Why, you've got the only indoor pump for three hundred miles. And that fancy brass bed had to be hauled by wagon all the way from Billings."

"But the furniture was already there when I arrived," she cried as he slammed the ledger shut. Her shoulders drooped in defeat. "If I'd been given the choice, I'd have spent the money on medicine." She raised her head at a sudden thought. "Why don't we write to the commissioner of Indian Affairs?" she suggested. "He's the one who wanted an agency doctor at Lame Deer. Surely Mr. Price will see the need for these medical items."

Corby jumped to his feet, his face red, his eyes bulging with indignation. "Don't you dare!" he exploded. "Don't you even think it!"

Surprised at his violent reaction, she backed slowly away until she bumped into the solid frame of War Lance, who'd been advancing as she retreated. "What harm is there in asking?" she said in a shaky voice.

Corby moved toward her, livid with rage. He snarled through clenched teeth. "If I ever learn that you've been writing to Washington about anything having to do with this agency, you'll be leaving on the next train pulling out of Custer Station. Do you understand?"

With a lightning move, War Lance Striking was suddenly between her and the irate agent, whose head didn't quite reach the warrior's shoulders. The Cheyenne's strong hands were doubled into fists. As Corby looked up to meet the granite features of the menacing brave, Suzette took the opportunity to beat a hasty retreat.

"Come on, War Lance," she called in the Cheyenne tongue as she opened the door. "The agent's just cross because I asked him for money. That stingy old goat doesn't mean me any real harm."

Chapter 11

Less than an hour later, Suzette and War Lance Striking left Lame Deer for Fort Custer on the Big Horn River. They traveled fast and light, crossing rolling hills with their short native grasses and tablelands covered with prickly pear and sage. Interspersing the gradually sloping plains were the fertile valleys of the Little Big Horn's tributary streams. Not all of the going was easy. They were slowed crossing the rugged divides thrown across the countryside by the spurs of the Rosebud Mountains.

All day Lance hurried them along, for once they had crossed Rosebud Creek, they'd entered the Crow Indian Reservation. Although the Cheyenne were now at peace with the Crows, word of the white medicine woman might not as yet have spread through all the camps of their former enemies. A Cheyenne brave traveling with a beautiful *vèhoka* on Crow land would invite trouble should they stumble upon a small group of hot-blooded young hunters out looking for excitement.

This time Suzette had no cause for complaint about War Lance's lack of attention. He stuck by her side like a newborn foal with its mother. With Jacob's old Springfield slung across his back, he watched for the signs of sandhill cranes suddenly taking wing, or herds of startled elk or white-tailed pronghorns racing across the tablelands.

After leaving Horace Corby's office early that morning, Lance had questioned Suzette about the obnoxious agent's sudden loss of temper.

"He claims there's not enough money to buy medical supplies," she said, clearly in no mood to explain to her hired help that Corby had just threatened to fire her. She was in a fine, rare huff. She stomped across the compound to her cabin, the pointed toes of her high-buttoned shoes sending swirls of dust over his freshly brushed moccasins. It wasn't only the agent who'd perturbed her. She was still thoroughly displeased with her guide as well.

From his vantage point across Corby's desk, Lance had been unable to read the figures tallied in long columns down the ledger page. "Is that what he showed you in his big book?" he questioned her. "You haven't any more green paper to trade for your remedies?"

When she raised her russet eyebrows and looked at him in disdainful silence, he ignored her aloofness and continued to press for information. "What exactly was written on the agent's long pages?"

"What difference does it make to you?" she snapped. "You don't understand the white man's money anyway."

They stepped into the covered dogtrot that separated the cabin's twin buildings. Bending over, she shook out the pleated flounces of her green morning dress with quick, irritated movements.

"There is a doctor at Fort Custer," he told her with studied disinterest. He looked over in seeming fascination at the horses and mules milling about behind the corral fence. "Perhaps he has some government paper for the *vèho* healing potions."

At that moment, Suzette had made the decision to travel to Fort Custer in the hopes of borrowing from its hospital provisions. Exactly as Lance had expected her to.

Riding due west, he purposely avoided the site of the battle, located only a few miles to the south, that had claimed the lives of Custer and his raw recruits. Lance's high-strung companion was already upset enough. She didn't need to see that painful reminder of her loss, with its tall granite monument standing in solitary mourning against the blue Montana sky. In the afternoon they enjoyed a brief stop in the cool, fragrant shelter of western yellow pines and mountain balsams along a high ridge, and while the horses rested, they made a quick meal out of the baking powder biscuits and plum jam Anna had packed for them, in such a hurry.

When they forded the river with Fort Custer in sight, Lance relaxed at last. High on a bluff overlooking the Big Horn River, the barracks, stables, ordnance buildings, officer's quarters, and storehouses were silhouetted against the darkening sky. He was familiar with the layout of the unpalisaded cantonment; he'd come through here as a chained prisoner on his way to Lame Deer. It was late in the evening, and most of the fort's occupants would soon be retiring. But Lance decided against waiting until daylight before entering the post. He wanted his charge safely tucked in bed and out of his keeping before they ended their journey.

They were stopped by the four sentries on duty. The enlisted men were surprised and delighted to send for permission from the commanding officer to admit a gorgeous redhead, who made the astounding claim that she was a doctor. Disgusted, Lance watched in silence as three chaw-bacon privates stumbled all over one another trying to get her a cup of coffee while she waited in the gatehouse. It didn't improve his spirits any to learn that he wasn't the only one to make a fool of himself over the sight of her slender curves encased in those ridiculous britches. The bumbling yokels couldn't take their eyes off her. Before she'd had time to finish the hot drink, Private Daggett returned with orders from the colonel to bring Dr. Stanwood and her Indian scout to the commanding officer's quarters.

Colonel John Hatch, renowned and decorated hero of

Antietam and present commander of the First Cavalry and Fifth Infantry troops stationed at Fort Custer, met his late evening visitors on the spacious veranda of his two-story frame home. His large, big-boned wife stood beside him.

"Dr. Stanwood," the colonel said, taking Suzette's outstretched hand and helping her up the step, "welcome to Fort Custer." He smiled broadly at his lovely guest, then briefly returned Lance's silent gaze.

"And welcome to our home, my dear," his wife added in her loud midwestern twang. "I'm Mrs. Hatch, but please call me Hattie." She grinned and mugged dramatically. "That's right. Hattie Hatch. Chose the colonel on purpose, just so's I could have his moniker." Without pausing for breath, she signaled a house servant to take the young woman's satchel and kept right on talking. "While you're at the fort, I want you to stay here with us. We heard about the lady doctor at Lame Deer. I'm just pleased as punch that I got to meet you before any of the other officers' wives."

Politely ignoring her guest's outrageous riding costume, the buxom woman took Suzette's elbow and guided her toward the front door. "I know you just came from back East. I'm so anxious to hear all about the political news." She allowed herself one sweeping glance down the audacious blue trousers, then met her young visitor's smile with a broad grin of delight. "And all the latest fashions."

"I appreciate your hospitality, Hattie, but I didn't come for a social call," Suzette explained. "I need to talk to the fort's physician. I hope to borrow a few of his drugs and other supplies until I can requisition some of my own."

"Well, Doc Gilbreath's probably over at the canteen this time of night, and in no condition to discuss medical terminology with anybody. I'm sure it can wait till morning," Hattie said with bracing cheerfulness. "You've had a long ride and you must be tired. I've got a soft feather bed all made up for you in the attic chamber."

Looking back over her shoulder, Suzette hesitated. "My guide . . ." she began. She looked across the wide porch and met Lance's impassive gaze with confusion. The need to go over and speak to him privately was almost overwhelming. Surely it would be acceptable for her to tell him good night. But he seemed to read her thoughts, and his eyes narrowed as if in warning.

The colonel's robust wife waved her hand in a casual gesture of dismissal before Suzette could say more. "Oh, the Indian can bed down in our stable after he takes care of your horses. Private Daggett'll show him the way." Without another look at War Lance, Hattie ushered Suzette into the house, her husband following with a patient, easygoing smile.

In the soft glow of a hanging coal-oil lantern, Lance groomed the large red stallion and the piebald mare with a rubber currycomb and a coarse bristle brush borrowed from Sergeant Haskell, who remembered the former prisoner from his previous stay at the fort. The methodical, repetitive motion required by the work was soothing, and Lance murmured quietly to the nickering horses in Cheyenne as he finished with a soft grooming cloth. He checked and cleaned the animals' hooves with an old hoof pick, carefully removing any rocks and mud they'd picked up on the journey. Then he combed the long manes and swishing tails. Despite his stubborn resolutions, thoughts of Suzette continued to plague him as he completed his chores. The image of her standing hip-deep in a stream, sopping wet, her disheveled hair darkened to auburn, her eyes alight with merriment at his antics, taunted him. The memory of her slim figure clearly revealed beneath the soaked blouse and trousers renewed the throb of desire in his groin, regardless of his unflinching conviction that he had to put her out of his mind, if only to end his own torment.

When the colonel's freckled houseboy brought out a tray with some soft-boiled eggs and three thick slices of buttered bread, he stopped and ate while the two horses had a treat of oats and timothy hay. He'd stowed the bridles, blanket pads, and Painted Doll's saddle in the tack room, where he'd piled up a bed of straw for himself in a corner. After checking to see that there was enough clean straw on the floor of the stalls, he wandered outside and leaned against the top rail of the stable's corral.

The cantonment appeared nearly deserted. Only the sounds of laughter and conversation coming from the home of the fort's commanding officer disturbed the evening peace. No doubt Suzette was being courted with pretty speeches and outrageous flatteries at that very moment. The fort's dandies were probably tripping over one another's highly polished boots to get to her. If they touched her, he'd break their soft, lily white fingers.

The roof of the post's little bandstand, directly across from the officers' quarters, shone silver in the moonlit parade ground. Lance gazed upward in solemn contemplation at the glistening September moon as he listened to the sound of booted footsteps moving stealthily toward him along the fence.

"Any luck so far?"

Lance faced the colonel. A huge Havana cigar was clamped in the commandant's white teeth, framed by his full, bristly gray beard and mustache. To anyone who should happen to pass by the stables that late at night, Colonel Hatch was simply out for his usual smoke and evening walk before retiring. He stopped several yards from Lance and leaned his elbows on the railing.

"Not yet," Lance answered, and the sound of his British accent seemed strange to his own ears. He gazed back up at the stars. "I haven't seen anything at Lame Deer I'd consider suspicious so far. Perhaps Commissioner Price was mistaken. Perhaps the deaths of the two special agents were really accidental after all."

Hatch drew on the cigar. The burning end revealed his face in a soft red glow. "Hell, I doubt that," he replied gruffly. With the sweet-scented Havana held between two fingers, he flicked the ashes in the dirt. "Horace Corby is a political appointee of the worst kind. He's greedy and lazy. But he's not stupid. Everyone knows that Indian agents usually retire with a small fortune after a few years time. It's a dirty shame that the reservations aren't still under the supervision of the army."

"From what I've heard, that didn't work out too well either, Colonel," Lance replied cryptically, and Hatch turned to meet his gaze with a wry grin.

Laughter rumbled in the officer's deep chest. Though not as tall as Lance, he was a big, strapping man in his early fifties. "You're right there, Mr. Harden. But I think it was a darn sight better than what's happening now. All around, I'd say the Quakers made the best agents. And just about anybody'd be better than a low-down weasel like Horace Corby."

Hatch moved along the rail fence, stopping only a few feet from Lance. His low voice was deadly serious. "Just don't forget that those two special investigators came to a sudden, brutal end. Keep your wits about you, man."

"I intend to do just that."

A cloud of smoke surrounded Hatch as he puffed again. He tipped his head back and studied the autumn constellations that sparkled in the inky canopy above them. "You probably wish you were back at our legation in London right about now, Mr. Harden, twirling some fat matron around the dance floor in a nice, safe waltz."

Lance smiled to himself. "Montana has its compensations."

"Yes, I've seen her." Hatch glanced over at his companion. "You could have knocked me over with a feather when I heard that you'd accepted the job as scout for Lame Deer's lady doc. Lord a'mighty, Harden, you're walking a tightrope there. I hope to hell there's nothing going on between you and that young woman."

Lance bristled at the inference. "My relationship with Dr. Stanwood is strictly business. There's no personal involvement whatsoever."

"Hell's bells, man, don't get your dander up. I wouldn't blame you if there were. She's a real beauty. Just don't go forgetting that out here, you're a Cheyenne buck. If any white folks—cowboys or soldiers—suspected that there was the least idea in your mind about getting personal with a white woman, they'd hang you without a moment's hesitation. Any help you'd get would come too late. You'd already be swinging from the wrong end of a rope." Hatch threw the cigar stub in the dirt and ground it under his boot. "Keep your distance from that red-haired gal or the entire investigation will go up in smoke. And you'll be just one more dead Injun."

Lance stepped away from the railing and turned toward the stable. "Don't worry, Colonel, it's not just my own skin I'm concerned about. The well-being of my father's whole tribe is at stake. I don't intend to do anything foolish."

Dr. Michael Gilbreath was an elf of a man with a plucky Irish grin. He peered at Suzette over his round spectacles and sucked on his meerschaum pipe. "Well, saints preserve us," he said as he led her across the wooden porch that ran the whole length of the post hospital. "A female doctor. If that don't beat all. Guess I've been away from civilization too long."

Suzette returned his teasing smile and crossed the threshold beside him. "It looks like you brought some civilization out here with you, Dr. Gilbreath," she said in admiration. She glanced about the center hall of the long frame building. Two wards of twelve beds each extended in opposite directions from the main entryway. "I was hoping that you might have also brought some extra medical supplies with you as well."

"So I understand, lass," he said, scratching behind one oversize ear with the stem of his pipe like a leprechaun who's just been asked to share his pot of gold. "But before we talk business, let me show you my hospital."

He pointed out with pride the spotless wards, the few patients being cared for by uniformed orderlies. Several convalescents were in a sitting room, occupied with reading and card playing. At last he ushered her into his office and sat her down in his own deep leather chair. Then he went to the open window and propped himself against the sill.

"I hate to disappoint you, Dr. Stanwood," he said with unmistakable sincerity, "but I'm mighty short on things myself. I've requisitioned everything from acetanilide to calomel, but I won't receive my next shipment until late October, early November at the earliest."

With a sinking heart, Suzette handed him her long list. "Anything you could spare would be sincerely appreciated," she told him. She tried, to no avail, to keep the disappointment out of her voice. "At the present time, I have almost nothing. If the Indians start depending upon me to be their doctor, as I hope and pray they will, the little I was able to bring from Pennsylvania won't last a month."

"I can loan you small amounts of morphia, arnica, paregoric, and belladonna," he said, ticking off the items as he read them. "But I don't keep a large stock of quinine on hand. There are no outbreaks of malaria this far north. It's just plain too cold." He looked up at her over his glasses. "Have you no funds of your own then, lass?" he asked in amazement.

Embarrassed that she'd been reduced to begging, she bent her head and stared at her fingertips. "Apparently not. Agent Corby claims there's been no money budgeted for me." She pursed her lips and met his blue eyes in honest confession. "So anything I borrow from you may be a long time being paid back."

"Write to Washington, mavourneen," he told her, bending forward and resting his hands on his thin knees. "Tell those needle-nosed bureaucrats back there you need more than just their good wishes to practice medicine."

Her shoulders slumped in defeat, and she leaned her

head back against the smooth leather chair as though suddenly exhausted. "I can't. I mentioned the idea to Horace Corby, and he became enraged at the very thought. I guess he feels it would be seen by the Indian Bureau as a criticism of his supervision of the Tongue River Reservation."

"What about someone back home who could help, macushla?" he suggested kindly. "Sometimes charities or church congregations will collect money for the reservations."

She sat up straight and stared at him in astonishment. "That's a wonderful idea! I'll write my sister and ask her to approach the Mennonite community of Lancaster County for help. I came out here with two of their missionaries. Surely if the Grabers' friends and relatives learn about the terrible straits we're in at Lame Deer, they'll want to help."

The diminutive man rose and walked over to his desk, laying her list down on its cluttered top. He picked up a piece of paper and a pen and offered it to her. "You write that letter, lass, and I'll walk you over to the post office, where you can mail it. Then I think you're due back at the colonel's quarters for lunch, Mrs. Hatch has invited some officers and their wives to meet you." He winked at her conspiratorially. "Sure, and if I know Hattie, there'll be a few unmarried officers there to round out the roll call."

Gilbreath's prediction proved to be correct. When Suzette returned to the colonel's home on the white-headed doctor's arm, the parlor was overflowing with men and women eager to meet the post's latest visitor.

"Now, don't you spalpeens go pushing yourselves forward," he warned a pair of handsome cavalrymen as they bore down on Suzette the moment she appeared in the room. "We'll have none of your bold-faced shenanigans here. Stand back and give the little darlin' room to breathe."

But the two men, in dark blue jackets decorated with

officer's stripes, and dress sabers belted over their orange sashes, grinned unabashedly and begged for an introduction, not retreating until the doctor complied.

Second Lieutenant Corwin Roe was a Virginian with a full, golden beard that brushed against the front of his tunic as he bent over Suzette's hand and bowed romantically. Captain Alex Spaulding, formerly of Minnesota, sported a thick shock of dark brown hair and not even so much as a well-trimmed mustache on his boyish face. Once the formalities were over, they both proceeded to ignore the tiny post physician and crowded around Suzette, openly and good-naturedly vying with each other for her attention. Within minutes, each had confided to her in a hushed, theatrical tone that he was single. And while his bachelor friend was far from being ready to settle down, he certainly was.

Suzette laughed at their high-spirited rivalry, purposely ignoring the unpleasant thoughts that kept intruding on her enjoyment of the happy get-together. She struggled in vain to set aside the feeling that somehow she'd been tried and found wanting. As she and Dr. Gilbreath had left the hospital and approached the colonel's quarters, they'd passed War Lance Striking. He was perched nearby, atop the rail fence next to the stable, repairing a braided horsehair halter.

"War Lance is my guide," she'd explained to the little Irishman beside her. They paused, and Gilbreath, clucking his tongue in surprise, had looked up at the strong, well-built Indian.

"Well, now, I think I've seen this handsome bucko before. But the last time, he was trussed up in chains like a horse thief just 'fore his own hanging."

A chill went through Suzette at her colleague's bald statement of fact. She looked in astonishment at Gilbreath to find him chuckling in wry amusement, then up at War Lance to discover his reaction. But of course there was none. He hadn't understood a word. He only stared down at her with that unreadable expression, though for some inexplicable reason she sensed his disappointment in her. Was there really an indefinable sadness behind that air of total indifference? Or was she merely allowing her own romantic fancies to play on her imagination? Certainly he had to be aware that he would never be invited to socialize with the white inhabitants of Fort Custer. He belonged to a different world. Good Lord, the thought of her Cheyenne scout being included in Mrs. Hatch's soiree was preposterous.

She had smiled up at him weakly. She'd opened her mouth, but uncertain what to say, closed it again. As Dr. Gilbreath had guided her once more toward the Hatches' residence, she'd felt War Lance's gaze riveted on her back. During the entire encounter, he hadn't spoken a word.

Now, surrounded by the laughing, chattering company, she still couldn't shake that vague feeling of uneasiness and discontent. The other guests in Hattie's salon, though not nearly so boisterous as her two self-proclaimed escorts, were every bit as friendly. She was deeply thankful that she'd thought ahead enough to stuff a dress into her carpet bag before leaving Lame Deer in such haste. Hattie had considerately ordered that the twenty yards of wrinkled buttercup-embroidered muslin be pressed for her early that morning. With a vanity she seldom indulged in, Suzette smoothed the fashionable puffs that drooped from the pointed waist of the fitted basque to a bouffant fullness in the back. Laughing in response to the witticisms of her two self-appointed escorts, she allowed herself to be pulled from one congenial group to another, until Hattie tinkled a little silver bell and announced that it was time for the luncheon.

During the meal, she was seated between Spaulding and Roe at one of the small tables set up on the veranda. She was unable to keep from comparing the young officers' carefree behavior with War Lance's undeniable aura of quiet power and inner strength. Next to him, the two lieutenants seemed like immature schoolboys out on a lark.

"Why, ma'am, I do hope you'll come to the post often," Lieutenant Roe drawled as he lifted a glass of lemonade in a toast. He drank deeply and wiped the sparkling drops from his golden mustache with his linen napkin.

"Probably not too often," she explained with a flattered smile. "I'm going to be pretty busy with my work as Lame Deer's physician. But perhaps I can come again sometime."

"We're going to have a grand ball next month in the post hall," Captain Spaulding promised from her other side. "Under the old commandant, the hall was reserved for the chaplain's Sunday services and temperance meetings for the women. The men of the garrison have never been allowed to use it before. When Colonel Hatch said we had the right to hold events there, too, we started a Rounders' Club, and one hundred of the men have kicked in five dollars each out of their own wages to pay for the food and decorations." He leaned toward her, his brown eyes aglow with all the heartfelt entreaty of a beagle pup begging for attention. "Say you'll come."

Suzette frowned uncertainly. Some niggling doubt in the back of her mind told her that War Lance Striking would be less than enthusiastic about returning to the fort without an imperative reason. And getting him to do anything against his will would be like trying to teach an army jackass how to dance the polka. "Goodness, I don't know," she said. "I'd have to arrange for my guide to bring me back here."

"No, you wouldn't," Roe assured her with brash optimism. "I'm sure Colonel Hatch would let us send a wagon with an escort for you. I'd come to pick you up myself."

"We've bought some turkeys and ordered lemons, oranges, and grapes," Spaulding added. "It'll be a bang-up affair. All the ladies on the post will be there."

She laughed at his exuberance. "You make it sound very inviting, Captain. But let me think about it."

"Here's to the ball," Spaulding said with a carefree smile, lifting his glass high.

"And to the beautiful doctor," Roe added as he joined in the toast.

Mrs. Hatch was a marvelous hostess, and Suzette's day was filled with social activities. After the luncheon, she joined a group of ladies who took her on a walking tour of the fort. They showed her the bakery, the stage office, the guardhouse from a distance, the post headquarters, where she visited briefly with Colonel Hatch, the telegraph station, and the post exchange with its library, billiard room, card room, and gymnasium. They even showed her the canteen, though at that spot on the itinerary, the chattering women only peeked in from the open doorway. Then everyone walked out to the target range and watched the enlisted infantrymen at rifle practice. The young women were a lively bunch, indulging in high-spirited giggling and raillery among themselves. The officers, who just happened to meet them at every stage of their outing, engaged the gaggle of females in good-humored, bantering conversation.

Suzette almost ran into War Lance Striking as she rounded the corner of the blacksmith's shop on her way back to the Hatch residence.

"I didn't see you coming," she apologized in Cheyenne. She folded up her borrowed parasol and rested its tip on the ground in front of her.

He inclined his head toward the leather bag balanced easily on his shoulder. "I had a buckle on your saddlebag repaired."

The six young ladies accompanying her grew silent, listening with apparent unease to their conversation in the strange language. Slowly the other women drifted away to close ranks in a tight little circle nearby, where they waited politely for Suzette to re-join them. Only the boldest one peeped up from under her long lashes, obviously both curious and frightened.

Hesitant, Suzette looked over at the group of females and then back to her guide. "Thank you."

He lifted his brows as though to tell her he had nothing better to do with his time. And, after all, he was being paid to wait.

She glanced once more at her new friends. All half dozen had been openly staring at the two of them, but looked quickly away. "Well, I should go now." She paused. She wanted to tell him something, but she wasn't sure exactly what. She missed him, but she couldn't tell him that. She wished he could have been at Mrs. Hatch's party the previous night, but she couldn't say that either.

"I'll see you tomorrow," she said at last. When he pointedly stepped out of her way, she opened the yellow parasol and hurriedly joined the others.

That evening there was a supper at the commanding officer's quarters, and though only a few of the colonel's staff and their wives were invited, Suzette had met most of the men and women there earlier in the day. Everyone treated her like an old friend. But despite their warm hospitality, she was constantly aware of the fact that the one person she most wanted to talk to had been relegated to the colonel's stable.

The next morning, Lance was waiting for her in front of the stable, where he'd slept for the last two nights and wasted an entire day. From his spot on the top railing of the corral the previous afternoon, he had watched her parade across the post grounds in her fancy yellow gown. One of the other ladies had even lent her a ruffled parasol to match. The unmarried officers, who obviously didn't have nearly enough to keep them busy, had followed the women around like groveling puppies, totally devoid of pride, lapping up any attention the females doled out to them. What went on inside the colonel's house at dinner and supper, he could only imagine, for

he'd certainly not been invited to step through the door—
front or back. But he could guess easily enough. The
blond lieutenant with the curly beard and the southern
drawl would have hovered around Suzette and drooled
all the way down the front of his blue dress tunic. And
the dark-headed, baby-faced captain probably caught one
whiff of the delicate scent of violets that always surrounded her and engaged in a bout of heavy breathing.

Now Lance stood beside Red Wind and Painted Doll
and waited for Suzette to finish her preparations for departure. The two idiot officers walked beside her, escort-
ing her from Mrs. Hatch's front porch to the stables as
though she were too weak-brained to find her own way.

"Woo-ee, she's a prime looker," one of the privates
who'd been mucking out the stable that morning said to
his partner. They'd both emerged from the building to
have one last covetous look at the lady doctor. Leaning
on their shovels, they stood just behind Lance and
watched their superiors approach with the woman between them.

"Shit, those officers git all the fun, don't they?" the
other man replied as he spat in the dirt. "Lordy, Lordy,
wouldn't I jest love to be examined by that bodacious,
long-legged sawbones."

Lance clenched his fists. Wouldn't he just love to
smash the foulmouthed runt's pug nose all over his
homely face. But he didn't so much as turn around. The
two enlisted men would be flabbergasted to think an Indian could even understand their crude remarks, let alone
be enraged by them. The pair of stable hands became
quiet as the gaily chattering trio drew near.

"Say you'll come, Dr. Stanwood," the dark-haired officer pleaded into her pink little ear. "The colonel has
given us permission to go to Lame Deer and get you.
And Mrs. Hatch said you'd be welcome to stay overnight."

She laughed in delight at his flattering pleas. "Very
well, Captain Spaulding. You and Lieutenant Roe have

talked me into it. The dance sounds like a wonderful idea, and I'll come if it's at all possible."

"We weren't going to take no for an answer, ma'am," the blond southerner drawled.

Suzette flushed becomingly. Her eyes sparkled with happiness. She fairly bloomed beneath their unbridled flattery, their overeager attention. As they drew near, Lance could see the flirtatious smile that skipped about the corners of her delectable mouth. In her mock military riding outfit, with its gold buttons and braided trim, she was absolutely adorable. How Lance could have ever thought she was too thin or too tall mystified him. The top of her head fit right under his chin. They were a perfect match.

What she saw in the two thickheaded dolts who were hanging on her every word would be a mystery to anyone. Except that Suzette had a well-known weakness for U.S. Cavalry officers. As he watched the animated threesome come up, Lance felt a wrench of pure jealousy, like a mule kick square in the gut.

She turned to him, and the musical laughter died on her lips. "I'm ready to go now," she said stiffly in Cheyenne, suddenly aware, no doubt, that he was the only one who wasn't smiling.

"We're starting late enough," he replied curtly in his native tongue as he mounted Red Wind. "We'll have to travel fast to reach Lame Deer tonight."

Both officers looked up at him in consternation, uncertain what he'd said to their lady fair, but aware that his tone had been cold and insolent. He met Roe's icy stare with blatant defiance, hoping, praying, the man would be foolish enough to try something. But under Lance's overt challenge, the golden-haired lieutenant only scowled and glanced away.

Then, with a gallant bow, Captain Spaulding cupped his gloved hands for her boot and tossed her up into the saddle. "We'll plan to see you next month at the ball, Dr.

Stanwood," he said, taking the ground-tied reins and handing them to her with a flourish.

"And we'll both come to get you, ma'am," Roe added with a wide grin.

The two officers walked on either side of Painted Doll as Suzette followed Lance, mounted on Red Wind, past the row of officers' quarters, where Hattie and some of the other wives stood on their porches and waved good-bye. When the entourage passed the post hospital, with the Stars and Bars flying high from its cupola, Dr. Gilbreath saluted her from his open window. The few drugs, bandages, and rolls of gauze he'd been able to spare her were to be carefully wrapped, packed in wooden crates, and sent over by wagon the next week.

Once they were past the long line of infantry barracks, Lance urged Red Wind into a gallop, and Painted Doll followed suit, hurrying to catch up with the great stallion. When Lance looked back, the coquettish smile on Suzette's face had disappeared, and she was hanging on to the piebald mare as though her life depended on it. Behind her, the two blue coats of her erstwhile beaus were covered with the clouds of dust kicked up by the flying hooves. For the first time in thirty-six hours, Lance felt a small measure of satisfaction.

Chapter 12

Suzette followed War Lance across the rolling sweep of shortgrass country, vividly aware of the sheer immensity of the land that surrounded them. The vastness of the prairie seemed eternal, the earth so big, the sky so wide, that she was unable to comprehend it. In the bright sunshine of Indian summer, kildeer arched in flight across the brilliant blue sky, while tufted golden plumes of little bluestem, buffalo grass, and bluejoint swayed in the breeze. As they crested a hill, a startled pronghorn bounded away in graceful leaps, while western meadow larks exploded into the air all around them.

In the warmth of late morning, she'd removed her short blue jacket and slipped it into the satchel behind her saddle. She'd opened the collar buttons on her dull gold blouse and rolled up the lace-trimmed cuffs. Once again, she rode with only the back of her guide's faded cotton shirt and the old rifle slung over his shoulder in view. War Lance, with unswerving tenacity, kept his position directly in front of her. Though he remained close enough to hear her call if she needed him, he was too far away to be engaged in conversation of any kind. He hadn't spoken to her since his few, curt words at Fort Custer, just before they'd left. But the delicious afterglow of her pleasurable stay at the fort kept at bay the increasing awareness of their total isolation, which would have otherwise threatened to overwhelm her.

Nothing could bother her this morning. The long, intense years spent poring over her studies had left little time for frivolity or self-indulgence. Even more exacting had been the harried months of internship at the Women's and Children's Hospital. And the death of her father only the previous summer had cast a pall of sadness over Pauline's marriage and the birth of her tiny daughter.

The spontaneous, warmhearted attention of Fort Custer's residents, particularly the unmarried officers, had coaxed into full bloom the dormant sense of childlike playfulness that War Lance had awakened within her. Suddenly she felt much younger than her twenty-eight years. And if in the time that had passed since Jordan's death, she'd begun to view herself as an unwanted spinster on the shelf, that had certainly changed since her arrival in Montana territory. Today she felt youthful and attractive and gloriously alive. She smiled gaily to herself as she recalled the extravagant rivalry Spaulding and Roe had engaged in. Like knights of old jousting in a tournament, they'd openly competed with each other for her favors.

Ahead, War Lance finally slowed Red Wind to a walk, and her pleasant reverie was ended. Bursting with an unbounded energy, she urged Painted Doll into a fast trot and quickly caught up with her taciturn guide.

"Did you see that antelope back there?" she asked in an attempt to make conversation. She had to share her happiness with someone. She favored him with a provocative, teasing smile.

War Lance's rugged face remained the mask of indifference he'd maintained during their entire stay at Fort Custer. Here, with a vengeance, was the stoical red man she'd read about in the eastern newspapers.

"Of course," he replied sardonically. One corner of his wide mouth turned up in a mocking half grin. "We almost rode over it."

Ignoring his foul mood, she looked about the lush September landscape as it rolled away into a hazy, golden billow of sage and grass. Thickets of silvery buffalo berry in the draws trailed amongst the sandbar willows that lined the streams. Along the banks, cottonwoods rattled and shook in the wind. Western junipers stretched across the faraway hills like sentinels guarding them in the distance.

"I can't help but wonder," she said with a melodramatic sigh, waxing poetic in her high spirits, "How many driving rainstorms, how many unremitting gusts of wind, how many bitter winters melting into warm springs, have chiseled and shaped this wondrous landscape."

He made no comment.

She refused to let his bad humor bother her. She was filled with a sense of jubilation, of amazement and awe at the land they were crossing. Her tone was light and frivolous, just the way she'd felt since yesterday's welcome fling of socializing. "This wilderness is so vast, we haven't seen a trace of a human being since we left Fort Custer."

"Or an Indian either," he said sharply.

She straightened the wide brim of her hat and scowled at him, disgusted with his grumpy attitude. "What's the matter with you?" she demanded in irritation.

In a lightning move, he reached over, grabbed Painted Doll's reins near the halter, and kicked his great stallion into a wild gallop. Suzette clung to the saddle horn in startled dismay. Together both horses, solely under War Lance's control, flew over the grass to a nearby sheltering stand of cottonwoods, where he pulled them to an abrupt stop. He dismounted in one fluid, graceful motion and turned to her. His narrowed eyes were glittering shards of black ice. Before she could even guess his intentions, he yanked her off Painted Doll, his actions quick and rough and predatory.

"What are you doing?" she screeched. Finding herself in midair, she automatically braced her hands on his wide shoulders. His powerful muscles tensed and knotted beneath the blue cotton shirt at her touch.

The moment her feet hit the ground, she tried to break free and run. Her decision to take flight caught him off guard, for he'd released his hold on her momentarily, believing, no doubt, that his wrath alone was frightening enough to hold her captive. Before she could escape the reach of his arms, he caught her hand and effortlessly swung her back around to face him. He was no longer the impassive warrior she'd spent the entire morning with. His arrogant face was taut with a cold rage. Ruthlessly he clamped his fingers on her upper arms and shoved her backward until she was pinned against a tree trunk, her body trapped between the rough bark and his sinewy frame.

"Stop it," she cried as she tried to shove him away. Her heart pounded wildly in her chest. "Let me go."

"Ahh, no, *náevehoka*," he said, his low, bitter words betraying the turbulent emotions that had raged behind his facade of cool indifference all morning. "Not until I show you what is wrong with me."

She struck at him, pummeling his head and shoulders and chest with her clenched fists. When he merely ignored her futile attempts to fight him off, she smacked his face resoundingly with her open palm. He shook his head once at the unexpected force of her blow and grinned mirthlessly. His dark eyes lit up with the anticipation of certain revenge, as though he'd wanted her to hurt him, so that he'd have an excuse to hurt her back.

He caught both her wrists in one strong hand and lifted them above her head, pinioning them against the tree in his powerful grasp. With the other hand, he caught her jaw and forced her face upward to meet his. Under the relentless pressure of his steely fingers, her lips opened slightly. He bent his head and kissed her savagely, his tongue probing and entering her mouth at will. There was no gentleness in his touch, only a ruthless, insistent, remorseless need to conquer and possess. He released her chin and moved one hand to her side, bracketing her breast with his thumb.

With a sob of terror and confusion, she turned her face and broke away from the searing kiss. "You're frightening me," she said. Her shaky voice sounded as weak and pitiful as a betrayed child's.

He pulled his head back to look at her and grinned devilishly. Still keeping her wrists captive in his unyielding grasp, he slid his other hand brazenly up the front of her blouse and encircled her neck. With deliberate savagery, he pressed his thumb against the wildly beating pulse below her jawline. Her every sense heightened by fear, she could feel the blood pumping madly through her veins.

"You should be scared, angel," he purred in a low rumble of barely leashed restraint. He arched one black eyebrow in heartless mockery. "Out here in this empty wilderness, which you claim to admire so much, you are totally in my power. I can do whatever I want, and neither you nor anyone else can stop me."

Caught in the unexpected ferocity of his attack, she was stunned. She tried to reply, to beg him to think of the consequences should he harm her, but he smothered her words with his mouth and tongue as he pressed his hard length against her.

His large hand slid over her chest in a fiercely possessive movement. One by one, he methodically released the small buttons down the front of her blouse. Moving his hand inside the flimsy cotton barrier, he cupped her breast, its fullness enhanced by the position of her arms held securely above her head. Then he skillfully, knowingly, slipped his long fingers beneath the lacy white camisole. The feel of his rough fingertips flicking across her soft nipple brought shock waves of pleasure. A whimper of submission escaped her bruised lips, only to enter his open mouth.

Her reflexive, involuntary response seemed to enrage him further.

His lips moved against hers, and as he spoke, their warm breath mingled. "Did one of those men touch you like this?" he demanded hoarsely. The fury in his voice was as jagged and raw as a cut from a serrated blade.

She turned her face so that his lips were pressed against her cheek. "No," she said, panting for breath, desperate for some means to strike back and regain her equilibrium. "They're much too civilized to do that."

With a low growl of undisguised satisfaction, he slid his open mouth down to the base of her neck and lightly nipped her bare skin with his even, white teeth. There was a hint of cynical laughter in his reply. "How unfortunate for you that I'm not."

As he spoke, he pressed his muscular thigh between her legs, lifting her slightly and letting her ride him. Through her broadcloth trousers, she could feel his manhood, taut and hard and fully aroused, pressing against his denim jeans. He pushed the white camisole deftly aside to free one breast, then bent his head and suckled her. Next to his bronzed cheek, her pale skin looked incredibly soft and creamy white. The intense erotic pleasure as he stroked and encircled the tight bud with his moist tongue awakened deep within her all the aching desire she had felt the night he'd touched her so intimately. For an instant, the universe halted. All she could feel was the gentle tug on her engorged breast.

"Please, you must stop," she said, moaning. She moved her head back and forth in her denial of what they both wanted. Trapped against the tree, her pinned arms lifting her exposed breast higher to his devouring mouth, she felt jolts of pure, exquisite pleasure lance through her. Despite her words of refusal, her body betrayed her, and she rubbed her hips and thighs against him in a movement so primal, so instinctual, that she was barely aware of her own actions. Vaguely, as though drifting on a magic carpet, she realized that he had released her imprisoned hands. His strong fingers slid down her back and over her buttocks, pulling the core of her throbbing need ever tighter against him. Instead of pushing him away, she threaded her trembling fingers through his black hair and brought his mouth closer to her breast, unable and unwilling to seek freedom.

Lance moved to suck the pink crest of the other, waiting breast that had been revealed by his questing fingers. Suzette tilted her head back, half sobbing in her passionate response to his touch. As he covered the tight bud with his hungry lips and laved it greedily with his tongue, he could feel her sweet female body surrendering. He was in glorious, fiery torment, and only she could bring the cooling balm that would soothe the flames raging inside him. He could feel the delicate bones and nubile curves melt in compliance against his lusting body, and his bunched muscles spasmed and clutched. He was rocked by a carnal need greater than he'd even known before.

What he'd just told her was true.

He could do anything he wanted with her.

And he wanted this redheaded vixen more than any woman he'd ever known. Fantasies of schooling her naked, silken flesh in all the arts of erotic love had haunted him since he'd first touched her that night in the cabin. He longed to erase every memory from her mind of the inept fiancé who'd failed to teach her even a lover's kiss.

Like the wild thunder of a thousand hoofs pounding across the prairie, his driving male need threatened to smash and obliterate his own carefully fortified sense of duty, honor, and personal integrity. He knew he must stop now, or he would never be able to stop at all.

Lance called forth every measure of the iron resolve he'd learned as a young warrior, who'd willingly suffered the excruciating pain of the Great Medicine Dance, and brought himself to a wrenching halt. It took all the brutal determination of a man throwing a stampeding buffalo to the ground. By sheer strength of will alone he forced himself to raise his head and release his hold on her.

He straightened, allowing her to slide down his thigh and lean back against the cottonwood for support.

Roughly he cupped her fine-boned face in his large hands. Her marvelous violet eyes were heavy-lidded and dazed, as she slowly became aware of her surroundings and of the fact that he was no longer kissing and suckling her.

His breath came in deep, rough drafts. He was infuriated with her for flirting with the two officers. And at himself for caring. But worst of all, he was half-crazed with the knowledge that both men had a right to court and woo and marry her, while he could not. He knew, without a doubt, that—given enough time—one of them would succeed in doing just that.

"It is only by my choice alone, angel, that I do not throw you to the ground and take you here and now. If you think that I am afraid of that pair of fools back there at the fort, or what they might do about it, you are completely mistaken. I will decide what will be between us."

Slowly he squeezed his fingers against her delicate cheekbones with just enough pressure to allow her the uncomfortable awareness that he could crush her skull without ever exerting his full strength. Her expressive eyes were enormous with unfulfilled need and a burgeoning fear of him. He could feel her trembling and fought the urge to enfold her tenderly in his arms and reassure her that he'd never, ever hurt her. Instead, he left her thoroughly frightened.

Her cheeks were flushed with thwarted passion and a rising anger. "There is nothing between us," she said with disdain. "And there never could be."

At her biting words, he stepped back. "I am well aware of what you think of me, little white woman. But in the future, remember that I will take only so much of your taunting ways. And then I will strike back."

The Crows had been invited for a horse race. They came to Lame Deer early in the morning on the first Tuesday in October. Below the agency, the visitors put up their canvas cone lodges near the swift-running creek.

Only a few families of either tribe had managed to retain their buffalo-skin tipis during the past few tragic years. It had been a long time since they'd killed enough buffalo to renew the comfortable dwellings they liked so well. In the midst of the milling crowd, small groups of Indian women and children sat outside the trading post and general store, waiting patiently for the day's festivities to begin.

From her spot on the corral's top railing, Suzette looked around her in fascination. The agency buildings were all one story and built of logs, except for Corby's office, which was frame. These were gathered around a wide, rectangular space of dirt into which supply wagons and the weekly stage from Miles City were driven. At the south end of the dusty plaza area was a blacksmith shop, over which old Mose Purvis presided. Next to it was the commissary, where the government-issued rations were housed, and the wood shop, run by Clarence Boan, the carpenter. To the north were the homes of the agency's staff. Suzette knew that the list of employees under Corby's supervision also included the issue clerk, the wheelwright, the butcher, the stable man, the barber, and the trader—to whom she still owed a hundred dollars for her fancy new saddle. She and the Grabers were a part of the superintendent's responsibilities, as well, though he probably respected them the least.

Cheyenne from all over the reservation had come to Lame Deer for the race, and their lodges were scattered along both sides of the bubbling stream west of the agency compound. Many had chosen to wear their most festive regalia, complete with feathers, beads, bells, and paint. Most of the Cheyenne women had put aside their calico skirts and blouses and donned instead their fringed and beaded buckskin dresses with their flying sleeves. There were even some among them who proudly wore dresses tanned to a golden brown and embellished with a thousand elk teeth. As in days of old, a good husband still provided, through hunting or trade, these highly favored decorations for his wife to make a "one-thousand dress."

Wearing just such a garment, Blue Crane Flying sat perched beside Suzette on the top rail of the corral fence, and even she, who was usually so quiet and grave, was touched by the pervasive air of excitement and merry-making.

"Where will the race start?" Suzette asked, unconsciously raising her voice. Even though she realized by now that her mastery of the Cheyenne language was good enough for all to understand, she nearly always spoke more loudly and distinctly than was her normal manner in an effort to compensate for what she knew was probably a heavy accent.

"It will begin farther down this road," Blue Crane Flying answered in her gentle way. She pointed in the direction of Tongue River, toward the group of men and horses congregating in the distance. "They will have a straight stretch to race on and will finish here at the agency. The first rider to pass the corral and reach the center of the dirt clearing will be the winner. Two old men chiefs, one Crow and one Cheyenne, will judge the final moments of the contest."

Suzette met the lovely Indian woman's somber eyes and smiled at her with sincere fondness. During her son's convalescence, Blue Crane Flying had stayed in a small lodge she'd erected just behind the Grabers' cabin. She had cared for Young Wolf, who'd remained in his doctor's bedroom, with such Madonna-like tenderness that Suzette had been deeply moved. Though the Cheyenne medicine woman had brought her special parfleche painted with her own secret patterns and had sprinkled the sacred sage to purify the *vèho* cabin, she'd also followed Suzette's detailed instructions with scrupulous care. The Pennsylvanian's smug belief that the Cheyenne were a primitive people had been altered drastically in the short time since her arrival at the reservation. Never before had she seen parents as loving and giving to their children, or adults so respectful and caring to their elderly, as these so-called savages.

It was over two weeks since the appendectomy. News had immediately spread across the reservation of Young Wolf's amazing surgery. Shortly afterward, an old man chief, nearly blind with cataracts, and a woman who'd been crippled since childhood from a fall had presented themselves at the door of the white medicine woman's lodge, fully expecting to be healed. When Suzette had admitted that she was unable to help either patient, the Cheyenne had no longer been so impressed with the power of her medicine.

But the robust little six-year-old was up and about, and that was what counted. Today his grandmother, Prairie Grass Woman, and his sister, Yellow Feather, were also at the agency. They'd come with Bear Scalp and War Lance Striking, who were both riding in the race. Yellow Feather was carrying a sack of hard candy, purchased by her uncle at the trader's store, and she was happily sharing the sweet rocks with her little brother.

"Will you bet on the race, *náevehoka?*" Blue Crane Flying asked.

Suzette flushed, knowing that the astute woman had observed the distance that had arisen between the white woman doctor and her paid guide. Surely War Lance Striking's sister-in-law was aware that there was something far more personal and serious between the fractious pair than a mere occupational disagreement.

"No, I'm not betting," Suzette replied with a breezy air. "Since it makes no difference to me who wins, I will just watch and enjoy the race." She grinned in a teasing fashion at the thin woman beside her. "But I'm sure you'll be betting on your husband's beautiful Appaloosa."

On the grass behind the stable, someone had spread a striped blanket and was calling out to one and all for bets on the race. The Indians, men and women alike, crowded around, depositing their stakes on the open blanket. In no time, there were piles of silver coin, paper currency, pistols, rifles, belts, cartridges, shawls, moccasins, tobacco pouches, medicine pipes, smoking tobacco, bridles, picket ropes, and bands of sleigh bells. Tied to the railing beside the stakeholder, there was even a bunch of mustangs.

"Little Red Fox," her companion said with gentle compassion after a moment's pause, "I am sorry that you are angry with all of us again, even on a happy day like this."

At a loss as to her meaning, Suzette turned and stared at her new friend. "What do you mean?" she asked. "I'm not angry."

Blue Crane Flying looked at her in disbelief, as though not quite certain that the lady doctor could be so totally unaware of how cross she really sounded. "You always speak as though you are irritated with everyone around you."

"Why?" Suzette demanded. She leaned toward her, bracing one hand on the railing. "Why do I sound as though I'm angry? Is it the words I use?"

Her friend smiled quizzically, the nut brown eyes filled with a sympathetic amusement. "Then you don't realize, *náevehoka,* that Cheyenne women never talk loudly unless they are very, very angry? We speak with much softer words than a man. Since you have arrived, everyone has wondered why you are always in such a bad temper toward all of us."

"I . . . I learned to speak your language from a man who learned it from other men," Suzette stuttered in mortification. She could feel a flush of embarrassment spread over her cheeks and neck. "I'm sure Jacob didn't realize that I sounded like a harping shrew."

Blue Crane Flying covered her mouth to smother her giggles. "From now on, Little Red Fox, you must speak our language much more softly. Then our little ones won't be so afraid of you."

Remembering the way Yellow Feather had first looked

at her with such terrified eyes, Suzette understood at last how she must have sounded to the Cheyenne: like a sharp-tongued harridan, for goodness' sakes. It was a wonder that anyone had allowed her to treat them.

She shook her head and grinned self-consciously. "From now on," she said in a stage whisper, "that's exactly what I will do."

Their mutual smiles faded at the abrupt appearance of Horace Corby. "You girls seem to be in good spirits today," he said with oily charm. Tipping up the brim of his oversize slouch hat, he leaned his elbow casually on the top railing of the fence.

His shoulder brushed against Blue Crane Flying's thigh, and she shifted her weight and scooted deliberately closer to Suzette. A look of distaste marred her usually serene features. With a quick gesture, she tossed back both of the long braids that rested against her breasts, as though wanting to hide their thick, shiny beauty from Corby's eyes and give him no excuse for his gaze to linger. Unable to understand his *vèho* words, she made no attempt to answer, but looked out past the dusty plaza area to the road down which the horses and their riders would soon be galloping.

"We're enjoying the festivities," Suzette replied noncommittally. Corby didn't even glance her way. His eyes were fastened on the tawny Indian woman, his overt gaze sweeping over the deerskin dress, decorated with the shiny white elk teeth. "Blue Crane Flying's husband will be riding his horse in the race," Suzette added for his edification. "She's very excited for him."

Corby scowled at this unwelcome news. "Oh yeah, which one of those good-for-nothin' bucks is her husband?" he said with a sneer.

"War Lance Striking's brother," Suzette replied, hiding a telltale grin at his sudden discomposure. "Bear Scalp is nearly as big as my guide. And looks just as fierce and short-tempered."

The agent straightened to his full five feet four inches.

He hooked his thumbs into the armholes of his brown vest and puffed out his chest like a strutting cock in a barnyard full of hens. "Well, you just tell the pretty little squaw here that when the rations come in next week, if there's anything extra she needs, she can come and see me. I'll be sure she has everything she wants." Corby smiled up at Blue Crane Flying, his crooked teeth flashing beneath his huge mustache.

When Suzette translated the agent's crass offer, the unruffled young woman didn't so much as glance at the short, stocky *vèho*.

"Tell Major Hairless Head that my husband sees that I and our children are well taken care of," she said in soft Cheyenne syllables. "We have everything we need."

As Suzette repeated the woman's answer, including the unflattering sobriquet, Corby's thick, pug-nosed face turned red. Even the lobes of his ears were scarlet. Too late, she wondered with dismay if the snub would cost her dearly in the needed medical supplies. His pale green eyes glittering with rage, he turned to leave, but was halted less than a step away by one of the ranchers who'd come to see the horse race.

"I was hoping you'd introduce me to Lame Deer's new doctor," the man said, grabbing hold of one of Corby's elbows. The middle-aged rancher smiled up at Suzette engagingly as he spoke, his twinkling blue eyes bright with a friendly, easygoing charm.

"Introduce yourself, Rumsey," the reservation's unhappy superintendent snarled. Without a backward glance, he stomped away in his high-heeled snakeskin boots.

Undaunted, the stranger chuckled and approached the two females perched side by side on the fence. "Guess I'll have to do just that, ma'am," he said, touching the wide brim of his Stetson hat and addressing Suzette. "Name's Lew Rumsey. I'm one of your neighbors."

Suzette smiled at the rancher. She liked him instantly. Dressed in the cowboy's habitual costume of denim jeans and plaid shirt, he was lean and wiry, despite the fact that he was probably in his early fifties. Deep creases framed the corners of his cheerful eyes, and his deeply tanned cheeks were leathered from years spent working in the sun and wind. A pair of shiny black binoculars hung around his neck.

She extended her hand. "I'm pleased to meet you, Mr. Rumsey. I'm Dr. Suzette Stanwood, and this is Blue Crane Flying. Are you a horse-racing fan?"

"I've placed a few bets today," he admitted, touching his hat and smiling at the Cheyenne woman. "Any suggestions?"

"My friend's husband will be riding a strong Appaloosa," Suzette told him. "Bear Scalp's gray spotted mare is probably the crowd's favorite. There's also a large red stallion that no one has seen race before. Many people seem to be betting on him, as well."

"Oh?" Rumsey queried in surprise. "I don't think I know the horse. Who's the owner?"

"My guide, War Lance Striking," she answered with circumspection, attempting to keep her voice even and natural. "He captured Red Wind only a few weeks ago. The stallion looks like he might have been sired by a Thoroughbred that escaped from some rancher's prize stock. When War Lance caught him, the horse was leading a herd of wild mustangs in the mountains."

The lanky rancher didn't seem to notice the tension in her voice. He hopped up on the railing beside her. "The stallion'll never win," he predicted with a shrug of his shoulders. "Studs are too unruly and undependable to make good racers. But I've seen the Appaloosa. She's going to be hard to beat. Horace is going to be madder 'n blue blazes if his breed interpreter, Big Nose, doesn't win on that fancy palomino gelding of his. Corby's put all his eggs in one basket there." Rumsey flashed her a crooked grin, obviously not the least bit worried about the agent's bets. Then he nodded toward the roadway. "Looks like they're about ready to start."

The road leading into Lame Deer was lined with people. Indian men and women, children on painted ponies, agency employees in wagons and buggies, and a few ranchers in covered hacks all crowded alongside the dusty thoroughfare. Behind a gentle old horse, three small children watched from a travois in their cozy nest of soft hides. All eyes were directed eastward, down the road to where the group of riders and their mounts congregated in the distance.

Suzette had seen the horses earlier that morning when their proud owners had paraded them through the plaza area. Many were fine animals, descended from good ranch stock. Not infrequently, valued quarter horses and fine cow ponies escaped from corrals and stables carelessly left unlocked to join bands of wild mustangs running free in the mountains of the West. Like many other tribes, the Cheyenne caught and broke the mixed-blood descendants of these horses with incredible skill. Most Indians learned to ride a horse at the same age they learned to walk.

During the parade, War Lance had spotted Suzette amid the throng of spectators. He'd pulled Red Wind to a halt in front of her and leaned forward to pat the stallion's glossy neck. "Did you place any bets, *náevehoka?*"

She shook her head. "Do you have any suggestions?"

"Don't bet against me."

With a cocky grin, he'd turned his mount and re-joined the other contestants.

Now, from her place on the fence railing, Suzette searched the cluster of horses and riders for her Indian guide. Dressed once again in his fringed buckskin vest, breechclout, and leggings, War Lance Striking was a glorious sight on his great red stallion. The polished shell-core collar glistened around the large warrior's throat; two white eagle feathers shimmered in his lustrous black hair. The bronzed muscles of his bare arms and shoulders rippled and gleamed in the morning sunshine as he guided his nervous mount through the crowd. Still half-wild, the regal horse pranced and curveted across the dirt of the open plaza. She doubted if anyone, except his powerful master, could control the spirited animal.

There was no judge at the starting line. The starter would try to keep them as near as possible at the beginning of the race. The first one to cover the approximate six furlongs, pass the corral, and enter the agency's compound would be the winner, all the stakes going to him.

As if by a prearranged signal, there was a sudden pause in the hum of activity. The faraway crack of a pistol announced the start. They were off! Down the dirt road thundered the wedge-shaped pack of horses, their riders bumping, crowding, and attempting to box in or otherwise hold back their competitors.

"Here, use these," Rumsey said. He took the pair of binoculars from around his neck and handed them to Suzette.

She accepted them with a grateful smile. As she focused the lenses on the far-off racers, she held her breath. Vying for the lead at the front of the pack were Bear Scalp's spotted gray Appaloosa and Big Noses's showy palomino. Desperately she tracked the glasses from the noses of the front-running horses backward over the flying field. Red Wind, with a stallion's mercurial temperament, had gotten a poor start. At the sound of the gun, he'd risen up on his hind legs and pawed the air. Then, issuing a shrill clarion call of challenge, he bolted. Headstrong and unpredictable, the great horse appeared to be fighting his rider for control as he plunged wildly after the other animals. Through the field glasses, she could see War Lance regain his balance and bend over the long neck, his face almost buried in the flying red mane. He was using the skillful pressure of his arms and legs, rather than a pony whip, to gain dominion over the mighty stallion.

"Come on, War Lance," Suzette muttered under her

breath. "Make him behave. He can win if he'll just behave."

Aware of her status as a borrower, and resolutely minding her manners, she pulled the binoculars down and politely offered them back to their owner. Rumsey flashed her an understanding grin and shook his head. "Go on. Keep them. I have a feeling you're more interested in the outcome of this race than I am."

Grateful, she returned his smile and peered though the lenses again. She caught her breath in awe. The majestic red horse and his stunning rider were the most beautiful sight she'd ever seen. Even as she watched, Red Wind's head came up; there was a flick of his small ears as he listened to his master, who was crouching forward and asking the great beast for more and more speed. The stallion lengthened his stride, stretching out fully as his hoofs devoured the ground. Now perfectly balanced and galloping full out, Red Wind was seizing every opportunity to fight his way through the bunched field, pulling steadily up between the densely packed horses. One by one, he overtook his opponents. Even from her vantage point on the corral fence, Suzette could see the red stallion straining to catch the vanguard horses, as though the blood of his Thoroughbred forebears had awakened inside him the urge to take and keep the lead. In the bunching muscles and straining limbs were the speed, staying power, and heart of a natural-born winner.

War Lance was bent low over his mount's neck, urging him onward, closing the distance between them and the two leaders. Neck and neck, the gray Appaloosa and the creamy palomino flew ahead. With his great body extended, Red Wind seemed barely to touch the track as he gained rapidly on the two in front of him . . . and then caught up with them.

All around Suzette, people were cheering madly, calling out encouragement to their favorite horse and rider, pleading for them to go faster and faster. Blue Crane Flying and Lew Rumsey, on either side of her, were hollering at the top of their lungs for their chosen horses. Less than a furlong away, the three leaders thundered down the straightaway, racing stride for stride. The entire crowd was on its feet.

"Come on, Red Wind!" Suzette screamed in exhilaration. "Pass them! Pass them!"

Chapter 13

As though hearing her cry, the mighty red stallion exploded with a burst of strength. His lightning-fast hoofs pounded the track in a blur of movement. With every muscle strained to the utmost, his head stretched out, his nostrils snorting, he flew down the final stretch in great, sweeping strides. He was going full bore for the finish line with all the incredible speed and stamina of a born winner.

"Go, Red Wind, go!" Suzette screamed in Cheyenne at the top of her lungs. She could barely hear herself above the roar of the onlookers.

Just as the three horses passed the corral fence, Red Wind surged in front with a final, tremendous explosion of speed, his legs reaching out in a leaping, bounding motion, devouring the ground and leaving his competitors behind his flying hoofs. The red stallion and his master flew into the open compound, past the two judges, to the frenzied thunder of approval from the crowd.

"We won! We won!" Suzette cried, waving the binoculars high over her head. She turned to Blue Crane Flying and hugged her. For an instant they both rocked perilously back and forth on the top rail. As she caught herself with one hand, still clasping the field glasses in the other, her friend regained her own equilibrium.

The Indian woman's dark brown eyes sparkled with a

wry humor. "I thought Little Red Fox did not care who won the race," she teased. A knowing smile turned up the corners of her mouth.

"Maybe I should have placed a small bet," Suzette admitted as she burst into excited laughter. With a word of thanks, she handed the glasses back to Rumsey and turned to watch the racers and their mounts milling about in the dusty quadrangle.

Heady with the first flush of victory, War Lance dismounted, his grin wide. A small group of well-wishers had quickly gathered around him, but over the tops of their heads he'd seen Suzette embracing Blue Crane Flying with wild abandon. He was certain she'd been cheering for him. As he accepted the words of congratulations and praise from his admirers—and the fine Winchester rifle he'd just won—he eased out of the closely packed circle of people and handed his reins to a young boy from Bear Scalp's camp. Spotted Deer and his friends would see that Red Wind was properly cooled down, given water, and brushed thoroughly.

Lance walked toward the corral fence carrying his new rifle. As he approached, he met Suzette's brilliant eyes. They glowed with joy and admiration at his success, the lavender gown she wore intensifying their usual color. When she realized he was coming straight to her, her creamy cheeks flushed with pleasure. Not only had she been rooting for him to win, but she'd also clearly forgiven him for the way he'd frightened her.

At that moment, he knew he was completely and irrevocably lost. Like a siren, she had lured him to the brink of self-destruction. He'd successfully fought off his driving need for her once, but he admitted now with perfect honesty and an unerring knowledge of himself that he could never do it again.

He wanted her.

And he was going to have her.

He was going to make her his, if only for one brief, blinding moment in a lifetime of emptiness. She was his life-mate, meant only for him. But though she belonged to him, he could never keep her. And when he returned to his post in London, leaving her behind—as inevitably he would—he could only hope that he would retain some measure of his sanity.

She sat on the fence's top railing between Blue Crane Flying and the rancher and proudly watched him come to her. Her slim body was straight and regal, the small, high breasts and tiny waist outlined by the soft sateen of her walking dress. Golden highlights, enhanced by the morning sunshine, glinted in the brilliant coppery curls piled high on the top of her graceful head. Seeing Suzette's slight frame, tense with nervous energy, he recalled the fading image of the lazy, voluptuous mistress who waited for him in Knightsbridge. There had never been anything between him and Melissa Montgomery other than a well-defined financial agreement. He'd expected nothing from the plump, greedy little blonde except what she'd been very generously paid for—a fine time in bed. As he approached the vivacious woman doctor, he studied her slight, willowy figure quivering in excitement and wondered just how much she knew of physical love between a man and a woman. Certainly she'd studied biology and anatomy, but he'd known from the first time he'd kissed her that when it came to practical knowledge of carnal matters, she was only a beginner, far more innocent and inexperienced than most women her age.

Since he'd frightened her so thoroughly ten days before when he'd pinned her against the tree and forced his kisses on her, she'd been cautious and wary. She'd crept around him like a timid little field mouse who expected a predatory owl to swoop down upon her with outstretched talons at any moment. He'd continued to take her from camp to camp, but a wall of suspicion and fear had separated them. A barrier he'd purposely constructed. Several times, he'd caught her watching him guardedly, as though trying to judge beforehand his possible reaction to anything she might say or do. Clearly she was taking no chance on getting him stirred up again. She had no idea that just the faint scent of violets that hovered about her aroused a need within him that had become impossible to deny.

The moment he was close enough to hear her, she spoke, her eyes sparkling with approbation. "You were . . ." She paused to search for the correct Cheyenne word, and he wasted no time providing one.

"Wonderful."

"Yes."

"Amazing."

"That, too."

Her enchanting smile told him without words that he was more than forgiven for frightening her so badly. She thought he was marvelous. His heart bounded inside his chest, as though trying to turn cartwheels between his ribs. He felt like a child at his own birthday party.

Blue Crane Flying slipped down from the fence to stand beside him. "If my husband had to lose to anyone," she said, "I'm glad it was to his younger brother. I wagered a quilled doeskin parfleche on his gray mare. Now I'm going to find Bear Scalp and listen to why he lost after he'd assured me that no one could beat him."

With the younger woman's departure, Suzette shook her head at Lance in wonderment. "Without actually seeing it, I'd never have believed a horse could come from so far behind to win. When I watched you at the start of the race, I didn't think you'd even finish."

Basking in the glow of her admiration, Lance looked up at her and smiled. He resisted the temptation to reach over and touch the coppery wisp of hair that had come loose from her coiffure to fall in front of her delicate ear. The urge to wind the shiny curl around his forefinger tantalized him.

"You should have known Red Wind would never allow any other horse to beat him," he chided her. "The stallion spent too many years leading his mustangs in freedom through the Wolf Mountains. All I had to do was hang on tight and keep from falling off."

He glanced at the rancher sitting beside her. The cattlemen watched with open curiosity, an expression of bafflement on his lean face as he listened to them speaking in the strange language.

"I see you've made a new friend," Lance added casually.

"Mr. Rumsey is a nearby neighbor," she explained. "He came to see the race."

Lance already knew who the man was. Lew Rumsey's big ranch sat right smack in the middle of Cheyenne land. Unlike other reservations, Tongue River was checkerboarded with ranches owned by whites. The bureaucratic fools in Washington had hoped the presence of white men would have a civilizing effect on the Indians, but so far, it'd only been the source of constant problems arising between hungry Cheyenne, out hunting on their own land for food, and angry cattlemen, who claimed the red men were killing and slaughtering beef that had wandered off ranch property. In his report to the BIA, Lance intended to recommend that the white homesteaders, who held the best bottom land, be bought out. But instead of trying to turn the nomadic Cheyenne into farmers, he wanted to see them raising their own cattle.

"I guess this big buck must be your guide, Dr. Stanwood," Rumsey interrupted in his western drawl. Unable to understand what they'd said, he could still easily deduce Lance's identity from her animated expression.

"Yes, this is War Lance Striking," Suzette replied, switching to English.

The two men eyed each other in silence, neither acknowledging the other's presence by the slightest nod.

Then Rumsey turned back to Suzette. "As you make your rounds on the reservation this week, Dr. Stanwood, have your Indian scout here bring you to my ranch." His weathered cheeks were etched with deep creases as he smiled at her warmly. "I'd like to show you my place. I'm mighty proud of my spread, even though my home's lacked a woman's touch ever since my wife died two years ago."

Suzette glanced cautiously at Lance, her worried look revealing her concern that he might think she was dallying with the middle-aged rancher. Since the time War Lance had warned her in no uncertain terms about her flirtatious behavior, she'd done nothing that could remotely be considered flirting.

"Goodness, I don't know," she told Rumsey dubiously, still watching Lance from the corner of her eye. She released a long, hesitant sigh. "I'm not sure my guide would want to leave the reservation and go on the property of a white man."

Lance wanted nothing better than the opportunity to do just that. Since he'd arrived at Lame Deer, he'd made almost no progress in discovering why the two special agents had been murdered. The bimonthly beef issue in the middle of September had come and gone without the slightest indication of any underhanded dealings. The cattle had been driven in from Billings by way of Fort Custer, the soldiers and cowboys delivering the herd right on schedule. There'd been a full quota the day they were issued to the Indians, with complete rations for every family on the reservation. But Lance had noticed that Rumsey had been at the agent's office for a long while the day before the cattle arrived. Whether this was simply a coincidence, he had no way of knowing, but he would relish the chance to have a close look at the cattleman's spread. Unfortunately, it seemed Suzette was about to turn down the rancher's invitation for fear of upsetting her volatile guide.

"Since you're paying his wages," Rumsey prodded persistently, "I'd think it'd be up to you where you went. Go ahead, tell him you want to come to my place. He wouldn't dare refuse while I'm watching."

Suzette looked at the rancher as though he were approaching idiocy if he really believed War Lance would give a tinker's dam what he thought. She cleared her throat nervously, still reluctant to speak.

"Go on," Rumsey insisted.

"The rancher would like you to bring me to his home next week," she told Lance in the softest, most enticing Cheyenne syllables he'd ever heard.

He grinned up at her in satisfaction. "Little Red Fox is in a sweet mood today." He made no attempt to hide his amusement that she'd finally learned just how ridiculously sharp and cross she'd always sounded to the Cheyenne ear.

"Why didn't you tell me that I've sounded like an angry old crone since the day I arrived?" she demanded, her words rising to their old, familiar level once again. "Or worse yet, a man?" She jumped down from the railing to land right in front of him and shook her finger under his nose. "You must have realized that I didn't know any better than to talk at the top of my voice."

He tried to look baffled by her outburst, but the smile tugging at the corners of his mouth gave him away. "Why, angel, I wasn't even here the day you arrived." He started to walk back toward the crowded compound.

"You know what I mean." She followed at his heels, just as he'd expected, yipping at him like an excited puppy. "You purposely let me go on half shouting, when it made me sound like an outraged female—or a foolish male."

"When you first rode into our camp on the Rosebud, you were dressed like a little soldier chief," he reminded her. He stopped, allowing her to catch up with him. "So when you talked just like a man as well, everyone thought you were pretending to be one. Naturally we were too good-mannered to mention that we knew better." He lifted his brows and grinned. "If you wanted to act like a little warrior, how could we deny you the pleasure?"

"Oh, you ... you ..." Suzette sputtered to a stop.

Speechless, she stared at him, wishing she knew a good swear word in his language. But that was one thing Jacob Graber hadn't taught her. The absurdity of it all hit her at last. Reluctantly she smiled and shook her head. "You big, crazy Cheyenne."

At his look of sham innocence, laughter bubbled up inside her, and she giggled in spite of herself. He joined her, and they laughed out loud like children. Suddenly remembering Rumsey, Suzette turned to find the rancher still waiting on the fence where they'd left him. He watched them in astonishment.

"We will be near the white man's home in two days," War Lance told her as he turned to go. "Tell him that I will take you there then."

Two days later, Suzette sat in Rumsey's ranch house parlor having a cup of coffee, while Lance prowled cautiously about the cattleman's stable. Lance had brought her for the promised tour of the ranch an hour earlier and had waited in the open corral area with their horses, hoping for a chance to be left alone. It was nearly time for them to leave before he could slip inside the stable undetected.

In the dim recesses of the steeply roofed building, several stock horses nickered from their stalls as Lance moved silently across the dirt floor. All along the stable walls, hanging on nails pounded haphazardly into the rough boards, were the usual paraphernalia of the cowman: dehorning clippers and saws, rawhide horse hobbles, miscellaneous spurs, extra lariats and stirrup straps, a pair of fancy Mexican *chaparrejos,* bridles, Spanish bits, hackamores, reins, and snaffles. Several stamp irons with the LR brand hung beside the door to the tack room. Nothing out of the ordinary.

Lance turned to leave and noticed a gunnysack thrown carelessly on top of a pile of straw in the corner nearest the door. He moved quickly to it. Turning the burlap bag over with his foot, he crouched down and found three running irons half buried in the straw. They were no more than long, straight pieces of iron with hooks at both ends, used to hold on to just about anything that would inscribe a rancher's brand on the side of a calf. Heated and applied through a wet sack, they left the original brand indistinct. Given the endless possibilities they offered the creative cowboy, carrying a running iron in Montana was considered a serious breech of western manners.

"What the hell are you doin' in here, Injun?" a loud voice demanded from the stable's open doorway.

Lance rose and turned to find three cowboys silhouetted against the bright afternoon sunshine. He smiled and raised his hand, palm forward in the universal sign of peace.

"Hou," he said, and walked toward them. "Injun lookin' smoke pipe. You got tobacco?"

"Tobacco, my ass." The largest cowhand, standing in the middle, sported a huge, drooping black mustache. He took one step forward, hooked his thumbs under his gun belt, and spit a stream of chewing tobacco on the toe of Lance's right moccasin. "There's only one thing a dirty, sneakin' Injun's lookin' for in a stable, and that's a hoss to steal. And we hang hoss thieves."

Unable to give a response to the threat spoken in English, Lance remained still, watching the three for any sudden movement. His dumb Indian act hadn't impressed them one bit. He hadn't planned on a fight and would avoid one if at all possible, but he sure as hell wasn't about to let them put a noose around his neck. The hanging of an Indian, even by mistake, would go unpunished. There probably wouldn't even be a trial. The three could corroborate one another's alibis at the investigation.

The big man turned to glance back at one of his partners. "Git a rope, Bouten."

Thankfully, Bouten shook his head. "Naw, we can't hang him in here. The boss wouldn't like it. He's entertainin' female company." His two friends responded with snorts of derisive laughter.

The burly man in the center smacked one gloved hand into the palm of the other and grinned. "Then I guess we'll just have to teach the big buck here a lesson 'bout sneakin' round white folks' property. One he'll never forget." His ham-sized fist shot out, smashing into Lance's gut.

He doubled over, caught by the impact of the sudden, vicious blow. Keeping his head lowered, he rushed the big man like a charging bull and knocked him off his feet. Together they flew out the stable door, hit the ground, and skidded across the dirt, the cowboy's filthy Stetson smashed flat beneath them.

"Get 'em, Troxel," the second cowpoke hollered. He unbuckled the gun belt hanging below his huge belly and threw his pistol and holster, along with his own wide-brimmed hat, safely aside. "He ain't nuthin' but a yella-livered coyote."

Together Lance and Troxel rolled over and over in the dusty stable yard. Each man sought to improve his hold, grasping and twisting in the other's rough embrace. Pinned beneath his opponent, Lance felt Troxel's meaty thumbs sliding toward his eyes. He reached up and grabbed the man's hair, jerking him sideways to the ground. Twisting, he wrenched himself free and started to rise. Lance was still on one knee when Troxel's big-bellied friend emitted a ferocious roar and jumped on his shoulders.

With a fluid movement, Lance doubled over, taking his attacker with him and smashing the obese cowhand to the ground with violent force. The fat man's boot hit Troxel in the head as he flew over. Lance jabbed a punishing elbow into the soft paunch and bounded to his feet.

Standing to one side, Troxel held a huge hand to his lacerated face. The pointed toe of his friend's boot had split his temple just above the eyebrow, and blood was oozing into his eye, over his fingers, and across his thick black mustache. "Hit the bastard, Bouten," Troxel hollered to the third cowboy.

Lance dodged as the pale-haired Bouten lashed out at him with a right jab. In addition to the early Cheyenne training he'd had in basic survival, Lance had spent the past twenty years perfecting the arts of wrestling, boxing, and fencing. But there was nothing he liked better than a no-rules, nothing-barred free-for-all. He grinned in anticipation, his tense, frustrated body aching to mete out physical punishment. He parried Bouten's blow with ease, then feinted with his right, double-feinted, and caught Bouten with a perfect left upper cut. The force of the blow nearly snapped the cowboy's blond head off. Lance followed up with a right punch to the exposed midsection and a jab to the freckled nose. Stunned almost to the point of unconsciousness, the man staggered backward, out of reach of Lance's punishing fists.

A shrill whistle pierced the air as several more ranch hands rode into the yard. "Hey, there's a fight!" someone yelled. Although the men dismounted, they made no attempt to interfere.

"Stand back," several men called at the same time. "Stand back and give 'em room."

Three of the bystanders climbed up on the corral fence for a better view. "Well, I'll be damned. It's an Injun," one of them exclaimed.

At the sounds of the commotion, people hurried out of the bunkhouse. The cook, in his long white apron, came from around the corner to watch, still holding a plucked chicken in one hand.

"Rush the son of a bitch, Kraus," Troxel called to his fat friend. Both cowboys stalked cautiously around Lance, while their stunned yellow-haired partner staggered about blindly, his head tipped back, his hands nursing his bleeding broken nose.

Balanced lightly on the balls of his feet, Lance waited

for the two cowhands to make their move. They advanced crouching, slowly and cautiously.

"Now!" Kraus yelled, and they sprang at him.

With a lightning reflex, Lance's foot flashed to Troxel's groin and the man doubled over, howling in agony.

"Stop it! Stop it!" came a woman's shrill, nearly hysterical scream. Lance recognized Suzette's voice and turned his head slightly to catch the blue of her riding clothes in the corner of his eye. In that split second, Kraus came up from behind. He seized Lance in a hammer lock, twisting his arm up painfully behind his back. Then Kraus pressed his other arm against Lance's throat like a vise.

In front of Lance, Troxel straightened slowly, painfully, nursing his injured crotch. An evil grin spread beneath the shaggy black mustache.

"Hold that son of a bitch still," he said in a hoarse whisper. He was breathing in great, raspy gasps. With ham-sized fists he delivered battering-ram blows to Lance's stomach and ribs as Kraus applied increasing pressure to his throat and right arm. A strangled grunt escaped Lance's lips.

Suzette, held fast by Lew Rumsey, struggled wildly to intervene. "They'll kill him," she cried, desperate to pull her elbow free from the rancher's grasp. "You've got to stop this." Tears poured unheeded down her cheeks.

"He was doing okay," Rumsey said with curious detachment as he watched the unfair bout. "Let's see how the big buck does."

The potbellied man, sweat dripping down his florid face, continued to apply relentless pressure to War Lance's right arm as Troxel pulled back his large fist for another vicious blow to their opponent's face. In a quick, unexpected move, War Lance Striking dropped down on his left knee, pulling the corpulent assailant behind him forward and off balance. The Cheyenne reached up with his free arm and grabbed a handful of Kraus's stringy brown hair. With a powerful yank, he jerked the cowboy forward, flipping him neatly over his shoulder. Kraus landed on the ground with a sickening thud. One expertly placed kick below the ear and the fat man's body went limp, unconscious at War Lance's feet.

From her place beside Rumsey, Suzette could hear War Lance's breath coming thick and fast. It was down to just the two men now: War Lance and the big, mustached man they called Troxel. She covered her mouth to still her broken sobs.

The burly cowboy was several inches shorter than War Lance Striking, but he was built like a prize bull, with broad shoulders and a barrel chest. He still wore his Colt strapped to his hip. Suzette could only surmise that, in the anticipation of administering a sound beating to the lone Indian, both he and his partners hadn't even considered the possibility that their adversary would inflict more harm on them than they did him. For an instant Troxel's fingers crept toward the handle of his revolver. There was a dozen growls of warning from the fascinated audience, none of whom intended to watch a cold-blooded murder take place in front of them without trying to stop it.

"Keep it fair, Troxel," somebody yelled from his spot on the fence. His words were followed by the click of a cocked revolver. "He ain't nuthin' but a no-'count Injun. You should be able to lick him one-handed."

Hoots of derision came from the crowd, and the cowboy's hand pulled back from the holster and clenched into a fist.

The opponents circled each other warily. Then War Lance moved in a blur as his solid, well-trained body attacked with the relentless precision of a machine. Again and again, in a flurry of quick, sharp jabs, he struck Troxel's jaw and cheeks only to retreat nimbly, easily dodging his opponent's wildly inaccurate punches. The cut just above the cowhand's eyebrow split further, the blood nearly covering one eye. Under the well-aimed blows, the other eye was soon swollen shut and turning blue. Troxel stumbled, and War Lance caught him with a powerful right to the chin. Unable to even see the lethal blow coming, Troxel staggered, fell to his knees, and pitched forward in a heap in the dirt.

War Lance Striking stood in the center of the stable yard and gently rubbed his split, swollen knuckles with his fingertips, while the surrounding crowd watched in awed silence.

"Get him out of here," Rumsey said succinctly. He never took his eyes off the tall warrior as he released Suzette's elbow.

"But ... but I should look at those cowboys first," she stammered. "I'm ... I'm a doctor, and they're ... they're injured pretty badly."

Rumsey's blue eyes softened. "They're not so bad we can't handle it ourselves. Fistfights are pretty common out here. It's nothin' we haven't taken care of before. Now, get that big buck outta here before someone else decides to try his luck." Rumsey turned her around and pushed her gently toward Painted Doll, tied beside the red stallion in front of the ranch house. "Go on, now. Git."

War Lance followed in her wake, right through the hole she opened up in the dumbfounded audience. She could feel the tremendous aura of his presence behind her; every nearby spectator took an involuntary step backward as the large Indian passed. The sight and sound of the brutal fight had shaken her badly. She'd been certain War Lance would be gravely injured, if not killed outright. Her legs trembled beneath her, and she fought the nausea that threatened, afraid her knees would buckle and she'd fall to the ground in an ignominious heap. With the tracks of the dried tears tight on her cheeks, she forced herself to keep moving till she reached Painted Doll. For a brief moment she rested her forehead on her arm placed against the saddle. Then, summoning every bit of willpower she possessed, she put her foot in the stirrup and mounted. When she looked over at Red Wind, War Lance was already up and turning his horse toward home.

"Let's go, angel," he said under his breath with startling composure. She met his glance. His chiseled face was battered and dirty and splotched with blood. The plaid shirt was ripped down the front, exposing the scars on his bronzed chest, and the denim jeans were covered with dust. But all she could read in his midnight eyes was a deep, abiding concern for her.

He kicked his heels into the stallion's flanks and galloped out of the ranch yard and down the road. The piebald mare gave a shrill whinny of protest at being left behind, and chased after her fleeing partner.

Suzette and War Lance rode side by side for miles without speaking, till they were safely off Rumsey's property and back on the reservation lands. After doubling back to make certain they weren't being followed, War Lance led her into a small, sheltered canyon protected by sheer cliffs on three sides. Lodgepole, western yellow pine, and mountain balsam followed the banks of a clear-flowing stream, offering a cool shelter from the afternoon sun. Scattered throughout the thick grasses that covered the canyon floor were the fragrant blossoms of a few late-blooming wildflowers.

Before she could dismount, he was on his feet and lifting her out of the saddle.

"What happened back there?" she demanded, still badly shaken. "Why did those men attack you?" She gripped his forearms in a determined attempt to hold him still in front of her.

He lifted his raven eyebrows in bafflement. "I do not know, Little Red Fox. They were trying to tell me something, but I couldn't understand what they wanted."

She studied his perceptive eyes, wondering briefly if he'd really been so unaware of their hostile intentions. Then she released his arms and tipped her head toward the stream. "Sit down on the bank and take off your shirt. I want to have a look at you. You probably have some cracked ribs."

War Lance smiled, then jerked his head in a grimace of pain. He touched his lower lip tenderly. "There is nothing wrong with my ribs," he said, "but my knuckles hurt worse than the wounds of a Great Medicine Dance."

She stubbornly pointed to a spot on the grass. "Still, I want to examine you. Go sit down like I told you." She moved to her horse and unfastened the black medical bag from behind her saddle. "When I heard the shouts from the stable yard, I was afraid of something like this. You're going to have to learn to speak our language, War Lance. Otherwise, the same thing will keep happening over and over again." She turned to find that he'd spread his blanket on the ground. He was sitting placidly in the middle of it with his legs crossed, waiting for her.

"Take off your shirt," she ordered. The tension in her voice betrayed her turbulent feelings. "Those three men could have killed you," she scolded as she knelt in front of him. Her voice broke, and to her horror, two large tears rolled down her cheeks.

"No," he replied with exasperating serenity, his words calm and reassuring. "They could not have harmed me, vèhoka." He slowly unbuttoned the faded plaid shirt with stiff fingers and slipped it off, leaving only the shell collar around his neck, gleaming white against his bronzed skin. "I was never in any danger." He reached over and gently touched her cheeks, his thumbs brushing away the tears. His deep baritone softened to a caress. "There is no need to cry, angel. I'm sorry you were so frightened."

Batting his hand away, she jerked her head aside in irritation. "One of us has to have enough sense to recognize danger when we see it. Now, lie down on your back," she snapped.

He grinned, then winced again, but his black eyes sparkled as he eased to a recumbent position. "Whatever you want me to do, náevehoka, I will do. After all, I am your paid servant."

She met his teasing eyes and flushed at the brazen insinuation in his words. Although she truly was his employer, he'd always behaved on every previous occasion as if he were the one in charge. Now, of all times—as he lay on the blanket beneath her—he chose to imply that he was at the mercy of her every whim. Assuming her most professional bedside manner, she bent over her patient. Despite his blasé attitude, she feared the worse. Gently she explored his lean, muscular torso, anticipating his groans of excruciating pain at any moment.

"Does this hurt?" she asked as she carefully felt along the length of his rib cage on each side, moving methodically from the sternum to the spine. She made her examination as tender and light as possible. "How about here?"

But he'd been right. There wasn't a sign of a fracture—no pain as he breathed deeply for her, no tenderness or swelling of the overlying tissues. There wasn't even a bruise to show the horrible pounding his body had taken. Once she realized that his ribs were, indeed, completely unharmed, she started pushing, poking, and prodding less gently and with more irritation. With the awareness that he'd escaped without serious injury, her temper rose. All the terror she'd felt for his safety now crystallized into a furious sense of righteous indignation over the awful fright he'd put her through. She kept talking as she worked, her tongue as busy as her skilled fingers.

"The only reason you don't have two or three broken ribs, War Lance Striking," she said, jabbing at him with each word for emphasis, "is that you're just too pigheaded stubborn to get hurt, too muleheaded ornery to lose a fight, and you happen to be built like an old bull buffalo."

Lance lay still, in ecstasy beneath her silken touch. The feel of her small, graceful hands moving over his bare flesh, the accidental brush of her smooth fingertips on his flat nipples, made his muscles leap in glorious an-

ticipation of each titillating encounter. Though she probably thought she was inflicting at least a little punishment on his bruised body for what he'd done, her utterly
feminine touch was as soft and harmless as the flutter of
a bird's wing.

"My large size is not my fault, angel," he protested,
doing his best to keep from smiling in delight at her ministrations. "I was born big. When I was thirteen years old
I had the stature of a grown man."

She sat back on her heels and looked down at him in
exasperation. "You must have strong medicine, War
Lance Striking. I would never have dreamed any man
could take such a thrashing and escape unhurt."

Ignoring the cocky grin he gave her, she rose and
walked to the stream. He sat up and watched as she
crouched over in her blue trousers and rinsed a cloth in
the cool water.

"Let me check your face," she said when she returned
once again to kneel in front of him on the striped blanket. "You're covered with dirt and dried blood."

He obediently lifted his face for her inspection, while
he wisely placed a hand on each of his own knees to
keep from pulling her into his arms. Tenderly she washed
off the smudges, obviously expecting to find innumerable
scrapes and contusions. She was wrong. There was only
one minor cut on his right cheekbone, plus a swollen
lower lip with a crack at the corner of his mouth. He was
sure he'd also have a bruise on his jaw by morning. She
applied an antiseptic solution on the raw lesions, meeting
his eyes with a satisfied I-told-you-so scowl, and was
clearly disappointed when he didn't so much as wince.
Her lovely face was only inches above him, and he studied every detail of her fine, classical features with a con-
noisseur's fascination. Aware of his scrutiny, she lowered
her russet lashes and refused to meet his gaze again.

Finally she took one of his hands in her tapering fingers. His knuckles were split and raw and swollen. She
flashed him a victorious glance. Here, at last, was some-

thing she could tend to. The whole time she was washing the wounds and administering the stinging solution, she berated him.

"You should never have allowed yourself to be dragged into a brawl with three strangers, War Lance," she chided. "The whole misunderstanding was your own fault because you weren't able to convince those cowboys that you meant no harm. I've tried over and over again to teach you my language, but you've never made the least effort to learn it."

"You are like the little redheaded woodpecker, *náevehoka*," he teased her at last, trying to take her mind off her unfounded fears. "You keep tapping at my head with your sharp little words. *Tek, tek, tek.*"

Her head snapped up and she met his eyes. Her full lips trembled as she lost her thinly stretched composure. "That's it," she said, releasing his hand and pulling back. Tears sparkled on the tips of her long lashes. Her voice broke on a sob. "Go ahead. Make fun of me. When I was scared to death they were going to kill you."

Chapter 14

War Lance's rugged features softened when he heard the sob she tried unsuccessfully to hide. "Don't cry, little angel. I didn't mean to hurt your feelings. I only wanted to show you there was no reason to be so frightened." The corners of his mouth turned up in a half smile. Tender amusement lit his eyes. "I was never in any danger from those bumbling idiots. And I took great care not to hurt them badly. It would be foolish to start trouble between my people and Rumsey's cowboys. And most of all, I didn't want Little Red Fox to waste her sweet healing medicine on one of those ugly brutes instead of saving it all for me."

In spite of herself, Suzette smiled through her tears at his cajoling words. She'd been deeply shocked by her own reaction to the violent brawl. Medical training or no, she hadn't cared in the least what horrible injuries Lance inflicted on those three thugs. But the sight of him being throttled and beaten had frightened her terribly. The very real dread that he might be seriously hurt, possibly even killed, had nearly brought her to her knees. Surely she'd felt such overriding terror on his behalf only because she thought he was helpless to defend himself against three men at once. His inability to speak the white man's language meant he would undoubtedly be subjected to more vicious assaults in the future.

"You must learn my language, War Lance," she told

him with the presumptuousness of a general. "I know I can teach you, if you will only make a little effort to learn."

"No, *náevehoka*. I cannot learn your language."

"Of course you can't," she answered with unveiled sarcasm. She pushed against him in exasperation, and when he reluctantly released her, she rose and stood over him. Leaning down, she lashed out in frustration with bitter words she only half meant. "You're too wrapped up in your own self, War Lance Striking, to try to learn anything from me. You think this reservation is the only place on earth to live, and the Cheyenne are the only people in the world who matter. It would never occur to you that I could have something to offer. Something you might need."

She snatched up her medical bag and closed it with an annoyed snap. Without another look at the self-assured man sitting at her feet with all the born arrogance of a bejeweled pasha on his Turkish carpet, she whirled and stomped away.

"Wait, Little Red Fox," he called after her. There was a hint of laughter in his deep voice. "Come back here. What you say is not true."

She ignored him. With indignant resolution she fastened her black satchel in place on Painted Doll's back. Grabbing the piebald mare's reins, she started to mount, fully determined to ride away without him.

He caught her in midair, one booted foot in the stirrup and the other ready to swing over her horse's back. His hands encircled her waist, and he lifted her bodily away from the saddle, as though she weighed no more than a porcelain doll. Caught completely by surprise, she let the reins slip through her fingers. He swung her around in a wide arch with maddening ease and placed her on her feet in the short grass.

"White woman no happy," he said in fractured English. "Injun's heart cracked to pieces."

"You mean 'heartbroken'?" she asked in stunned disbelief. Good Lord, why shouldn't she be shocked? It was only the second time she'd heard him speak her language.

He tapped his chest with one finger. "The Lance's heart broken," he assured her, continuing to mangle her native tongue. His eyes lit with pleasure because she had understood his meaning. Without warning, he swooped her up in his strong arms and tossed her lightly into the air. She gave a shriek of startled laughter as she landed snugly back in his stalwart hold. Her arms were wrapped securely around his neck before she had time to think.

"Angel's smile suns on Lance. Makes brave's heart hurry-hurry." He shifted her in his arms so that her ear rested against the bare wall of his muscular chest. She could hear his heart booming rhythmically.

He grinned in mischief and, as if she were a small playmate, bounced her higher and higher with each English phrase. "Lance winter. All time cold. Angel summer. Melt Lance puddles."

She burst into delighted laughter at his crazy, mixed-up words, then switched to his language once again. "Do you even know what you're saying?" she asked in a giggle as she took his handsome face between her hands and leaned forward till they were nearly nose to nose.

His jet gaze swept over her face with the sudden, predatory hunger of a stalking wolf. The timbre of his deep voice was husky and impassioned as he slipped into the low, soft-spoken Cheyenne syllables. "I'm saying, angel, that your beautiful smile has melted my heart like sunshine on winter snow."

Her breath caught high in her chest at the romantic speech. Moving back slightly to study his chiseled features, she read the unutterable tenderness in his eyes. She knew without words that she had no reason ever to be afraid of him. Her gaze drifted down to linger on his firm, generous mouth. And suddenly the compelling urge to kiss him was all she could think of. Goodness knows, she had tried to ignore the unexplained need for him that she'd felt since the first day they'd met. But the yearning she'd tried vainly to keep hidden from his perceptive eyes now welled up inside her.

Still cupping his face in her hands, she leaned forward and gently touched her lips to his. It was a brief, chaste kiss. One of curious, almost childlike exploration, testing the feel of his mouth against hers. The immediate, spontaneous pressure he returned was warm and welcoming, telling her with silent reassurance that she could explore his lips, his mouth, his whole body, to her heart's content. She drew back, and their gazes locked.

Desire, raw and hot, had replaced the tenderness in his midnight eyes, glowing now like smoldering embers. He'd become very still, hardly breathing, but she could feel his muscles flex as he shifted her a tiny bit higher in his arms, giving her easier access to his lips. She slipped her arms around his neck and kissed him once more. This time, tentatively, hesitantly, she ran the tip of her tongue across his lower lip to discover once again the wonderful taste of him. Wary and skittish, she was prepared to disengage quickly. But War Lance waited, unmoving and patiently submissive, allowing her time to feel her way. The only indication of the emotions raging inside him was the steadily increasing tempo of his warm breath as it brushed softly against her cheek.

Her trembling fingers slipped into his shiny black hair to pull his head still a fraction of an inch closer. This time, as she ran her tongue across his lips, he opened them. The firm touch of his tongue, vibrant and urgent and responsive, invited her in and insisted that she stay there. Her soft tongue grazed the hard edges of his teeth as she memorized every fold and curve of his mouth.

With a pang of guilt, she suddenly recalled the cuts he'd suffered earlier that day. She drew back and touched his swollen lower lip lightly with her fingertip. "I shouldn't be doing this," she whispered in apology. "I must be hurting you."

"I'll tell you if it hurts too much, little angel," he said with a throaty laugh. He took the tip of her finger in his strong white teeth and nipped it lightly, then brought it further into his mouth, only to slide it back out again in a provocative, symbolic gesture. A teasing grin played at the corners of his lips. "Maybe after an hour or so, I'll have to beg for mercy from such agonizing torture. But for right now, I think I can bear the pain."

Unable to hide her answering smile, she snatched her hand away to place it safely behind his neck. Lifting her chin slightly, she met his twinkling eyes. "I wouldn't want to cause any further injury to such a brave Cheyenne warrior after what you've already been through today," she told him with saucy pertness.

"I trust you to be gentle with me," he murmured in a voice thick with desire as he bent his head.

This time it was his turn to kiss her. And where she had been timid and inexperienced, he was sure and knowledgeable. His questing tongue pressed insistently between her lips, then entered with expert boldness. As they kissed, he slowly released her legs and set her down on her feet, allowing the soft curves of her figure to slide down the rock-hard length of him.

His hands moved to her sides, gliding up over hips and waist to bracket her breasts. As he cupped their fullness hidden beneath the yellow blouse, his thumbs circled their tight, aching crests. Wherever he touched her, a current of sensual arousal swept from his skilled fingers across her responsive body. With facile expertise, he was unleashing within her all the hidden yearnings she had locked away and repressed for so many years. Silently her pliant body begged him to release the covered buttons on the yellow shirt, to bring his mouth down to replace his fingers, to flick over her taut nipples with his moist tongue. With a ragged sigh, she raised up on tiptoe, lifting herself higher, stretching her arms to pull him closer.

As if reading her thoughts, he slipped one powerful

arm around her and brought her tight against him. Lifting her slightly, he brought her hips snugly against his lean frame.

"Spread your legs and ride me, angel," he said, breaking the kiss to murmur in her ear. Beneath his blue denims, he was fully aroused.

She shook her head. "I don't understand . . ." He lifted her higher, his strong hands sliding under her buttocks to open her thighs and guide her legs around him. As she realized what he wanted her to do, she wrapped them about his hips and clung to him.

"Ride me like a wild stallion," he urged. "Teach me the feel of your thighs around me. You can tame me with a touch."

Cupping her bottom with both large hands, he lifted her up to claim her lips with his open mouth. She pressed herself against him and moved in a slow, sinuous, instinctual dance of eroticism. She wound her fingers through his hair and returned his kiss, her tongue caressing and stroking his with all the longing, the fervor, that burned inside her.

She broke the kiss, her breath coming hard and fast, and placed her cheek against his. "War Lance," she panted in his ear, almost pleading in her desperate need, "I want you."

"I will pleasure you as I did before," he told her, as his hands slid back and forth beneath her buttocks. With unhurried deliberation, he began to unbutton the waistband of her trousers.

"No, no," she cried. She rocked against him in a movement as old and instinctive as mankind. "I want to pleasure you also."

At the soft words whispered in his ear, Lance stopped, frozen in breathless silence. For a brief moment he bent his head and buried his face in the graceful curve of her neck and shoulder. Then he slid his hands up to her tiny waist and lifted her down.

"Do you know what you're saying?"

She looked up at him through enormous violet eyes hazed with passion. "Yes."

Slowly, carefully, he stepped back, allowing her time to gain control over her rampaging emotions. "Be certain, little doll. For once you step out into the rapids of this river, you lose all control, and the headlong rush over the falls becomes a certainty."

"Then we'll drown together."

It had not been his plan to rush her so quickly. Rather, he'd foreseen a long, patient siege that would test the limits of his willpower. He wanted her body, as she wanted his. But he wanted more than just her willing flesh. He wanted her mind and heart and soul. He could rush her headlong into physical consummation, seducing her so swiftly that the unfulfilled hunger coursing within her would block any doubts she might have. Instead, he forced himself to give her time to be sure. Gradually her breathing calmed and she stepped back, releasing his arms. The quivering shudders that racked her slowly subsided. Still he waited as she gained control of her emotions.

With uncompromising determination, he met her confused gaze. Then, without touching her, without speaking, he held out his hand.

She understood what he was asking. He could read the sudden glitter of comprehension in her luminous eyes. He wasn't going to allow her any half-truths, any excuses to be offered later, any evasions to be cited the next day. If she yielded to him, she could never explain it away as a moment's weakness, or the unwilling surrender to an expert seduction. If she took his hand, she would be taking him as he was. Completely.

As she had that day so long ago, when he'd first asked her to trust him, she reached out, ever so slowly, till their fingers were only inches apart. The sight of their hands, his large and hardened and bronzed, hers small and soft and pale, seemed to symbolize the enormous differences between them. Differences that could never be bridged in a lifetime of trying—only willingly set aside for a brief autumn afternoon.

She drew a long, steadying breath and placed her smooth hand in his callused palm. "As a woman wants a man, War Lance Striking," she whispered achingly, "I want you."

Lance caught both her hands in his and brought them to his lips. Slowly, almost reverently, he unbuttoned each lace-trimmed cuff in turn and traced a hot path across the silken smoothness at the inside of her wrists. "Little angel," he murmured. "You don't even know what wanting is."

The delicate, feminine scent of her rocked him. He was like a man driven wild with thirst at the first sight of an oasis. Shaken, nearly crazed with the certain knowledge that she would disappear from his life all too soon, he wanted to imprison her cool softness beneath his hot body, to slake his need for her over and over, till at last he was sated and replete and whole again. And all the while, a small voice from within warned him that he would never get enough of her; that at her inevitable departure, he would be left with no more than an empty shell.

"I will go as slowly as I can," he promised her with a hoarse laugh. He could feel his lungs constricting as his breath grew embarrassingly short. "I shall go as slowly as my tortured body will allow."

He unbuttoned her shirt, his long fingers shaking with heady anticipation. Pushing aside the material, he revealed her smooth, white shoulders and the soft mounds that rose above the lace edges of the camisole. Then he removed the blouse completely, pulling it down her arms and over her graceful hands to drop, forgotten, on the grass at their feet.

She met his gaze with a tremulous smile. There was no fear in her eyes, only desire and a curious expectation. She reached up to touch him, her fingers skipping lightly over the collar of shells that encircled his throat, to rest trustingly on the muscles of his upper arms. He turned his head and ran his tongue up the inside of her arm, then nipped the pale skin of her shoulder.

"My heart's desire, how I have wanted you," he murmured. "You are a feast for my famished body. I shall devour you with my lips and my tongue and my hands till I have tasted and learned every curve, every hollow, every bone, of your sweet body."

At his whispered directions, she braced her hands on his shoulders while he knelt on one knee and removed her boots. Then he unbuttoned her trousers and slid them over her slim hips, down each shapely leg, and over her feet. Remaining on both knees in front of her, he moved his hands up the backs of her silken calves and thighs. She stood before him, clad in only thin muslin drawers and a lace-trimmed camisole. The reddish brown triangle of down between her legs was visible through the flimsy underwear. Clasping her soft, round buttocks in his hands, he pulled her to him with a growl and pressed his hungry lips against her female softness.

"War Lance," she protested in bewilderment. She tugged gently on a handful of his hair. "Don't . . ."

He nuzzled the springy curls hidden beneath the sheer cotton, then lifted his head and met her look of astonishment with a smile.

"You're right," he said. "That's something we can save for later."

Sliding his fingers up across her flat stomach, he covered her small breasts with his large hands. She took a quick, indrawn breath and stopped pulling on his hair. One by one he released the tiny ivory buttons that ran down the front of her delicately embroidered underwaist, his fingers barely stumbling over the exacting task.

He rose as he pushed the garment aside. The silken globes of her breasts were revealed, and he held them cupped in his rough hands. She was perfectly formed, her uptilted breasts high and firm, with round, taut nipples. The raging, mindless, primal drive to dominate, to take at will and keep for his own, roared through his loins, threatening to destroy his iron control. With shaking hands he gently removed the delicate camisole, managing not to tear the sheer muslin, and then let the undergarment fall to rest beside the discarded yellow shirt. He moved slowly and precisely. He had no intention of frightening her away with his usual rough aggressiveness. Not now. Not when he was so close.

"My beautiful, beautiful angel," he whispered hoarsely as he encased her rib cage with his hands and lifted her up in front of him. Bending his head, he touched one pink bud with his tongue, and she stiffened with excitement in his grasp. He could hear her drawing in quickened drafts of air, and her breasts rose and fell rhythmically as she breathed. He suckled her greedily, moving back and forth from one swollen nipple to the other.

"Oh, my God," he heard her moan in English. "It feels so wonderful."

With a tender smile at her words of surprised naïveté, he let her slide slowly down the length of him before he swung her up in his arms and carried her to the blanket spread out on the soft grass of their sheltered bower. On the bank of the bubbling stream close by, the grazing horses nickered to each other in the warm, contented afternoon, while in the branches overhead two larks raucously scolded a nosy jay that had the bad manners to barge into their peaceful scene uninvited.

Kneeling on one knee, Lance laid her gently on the striped gray wool. He pulled away from her just long enough to remove his moccasins, denim jeans, and the breechclout he wore underneath. His engorged manhood was fully erect, springing from the black mat of hair that surrounded it. When he turned back to her, he found her watching him with fascination. He was a big man, and next to her slim figure, his broad frame and muscular bulk loomed even larger. He realized how frightening he must appear to her. Even though her medical training assured him that she had precise knowledge of the human male's anatomy, given his generous natural endowment and the likelihood that she had seldom, if ever, lain with a man, it was not surprising that she was having second thoughts about what they were doing.

She rose on her elbows and started to scoot away from him. "Wait, War Lance," she pleaded with a gasp.

A husky laugh rumbled deep in his chest. He grasped the smooth curve of hip covered by her thin muslin drawers and held her still.

"Don't be afraid," he cajoled in a thick, breathy voice. He lay down on the blanket beside her. Slipping one arm around her slender waist, he turned her toward him. He brought her face and shoulders above his head so she could brace her forearms on his chest. "See, little doll, you are in complete control," he said with a coaxing smile. He reached up and lightly stroked her cheek. "You are free to leave our secluded haven whenever you want. But stay here beside me, if only for a little while longer."

Tendrils of coppery silk, falling free from her severe chignon, framed her oval face. Her violet eyes sparkled with wariness and something more. She watched him with an almost eager anticipation, her full lips parted to reveal glimpses of her small, white teeth.

Looking up at her delicate features framed by the backdrop of green, russet, and gold leaves shimmering in the treetops above them, he spoke in a quiet, reassuring voice. "A moment ago, you were talking to yourself in your strange language. Teach me some more of your *vèho* words."

She flushed and smiled hesitantly. "What words would you like to know?" she queried in an obvious attempt to stall for time. He was certain she'd never translate her spontaneous reaction to the feel of his mouth on her breasts. But as he'd hoped, she was momentarily diverted from her natural caution by her overriding desire to teach him English.

He raised his head up and brushed his tongue against her lips. *"Vitanov,"* he said.

"Tongue," she replied in a suffocated voice.

Her rosy lips parted and he slid his tongue inside to sweep the soft, pink cavern. *"Màz,"* he demanded.

"Mouth," she whispered, and entered his in return.

Cupping the ivory globe of her breast in his hand, he bent his head and kissed its rosy crest. *"Matan,"* he said.

She leaned over him and caressed the flat nipples on his chest. "Breast," she instructed with a soft smile.

Whispering seductively in her ear, he took her small hand and guided it down to his engorged shaft.

Her musical laughter tinkled above him and she shook her head at his audacity. But her tapering fingers explored him with a gentle caress before moving away to rest on his abdomen. "Now you're just being naughty," she teased, as she looked down at him with sparkling eyes. "If you are not going to take our lessons seriously, we won't continue."

He reached up and took her lovely face in his hands. His thumbs rested on her fragile cheekbones; his callused fingertips were buried in her coppery hair. "Beautiful eyes," he said almost gruffly, "I take our lessons more seriously than you would ever know."

He removed the four small combs that held her chignon sedately in place and laid them, one by one, carefully on the blanket beside his head. Then he ran his fingers through the mass of reddish gold waves that cascaded over her shoulders. The silken strands wrapped themselves tightly around his long fingers as though vibrant with a life of their own.

When he spoke, his voice was hoarse with an ardent, undisguised desire. "And now it's time for me to teach you how a man worships an angel that's fallen to the earth at his feet."

Chapter 15

With his hands buried deep in her lustrous curls, Lance pulled her face down to his. His open lips covered hers, his tongue sweeping across her parted teeth and into her mouth. He rolled over on top of her, trapping her beneath him. He rained kisses over her brows, her lids, her cheekbones, and nipped her pert, dainty nose, then traced a hot path with his tongue across the delicate bone of her chin, down the silken column of her throat, and delved into the hollow of her collarbone.

As he moved across her creamy skin, he described to her in specific detail just what his tormented body wanted of her, and what he would give her in return. He spoke to her in earthy Cheyenne phrases, urging her to touch him, to traverse his male body with her soft little hands, just as he was discovering hers.

Suzette gazed up through shuttered lids at the magnificent male leaning above her. In a state of near helpless capitulation, she was assaulted over and over again with his all-consuming sensuality. She lay pinned beneath his hard body, like an exhausted swimmer sprawled on a raft, battered by wave after glorious wave of pure physical pleasure brought on by the touch of his mouth and teeth and tongue. She was drowning in a tide of passion. As through a mist, she could hear him talking to her, his beautiful deep voice telling her it was all right to touch him. Her body responded as though it had a will of its own. Her hands roamed everywhere, feeling the tense, corded muscles of his chest, his arms, his thighs, as they leapt reflexively in a lover's welcome to her merest touch. She ran her fingers across his lean flanks and timidly stroked the warm, firm velvet of his manhood.

Vaguely she heard his quick intake of breath each time she touched him so intimately, followed by a low, happy rumble deep in his chest like a mountain cat purring in contentment.

"I've wanted to touch you like this from the moment we met, War Lance," she confided. She spoke in her own language, knowing there was no way he could possibly understand what she was telling him. Languorously she moved her hands across the firm pectorals of his chest, up his strong neck, to trace his rugged jawline with the tip of her finger.

"You are absolutely beautiful, do you know that?" she whispered with a soft chuckle. "Of course you do. But you couldn't have possibly guessed how much I've longed to glide my hands over your marvelous body. Or that I've ached for you to touch me like this. Or how I've dreamed of us splashing together, naked and free, in the sunshine."

Through the haze of sexual arousal that engulfed her, she sensed that he was listening to her strange words as he bent and suckled her. She didn't realize he was removing her last remaining undergarment until she felt him ease the leg of her drawers over each foot. Then his long fingers slid up the sensitive skin of her inner thigh, and he touched the curly triangle that covered her mound, deftly opening her most secret parts to his exploring fingertips. He bent over her and gently kissed her there, as he slipped his fingers inside her. Suddenly filled with doubt, she started to rise up on her elbows.

"Let me pleasure you, angel," he crooned to her. "Lie back down while my hands caress your sweet body. Let me open your pink silken petals and prepare you for what we will be sharing together."

"Oh, War Lance," she breathed, no longer certain what language she was speaking in. She could feel her muscles clutching against him, involuntarily responding to his skilled manipulations. "I've never ... I haven't ever ..."

But Lance had already discovered that. Her passage was gloriously, incredibly, unbelievably tight. The primal male thrill of first possession stabbed through him. When he took her, she would be his completely.

He had brought her to full arousal. He positioned himself between her thighs, grasped her hips securely in his hands, and slowly sheathed himself in her vulnerable flesh. Bit by bit he drove into her, and the tightness of her virginal passage gradually stretched under the steady pressure he exerted. He moved in her gently, withdrawing and reentering, his throbbing shaft inching into her honeyed resistance a little farther each time.

Covered with a fine sheen of perspiration, he braced himself above her on his forearms. His breath came harsh and ragged. His body shook, struggling against the control of his iron will as he held back the unconquerable onslaught of pure male lust.

"I'm going to hurt you, angel," he whispered hoarsely. "There's no other way."

She met his gaze with unflinching acceptance. "I know," she said. Wrapping her arms around his shoulders, she lifted her head and kissed him. "Do it," she pleaded. "Take me now."

Imprisoning her beneath the weight of his large frame, he held her body secured for his thrust. He moved his hips against hers, sliding his swollen shaft in rhythmic strokes, building up the need within her. Then he drove his full length into her, tearing the last fragile barrier between them.

Just as he had marked her with his forceful invasion, she had victoriously breeched the wall he'd so carefully erected around the citadel of his heart. The caring words she'd spoken in English, believing he would never understand, were etched across that broken rampart, and nothing he could do or say would ever erase them.

Shattered, one physically, one emotionally, they remained in each other's embrace as her body slowly began to stretch and accommodate him. For Suzette, the initial discomfort was soon replaced by the wonderful feeling of completeness, as though, at last, the two partial circles of their physical selves were joined into one whole. Two halves meshed as one. Conquest and surrender changed to bliss. Aggression and submission into harmony. Male and female into love.

Filled with elation, she lifted her lids to meet his gaze. Teardrops sparkled on the tips of his thick black lashes. *He* was crying.

"I'm all right," she whispered reassuringly. She slid her hands to his face and caressed his cheeks. "It wasn't that bad."

He smiled down at her with an aching tenderness. "It's supposed to feel good, little doll."

As he spoke he began to move within her, plunging and retreating, in steady, rhythmic strokes. Her body responded, moving of its own volition, picking up the increasing tempo. Sparks of white-hot excitement ignited within her, fueled with each thrust and withdrawal. She was pulsating with a fierce, uncontrollable need, chasing after some unfamiliar goal. Her breath came short and fast. She panted like a runner, striving for the race's final trophy just beyond her reach.

"I can't," she confessed, almost sobbing. She shook her head in confusion as she felt the consuming sensations begin to slip away.

"Yes, angel, you can," he told her, and continued his driving onslaught. "I'll take you there. We have as long as you need."

His words of absolute confidence and selfless passion, coupled with his plunging ride, brought her to the edge of fulfillment. With each rapid thrust, the burning ache heightened till her senses were filled with only his presence. Every nerve in her quivering body reached for him. She breathed in his male scent, rubbing her face against his muscled shoulder, touching his skin with her tongue. His thrusts rocked her, jarring her body with jolt after jolt of mind-consuming pleasure. Each breath was a tortured gasp, coming faster and faster as she felt herself start to cross the brink, to feel the outermost edges of the explosion that was about to engulf her. The detonation consumed her, tossing her about in rolling shock waves of sheer, perfect, exquisite pleasure. Somewhere in the midst of the whirling sensations that enveloped her, she heard herself call out to him in a cry of total female surrender.

He continued to drive into her, hard and wild, increasing and extending the pleasure she reaped, until his great body suddenly stiffened and tensed with the convulsions of release. He withdrew just before his seed would have spilled into her. Gasping for air, he stretched out beside her and gazed at the branches above them. She turned and leaned up on one elbow to look at him, and this time she was the one who was crying. Even in the throes of consummate passion, this magnificent man she had so smugly labeled a savage had maintained his fierce self-control, continuing to place her needs above his own.

Suzette gazed about the sheltered bower, wanting a lasting impression of the lovely, shaded nook so that in the cold winter months ahead, she could remember in detail just the way it looked on this glorious autumn afternoon. For a long while they had lain quietly on the rough woolen blanket, sated and replete in each other's arms. Then War Lance had nudged her softly and tipped his head toward the stream. There on the other side, nearly hidden behind a cluster of sandbar willows, a doe waited cautiously while her nimble fawn stretched out its thin legs and bent its head to drink.

Astride her black and white spotted mustang, Suzette

was filled with a bittersweet sadness now that they were ready to leave.

"What is the name of this stream?" she asked, hoping they would have the chance to come back again one day.

War Lance swung up on his red stallion. Gathering the reins, he wheeled Red Wind around. But before he signaled his mount to start, he rested a hand on one thigh and turned to look about their tranquil sanctuary. His rugged features were softened, and a tender smile flickered over his face as he met her questioning gaze.

"This is called Hanging Woman's Creek," he told her, but offered no further information. Side by side, they rode their horses out of the small canyon at a walk.

The inappropriateness of the name had caught her by surprise, and turning it over in her mind, she scowled in disenchantment. "What a horrible name for such a lovely spot," she protested unhappily. "Why ever would anyone call it that?"

Laughter sparkled in his black eyes at her guileless disappointment. "It's been called that since before I was born. The story told when I was a small child was that a beautiful young maiden hung herself from one of the trees there beside the stream."

Suzette turned in her saddle and looked back in dismay. "An Indian girl? Why would she do that?"

"She'd fallen in love with a handsome young brave, who returned her affection. But her parents didn't like the man she'd chosen. They preferred an older man, who'd counted many coups in battle. One whom they were certain could provide for and protect her."

"Indian parents choose their daughter's husbands?" she asked with curiosity. She'd never given the courting customs of the Cheyenne much thought.

"Not always," he replied. "Most of the time a young girl is free to choose among several suitors. Some pretty girls can have more than a dozen love-struck fellows hanging around them. But a good girl, one who is brought up properly, is always guided by the wishes of her parents. She listens to them dutifully and takes their advice. This time, however, the girl would have no part of the marriage they proposed, and her parents wouldn't give in."

Suzette wrinkled her nose in disapproval at the maiden's woeful lack of fortitude. "Why didn't she just run off with the man she wanted?"

"An elopement among the Cheyenne is considered a disgrace," he explained patiently. "It is regarded as no marriage at all. Sometimes, after a couple has run away, the young man will send the parents the customary gifts, and the marriage will be considered valid. Then the erring pair is taken back, and all is forgiven."

"And so, rather than the disgrace of an elopement, the young woman went out and hanged herself?" Suzette asked with disgust. "What a foolish decision."

There was an unreadable expression on War Lance's face. "What would you have done, angel, if your father and mother had chosen a man for you, and you did not want him? Or denied you permission to marry the one you loved? Would you have refused to obey your parents?"

With a start, Suzette recalled her father's obdurate disapproval of Jordan. She had forgotten the many times Martin Stanwood had urged her to continue accepting the visits of potential suitors, even after her fiancé had returned to active duty out West. It had been the only significant disagreement between Suzette and her father. Had her cavalier dismissal of his assessment of Jordan been far too hasty? She wondered what her astute father had found missing in the young officer—a flaw she'd never noticed in her girlish infatuation. Had Jordan's blond good looks blinded her to major defects in his character that should have been all too obvious? Something told her that if she met him for the first time today, she'd understand her father's objections. She had the unpleasant suspicion that her memory of the glorious military hero was no more than a figment of her youthful imagination.

"Actually," she said, staring thoughtfully down at the reins in her gloved fingers, "my father did try to talk me out of my plans to marry Captain Maclure. But I wouldn't listen. Father said I was blinded by the fancy uniform and didn't see the real man inside."

"And you never had any doubts that your father might have been right?"

"Not at the time," she answered. She looked over at War Lance. Dressed in a faded blue shirt and Levis, with his primitive shell-core necklace, the short braid at the crown of his head decorated with hammered silver ornaments and the fluffy down feathers of an eagle, and his shiny black hair falling past his collar, he was the exact opposite of Jordan, who'd always played the role of the dashing cavalry officer with such gallant refinement and savoir faire. She chuckled softly. "I wonder what my father would have said about you."

But her companion failed to see the humor in her offhand remark. His raven brows snapped together in a frown; his answer was clipped and edged with a biting sarcasm. "He would have reminded you of what every white woman on the frontier is told repeatedly. It would be better to kill yourself than to be touched by a red man." Kicking the great stallion's flanks, he took off at a gallop.

Astounded by his rapid change of mood, she grabbed hold of the saddle horn and tried to catch her balance as Painted Doll whinnied in protest at being left behind and hurried after her partner.

Less than an hour later, Suzette and War Lance came across a milling herd of cattle. The wandering animals were Texas beef steers mostly, a crossbred stock that combined the hardy durability of the longhorn and the fatter, tenderer meat of the white-faced Hereford. But there were others mixed in, some Angus heifers and a few cows with their calves. The livestock spread out over the better part of the shallow valley, grazing contentedly.

To Suzette's surprise, her guide immediately turned his mount in their direction, with the faithful piebald mare following like any lovesick female. They were soon in the midst of the herd, some of the cattle bawling loudly in complaint at their intrusion.

Suzette hollered over the noise. "Why are we riding through the middle of them?" She brushed the dust from her eyes peevishly, stilled miffed at his last uncalled-for remark.

"I wanted a closer look," he explained cryptically. His gaze roved over the herd as though searching for a particular steer.

"Do you know anything about cattle?" Dubious, she made no attempt to keep the boredom from her voice.

His eyes glinted with amusement. For whatever reason, he'd regained his lost sense of humor. "Not much. Who do you think they belong to?"

She shook her head in open disgust at his ignorance. She was a mere greenhorn from the East, and even she knew the answer to that. "They're Lew Rumsey's, of course. See the LR brand on them?" She pointed to the nearest cow.

"What about the cuts on their ears?"

She squinted in concentration at the slow-moving cattle. The animals were all marked differently, with a random assortment of crops, bits, and bobs carved out of their long ears in no particular pattern. "Learning to speak Cheyenne was difficult enough," she replied sarcastically. "I'm afraid I haven't had time to learn how to read cowboy earmarks."

"How do you think the cattle got here?" he persisted, flashing her a wicked grin that was obviously meant to goad her.

She refused to rise to his bait and answered with studied disinterest. "They must have accidentally wandered onto the reservation lands. Rumsey's cowhands will be out looking for them."

"Then they'd better hurry," he stated with quiet, unflappable authority. "Because if any other Cheyenne finds them grazing on our grasslands, Rumsey's going to be missing a few."

"Cattle stealing is against the law," she informed him, shocked at his audacity. She inadvertently jerked on the reins, and Painted Doll sidled in confusion at her rider's contradictory signals. "If any of Rumsey's hands catch an Indian butchering a steer, they'll shoot him or hang him. That's why ranchers put their brands on their property. People are supposed to honor another man's mark."

"People are also supposed to keep their cows on their own land," Lance replied. Scorn for the white man's greed and selfishness surfaced once more, a feeling he'd known for twenty years. As an adolescent who'd been raised in a culture that believed in communal responsibility, he'd been appalled to see the poverty and degradation of the slums of New York and London. In his father's village no one had ever gone hungry, not even the widowed or elderly. The fruits of the hunt were shared by all, for once the buffalo was killed, the butchered meat belonged to the women, who distributed it as needed. Generous gift giving had always been an important part of Cheyenne life, and all contributed their skills for the welfare of the whole band. A chief was esteemed not for what he accumulated, but for what he gave away. How different from the self-serving avariciousness of the white man, whose primary goal was the acquisition of money. It made no difference what class—the aristocracy, the merchants and shopkeepers, or the poor—they were always ready with an open palm, and everything had a price.

Brushing aside his negative thoughts, Lance shifted in his saddle, ready to leave, and Suzette reached over and grabbed his elbow.

"You're wrong about my father," she blurted out. "I

never heard him say one derogatory thing about the color of a person's skin. He always told me to watch what a man does and judge him by his actions. He would have treated you fairly, War Lance. That much I can promise you."

"I doubt he'd have welcomed a Cheyenne brave as a son-in-law, *náevehoka*," he replied with cynicism.

Suzette regarded him in shock. "I guess not!" she exclaimed. The thought of marriage to an Indian had never even crossed her mind. Not in a million years would she have considered such a preposterous idea. Good Lord, they were primitives, hundreds of years behind the technology of the whites. Unable to read or write, they lived in tipis and cooked over open fires. And every so often they went on the warpath, murdering and scalping innocent white people.

"Then your father was fair," he clarified, bitter irony twisting his smile. "But not crazy."

He met her gaze with an expression of cold disdain, and a blinding, painful realization whipsawed through her. *She hadn't meant him.* She no longer thought of War Lance as an Indian. He was a man. A very brave, very handsome, very special man, who also just happened to be Cheyenne. Speechless, she flushed in mortification at her bigoted, thoughtless remark.

As he rode on ahead of her, War Lance's words echoed in her mind: *a Cheyenne brave as a son-in-law.* She smiled to herself in surprise. The idea of marrying War Lance brought a warm glow in the region of her heart. Although it would mean spending the rest of her life on the reservation—for he clearly had no intention of learning the ways of the white man—the sacrifices involved might be worth the treasure gained. He would be a wonderful husband: passionate, protective, gentle yet strong. She could think of no one who would be a better father to his children.

Children.

If the two of them continued what they'd started that

afternoon, the conception of a child was a very real possibility. What would they do if she became pregnant? Among the Cheyenne, there was no such thing as a child born out of wedlock. If a man slept with a woman, she was considered his wife and his responsibility. He was expected to provide for her and any children she might conceive. Of course, a man could have more than one wife. Many older men on the Tongue River Reservation had two or three.

A feeling of unease smothered the warm glow inside. Would War Lance want to have several wives? She could read in his eyes how deeply he cared about her. And everyone knew just how much Cheyenne people loved their children. But if she became pregnant, would he marry her and move into her cabin, or would he expect her to share him with other women?

That evening, War Lance deposited his charge safely at her front door and left for his brother's camp at once. He was distant and remote when they parted, for the moment they were once again in the presence of white people, his demeanor changed to one of guarded reserve. Not by a gesture or a look could anyone observing them have suspected their secret. From all outward appearances, he was her hired Indian scout and nothing more. Confused and hurt by his unexplained absence, Suzette spent the next three days receiving patients in her cabin and wondering if she'd mistaken the emotions she'd read in his gaze.

On the second Monday of October, War Lance appeared with a message from his grandmother: Suzette was invited to a feast at the camp by the Rosebud. Late that afternoon she rode beside her guide into the camp's great circle just as the herald was calling out for all Cheyenne to open their ears and listen to the news of the day. A group of young women were returning from gathering roots, giggling among themselves, while several conceited dandies, their long black hair meticulously combed and braided, rode around the village showing off their finest clothing. Suzette had learned from War Lance that the men used a pair of tweezers, called an eyebrow plucker, to remove the hair from their cheeks and above their mouths. In the old days, they'd also plucked out their eyebrows and lashes. Hairy faces were considered unappealing by the Cheyenne.

She'd also learned that daily washing was a common practice. The men would go down to the nearby stream to bathe every morning. It was a habit that many white men would have benefited from, for a Saturday night bath was just about the most one could expect from the rough, hard-riding cowboys who worked on the nearby ranches.

"I am glad you have come to my feast, Little Red Fox," Prairie Grass Woman said kindly when Suzette rode up with War Lance. "Bear Scalp and his friends brought in three elk this afternoon." She turned to her grandson and smiled merrily. "And we will roast the beef you brought in this morning, *nixa,* though everyone much prefers wild game to the white men's tame cattle."

Suzette looked at War Lance with open suspicion. He had the effrontery to return her stare with a dazzling grin. It had been four days since the two of them had discovered Rumsey's herd wandering across agency land.

"But Little Red Fox will enjoy the beef, *niscehem,*" he said as he dismounted and came to stand beside his tiny grandmother. He made no attempt to hide the amusement in his voice. "I brought it especially for her."

Suzette ignored his taunting words and looked about the village. The unusually warm, clear weather of the week before had been replaced by the briskness of autumn. The day had been cool and cloudy, and with sunset, the air would grow chillier still. People had added flannel leggings and blankets to their summer clothing. Many women wore red woolen dresses. Some of the men wore the indigo Levis popular with the cowboys, but to Suzette's astonishment, they also continued to keep their breechclouts as part of their outerwear. They'd simply cut away the crotch and turned the denim trousers into leggings. And everyone still wore the comfortable, beautifully beaded Cheyenne moccasins.

"Come, Little Red Fox," Prairie Grass Woman said, a look of glee on her wrinkled face. Suzette was certain her hostess was fully aware of the illegal source of her grandson's largess. "There are some sick members of the tribe who are waiting to see you," the elderly woman continued. She grasped her visitor's arm and waved War Lance away with a gesture of dismissal. "My grandson can see to your horse and then visit with his friends."

By nightfall, the camp was a hubbub of activity. Horses were brought in from the nearby hillsides and picketed. Fires burned in every lodge as meals were prepared. People scurried back and forth from home to home, where families joined one another to share the food and enjoy the latest news. Suzette had learned that the Cheyenne were great gossips, carrying reports of the entire reservation through the village with a speed that would have been the envy of Lancaster society's most proficient tattlers. Later in the evening, a social dance was to be held for the young men and women, and this time Suzette had been invited to join them.

Little by little, War Lance's people had come to accept the white medicine woman he took from camp to camp. Although only a few allowed her to treat them as patients, she found that everyone was friendly and willing to talk with her. Most were not ready, however, to give up their trust in the honored medicine men who had cared for their needs for so many years. They saw no reason to rely on the strange *vèho* remedies when there was very little proof that hers were any better than the ones that had been given to their people in dreams and visions by the Great Wise One Above.

"I will take Little Red Fox to see the dancing," Blue Crane Flying announced to the others when the evening meal had been eaten and the dishes cleaned and put away. "Touching Cloud's family has invited her to their lodge to enjoy the festivities."

"May I come too?" Yellow Feather asked, her light brown eyes glowing with anticipation. The shy young girl had come to sit beside Suzette during the meal, listening quietly to the conversation of the grownups. Once again Suzette wondered about the child's half-white heritage, but was too polite to question the mystery aloud.

"Not tonight, *nàtóna*," her mother answered with a gentle smile. "Your great-grandmother is tired and wishes to rest, so you must stay here and keep her company. You can also care for your little brother, should he need any help."

Young Wolf, who sat proudly between his father and uncle, looked up in surprise. "My sister does not need to help me. I am old enough to take care of myself."

"Yes, at six summers you are very responsible, my son," Bear Scalp said as he rose. "But your uncle and I are going to walk around the camp and look at our horses, then smoke your grandfather's medicine pipe."

"If you and your sister will stay with *niscehem* and take good care of her," War Lance added, "I will give you both a ride on Red Wind tomorrow morning." The children exchanged gazes of delight and hurried to discover if there was anything their great-grandmother needed.

When the men had left, Suzette walked with Blue Crane Flying to the home of an unmarried young woman named Touching Cloud, who was a close friend of War Lance's sister-in-law. The dance was being held in the camp's largest tipi. Nearly thirty feet in diameter, the dirt floor had a fire pit in the center. The lodge was already filled with people, some chatting and visiting together, others in tight groups telling funny stories and laughing uproariously, while the older, more mature visitors looked on quietly. Suzette was given the place of honor opposite the entrance, and several of the young women, whom she'd met previously, brought her gifts and in-

sisted she wear them. Gift giving was extremely important to the Cheyenne. It was considered a terrible show
of bad manners to refuse to accept a present. So she put
on a wide leather belt, intricately decorated in bright ge-
ometric patterns of blue, white, red, and green beads,
over the waistband of her brown wool trousers. If the
women thought it was peculiar that she rode about the
countryside attired in white men's clothing, they were far
too courteous to mention it. In the midst of Suzette's red
curls, Blue Crane Flying fastened an ornament cunningly
wrought of blue jay feathers and tiny sapphire beads.

Fascinated, Suzette looked on as the dancers moved to
the rhythm of the music provided by two drums and the
accompaniment of six voices, male and female. The first
dance started slowly, increasing in tempo to a final exhilarating pace. The feet of the men and women seemed to
fly as the beat of the music went faster and faster and
then suddenly stopped.

Since early childhood, Suzette had loved to dance.
Whenever she'd been allowed to watch the adults at parties in her parents' home, she'd inevitably end up
twirling around the parlor with her father at least once
before being sent up to bed. Later, as an adolescent,
she'd outlasted all of her friends, seldom missing a set,
whether the musicians played a waltz, a schottische, or a
polka. So as she listened, she followed the steps carefully, scarcely aware that she was swaying in happy
rhythm with the music.

"Come, Little Red Fox," urged Blue Crane Flying. Her
nut brown eyes twinkled merrily at her friend's obvious
delight in the dance. "I will show you the steps."

Without thinking twice, Suzette jumped up and joined
the merrymakers.

Chapter 16

It wasn't long before Suzette's feet were moving to the music in a fairly close approximation of the steps that Blue Crane Flying cheerfully demonstrated. Once the men realized that the *náevehoka* could dance remarkably well for a white person, they were happy to join her. Unlike the white man's ballroom etiquette, it was customary for the Indian women to choose their partners at social dances. She didn't miss a set, switching partners one right after the other in gay-hearted abandon.

After a particularly fast-paced dance, everyone sat down for a brief rest while the pounding drums and the prattling mouths continued without a pause. Twelve young men rose and left the tipi, only to come quickly back wearing masks of various wild animals. There were foxes, bears, deer, mountain lions, wolves, and antelopes. Each mask was cunningly made of the real creature's fur and teeth, and fit completely over the head of its wearer. These costumed dancers leaped about the lodge's fire, imitating the different animals in stunning and clever movements. Twelve girls joined the capering menagerie to sway and twirl in a circle around them. Then each maiden stopped in front of a masquerader and tried to guess his name. If, on the first try, she correctly identified her counterpart, he had to wear the mask for the rest of the evening. Two braves were unfortunate enough to be caught immediately, and the sheepish pair were the butt of many uproarious jokes. But they took all the rail-lery in good spirit.

"The next dance will be the last," Blue Crane Flying told Suzette over the laughter and the spoofing. Her thin face was alight with merriment. "Some of the young women will leave the tent and disguise themselves. Come with us, Little Red Fox, and you can take part in our game."

"Thank you for wanting to include me, but why should we bother?" Suzette asked. She grinned at the lovely woman and pointed to herself in lighthearted self-mockery. "Anyone could guess who I was without even trying."

"Wait and see," her friend persisted as she tugged on Suzette's hand.

A group of high-spirited women flew out of the tent, dragging the dubious *vèhoka* with them. In a lodge close by, everyone exchanged clothing as they chattered excit-edly. They even switched jewelry, wearing one another's brass and copper bracelets and necklaces of elk teeth and brightly colored glass beads.

Touching Cloud, whose family was hosting the dance that night, handed Suzette her own skirt and blouse of blue and yellow striped calico. "I am nearly as tall as you, Little Red Fox," she said with a friendly grin. "Give me your strange leggings and boots, and I will pretend to be you."

"You see, Little Red Fox," Blue Crane Flying added, a teasing smile skipping about the corners of her mouth, "you won't be that easy to recognize after all."

Surprised, Suzette looked at Touching Cloud once more and realized that they were nearly the same height. It was unusual to meet another woman so tall. "I'm sorry to spoil your plans," she said, and patted the curls piled on top of her head. "But what about my red hair?"

"We'll solve that problem," Many Magpies said. Her dark, almond-shaped eyes sparkled with mischief. One of the youngest in the group, she hopped about like a little sprite, filled with the unbounded energy of a sixteen-year-old, barely able to suppress her nervous giggles.

Touching Cloud shook out a blanket and lifted it up over Suzette's bright hair. "Pull it around you," she instructed, "and cover your face. Then just peek out. We'll all do the same."

With a doubtful shrug, Suzette followed her instructions. "I still don't think we'll fool very many people," she said, laughing. "But I'm willing to try."

"We will make it even harder," Blue Crane Flying said. "The men know that they have to guess not only which one of us is the woman they want to dance with, but also which secret name she has chosen. We will each take the name of one of the year's moons, so think of the time that is special to you. We will let you choose first, Little Red Fox."

The gaggle of animated females gathered around Suzette, eager to hear her choice.

"Let's see, which moon should I be?" Suzette debated carefully, then snapped her fingers. Her birthday was in early June. "I'll choose *Enanoesehe,* for the time when I was born."

"And I will take *Maxoxzeésehe* because my favorite games are the ones we play in the winter snow," Many Magpies decided, choosing the *vèho* month of February.

One by one, the other women picked the name of a Cheyenne moon, some explaining the reason for their choice, others bashfully keeping it a secret.

"Listen," Touching Cloud announced when everyone was ready. She waved her hands to signal the talkative females to hush. "The men are calling for us to return."

From the other lodge Suzette could hear a chorus of deep baritones, in accompaniment with the drums, singing a chant for the girls to come out of their hiding.

Many Magpies excitedly pushed Suzette to the center of the group. "Don't go in first or last," she advised, her happiness bubbling over in an uncontrollable giggle.

"Stay in the middle, so you won't be noticed right away."

With their noisy chatter muffled by the blankets pulled over their heads, the young women returned to the dance floor, where they each peeped out at the line of potential partners with one shadowed eye. Circling the fire, they danced slowly, in rhythm to the pulsating beat. The waiting braves stood on the outside of the circle, watching them in obvious anticipation.

Suzette looked out from under the protection of her striped blanket, careful to keep her face in shadow. She and Touching Cloud had purposely taken positions far away from each other so the slight difference in their height would be less obvious to the casual observer. The irrepressible Many Magpies, unable to contain herself any longer, burst into peals of earsplitting laughter, and several of the young men turned at once, knowing immediately who was hidden under the protective covering and the borrowed clothes.

With a start, Suzette suddenly realized that War Lance and Bear Scalp had come into the tipi in her absence. No doubt they knew just what kind of carefree romp the evening's last dance would be. The two large, well-built brothers stood shoulder to imposing shoulder beside the other men dancers. But her usually astute guide was thoughtfully studying Touching Cloud, whose tall, slim form was arrayed in the white woman doctor's brown wool riding outfit and leather boots. Secretly delighted that she'd fooled him so easily, Suzette covered her mouth with her hand beneath the blanket to make sure she didn't duplicate Many Magpie's girlish mistake. When the tempo of the music increased, the male dancers issued forth, heading toward the cloaked figure they believed was the person they wanted to dance with.

To Suzette's astonishment, War Lance agilely outmaneuvered the younger men around him and moved to stand directly in front of her. He'd acted without hesitation. Well, goodness, she hadn't fooled him for a moment.

One by one, each man danced in front of his chosen partner with quick, intricate, flying steps, and then stopped and loudly pronounced the secret name. Of course, none of them knew which moon a particular girl had selected. So even though they might be relatively certain which young lady, regardless of her disguise, they were after, the choice of the correct title was sheer guesswork.

Many Magpies was identified on the first round. The brave who'd easily guessed the moon she'd chosen led his lovely prize back to her seat with an air of smug self-satisfaction. There he exercised the privilege he'd won and, sitting down beside her, wrapped the blanket cozily around the two of them. Bear Scalp was just as quick to identify his wife's secret name and led her off the dance floor.

On his turn, War Lance's moccasins flew to the music. He was amazingly nimble and light on his feet for his size. *"Seene,"* he called out with absolute confidence the minute the drums stopped. The same look of contented male complacency that had shone on the first two winners' proud faces glowed on War Lance's rugged features.

A laughing Suzette, under the protection of her blanket, signaled in the negative. Then she twirled and lightly danced away to join the other women gamboling around the fire as gracefully as fawns. As she moved away, the tiny bells sewn on the hem of Touching Cloud's blue and yellow skirt tinkled impertinently at the tall warrior, who stood there in perplexed disappointment. Certain now that he'd guessed her identity, she knew why he'd chosen the month of October. He was thinking of the afternoon they'd spent in each other's arms. His choice told her that for him, it was the most important moon of the year.

His luck in guessing her selection, however, was terrible. Seven times he danced in front of her. Seven times he failed to guess correctly. The music grew faster and faster, and War Lance's feet struck the ground exactly to the wild, throbbing tempo of the drums. But it was only by a process of elimination, as, one by one, the other young women were discovered by their would-be partners, that he finally arrived at the answer.

"Enanoesehe," he said at last, and this time, with her signal of affirmation, he lifted the blanket that covered her. With a happy growl of success, he used the striped wool to pull her to him. "Why the Planting Moon?" he asked in her ear.

Laughing out loud, she looked up at his bewildered expression. "It's my birth month," she said simply.

With a wry grin of admiration, he slipped his arm around her shoulders and led her to their place. Once seated beside her, he wrapped them in her blanket. His strong fingers slid down to her waist, and he pulled her to him. With a sigh of pleasure, she relaxed, leaned comfortably against his powerful shoulder, and breathed in the intoxicating masculine scent of him.

Beneath the blanket, his hand rubbed across the curve of her hip in a gesture of gratified ownership. "At last," he breathed in satisfaction.

"Yes, it took you long enough to guess correctly," she teased, deliberately misunderstanding his meaning. "I'm not at all certain that it was me you really were trying to find. Perhaps you mistook me for Touching Cloud."

He flashed her a wicked grin. "There was never a doubt in my mind, angel, which clever little dancer was you. I simply went after the one who was making up the most absurd steps I'd ever seen in my life, with such simple-hearted enthusiasm."

At his gibe, she shoved her elbow into his side and tried to scoot away from him. "I haven't had the time to waste practicing dance steps like some people," she told him with sham haughtiness.

But instead of allowing her retreat, he drew her even closer, his long fingers splayed across her rib cage.

"I have arranged for us to have the privacy of a friend's lodge tonight," he murmured against her cheek. "We can practice a different dance when we are alone. Do not worry that it will become known at the agency. My people would never reveal what I have asked them to keep secret from prying white eyes."

Her cheeks burning at the unspoken meaning in his velvety words, she looked around the large tipi. She wondered uncomfortably which brave was the friend who'd so obligingly offered his own home for their lovers' tryst.

Everyone was busy gossiping or telling jokes. Couples wrapped in blankets were talking softly with one another. Several older women entered the tipi carrying great kettles of hot soup and carved wooden platters piled high with cakes made of dried chokecherries and pemmican. There were even six large wooden bowls of hot white biscuits made of milled wheat flour, and the wonderful aroma flooded the lodge. This was a special treat in Suzette's honor, as rare and costly to the Cheyenne as any exotic gourmet cuisine served in a fancy New York restaurant. Some older men had joined the party just in time for the food, and these were being courteously served by a bevy of bright-eyed young helpers. No one was paying the *náevehoka* and her partner any particular attention, aside from the two pretty girls who offered them some biscuits and then burst into shy giggles when War Lance, with his lazy, devastating smile, politely thanked them.

Suddenly shy herself, Suzette looked down intently at the wooden bowl of soup in front of her as if it demanded her full attention. Her mind raced ahead to the hours to come. The thought of spending the entire night in his arms was intoxicating. She could feel a flush of heat spread through her limbs. Her heart thrummed in wild excitement.

"What will Prairie Grass Woman say if I do not sleep in the tipi with her tonight?" she asked hesitantly, tearing her gaze from the broth she stirred to meet his look of tender amusement.

His mouth quirked in a wry smile as he lifted a biscuit to her lips and fed her. "My grandmother will scold and complain like a little black crow. But at thirty-four summers, I am far too old to be bound by the restrictions that constrain the unmarried youngsters. And since you are white . . . and not exactly a child either . . . no one would expect you to follow the customs of my people that govern the behavior of our young maidens."

She was biting into the warm, heavenly bun when he'd made the unexpected remark about her advanced age. Coughing on a speck of biscuit that lodged in her windpipe, she lifted her indignant gaze to his midnight eyes. They were brimming with laughter.

"I never claimed to be . . ." She floundered for the correct words in irritation, her voice hoarse.

"Under forty summers," he offered promptly. His lips twitched suspiciously as his gaze roved over her mussed hair. Tangled curls, knocked into complete disarray by the blanket she'd hidden under, spilled over her shoulders. He reached up and gently touched the feathered ornament that Blue Crane Flying had fastened in her hair. "I don't want a little girl," he said softly "I want a woman full grown." He slid his fingertip down her forehead and over the bridge of her nose, to tap lightly on its tip. "But at this moment, beautiful eyes, you look no more than sixteen summers."

She pursed her lips and tried to scowl at his preposterous flattery. "Eat your soup before it gets cold," she ordered primly.

"Yes, angel," he responded with mock subservience. But a grin of delighted anticipation flickered across his sensuous lips.

When the feast was over and the extra food was carefully stored in leather pouches, it was time for the storytelling. The partygoers quietly settled around the cleared outer area of the lodge's dirt floor. Red stone pipes em-

bellished with eagle feathers, and tobacco pouches decorated with porcupine quills, were brought out and shared
by the older men, while the camp herald rose and took
the floor.

Village Crier was a fat, cheerful man who loved to
talk. For the Cheyenne, he was a walking newspaper. It
was his responsibility to ride about the camp circle twice
a day, morning and evening, calling out the latest orders
of the chiefs, the important events that had taken place
throughout the reservation, or little tidbits of personal
gossip. He was also a consummate actor, portraying
naughty children, tottering old men, sweet young maidens, and harping shrews to perfection. So great was his
talent, people would give him presents just for telling
stories. The noise in the lodge, which had risen to a rau-
cous din during the dancing, now quieted as all eagerly
settled themselves to listen. For the next hour, Village
Crier entertained them with one marvelous tale after another, ending with the story of an old chief who saw himself in the white man's mirror for the first time and made
insulting remarks about the looks of the aged, ugly person in the glass. His comic style was so clever, the audience was soon laughing uproariously.

The camp's acknowledged storyteller was followed by
a wrinkled old man who rose abruptly, pulled out his
knife, and lifted it up high before the crowd. Flashing its
sharp blade about in the firelight, Beaver Heart yelled for
attention and then launched into a dreadful tale of fighting a Crow warrior in hand-to-hand combat. His account
of past glory was so brutal and specific that Suzette was
shocked. Mesmerized, the others around her listened in
silence to his story of personal bravery. No one paid the
least attention to the lady doctor wrapped in a blanket
with War Lance. It was clear they had forgotten that a
white woman sat among them, able to understand everything that was being said.

The next one up was Tall Bull, a deep-chested man
about War Lance's age who'd danced with Suzette earlier

in the evening. He immediately began to tell of a great battle in which he had killed many horse soldiers and counted many coups.

"My younger brother, Loose Bones, made a vow of suicide that day," he boasted to the enraptured audience. "He promised to fight until he was killed. Twenty others, who made a similar vow, died with him." As he circled the fire, the speaker, his long braids flying about his shoulders, imitated the Dying Dance in which these brave young warriors had made the time-honored vow to throw their lives away.

"The Long Knives were surrounded on a hillside," he continued. "We outnumbered them many times and rode our horses right over them. The fighting was so close, we couldn't even take aim, but just shot wildly in any direction. After emptying our guns, we used clubs and hatchets until every soldier was dead."

As Tall Bull reached the last part of his gory tale, War Lance's large frame grew stiff and rigid beneath the blanket he shared with Suzette. Even in her confusion, she sensed from his reaction of displeasure that Tall Bull was telling the story of the Custer fight. She moved restlessly beside War Lance, uncertain whether to get up and risk offending her hosts or stay where she was.

He moved his hand to the base of her neck and rubbed her tense muscles comfortingly. "It's all right, Little Red Fox," he said in a low voice. "It's just a war story. It could have happened anywhere, at any time." Despite his soothing words, he scowled at the man standing beside the fire and started to rise.

At that moment, Tall Bull pulled out a blond scalp from beneath his shirt and dangled it in front of his fascinated listeners. Horrified, Suzette jumped to her feet beside War Lance. She stood frozen, staring transfixed at the golden patch of wavy locks spilling from the brave's fingers, unable to move, unable to breathe. It was the exact color of Jordan's hair. A deathly, ominous stillness filled the lodge as its occupants turned from Tall Bull to the white medicine woman. With a furious jerk of his hand, War Lance signaled the warrior to remove the scalp from sight, and Tall Bull hurriedly stuffed it back inside his flannel shirt, a look of dread on his startled face.

A woman's high wail pierced the silence, only to be quickly muffled by someone's hand clamped over her mouth, and Suzette realized, with a sickening lurch of her heart, that she had witnessed something no white person was meant to see. The identities of the warriors who'd actually fought in the Custer battle had been kept a secret, for many Indians, Cheyenne and Sioux alike, feared that the cavalry soldiers would still take reprisals after nine long years.

In a daze, Suzette looked around the tipi and met the shocked gazes fastened upon her. For the first time since she'd come to the camp of Bear Scalp's band, there was no warmth or friendship in their eyes. Only suspicion and fear. Appalled at what she'd seen and heard, and angry that they would dare to look at her with accusing stares, as though she were the one who'd committed the foul atrocities perpetrated at that infamous battle, she bolted across the floor and left the lodge. Behind her, she could hear loud voices raised in angry disagreement.

Lance was only a step behind her. He called her name, but she ignored him and raced across the open camp circle and into the nearby stand of trees that lined the creek. He could have stopped her easily, but he allowed her to reach the privacy and solace of the woods, content to remain a mere arm's distance away. At last she slowed. Reaching out, she braced one hand against the crackly bark of a river birch, bent her head, and tried to still the sobs that racked her slight figure.

"I'm sorry, angel," he said. A dull ache spread through him at the sight of her anguish. He placed his hand on her shoulder, hoping she'd allow him to comfort her. Instead, she jerked away and whirled to face him.

"Don't touch me," she cried with loathing. "Don't you ever touch me again."

He ignored her warning and roughly grasped her upper arms. "Stop being so foolish," he said hoarsely. He shook her like a spoiled, overwrought child. "What happened back there in the lodge doesn't have anything to do with us."

"It has everything to do with us," she cried. Her eyes were enormous and dark in the moonlight. "Everything!" She pushed against his chest, trying desperately to shove him away, but he refused to release her. "You were there with Tall Bull at the Little Big Horn, weren't you?" Her voice grew shrill with mounting hysteria. "You helped him hack and bludgeon and mutilate those poor innocent soldiers. Didn't you? *Didn't you?*"

Lance searched her beautiful features, distorted now with an unreasoning hatred, and his heart sank. There was no way he could tell her that he hadn't been with his people at the time of the battle. That he'd been thousands of miles away in England. He couldn't tell her the truth. Nor did he want to. Stubbornly he clung to the hope that she would accept him as he was and not because he'd been "civilized" in the white man's way. He released her, and she quickly backed up against the tree, staring at him as though he were some marauding Hun.

"Say something," she begged, wild-eyed and distraught. "Tell me it isn't the truth."

"There is nothing I can say, Little Red Fox. That part of my people's history is over and done with. We are no longer the fierce plains fighters who once roamed freely across endless stretches of open grasslands, but a subdued and peaceful tribe willing to remain here on our small reservation. I can't tell you about any warrior's part in the fight with Custer. You will have to accept me as I am."

He could see the tears glistening on her lashes like silver sparkles in the dappled moonlight. Her lower lip trembled uncontrollably, and her high-pitched voice cracked like a heartbroken child's when she spoke. "Accept you? With the blood of the only man I ever loved on your hands? Never."

Her words cut, deep and painful. Had he ever really been crazy enough to hope that one day she might learn to love him? God, he was such a fool. He knew all about white women. He had no reason to be surprised at her hatred. And no one to blame but himself for the searing ache of despair that tore through his chest.

"It is your decision, *náevehoka*," he said in cold rage. He was furious at her prejudice and stupidity. Furious that she still considered the soldier who was dead and buried her beloved, while he—War Lance Striking—was alive and blazing with desire for her. Fighting the urge to retaliate in kind, he turned on his heel and left before his white-hot anger drove him to say something he'd regret.

He could hear her footsteps in the dry grass as she raced after him. She grabbed his elbow, and he stopped reluctantly. Clenching his jaw to bite back the scathing words on his tongue, he looked down at her in icy, controlled wrath. "What is it now?"

"Take me there," she demanded shrilly. "Take me to the battleground. I want to see the place where Jordan was killed."

"Why? So you can prove to yourself what a vile savage I am? You must be burning with shame that you found me so attractive as a man," he taunted mercilessly. "That you actually let me touch you with my bloody, butchering hands."

She clenched her own small hands into fists. "Believe me, it will never happen again," she promised. "I won't let it."

It was obvious she considered her need for him merely a physical drive she could control at will. He'd experienced that before, when married ladies of wealth and rank had proposed to meet with him secretly for afternoons of lust-filled romps. Those same women reacted with shrill vindictiveness when he refused to become a part of their lies and deceptions.

Like them, Suzette viewed him as an ignorant, amoral creature far beneath her in every way. He wanted to hurt her for that. "How humiliating it must be," he sneered, "to think you surrendered your pure white body to nothing more than a scalping redskin."

She tried to slap him, and he grabbed her fragile, small-boned wrist. Nothing could have brought home so completely her real feelings about him. He smiled in derision as he brought her slim figure up against his large frame. "I could take you now, angel," he rasped, infuriated at the ache of lust that sprang up in his loins at the very touch of her. "And before I was even half started, you'd be begging me to come inside you."

She looked up at him with narrowed eyes, ignoring his threat and refusing to back down, though her slight form was shaking in anger and fright. Her fierce resolution reminded him of a spunky little prairie dog, standing up on its hind legs and taking on a venomous rattler. She had enough tenacity and courage for a Cheyenne war chief.

"Either you'll take me to the Custer battleground, War Lance," she said through clenched teeth, "or I'll hire someone who will."

He caught her stubborn chin in his fingers, and when she tried to pull away, he forced her head up, making her look him square in the eye. Then he leaned down, till their faces were only inches apart. "As you wish, náevehoka. I will take you there tomorrow. As for now, you'd better get yourself safely inside my grandmother's tipi, before I decide to ride you over the prairie tonight."

The instant he released her, Suzette turned and fled. He was a barbarian. A murderer. His very silence condemned him. He was one of the heathens who'd killed and mutilated Jordan. The filthy Indian had known it all along, yet he dared to make love to her. How he must have laughed at her foolish trust in him. She'd go with him to the battle site tomorrow, to the very spot where her fiancé died, and there, once and for all, she would exorcise War Lance Striking from her mind and heart and soul.

Chapter 17

"Come back to visit me again," Prairie Grass Woman told Suzette with a warm smile, as though nothing unusual had happened. They stood in front of the elderly woman's lodge, and she looked up at Suzette with eyes as bright and alert as a blackbird's. "When you return, all of this unhappiness and suspicion will be forgotten. I know, Little Red Fox, that you will say nothing of what you saw and heard last night to the agent or to the big soldier chief at Fort Custer. Tall Bull has a pregnant wife who needs him. Perhaps when you return you will use your strong medicine to insure the safe birth of their child."

Heartsick, and still in a state of shock, Suzette tried to return the tiny woman's smile, but the best she could do was a polite inclination of her head. "I am a doctor, Prairie Grass Woman. I have sworn to save lives, not take them. You have my promise that I will not mention Tall Bull's name to anyone." Dressed once again in her own riding outfit, she moved to Painted Doll, prepared to mount and leave. War Lance was already astride his great red stallion, waiting impatiently.

"Don't go yet, Little Red Fox," a sweet voice piped up. Out of the tipi came Yellow Feather, her coffee-colored braids swinging about her narrow shoulders. She was holding the wide beaded belt with its complex and fascinating designs that had been given to Suzette the

257

evening before. "You forgot to take this," the nine-year-old said with a gap-toothed smile. "I know Touching Cloud wants you to keep it. She said so last night when she returned your clothes."

Suzette looked at the girl through eyes suddenly blurred with tears. She had purposely left the belt behind, uncertain whether its giver would want her to still have it. Now the bashful half-breed child was extending to Suzette not only her own friendship, but also that of the tall Indian woman who'd so generously exchanged costumes with her the previous evening. Yellow Feather tipped her head to one side and gazed up at Suzette in doubtful apprehension, afraid she would refuse the painstakingly crafted gift. And once again, in the child's expression there was a tantalizing reminder of someone from Suzette's past. She tried to pull the vague image into clearer focus, then, unsuccessful, relinquished it.

"Thank you, Yellow Feather," she said. She stooped down to meet the child's enormous light brown eyes, and took the present. "I shall put it on right now."

As Suzette tied the multicolored sash around the waistband of her brown wool trousers, Blue Crane Flying came out of the tipi to join her daughter. She was carrying the gossamer ornament of sapphire beads and bluejay feathers that Suzette had sadly placed on her sleeping pallet alongside the beaded cummerbund.

"I want you to keep this also," Blue Crane Flying said with unruffled serenity, her nut brown eyes filled with kindness. "I made it especially for you, Little Red Fox. Please do not leave it behind." Without waiting for her answer, the gracious Indian woman reached up and fastened the delicate trinket in Suzette's red hair.

"Thank you for your gift," Suzette mumbled forlornly. Her lower lip trembled. She searched for something more to say, wanting to erase the feeling of constraint and suspicion that had arisen between her and the band of Cheyenne. Unable to find the words, she glanced about her. Bear Scalp, his arms folded across his massive chest, stood beside his grandmother, watching the white medicine woman with an unreadable expression on his pockmarked face. Young Wolf leaned against him, one chubby arm wrapped around his father's muscled leg. Moving to her black and white mustang, Suzette mounted and followed her guide.

They left Bear Scalp's camp at dawn, riding out of the circle of canvas lodges in the faint gray light. A dozen men and women came out of their homes to watch the *náevehoka* and her hired scout leave. Children stood quietly beside their parents, watching with big, frightened eyes, and Suzette could feel the hostile gazes follow them until they'd pulled out of sight.

All day long, War Lance Striking set a brisk, steady pace. They rode hour after hour in near silence. Not once during the disheartened pilgrimage did he make any reference to their terrible argument of the night before, or the spiteful animosity that stood between them like an unbridgeable chasm. He was as aloof and polite and unemotional as a stranger.

The Custer battlefield was located on the Crow Indian Reservation. Accompanied by her guide, Suzette reached the lonely, windswept site late in the cool, cloudy October afternoon. Side by side on the crest of a high ridge, they sat astride their horses and gazed out across the valley of the Little Big Horn. A natural, untouched loveliness encompassed the deserted battlefield, sweepingly primitive and hauntingly desolate.

"There were six tribal circles down by the water," War Lance said at last, pointing across a deep ravine to the stands of cottonwood that followed the meandering river below. "Five were Teton Sioux; the other, Northern Cheyenne. Plus a scattering of Santee and a few Arapaho. Their lodges stretched for a distance of three miles along the west bank."

Suzette turned her head to follow the path of his hand as it swept across the valley floor beneath them. "Where were the soldiers?" she asked in a tight, dry voice. Her breath caught high in her throat, and she swallowed to ease the uncomfortable feeling of near suffocation.

"Long Hair, the big soldier chief you call Custer, brought his bluecoats from the other side of Medicine Tail Coulee over there to the east," he answered. "He led them across Deep Coulee and right on down to the river bottom, planning to sack the village. Much of the Indian camp was hidden from view among the trees and the hills, so he probably had no idea he was facing about two thousand warriors." He shifted his position on his saddle blanket and pointed to the southwest. "The Cheyenne lodges were at this end."

Suzette slid down from the piebald mare's back and walked slowly across the grassy hillside. A glint of metal caught her eye, and she bent to pick up an empty shell. Rolling the shiny expended cartridge back and forth across her palm, she looked out over the battlefield once more. "Then what happened?" she called. She glanced back over her shoulder at War Lance, who still sat on his great red stallion.

As though reluctant to continue, War Lance slowly dismounted and, leading Red Wind beside him, came a bit closer. The steady autumn breeze whipped about them. It ruffled the white down feathers at the base of his braided scalp lock and tugged at the wisps of coppery hair that had pulled free of her chignon. Across the deep blue sky, huge cumulus clouds sailed in the wind, throwing patches of shadow over the network of ravines, gulches, and ridges that crisscrossed the rolling plain.

"Our warriors forded the river to meet them," he said simply. "The soldiers crossed the south end of this ridge and followed it down to the bottom. About forty or fifty Indians were firing at them from the brush along the river. So the bluecoats turned and raced back in the direction they'd come from. More and more Cheyenne and Sioux kept crossing the river as the soldiers hurried back up toward the top. But by that time, other warriors waited on the ridge above them. Long Hair rode into the center of that big basin over there, where his men dismounted and moved up the hill on foot toward where we're standing now."

"Which companies?" Suzette demanded, whirling to look down where he'd pointed. "Which companies were trapped down there?"

Lance hesitated. He could claim he didn't know, though Bear Scalp had taken him to the battle site five weeks before, when they'd been chasing the herd of wild mustangs, and had explained it all. His brother had been in the thick of the fighting that day at Greasy Grass.

She stood just a few feet in front of him, staring down at the base of the hill as though in a trance. Only her profile was turned to his view, but he knew there were deep shadows under her eyes. He doubted if she'd slept at all the previous night. Since they'd arrived at the site, her pale cheeks had turned chalky white, and a faint bluish color outlined her lips. He wondered how long it would be before she'd topple to the ground in a swoon.

"The gray horse company," he said.

"Company E," she replied without hesitation. "And Company C fell right alongside them."

At her automatic response, he was certain she'd read the lists of war dead in the newspaper accounts over and over again until she'd memorized the makeup of each battalion, each fallen company. She faced westward and looked down at the white markers on a small knoll between the hill and the river. The breeze carried her soft, stilted words up to him. "And then?"

God, he wasn't sure he could go through with this. He hated the cavalry officer who'd taken the past nine years of her life with him when he died that day. How much longer would she idolize this fallen soldier as her unblemished hero?

"Let's go back, angel," he said gently.

"What happened?" she cried, still staring out across the valley.

He lifted his voice so she could hear every word. Dammit, if she could stand it, so could he. "The soldiers who were still alive made a stand right here on this ridge. They were surrounded and shooting wildly in all directions. Then the Cheyenne boys, the ones who'd taken the vow to throw their lives away, gathered down at the river. They charged the bluecoats, starting the hand-to-hand fighting at the cost of their own lives, so that the warriors above could come in from the other side. After that, there was no time for the soldiers to even take aim. The Indians were right among them. Some of the bluecoats started to run along the ridge, some went down one side, some the other. But not far. Every one of them was killed."

She made no response, just waited there, listening, until he'd finished. For a while, they stood motionless, and the only sound was the rustle of the dry grass in the wind. Then she walked down the west side of the ridge. There in the high grass was a cluster of markers, nearly hidden from view. Late-blooming wildflowers covered the hillside, their yellow blossoms waving like a thousand tiny flags in the autumn breeze. One by one, she stood before each marker and read, in silence, the inscription carved into the headstone. Her slim shoulders drooping, she reached out and touched the last one, and he saw the cartridge fall from her trembling fingers. Then she turned and climbed back to the top of the rise, where he waited for her beside the battlefield's tall monument. In her hand she carried a bouquet of sunflowers.

She stood dry-eyed in front of the memorial shaft that rose up against the sky, bearing the names of all the dead soldiers heavenward. Stooping down, she reached through the iron picket fence that protected the shrine and laid the flowers on the ground at its base. She rose, gripping one of the thin bars as though to steady herself, and Lance moved toward her.

"Jordan's remains are not here," she said, so quietly he wasn't sure she was even talking to him. Her faint words were nearly lost on the wind. "His body was exhumed eight years ago and returned to Pennsylvania at his parents' request."

She turned and looked out over the empty valley. "But his soul is still here. And those of the friends who died with him. I can feel their presence, as surely as if they'd spoken to me." She bent her head, and he could see the graceful line of her white neck curving like the stem of a flower whose blossom is too heavy to support. "What I don't understand," she said, and he had to move even closer to catch the hushed, plaintive words, "is that I also feel the presence of the Indian warriors who died here. Why do you suppose that is?"

All the anger and resentment he'd stored inside himself, harboring it tightly throughout the day like a miser his gold, dissolved at the sight of her fragile, aching vulnerability. If only she'd cry, he could comfort her. But the dazed bewilderment that surrounded her, as though she herself were suffering from battle shock, ripped away his mask of indifference. He tried to speak, and the words caught in his throat till all that came out was a hoarse, painful groan.

She looked up at the sound. "You must think I'm crazy," she said, her lips trembling.

"No, you're not crazy, little angel," he assured her softly. "Every one of my people would understand what you're feeling now. The Cheyenne believe that all life is continuous and ongoing. We are surrounded by a life force that is moving in an eternal stream. It encircles us and binds us together, making us one with all the earth. Its steady, unending flow includes mankind, the animals, the trees, the sky and clouds, and even the very rocks at our feet, and all things that have ever been in a place are always in the present there. For my people, the things that happened here that day so long ago are always happening. What has been done in this valley is here forever."

Inclining her head at his words of comfort and understanding, she reached out to touch his arm, and he immediately moved to stand beside her. As she placed her fingers lightly, tentatively, on his sleeve, he swept his other arm around her waist and drew her gently to him. She leaned her weight against him, using his solid bulk for support. Her whole body quivered. Together they walked down the grassy hill till the white markers and the tall granite monument were lost to view, and all they could see was the sweeping beauty of the deserted countryside, with its grass-covered ravines and coulees, and the line of cottonwoods that followed the winding river as it cut its way through the heart of the valley.

They sank down together in the dry grass. He put his arm around her, and she rested her head on his shoulder. Gradually her slight frame stopped trembling, and her lids drooped till her russet lashes lay like thick fans on her pale cheeks. Lance felt her body slowly relax against him, and he bent his head and brushed her temple with his lips.

He knew she believed that the Indians had perpetrated a monstrous crime at this site, and he wanted her to know that the blame was not all on one side. "The soldiers who died here were not without guilt," he said quietly. She stirred in his arms, and he held her against his heart with an abiding tenderness. "Had the village been as small and defenseless as Long Hair at first believed, the horse soldiers would have attacked just as they'd planned that morning. They would have ridden through the lodges, cutting down innocent women and children as they tried to run and hide."

She straightened and lifted her head to meet his gaze. "No!" she gasped in horror. "Jordan would never have killed women or children. I can't believe that."

"I know nothing of your golden-haired soldier, angel. I am only telling you what would have happened that day, had the bluecoats succeeded in reaching the camp. Long before this battle took place, the Long Knives had a history of butchery, of lies and broken promises."

She bit her lower lip and frowned, her violet eyes filled with immeasurable pain and sorrow and confusion. Then she slumped against him once more, as though unable to bear the things he needed to tell her. With a ragged sigh she lowered her head, till the top of her silken hair brushed against the base of his neck. She stroked his hand, running her smooth, pale fingertips down his long fingers. Her voice was choked with unshed tears. "Tell me about it, War Lance. Help me understand what it was like for your people."

"The Cheyenne, like our allies the Sioux, at first befriended the white men who came into our hunting grounds. But as the beginning trickle of the *vèho* turned into a great flood, we began to clash with them more and more often. We were unwilling to give up the lands we'd called our own for generations. And so we fought back. The whites claimed my people were dirty, treacherous, bloodthirsty savages, though it was always the *vèho* who first broke each treaty between us.

"Twenty years ago, a peaceful village of Cheyenne—men, women, and children—were massacred at Sand Creek, and no one, not even the Great Father Lincoln, objected. The next summer the big soldier chief Connor, who led his troops up the Powder River against the Sioux and Cheyenne, ordered his soldiers to refuse any offer of peace or surrender from us. The bluecoats were instructed to attack and kill every male Indian over twelve summers."

"Dear God," Suzette said as she stiffened in his arms.

"Four years after that," Lance continued in a harsh voice, "Long Hair Custer fought the Cheyenne at the Washita. Though he brought in many captives, there wasn't one male left alive over the age of ten. And at the Sappa seven years later, the big soldier chief Henely took no prisoners at all, not even the youngest child. The buffalo hunters with him pulled the babies out of their hiding places and clubbed them. Then they threw the bodies of the Cheyenne, dead and dying, upon their burning lodges."

She turned in his arms, gazing up at him in horror. "That can't be," she whispered in a hoarse croak. "Jordan was with Henely ten years ago. He went on that summer campaign after his leave was over."

"I'm telling you the truth, angel," Lance said, meeting her stricken eyes with sorrow. Even if he lost her now, he had to tell her what terrible atrocities his people had suffered from the U.S. Cavalry.

"Only seven short years ago," he persisted, "the Northern Cheyenne fled the reservation in Indian Territory far to the south, fighting their way across lands settled by white farmers, lined by telegraph wires and cut by the railroads' iron tracks, straight through the army that waited to trap them. All that my people wanted was to return to their own country here beside the Tongue River, as they had been promised they could do by the soldier chiefs. Two of my brothers died on that bloody journey. Blue Crane Flying's little sisters were hacked to death in the snow at Fort Robinson and their bodies mutilated. This time the cattlemen and traders joined the soldiers, tracking down and shooting the wounded. Even the children were stripped and scalped."

At last, at last, the tears came. Long, heartbroken sobs. Suzette knew she was crying for the helpless children, the murdered mothers, and the brave fathers who had died trying to protect their families and their age-old way of life. She was crying for the dead soldiers, who had been led into battle by glory-seeking officers to carry out a callous government's brutal policy that would settle for nothing less than the extinction of an entire people. But most of all, she was crying for herself. For all the time she'd wasted grieving for a man who had never existed. For the false image of a dashing, blue-eyed cavalry officer, who had sweet-talked his way into her heart, where she'd enshrined him without question for nine long years. For the caustic feelings of anger and hatred she had turned against the Indian people, blaming them for the loss of her beloved, when the fault lay with her own kind.

War Lance rocked her gently in his arms, surrounding her with his unyielding strength and total acceptance. Eventually her sobs eased. She wiped her eyes with the palms of her hands and looked up to meet his tender gaze. When she was finally able to speak again, her throat was constricted with pain and sorrow. "I ... I thought Jordan—with his handsome face and his perfect manners—was the most wonderful man I'd ever met. He was my ideal of a true gentleman and officer. And all this time, I've been grieving for an elegant ... refined ... butcher."

"Shh," he whispered, pressing his lips to her temple. "It's over now, angel. It's all over."

"My sister tried ... tried to tell me. She said I was the one who should ask for forgiveness. Not ... not your people. Paulie told me I had turned a soldier, paid to kill and maim and slaughter, into a golden idol. I only pray to God that he didn't murder innocent women and children. But I'll never really know."

"I think the Wise One Above brought us both here today for a reason," he said gruffly.

Suzette sat up in his arms and cupped his face in her hands. Tears rolled unheeded down her cheeks. "Can you forgive me, War Lance? Can you ever forgive me?"

"Ahh, my beautiful angel," he murmured, "let us forgive each other."

He enclosed her in his strong arms and pulled her back with him, until they were lying side by side in the grass. His lips sought hers, and she offered them gladly, sharing the salty taste of her tears. He probed her mouth hungrily with his warm tongue, stroking her and filling her with a sweet, sensual longing.

Clinging to him, she returned his kiss. She threaded her fingers through his straight black hair, touching the silver disks and the downy feathers fastened at the base of his scalp lock. Then she pulled away with a long, drawn-out sigh of delight to scatter adoring kisses over his high forehead, his raven brows, his thickly lashed lids, his high-boned bronze cheeks, his slightly hooked nose, his strong, angular jaw.

"I take it I'm forgiven?" she said with a tremulous laugh. She leaned her elbow on his broad chest, supported her head on her hand, and gazed down at him with a trembling smile.

He looked up at her with unutterable tenderness. He stroked her cheek with one rough fingertip, then placed it on her lips to keep her from saying more.

"Voice of my heart," he whispered huskily, his eyes shining with an unspoken devotion, "I could no more withhold my forgiveness from you than I could withhold my very self."

Without a shadow of a doubt, Suzette knew that he would never, no matter what the provocation, no matter what the circumstances, hurt her or any other weaker person.

Lance looked into her violet eyes, swollen now from crying, and read in them the total trust and acceptance he had yearned for, for so long. Released from its bonds of bitterness and distrust, his spirit soared within him like an eagle taking wing. She had accepted him on faith alone. Gathering her in his arms, he pulled her down and kissed her with all the love he could never reveal. He longed to tell her how much he adored her, just as he wanted to share his true identity. But that could never be. The greatest gift he could give her was to set her free.

Ruthlessly he slammed the door shut on the voice within that pleaded for a chance to spend the rest of his life with her, regardless of the consequences. He ignored the longings of a tortured soul that cried out for a companion to share his sorrows and joys. He loved her more than his own self, and the knowledge that she loved him in return would give him the courage to return to England alone. His heart ached at the deception he was forced to play, yet he had to continue to keep his secret from her—for her own sake.

Chapter 18

I t was the middle of October, and the weekend of Fort Custer's grand ball had arrived. It was also time, once again, for the bimonthly beef issue on the Tongue River Reservation. Standing beside the high wheel of Jacob and Anna's old-fashioned calash buggy, Suzette watched the steers being herded into the huge open meadow that lay between the edge of the Crow Reservation and Rose-bud Creek. The Grabers were to accompany her to the fort.

Although they couldn't attend the dance, since their religious beliefs proscribed it, the Mennonite couple were happy to accept the invitation of Colonel and Mrs. Hatch to come for a visit. Anna, who hadn't left Lame Deer since they'd arrived the first week of September, had plans to shop at the post's general store, armed with a long list of such exotic items as needles, pins, and yards of calico curtain material, as well as the more basic necessities, including hundred-pound sacks of flour, sugar, and rice, huge tins of Arbuckle coffee, thick sides of bacon, and canned goods by the case. Not to be distracted by the mundane requirements of everyday life, Jacob had declared that the post bakery, known for miles around for its mouth-watering cinnamon rolls and raisin bread, was the first stop on his list.

On the other side of the creek, nearly hidden by the tall stands of cottonwoods, alders, and birches, as well as the thick growth of wild rose and berry bushes that lined the bank, Suzette could see the tops of the cone-shaped lodges of Bear Scalp's camp, where she and the Grabers had spent the previous night. The three of them would be leaving soon for the fort, but the excitement of the beef issue was too heady to miss entirely. Many of the Cheyenne had come from nearby camps to watch the arrival of the cattle.

"Did they drive these longhorns down from Miles City again this time?" she asked Jacob, who'd just come up to the buggy to stand beside her. He was dressed for visiting in his best black suit, neatly brushed and pressed, with a matching bow tie peeking out from under the tips of the high stiff collar on his spotless, heavily starched white shirt.

From his shorter stature five inches below her, he looked up to meet her curious gaze, his bright eyes twinkling. "These cowboys came all the way from Billings with this herd, Dr. Fräulein," he said. "The government contracts the beef from the neighboring ranchers, or whoever makes the lowest bid. They'll hold the cattle here for a day, just like before, and then take them on over to the agency's ration station on Muddy Creek tomorrow."

Anna joined them, smiling broadly. Beneath her black bonnet, her blue eyes were tearing in the brisk autumn breeze, and her dimpled cheeks shone like polished apples. She, too, wore her Sunday best. Her severe black dress was cut with full, gathered sleeves; there was even a dollop of ivory lace pinned under her tightly buttoned collar to fan out across the top of her ample bosom.

"*Ja, Liebchen,*" she added cheerfully, "this is the best way to provide these people with fresh meat. On the reservation down in Indian Territory, supplying decent food was always the worst problem for the conscientious Quaker agent."

"And it's no wonder, Mama," Jacob said. He stroked the tips of his fingers across the edge of his neatly trimmed beard in thoughtful contemplation. "For centuries the Indians lived by the fruits of their hunting. All their customs of survival centered around the buffalo chase. Now the buffalo are gone, but the traditions surrounding it are deeply ingrained and hard, if not impossible, to change."

"Ach, du lieber, you would have been revolted by the government allotments we saw arrive at the Southern Cheyenne reservation, Dr. Fräulein." Anna clucked her tongue in dismay at the memory. "Stale army biscuits, wormy salt pork, moldy hardtack. Our stomachs would revolt at the sickening mess, let alone a people who'd grown up on a diet of fresh game. The Northern Cheyenne became ill on the putrid rations and died by the hundreds in Indian Territory. It's no wonder they fled the Oklahoma lands and fought their way back to their homeland."

The calls and whistles of the dusty trail drivers could be heard above the bellowing cattle. Dressed in vests and plaid shirts, with leather chaps over indigo Levis, wide-brimmed hats, bright bandannas, square-toed, high-heeled boots, and enormous, jangling spurs, the cowboys drove the herd into the wide pasture, where riders would hold the animals in close formation until the next morning. Across the grassy field, Horace Corby and his gangly clerk, Obadiah Nash, sat in the agent's buckboard, scrutinizing the scene. The noise of the grumbling bellows and the pounding hoofs was continuous. Suzette wondered how the cowhands, or the Indians in the nearby village for that matter, would get any sleep at all that night. She didn't hear War Lance riding up to Jacob's buggy until he was almost beside them.

It had been three days since he'd escorted her to the valley of the Little Big Horn; she'd spent the last two of them at her cabin with the Grabers. Her waking hours had been filled to the brim, for on both days several Indians and a few of the agency staff had presented themselves as patients. In addition, she'd helped Anna with the household chores of washing, ironing, making bread, milking, and churning butter. It was the empty hours of darkness that had seemed to stretch endlessly. Each night she dreamed War Lance came to her. Each morning she woke up cold and alone on the feather mattress of her brass bed.

She looked up to meet his dark eyes and felt her cheeks grow warm as a poignant, irresistible longing to be held in his strong arms knifed through her. He was magnificent, sitting astride his great red stallion and framed by the limitless backdrop of cloudy Montana sky. The collar of his flannel shirt lay open against the denim jacket that stretched snugly across his broad shoulders. Worn Levis hugged his corded thighs. Moccasins and the shell-core collar proudly proclaimed his heritage, as did the feathered ornament in his ebony hair.

"I thought you would have been gone by now, *náevehoka*," he said briefly, then turned to watch the rest of the herd being driven in.

Her heart fell at his wintry detachment. He hadn't even returned her smile. Despite the intimate moments they'd shared together, his aloof, indifferent manner was the same as before. Whenever there were other whites nearby, he reverted to his most stoical cardboard-Indian demeanor. Even last night, when she and the Grabers had eaten their meals with his family and slept in Blue Crane Flying's lodge, he'd been distant and remote. He'd slipped away to stay in the shelter of the unmarried braves without even saying a private word to her.

She answered cheerfully, speaking as he did in Cheyenne, but with all the forced bravado she could muster. "Since I'm going to miss most of the excitement in the next two days, I wanted to at least see the cattle being brought in before I left for Fort Custer."

He swung his frosty gaze back to her. Silently his eyes swept over the pert feathers that trimmed her small-brimmed black hat, down past the hem of her forest green traveling dress to the tips of her black kid buttoned boots. Since she was riding in the dubious luxury of the

Grabers' old four-wheeler, she'd exchanged her jacket and trousers for a tunic of grenadine wool and a pleated skirt of cashmere. In her small trunk, squeezed between Anna's carpetbag and her own black leather medical case behind the wagon seat, she'd packed an exquisite ball gown of pale blue surah, trimmed with matching tulle lace and satin ribbons.

His glance flickered over the calfskin-covered traveling trunk. When he met her gaze again, the understanding in his shrewd eyes assured her that he knew she had packed her finest, most flattering gown for the ball. The image of the two handsome cavalry officers anxiously waiting to dance with her at Fort Custer rose up between them. She longed to tell War Lance that it was only her female vanity that had made her bring her loveliest gown; that the men themselves meant nothing to her. She would have much preferred to stay at the Indian camp and share in any dances there might be with him. The thought of being wrapped in a blanket beside War Lance was far more tantalizing than waltzing with either of the two dandies at the fort. But the plans had been made and the invitations accepted over two weeks ago. It wouldn't be right to disappoint everyone: the Grabers, Colonel and Hattie Hatch, or all the other new friends she'd made at the fort and who were expecting her.

Jacob chuckled, unaware of the tension. He, too, spoke in War Lance's tongue. "The real fun will come tomorrow when the cowboys run those steer into the corral over on Muddy Creek."

Suzette agreed with Jacob. There'd be an almighty hoopla the next day. Twice before, she'd seen the way the steers were loaded, two and three at a time, into a small pen. From inside a little house above the wooden chute, a pompous Obadiah Nash would call out an Indian name in his high, piercing voice, and if a Cheyenne responded and was identified, the steers due his family were driven into the chute. The clerk would make the necessary marks in his accounts book with his thin, nervous fingers and then holler for the cowboys to release the cattle. When the gate swung wide and the frightened steers ran out into the open, there was a group of warriors with repeating rifles all ready for them. Some of the braves were stripped to breechcloths and moccasins and decorated with war paint. Their elated whoops filled the air and the panicked steers took off at a gallop. After them raced the small band of Indians, who brought the cattle down one by one after a heart-pounding chase of several miles.

"Why don't they just butcher the cattle right there in the corral, or build a slaughterhouse?" Suzette asked with a puzzled frown. "Why ride after them in the first place?"

War Lance Striking looked down at her with an enigmatic smile. "For generations, *náevehoka*, my people have ridden after the buffalo. We believe that the meat is no good unless the animal has run many miles at great speed. So it is not until the blood of the white man's buffalo has been heated that we shoot it."

"I'm sure it's no stranger than some of our customs surrounding food and eating," Jacob said with a hearty laugh. He straightened his slouch hat on his gray head and turned to Anna. "We'd best be going, Mama."

"*Ja*, Papa, time to go," the plump hausfrau agreed. "I'm looking forward to visiting with all the ladies at the fort."

Jacob helped his wife up into the high spring vehicle and then turned to Suzette. "Up you go, Dr. Fräulein. We want to get there in plenty of time for you tp put on that fancy dress of yours before the party starts."

Taking his hand, Suzette bent her head to miss the buggy's black canvas top and hopped up beside Anna on the wide, padded seat. The day was chilly, and both women immediately placed tartan shawls around their shoulders.

"You should hurry," War Lance said to the little missionary, "or you won't get to the fort before the rain starts."

Jacob looked at the darkening sky above the western horizon. "We'll make it," he said with confidence. "This old team doesn't look like much, but Blaze and Billy will get us there, all right."

At his words of inordinate pride, Suzette looked down at the rumps of the mismatched pair and tried to keep from smiling. Blaze was a heavy chestnut roan with a patch of white on his forehead; Billy was a smaller, rawboned sorrel. But she'd learned during the trip out to Bear Scalp's camp with the Grabers that, though poorly matched in size and appearance, the two horses pulled together like a set of perfectly matched bays.

War Lance was scowling as he took in the dilapidated old buggy and the two unsightly nags. "I should be going with you," he stated in a voice taut with concern. He shifted his position on the saddle pad of antelope hair and looked out over the herd, as though torn by indecision.

"We'll be just fine," Jacob said. "Those two young officers who brought the invitations for Mama and me will be coming up the road from Fort Custer to meet us. They've promised to escort us safely to the post, so we won't be going that far alone. There's no sense in taking up your time. You stay here and enjoy tomorrow's fun."

"I will see you in two days then," War Lance said with dispassion, as though speaking to all three of them. But his gaze was on Suzette. For the span of a heartbeat, his eyes revealed just how worried and unhappy he was to see her go. Then the shuttered expression returned, and before the buggy had even started to move, he was riding off toward the milling herd of cattle.

The rain came before twilight, accompanied by thunder and lightning. The steers ambled nervously about, bawling in fright, while the night herders rode around the edge of the shifting, jostling mass, singing softly and trying desperately to keep them calm. The cowboys, in voluminous yellow slickers, fretted over the weather, cursing the storm—but quietly, so as not to disturb their restless charges.

In the waning light, Lance watched from the cover of the wild rose bushes that lined the bank of the Rosebud. His vigil was rewarded much sooner than he'd expected. Three riders came in from the north, skirting the Indian camp on the east side of the creek by a wide margin. He didn't need the crackling streak of lightning that lit up the night sky to recognize them: Troxel, Kraus, and Bouten. He'd have known Rumsey's slimy trio anywhere.

The cowboys from Billings had built a rough lean-to out of birch limbs and brush at the edge of the open meadow, where the ramrod and several hands were crouched over a small fire. Rumsey's three men pulled up in front of the shelter, and the tall, lanky foreman in charge of the herd rose and came out to meet them. After shaking hands, Troxel reached beneath his slicker and pulled out a paper. The foreman took it over to the fire, out of the pouring rain, and studied it briefly. Then he nodded his head and issued orders to his men nearby. In no time, Rumsey's trio and a few of the Billings cowboys had separated about twenty head of cattle from the herd. With a satisfied wave of his hand to the ramrod, Troxel and his cronies drove the batch of steers out of the pasture.

Lance had no need to follow them. He knew they'd be taking the bunch to join the large, mixed herd of Holsteins and Texas longhorns he'd found the day he'd gone with Suzette to Rumsey's ranch. By tomorrow afternoon, the cattle from Billings would be wearing the LR brand. If his hunch was right, they'd be driven up to Miles City in less than a month and sold at the railroad stockyards there. The profit would be neatly split between Lame Deer's agent and the neighboring rancher. Sales from twenty to thirty head, two times a month, year in and year out, would amount to a nice, steady little income. But how Corby covered up the number of missing cattle, bought and paid for by the U.S. government as part of the Cheyenne's rations, was something he hadn't figured out yet.

Booms of thunder reverberated in the sky, followed by slashes of lightning. The restive cattle rose and pawed the ground. Lance tipped his head back in the pelting rain and gave a long, piercing wolf howl. Across the meadow, Bear Scalp, hearing his brother's signal, joined him. Suddenly the stormy night was filled with the hair-raising sound of the hunting calls of a pack of hungry wolves. Every steer was on its feet. The noise of their frightened bawling, and the hollow clattering of their long horns as they bumped into one another, competed with the shrill, ululating barks of the wild predators. One more explosion of thunder and lightning, and the steers bolted after the small bunch that Rumsey's hired hands were driving toward the northeast.

"Stampede!" an outrider hollered, and the cowboys raced after the thundering herd in a futile attempt to turn them. It was hopeless. The cattle spread out across the grasslands like a giant, moving fan, scattering in all directions and racing through the ravines and coulees as though chased by a ghost herd at their heels.

Lance grinned to himself as he watched them go. It would take days for all of the cattle to be rounded up.

By morning the rain had stopped, and the Cheyenne awoke to wonderful news. If they wanted their bimonthly ration of beef, they would have to scour the wet, rolling hills of the reservation to find the stampeded cattle. The opportunity to put on their strong medicine paint, grab their rifles, and mount their fleetest horses revived in them the ancient patterns of the hunt. The thrill of the buffalo chase, even if it was after the white man's puny buffalo, heated their blood. They hadn't had this much excitement since a war party of Piegans had sneaked onto the reservation and tried to make off with a small herd of horses five months before. They'd chased the trespassers down, killed some of them, and brought three scalps into camp for a victory dance. Though the cattle hunt would not end in fresh scalps, or be nearly as much fun as horse stealing, there might be a chance for some heroic deeds as they used all the old buffalo-hunting skills to scout for the lost game and organize the attack. And in the end there would be fresh meat, shot by the warriors, and skinned and dressed on the open prairie by the women in the time-honored way of their ancestors. All across the Tongue River Reservation that day could be heard the whooping and shouting of hunting parties as they took off in quest of the lost herd.

"Good Lord a'mighty," Obadiah Nash said under his breath, his Adam's apple bobbing up and down as he swallowed nervously. He gazed out over the grasslands and chewed his gum with a vengeance. "Sorta makes the hair on the back of my neck stand on end."

Horace Corby wiped his bald head with a grimy bandanna and looked over at his employee with a ferocious scowl. "It should, dammit," he snarled, jamming his oversize slouch hat back on. "When these filthy heathens get their blood up, it's a short step from shooting and butchering a steer to God only knows what."

The two white men sat in the agent's buckboard and watched with dread as the hunting parties scattered out across the plains. Bear Scalp on his showy Appaloosa, and his brother, War Lance Striking, on the big red stallion, were each leading a group of warriors. Dressed in breechcloths and moccasins, most of the Indians were bare-chested and bare-legged even on that cloudy October day. They were smeared with ghastly streaks of bright war paint. Wearing quilled collars, beaded necklaces, brass armlets and bracelets, they waved their rifles above their heads in wild exhilaration. Feathers crowned their scalp locks, and their long black braids, tied with beaver and otter skin, flapped behind them in the wind. One gray-haired old man chief had donned his war bonnet, and even from horseback, its long tails nearly reached the ground.

"I don't need an uprising on my hands," Corby continued sourly. "Sure as hell they'll shoot some of Rumsey's cattle in the bargain. Never known a buck yet to ask questions about ownership when he's out hunting fresh meat. Next thing you know, they'll get so all fired up, they'll try sneaking over to the Crow camps and raiding horses."

"Yeah, and if they butcher any of the ranchers' cows, our white neighbors are going to be madder'n blue blazes," Obadiah said consolingly. He knew from past experience to agree with his cantankerous boss, especially when he was in such a foul mood. "I ain't never seen an Injun that could pass up the chance to run off with a horse. Sorta looks on it as a moral obligation."

Corby glowered at his clerk in disgust. "Sometimes, Nash," he said with biting sarcasm, "your idiocy amazes me."

Obadiah hunched his shoulders and ignored the nasty remark. Miserable with a head cold, he blew his nose loudly on a handkerchief. "What'r ya goin' ta do now, boss?"

"Do?" Corby exclaimed as he cracked his whip over his team. "What *can* I do, you imbecile, except ride around out here in this godforsaken wilderness for the next few days and try to keep things from going to hell in a hand basket?"

That Sunday evening, Suzette and the Grabers drove into the Lame Deer agency well after dark. Tired and sore from bouncing about on the antiquated buggy's high seat, she felt a surge of relief as Jacob pulled the team into the muddy compound and drew up in front of their home. Together they unloaded the small amount of luggage they'd taken with them and carried it inside. Then, while Jacob drove the carriage over to the stable and un-hitched the horses, Anna and Suzette said a tired good night in the covered dogtrot and retired to their own set of rooms on opposite ends of the log dwelling.

Suzette crossed the plank floor of her darkened office, entered her bedroom, and, with a sigh of pleasure, set down her small trunk and medical case beside the door. She lit the kerosene lantern that sat on her bureau. Glancing in the mirror, she removed her feathered black hat and withdrew the pins from her hair. With a shake of her head, she let the tangled curls fall loosely about her shoulders. Humming the refrain of a popular waltz, she opened the traveling trunk, withdrew the blue ball gown, decorated with lace and ribbons, and draped it across the top railing of her bed's brass footboard. Then she walked to the westerly window that faced the creek and drew back the chintz curtains. Absently she looked out at the darkened landscape, deep in thought.

After a pleasant visit at the fort for the two missionaries, and a delightful ball for Suzette, the three had spent the next night back at Bear Scalp's camp, where Jacob had planned to give an early morning service for any Indians interested in the white man's religion. But no one, man, woman, or child, had been the least bit intrigued by the Mennonite service that Sunday morning. The cattle chase continued, and the hunting parties were still busy scouring the hillsides. The women butchered the beef right out on the open prairie. Tall drying poles stood beside every lodge in the camp, with strips of fresh meat being jerked over low-burning fires. Green hides were staked out on the dry grass, and several older women fleshed the skins with scrapers. But Suzette hadn't caught a glimpse of War Lance all day. When Prairie Grass Woman invited the missionaries and the white medicine doctor to stay for a feast that evening, all three declined, anxious to get back to their own cabin.

The agency itself was peaceful now, after all the commotion. So quiet, she could hear Jacob go into the Grabers' rooms and close the door. She leaned an elbow on the windowsill and rested her chin in her hand, absorbed in her pensive thoughts. She'd returned from Fort Custer more worried than ever about her dwindling medical supplies. It was too soon to expect an answer to the letter she'd written to Pauline three weeks ago. Somehow, though, she'd hoped for a miracle. While at the fort, she'd spoken to Dr. Gilbreath about the problem once again. The little Irishman had been sympathetic, but he was in no better position to help her now than before. For the second time, he offered to write to the commissioner of Indian Affairs, but she insisted that he wait. She had no desire to upset Horace Corby. It was possible the irascible agent would make good his threat to fire her if he learned Michael Gilbreath had written to Washington at her instigation. Being forced to leave Lame Deer was the last thing she wanted to happen.

She straightened with a sudden idea. As she and the Grabers had driven into the agency compound, she'd noticed a light in Corby's office, though she'd barely paid any attention to it at the time. No doubt he and Obadiah were working late in a frantic attempt to catch up on the paperwork that would have been set aside during the hubbub of the cattle stampede and the ensuing hunt. She decided to go and talk to the agent right then. If she waited until morning to plead her case, she'd never be able to sleep. Why not catch him when he wasn't expecting her? He wouldn't have all his excuses ready about skimpy budgets and lack of funds.

With her lips tightly pursed in unhappy expectation of the agent's nasty welcome, she picked up the lantern, grabbed the plaid shawl she'd thrown on her bed, and quietly left the cabin, careful not to disturb the sleeping Grabers. She hurried across the rain-soaked quadrangle and found the door to the agency headquarters unlocked. With a smile of satisfaction, she entered. To her surprise, there wasn't a sign of Obadiah, though his desk was littered with stacks of papers. She quickly crossed the vacant outer office. Not wanting to give Corby the opportunity to avoid her, she flung open his office door without knocking and stepped inside. She lifted the ruby lamp, flooding the room with a soft light.

But it wasn't Horace Corby behind his big oak desk. It was an Indian brave, large and frightening, complete with war paint and feathers. The Cheyenne stood up straight as she entered, and his hand flew to the hunting knife at his side. He'd been rummaging through the agent's drawers, clearly searching for something. And he'd been so involved in his task, she'd managed to catch him by surprise.

His savage ferocity left her breathless. He was nearly naked, dressed only in breechcloth and moccasins, with the primitive collar around his neck, and copper armlets on each bulging bicep. Streaks of black, white, and scarlet paint zigzagged in horrible patterns across the sharp features of his face and over the muscles of his bare chest. In the rosy lantern light, his black eyes glittered.

Frozen in terror, she stood in the office doorway and wondered if she could possibly reach the cabin's outer door before he caught her. She took one small, cautious step backward, ready to hurl the lantern at him, if necessary.

"Close the door, angel, and put out the light," the tall warrior said with a grin of irony.

Chapter 19

At the sound of the familiar voice, her heart jerked like a bell on an invisible tether, banging back and forth against her ribs in painful reverberations. "War Lance!" she gasped, and slammed the door shut behind her.

But she didn't turn out the kerosene lamp. Instead, she raised its ruby shade even higher to bathe the small office in a soft glow. She walked into the center of the room and looked about, half expecting to find either the baldheaded agent or his officious clerk there with War Lance Striking.

"What are you doing in here alone?" she asked in confusion.

He casually pushed the center drawer of Horace Corby's cluttered desk shut. Picking up the small lamp he'd placed on the floor beside him, he blew out the flame and returned it to its normal spot amidst the stacks of papers on the desktop. Then he walked around the battered oak desk to stand in front of her. As he moved, the sinewy muscles of his bronzed thighs and calves extended and flexed with the grace of a mountain cat, and Suzette found herself staring in fascination at his near naked, marvelously painted body, with all its primitive accoutrements of feathers, beads, shells, and hammered metal. Goodness gracious. Here, indeed, was the virile, full-blooded male of the species in all his formidable glory.

"Lower your voice, *náevehoka*," he said with maddening nonchalance, as though they were neighbors who'd met by chance on a street corner and stopped to exchange pleasantries. Below the heathen slashes of red, white, and black on his high cheekbones, a delighted smile played about the corners of his mouth as he took in the disheveled curls that spread over the shoulders of her rumpled green traveling dress.

"I'm glad you're back safely," he continued. "Bear Scalp told me this morning that you and the missionaries had spent the night at his woman's lodge. When we have more time, you must tell me all about dancing with the little soldier chiefs." He raised one hand as though to caution her. "But at the moment you must put out the light and speak softly. Otherwise, I'll have more uninvited guests. And although I'm always happy to see you, Little Red Fox, right now I'd rather not have anyone else interrupting me."

"What are you doing in here?" she repeated, though she followed his example and spoke in a quieter tone.

He raised his raven eyebrows in teasing mockery. "That must be obvious. What does it look like I'm doing?"

She refused to rise to the bait. "I don't know," she snapped. "Suppose you tell me."

"You caught me, angel," he said, leaning one hip against the front of the desk and folding his arms across his painted chest. "I was looking for the agent's little green pieces of paper."

"You were stealing money? I don't believe it!"

He met her incredulous gaze with infuriating calm. "I'm afraid so, beautiful eyes. Since Major Hairless Head and his foolish clerk were out chasing after the hunting parties, trying to keep all of us Indians from going back to the good old ways of scalping any whites who dared to trespass on our lands, I decided it was the right time to help myself to whatever I could find of the agent's government dollars. Now, would you put out that light? If someone finds us in here, they'll hang me for stealing, even though I haven't taken anything—yet."

His words were preposterous. The whole idea went against everything she knew and believed about him. He was totally incapable of such underhanded behavior. Besides, his pilfering money didn't even make sense. He had no understanding of the white man's currency or its value.

"No, I'm not putting out this lamp, War Lance Striking," she declared, raising her voice again, this time to an even louder volume, "until you give me a better explanation. I don't believe you were trying to steal money. So until you tell me the truth about why you were going through Horace Corby's desk, I'm going to stay here talking as loudly as I wish. With the light on."

Lance looked at the gorgeous redhead and scowled in frustration. Her unexpected arrival couldn't have been more ill timed. If he revealed his true identity, he might be placing her in great danger. But if they were discovered in Corby's office, his entire mission would be in jeopardy. "We can talk about it later, angel."

"No, we'll talk about it right now."

Lance moved closer, and she glared a warning. If he grabbed her, she'd scream her head off. And if he told her the truth, she'd probably still shriek like a banshee—or never speak to him again. That thought left an icy lump in the region of his heart. He wasn't certain she'd ever forgive him for his deception. But he was left with little choice. He had to get her out of the building at once.

"Angel," he coaxed.

"Are you going to tell me what's going on?" she demanded, refusing to budge an inch.

She stood stalwartly in front of him, holding up the ruby streetlight shade for a closer inspection of his person, while she interrogated him with the righteous tenacity of a cheated landlady who's just found her shiftless tenant about to bolt without paying the rent. The determination in her violet eyes told him that she'd never believe his explanation of trying to take money from the agent's desk. She thought she knew him too well. In reality, she didn't know him at all.

"All right," he said, realizing he had no choice but to reveal the truth. He leaned back against the desk, braced his palms on the edge of it, and gave a long, ragged sigh of concession. "I'll tell you. But not here. The longer we stay in this room, the more chance someone will notice the light and come checking. We can finish this talk in your cabin."

She tilted her stubborn little chin toward the ceiling. "Very well," she replied stiffly. "But I want the whole truth. And I'm not leaving this room until you promise to tell it."

"I promise." He straightened, moved to her side, and blew out the light. Then, clasping her elbow firmly in his hand, he led her to the door.

Apparently willing to accept his word, Suzette nodded her agreement and allowed him to guide her through the dark outer room to the front entrance of the agency headquarters.

"You go on ahead," he said quietly in her ear, "and I'll join you in your cabin. Just open the back window for me."

In less than five minutes, War Lance silently slipped through the open window of Suzette's bedroom, closed it, and pulled the curtains shut. Standing beside her brass bed, she watched him in the cozy glow of the lamp she'd relit and placed once again on her bureau. He padded softly across the floor in his moccasins and closed the door of her bedchamber, after first glancing out at her empty, darkened office. As he turned, his eyes lit on the opened traveling trunk sitting just inside the doorway, then moved to the pale blue ball gown she'd thrown across the footboard's top rail.

"Did you have fun at the dance?" he asked in an annoyed tone, as though she were the one caught behaving in an improper manner. His twisted half smile was forced and bitter. He stepped over to the bed and picked up the eighteen yards of twilled silk, lace, and ribbons.

"That's hardly important at the moment," she scolded, trying to keep her voice low despite her growing irritation. "Now, what were you doing in Mr. Corby's private office?"

His long fingers stroked the rich fabric absently. Then he tossed the gown across the shiny brass railing and stared at her, as though unsure how to begin. "I was looking for proof of cheating by Corby," he said at last. "The head chief of Indian Affairs sent me here to discover who killed two of his big-cat agents this past spring."

She frowned, trying to assimilate what he was telling her. "You mean you were released from a prison cell in Indian Territory and sent to Lame Deer to catch Horace Corby stealing government allotments?" she asked with disbelief.

He shook his head with a wry smile. "No, angel, I was never in prison. Nor was I ever on the Southern Cheyenne reservation. I came here from Washington. Before that, I worked for the Great Father across the ocean in the great village of London."

"No," she said with absolute certainty. "That's impossible. You couldn't. You can't even speak English."

"I'm afraid I can, sweetheart," he replied in her own language with the most refined, cultured British accent she'd ever heard. "And they tell me I speak it bloody well for a red man."

For long, heart-stopping seconds she stared at him. She couldn't have been more shocked if he'd suddenly and inexplicably conjured up a rabbit out of thin air like a carnival magician. Or floated off the floor on an India carpet in front of her very eyes like some exotic Hindu snake charmer.

"I don't believe this!" she gasped, still speaking in Cheyenne.

She walked blindly to the bed. Her legs started to give way beneath her, and she turned and sat down on its edge, transfixed and incredulous. He frowned and took a step nearer, and she knew from the stark anxiety in his black eyes that she must be deathly pale. She held up one trembling hand to ward him off. When he stopped a few paces away, she covered her face with her hands, while the world tilted crazily on its axis. Bits and pieces of their past conversations spun around in her mind, like a puzzle tossed to the floor and scattered about in wild disorder, without apparent rhyme or reason. It made no sense. Why would he keep such an incredible secret from her?

She looked up to find him watching her with profound concern. His scowling features distorted by the heathenish war paint, he waited tensely for her to realize the enormity of what he'd just confessed. Impulsively she sprang to her feet and darted past him to stand in front of the window, where she stared at the curtains with unseeing eyes. Then she turned and met his gaze again, hoping to make some rational sense out of the insanity of his sudden disclosure.

"All those times I tried to teach you my language," she said in a stunned voice, speaking to him in English at last. "You already knew how?"

"Yes."

"And everything I said in my own language, you understood?"

"Yes."

She walked over to grasp the tall post of the brass footboard, holding on to it like a lifeline in the midst of a hurricane. Her throat was constricted with tears. "I can't believe this. You're a Cheyenne. A full-blooded Cheyenne."

"I'm a half-breed, Suzette," he said softly in his flawless English. "When I was thirteen years old, I went with my white mother to live in England. I was educated there. I've been a member of the U.S. diplomatic corps for the last twelve years. While I was in Washington, D.C., on leave, I was asked to come out here to the Tongue River Reservation and investigate the swindling of money from my father's people. I hadn't seen my Cheyenne family in all those intervening years."

She looked blindly at the rough, chinked wall above her bed. Her lips trembled. "How could you do this to me?" she asked as she fought back the tears. Suddenly she felt used and violated and terribly angry. "To trick me like this? And . . . to . . . to . . . while all the time you were lying. Just plain lying."

He took a step nearer, and she moved quickly away, turning her back to him.

"I'm sorry, angel," he said, and the sound of his perfect, polished diction cut like a fine-bladed surgical knife. "I had no choice. I came here as a secret agent. Had I told you, you might have given it away, endangering your own life as well as others. I couldn't risk that. Even now you could be hurt if Corby finds out about the investigation and suspects that you are somehow involved."

Mortified, she refused to look at him. The memory of the poetry reading and the lesson in kissing rose before her. "I must have been quite a source of levity. I bet you laughed yourself sick every night when you went to bed. And all the while I was trying so hard to teach you my language. Good God, what a fool I've been."

Moving to stand directly behind her, he placed his hand on her shoulder in a misguided attempt to console her. She jerked away and turned to face him, furious at the sneaky, conniving trick he'd played.

"Just go now," she told him with icy contempt. All she wanted was to be left alone, so she could sob her heart out and tell herself how much she despised him.

"No," he said tersely, "not like this."

He captured her waist in a swift, easy movement. Pulling her to him, he slipped one hand to the small of her back and bent his head to kiss her lightly, coaxingly, on the temple. She started to jerk her face away from his lips, and he reached up and held her chin in his strong fingers. His calm voice was filled with implacable determination. "I'm not leaving until you understand my side of it. I never meant to hurt you, Suzette. Nor did I ever laugh at you."

His stern features softened as his gaze roved over her defiant expression and came to rest on her tightly clamped lips. He covered them with his open mouth, ignoring her muffled demand that he release her. She fought him, angry and hurt, and determined to lash back. But he continued the kiss, moving his tongue against her closed lips, while his relentless fingers held her face up to his. With a groan torn from deep in his throat, he released her chin to slide his hand to the nape of her neck, where he buried his fingers in her unruly hair. Cupping the back of her head in his wide palm, he maintained the unyielding pressure of his kiss while she pushed futilely against his bare chest with her splayed fingers. She could feel the merciless strength of his thighs and abdomen and the hard bulge of his male arousal through the plush cashmere pleats of her skirt.

They struggled breathlessly, matching the power of their obstinate wills, as he continued to pull her closer and she attempted to shove him away. But his physical strength made the end inevitable, and she finally ceased her part of the battle. The moment she abandoned the struggle, he broke the kiss to move his open mouth down her neck, tracing a hot path on her skin with his warm, moist tongue. One strong hand slid down to cup her buttocks and bring her even closer to his solid frame. Desire flared up within her as she felt him rub his hardened manhood enticingly against the juncture of her thighs. She forced herself not to respond, infuriated at the betrayal of her own body to his aggressively masculine seduction. But the satisfied light in his eyes when he lifted his head to meet her gaze told her he was aware of her unwilling reaction.

"Stop this," she whispered angrily. "If you think I'm going to forget about the way you tricked me, you're mistaken. I want you out of here. Right now. You're nothing but a fraud and a cheat."

But he continued his sensual onslaught, as though deaf to her contemptuous words. With one steely arm anchoring her securely against his lean hips, his searching fingers found the ten covered buttons that extended down the front of her long green tunic. He released them with slow, practiced deliberation. She tried vainly to hold the bodice front closed in her tight grasp, and an amused smile sprang to his lips at her childish tactics. Using both hands, he pried her fingers gently but insistently away and pushed the grenadine wool top of the traveling outfit open. Sliding it over her shoulders and down her arms and wrists, he allowed the tunic to drop at her feet.

"What are you doing?" she exclaimed as she bent and scooped up the top half of her dress. She held it in front of her embroidered white camisole in two tight fists.

"It's late, angel," he replied in a voice taut with strained patience. "I'm getting you ready for bed. I've had a long day, and you look pretty tired yourself." He snatched the green jacket from her grasp and tossed it toward the end of the bed, where it landed, neatly hooked on the post of the brass footboard.

"If you think I'll forget . . ." she repeated hoarsely.

His long fingers released the tiny buttons of her camisole and slid the lace straps over her bare shoulders to free her breasts to his sight. With a casual flick of his wrist, the undergarment joined her tunic at the foot of the bed. Then he slipped to one knee in front of her, grasped her hips in his hands, and brought her to him.

"I'm not asking you to forget what I did, Suzette," he murmured huskily. He traced his lips across the softness of her breast. "Only to forgive." His mouth found her nipple and he laved the rigid bud with his tongue.

The feel of him licking her, slow and seductive, rocked her with an inner explosion of need. She was suddenly breathless and off balance. Sparks of desire flashed, white and hot, inside her, as he flicked his tongue over the pink tip and tugged on it gently with his teeth.

She tried in vain to cling to her righteous anger. "What you're asking is . . ."

He moved to suckle her other breast, and despite her frantic intention to send him away, she moaned with pleasure. His hand slid up, to cup her breast and bring it closer to his mouth. Rivulets of paralyzing excitement spread through her body. Skillfully, expertly, rapaciously, he trapped her in the sensual currents of erotic hunger and unfulfilled need he built within her.

Flicking the pads of his thumbs back and forth across the swollen crests, he tipped his head back and looked up at her. His ebony eyes smoldered with passion. "I'm only asking that you try to understand my side of it, darling Suzette. I never meant to hurt you. I would sooner hurt myself."

She bent her head forward and released her held breath in an aching sigh of surrender. When she rested her hands on his broad shoulders, he reached down and removed her black kid boots, then slid his hands up under her cotton petticoat, following the outline of her stockinged legs with his searching fingers. Deftly he unbuttoned her muslin drawers and pulled them down over her ankles as she lifted one foot and then the other.

Grasping the hems of her skirt and petticoat together with both hands, he pulled them up to her hips as he rose to his feet. With the material gathered at her waist captured beneath his long fingers, he lifted her up and set her on the edge of the bed, and the yards of cotton and cashmere puffed out in soft billows around her bare hips and buttocks. The black silk of her stockings and garters made the naked flesh above them appear as white and fragile as fine china. He knelt between her legs, running his bronzed hands hungrily up over her calves and thighs and pushing back the folds of her skirts to reveal the curly russet triangle that covered her mound.

"Let me show you how sorry I am, sweetheart," he said, his velvety voice low and coaxing.

The sight of him kneeling in front of her, the corded muscles of his chest and arms slashed with war paint, and the white shell-core collar encircling his bronzed throat, brought a surge of wanton, carnal desire. She felt her doubt and hesitation being ruthlessly swept aside by the strength of his willpower alone.

He bent his head and tenderly kissed the soft skin on the inside of her thighs, and her heart thudded wildly. The sharpness of his chiseled features was heightened by the primitive adornments. Bright bars of paint slashed across his high cheekbones, and one line of black followed the bridge of his strong, slightly hooked nose.

"Wait, War Lance," she whispered breathlessly. "You're going too fast. We need to slow down so I can think about what you've told me."

"You can think about it in the morning," he said with sweet, honeyed seduction. He lifted one silk-stockinged leg, and then the other, over his powerful shoulders. She felt herself tip backward slightly and braced her palms against the quilted coverlet to keep her balance.

"Suzette, Suzette, Suzette," he crooned as he gently, expertly, opened the silken folds of her womanhood. "You're as beautiful as your name." He bent his head and stroked her with his tongue, while his callused fingers reached up to rub the sensitive tips of her breasts, already rosy and swollen from his suckling.

At his bold, knowledgeable touch, she felt her eyelids grow heavy. She slipped into a world of erotic pleasure beyond her wildest imagination. Unable to do anything but float on the tide of feelings that lifted and rocked her, she drifted deeper and deeper toward the impending whirlpool he was creating with such astonishing expertise. Languidly she lifted her lashes to see the top of his head bent over her, the downy white feathers and the hammered silver ornaments at the base of his scalp braid glistening against his black hair in the soft lamplight. His bare arms and shoulders were decorated with stripes of black and red and white. Polished copper bands encircled the bulging muscles of his upper arms. His bronzed hands were startlingly dark against the creamy skin of her breasts.

She rose and fell on the tide he created, her body and mind completely within his power. With each incredibly soft, gentle movement, he eased her into the swirling eddy, loosening the bonds of the outside world, setting her adrift with him, until there was only the two of them, as he sent her spiraling toward the brink of fulfillment.

With a deep sigh of mindless bliss, she leaned on her elbows and closed her eyes. Then, lying back on the bed, she allowed him to have his way with her, knowing that she could deny him nothing as he tugged and nudged and guided her over the cascading rapids and down, down, down—until she was drowning in a whirlpool of ecstasy. She called to him in a plaintive cry of abandoned surrender. As though from leagues away, she heard his throaty chuckle of delight at her honest, spontaneous response, and at last her lashes fluttered open as she found him leaning over her.

Lance had slipped off his breechcloth and moccasins, and his heavy shaft sprang from his loins, aching to be inside her sweet warmth. With quick, deft movements, he unbuttoned the skirt and petticoat that had been hiked up about her hips and pulled them down over her stockinged legs to be forgotten on the plank floor. He reached up to the head of the bed and yanked the coverlet down. The scent of violets wafted around them as he scooped her up in his arms and deposited her in the middle of the feather mattress. Her loose hair cascaded across the white pillowcase like living flames of molten copper. Gently lifting her knees, he positioned himself between her thighs.

She reached out and caressed him, and his starved

body tensed with the glorious pleasure of her silken touch. He was hot and turgid and hard. The sight of her tapering fingers stroking his engorged manhood drove him nearly mad with desire. Willing himself to slow down, he caught his breath and watched her guide his swollen shaft inside her.

"Suzette," he called softly as he buried himself in the moist, silken folds of her, feeling the warm, velvety flesh close around him. He braced his arms on either side of her head, and she looked up in wonder to meet his gaze.

"Hello, my love," she whispered, and his lonely heart skidded to a halt.

Her violet eyes were heavy-lidded and dreamy. A beautiful smile tugged at the corners of her luscious mouth. She explored his body with her small hands, running her graceful fingers across his chest and shoulders and upper arms. His muscles leapt in joyful anticipation of her shy, delicate touch. He nearly withdrew, only to plunge inside her, and then withdraw again. He watched the play of emotions on her love-softened features as the pleasure of his movements spread through her with each slow, measured entry and withdrawal.

"Darling angel," he teased, "say you'll forgive me."

She leaned up and met his open mouth with her lips and tongue, entering eagerly. He thrilled to the feel of her silken breasts brushing against his own hard chest. Bracing his forearms on the bed, he moved rhythmically, building to a feverish intensity once more as he guided her to a crescendo of sensual gratification. Her breath came ever faster, and she turned her head to gasp for air. He could feel her heart gallop to the increasing cadence he set with his body. He talked to her in Cheyenne, breathless phrases of sex, and she writhed with uncontrollable excitement beneath his driving, insistent strokes. Once again she surrendered to his complete control, allowing him to launch her into that swirling abyss of earthly delight. She held back nothing as she clung to him and moved her hips to the beat he set. With deep, rhythmic thrusts, he taught her his marvelous dance of eroticism.

And the long, slow culmination, beginning as a gentle ripple, built inside her, till the spasms of her climax clutched and pulled at his throbbing shaft. Her soft, female cry of fulfillment heightened his own pleasure threefold. His body jerked convulsively as he drove into her, and the throes of ecstasy reverberated through him again and again.

Tossed about on waves of carnal bliss, Suzette landed at last like an exhausted swimmer, thrown carelessly by the tide upon the smooth shore of spent emotions. War Lance lay on top of her, winded and drawing in huge drafts of air. Just when she thought she'd be crushed by his weight, he rolled to his side, taking her with him. But they were no longer joined, and exactly when he'd withdrawn, she wasn't certain, though she felt the warm, wet evidence of his semen on her thigh. This time she knew a sharp disappointment and realized, with an ache of longing, that she wanted to spend the rest of her life with him and bear his children.

She was in love with him. And she yearned for him to tell her that he felt the same.

He rose and poured water from the red-striped pitcher that sat on her bureau into its matching basin. Then, wetting the linen cloth beside it, he came back to the bed and tenderly cleansed her. Their eyes met, and she slid her trembling hand up his arm, praying he would tell her how much he cared.

"You look gorgeous in war paint and silk stockings, angel," he quipped, his eyes sparkling like jets in the lamplight. A bantering smile played about his mouth. "In fact, I don't think I've ever seen you look quite so adorable."

Surprised, she looked down to see that some of the greasepaint from his body had left smudges of red and black on her bare white breasts. He started to wipe it off with the wet cloth, but she caught his hand and shook her head.

"Leave it," she whispered huskily. "I'll only get more on me later."

He lifted one raven brow in wry amusement and tossed the washcloth neatly into the basin. It landed in the water with a soft splash. Then, with practiced efficiency, he slid her garters and stockings down her legs and dropped them over the side of the bed. Lying down beside her, he gathered her in his arms, and she pillowed her head on his shoulder. Together they sunk deep into the center of the feather mattress, and he pulled the coverlet up over them.

"I take it this means I'm forgiven," he murmured in her ear.

She turned her head and sharply nipped his flesh, and he chuckled deep in his chest. It was the sound of pure, unadulterated male satisfaction.

"Only if you tell me everything about yourself," she corrected with insouciance, quickly covering her dissatisfaction at his words. She'd hoped to hear a declaration of love. "I now realize how very little I know."

"What would you like to hear?"

"Let's begin with the name you use in the *vèho* world."

"Lance Harden," he said. He ran his large hand contentedly down the length of her side and rested it on her hip, then bent his head and nibbled on her earlobe. "What else?"

"Start with the day you were born and just keep going," she ordered as she snuggled up against him. She placed one hand on his broad chest, her fingertips grazing the scars of the Sun Dance above his dark nipples, and brushed her lips across the hollow of his collarbone.

"Yes, *náevehoka,*" he agreed with feigned submission.

Suzette listened in fascination as he told of his Cheyenne childhood and how, when his father died, his white mother had taken him back to her family in Virginia. He related his amazement the day the two of them had arrived in the great metropolis of London, and how he'd studied under private tutors at the home of his wealthy and influential great-uncle. She listened to his quiet, understated words and wondered what he'd left unsaid about his treatment as an Indian boy in his early teens at the hands of bigoted, ignorant white people.

When he finished the story with his appointment as chief political attaché of the U.S. legation in London, he bent his head and pressed a kiss on her forehead. "Satisfied?"

"Were you ever promised to a woman?" She tried to keep her tone casual and detached. Not once had he alluded to an involvement with a member of the opposite sex.

"No." He ran his fingers across her stomach to cup her breast, and lightly teased the pink tip till it became erect and firm once again.

She'd heard the sudden distance in his voice and realized that he was trying to distract her thoughts by his seductive caress, but she charged ahead recklessly anyway.

"You mean you never asked a woman to marry you?" she scoffed.

He smiled with self-deprecating irony and met her gaze. His response was brief, almost curt, his voice gruff. "I didn't say I never asked someone to marry me. I just said I'd never been engaged."

Incredulous, she leaned up on one elbow and propped her palm on his chest. "You asked a young woman to marry you and she refused? I don't believe it!"

He touched the tip of her nose with his forefinger and flashed her a wicked grin. "Thank you for the vote of confidence, angel, but it's the truth." Sliding his long fingers into the tousled hair at her nape, he pulled her face toward him and covered her astonished lips with his own.

But she wouldn't be distracted. She broke the kiss,

flung one arm across his wide chest, and nestled her head under his chin. "What was she like?"

"Who?" She could hear the laughter in his voice at her single-minded persistence.

"The girl you asked to marry you. Was she anything like me?"

"Not a bit."

She waited in silence for a further, perhaps flattering, explanation. When she realized that was all he intended to say on the matter, she sat up beside him. Staring down at the infuriating male with a scowl of displeasure, she spoke in a frigid tone. "I see."

"No, you don't." He pulled her into his arms and rolled over to pin her securely beneath him. At the soft chuckles of amusement at her expense, she glared up at him.

"I have never met anyone like you, Suzette," he told her with a devastating grin. "You are, without a doubt, the most unique, most strong-minded, most exasperating female I've ever encountered. I couldn't compare you to anyone, man or woman, I've ever known before. Does that answer your question?"

He didn't wait for her reply. Instead, he proceeded to show her with his hands and lips and tongue how very special he thought she was. With a sigh of contentment, Suzette allowed herself to be seduced for the second time that evening.

Chapter 20

~ ⤳⤲ ~

Lance looked down at the bewitching enchantress asleep in his embrace and felt the heartache of a love he could never reveal. It was almost dawn, and they'd spent the night in each other's arms. A night he would treasure for the rest of his life. He smoothed the coppery curls lovingly away from her face. Beneath the quilted coverlet, his restless fingers slid over the white satin globe of her breast and down one sleek hip. She was curled up against him, and in her dreams, she'd stirred, called his name, and drowsily twined one silken leg between his two long ones without ever opening her eyes.

He'd been awake all night. Looking at her. Touching her. He hadn't been able to sleep, any more than he'd been able to keep his hands from moving over her beautiful naked body. He wanted to burn the satiny feel of her into his memory. Into his unconscious being. Into his very soul.

The pained disillusion in her violet eyes had told him without words that she'd fully expected him to declare his love for her. A declaration that would have inevitably led to an exchange of promises, for he knew that she believed herself in love with him, as well. Heartsick, he'd withheld the words of devotion that sprang to his lips, knowing that, in denying her what she wanted to hear so badly, he was denying the simple truth.

He loved her.

More than he'd ever dreamed it was possible to love anyone.

And he, more than anyone else, knew how foolish it would be to even contemplate a lifelong relationship with Suzette. The bitter experiences of the past had schooled him well in the hopelessness of his love. From the insensible bigotry of strangers, to the unreasoning hatred of his maternal grandmother, to the tragic, useless death of the innocent young woman he'd courted and lost, the lessons of white prejudice had shaped and forged his deep sense of personal alienation. He was a man apart. And any woman who dared to spend her life with him would be set apart as well.

He should never have touched her. But, God forgive him, he hadn't been able to carry out what his intellect had commanded. Instead, he'd let his emotions overcome his common sense.

Her questions earlier that evening had brought back all the aching, miserable memories, and in the fleeting hours, while she peacefully slept, he had relived, once again, the tragedy that had haunted him for the past twelve years.

He'd been a brash young pup, scarcely finished with his university studies, when he met Cecily Bancroft. Only a few months had passed since he'd received, through the combined efforts of his grandfather, a well-known and politically powerful Virginia judge and his great-uncle, a highly respected and influential London barrister, his appointment as a member of the U.S. diplomatic corps. Robert Schenck, the American minister to the Court of St. James, had directed him to attend the birthday ball of the only daughter of the British secretary of the treasury as one of his first duties.

Just eighteen, the petite brunette debutante was dimpled and curvaceous, with a winsome smile that could ensnare the wariest of hearts. And looking into her sparkling brown eyes as he danced that first quadrille with her, Lance Harden had felt anything but cautious.

In the next few weeks, he saw her several times, for their paths continued to cross. Her father was an important figure in the British government; Lance, as part of the U.S. diplomatic team, was required to attend all official Court functions. He pursued Cecily with all the rash determination of a cocksure young swain, and at last she graciously allowed him to call on her at her parents' town home in Hanover Square.

They fell heedlessly, recklessly, in love, as only the inexperienced and innocent can do, so totally engrossed in their feelings for each other that they were oblivious to the scandalized gossip of a horrified British upper class. He'd even had the temerity to call upon her father. Sir Clarence Bancroft not only refused Lance's offer of marriage to his daughter, he barely refrained from having the servants toss the reckless suitor out on his backside.

The next day the legation's new attaché was called into Robert Schenck's private office and instructed, in no uncertain terms, by the red-faced and embarrassed American minister that he was never again to call at the Bancroft residence.

Willful, stubborn, and deeply in love, Lance managed to arrange a secret meeting with Cecily at the home of a mutual friend. When he urged his sweetheart to elope with him, she broke down and sobbed in his arms.

"I can't, Lance," she told him, her high, clear voice breaking in despair. "I'm not strong like you. Even if I could face the wrath and disappointment of my parents, I couldn't bear to see our children taunted and reviled."

He held her out in front of him to look into her tear-filled eyes. "What are you talking about?"

"Don't you understand?" she cried. "Mother and Father explained how any children we might have would be treated. They'd be completely ostracized. Cut by polite society. How could I bear to see my sons go friendless? My little daughters never invited to parties or balls? Never sought in marriage? I could bear to be treated that way, Lance. Really I could. But not my precious children."

With agonizing clarity, he realized that she was right. To the snobbish elite of London, he was—as a native of the North American plains—an exotic figure. A fine example of the noble savage educated. He spoke fluent English with a perfect British accent. He held a university degree, an honorable position at the U.S. legation, and came from a wealthy, prestigious family revered on both sides of the Atlantic. The bored, jaded, highborn married ladies graciously invited him into their salons. They danced with him, flirted with him, and discussed politics with him over a table sparkling with silver and crystal. Some even invited him into their beds. As a red man, there was only one thing he absolutely couldn't be allowed to do: marry one of their daughters.

In the end, he'd had no choice but to agree with Cecily. He might have taught sons to fight back, to earn the respect of their fellow man as he had, by being the fleetest, strongest, and best in every sport he tried. He'd won the fair treatment of his young colleagues at the university by doing just that. But innocent, sensitive little girls would never be able to handle the kind of backstabbing gossip that vicious society matrons and their spoiled daughters handed out.

And so he reluctantly acceded to the commands of her parents: He and Cecily would never see or talk with each other in private again.

Three evenings later, Lance attended a Court ball at St. James's Palace as the American minister's representative. Cecily was there with her mother, and he nodded to her briefly from across the dance floor. Trying to keep his unhappiness from interfering with his duties, he danced with the ladies as his diplomatic position required. Several married women flirted outrageously, and he did his best to remain charmingly unavailable. By the end of the night, his nerves were raw with the strain of pretense. Preparing to leave, he said a quiet good-bye to a small group of friends, turned, and met Cecily's dark brown eyes.

Deep blue shadows framed those tear-filled eyes, and her face was deathly white, as though drained of every drop of blood. She stood beside Lady Bancroft, watching Lance in abject misery. She opened her mouth to speak, then closed it again with a look of utter despair. A single, crystal tear slid from the dark lashes and rolled down her pale cheek. Then, without a word, she left the room with her mother.

Lance started to go after her, wanting to ease the stark pain he'd read in her eyes. But there was nothing he could say that would change the fact that they would never be allowed to marry. So he let her go without a word of hope or consolation.

It was the last time he'd seen her. Early the next morning a close friend came to his apartments to break the news. Cecily had gone obediently home from the ball and, while her parents slept soundly in their beds, quietly hanged herself. The Bancrofts' dutiful and compliant daughter, when faced with the decision of either disobeying their commands or accepting a future without the man she loved, had solved her unbearable dilemma by choosing neither. For the first time in his life, Lance tasted the bitter poison of self-hatred. He was certain that had he talked with her the night before—given her some tiny whisper of encouragement and hope—she would have had the courage to choose life over death.

He'd attended her funeral. No one would have dared to turn a representative of the U.S. legation away from the church or the grave site. Bereft, a stricken Clarence Bancroft met Lance's gaze over the flower-draped coffin, and the bewilderment and anguish in the older man's eyes was as deep as Lance's own.

Filled with guilt and self-reproach, Lance had, himself, barely managed to stay alive in the months that followed. He sought oblivion, night after night, by drowning himself in a bottle. Whole weeks were lost in a blurred haze of brandy and self-pity as he staggered through the brothels and gambling hells of London's stews. In waterfront taverns along the Thames that no sane man would enter, he courted knife fights and bare-knuckled brawls in the vain hope that someone would kill him. It was only by sheer luck or the intervention of angels that he hadn't maimed or murdered anyone during the first few months after Cecily's death.

Several married friends and their spouses tried again and again to comfort him in his grief, but he spurned their well-intentioned solace. One compassionate wife, who'd known Cecily since childhood, tried to tell him that the high-strung young woman had suffered periodically from deep, enervating bouts of melancholy. He refused to listen. He knew that he alone was to blame for Cecily's death. He should have realized that polite society would never allow a genteel white woman to marry an Indian half-breed, no matter what the level of his status or education or accomplishments.

The memory of Octavia Harden's words tortured him. His white grandmother had been right. It would have been better if he had never been born, or if his mother had drowned him at birth, than that he should ever have courted the gently reared beauty.

Eventually time dulled the pain, and Lance resumed his former habits of hard work, personal sacrifice, and dedication to duty at the legation. Yet even now, twelve years later, one thing was still absolutely certain: If she had never met him, Cecily Bancroft would be alive today.

Pushing the painful thoughts aside, Lance gazed down at the most exasperating creature he'd ever laid eyes on, sleeping peacefully in his arms. No one had ever moved him to such heights of emotion as this slender, obstinate, lovable, red-haired lady doctor. Since the day he'd met her, he hadn't known a moment's peace. Suzette's lighthearted flirtation with the two cavalry officers had angered him beyond words. He knew it was the fierce possessiveness of his nature that she had so thoughtlessly stirred up, with such passionate results. Nor had he ever felt such exuberant joy as he did with her. She brought out all the fun-loving playfulness and freedom of his Cheyenne childhood. And never, with any woman, had he known such a complete communion of selves. Their physical love had joined them together in a bond that united both their bodies and their souls. A doomed love that could never be.

Why had the Great Spirit Above allowed this to happen?

For Suzette's sake, Lance had to leave soon. He dared not allow their relationship to become known to the outside world, or she would be trapped between her feelings for him and the demands of white society. The castigations and shunning of her relatives and friends, perhaps even by her only sister whom she loved so dearly, would bring a suffering so deep, so painful, that, like Cecily, she would one day be tempted to take her own life.

The early morning light gradually suffused the room to reveal the scattered garments that had been hastily removed and tossed aside. The coming day's soft glow spread over the exquisite woman resting in his arms. Her head was pillowed on his shoulder, the rippling waves of flame-colored hair framing her delicate features. Her russet lashes lay against her creamy cheeks; her sensuous lips were slightly parted in sleep. Pulling her supple, nude body closer, he bent his head and softly kissed her. She murmured something unintelligible in Cheyenne as she snuggled up against him, and he smiled in tender delight.

"My violet-eyed sorceress," he breathed, "how in the world shall I ever leave you?"

When Suzette awoke in the morning, War Lance was gone. She drew the pillow he'd slept on to her and buried her face in its softness, breathing in the heady male scent of him. The white linen was smudged in random splotches of red and black. She smiled at the visible traces of her Indian lover. But the lingering memories of their passionate embraces were bittersweet, for though he'd demonstrated in every physical way how much he cared, not one word of love had been spoken.

The weather grew steadily colder that third week of October. The temperature dropped below freezing at night, with gray, cloudy skies and occasional rain during the day. On the weekend, Anna came down with influenza after being thoroughly drenched in an icy shower. She developed a high fever and chills by Saturday afternoon, and Suzette ordered complete bed rest.

Procuring four bricks from the agency's carpenter, Suzette placed them in boiling water for a while, then removed them and wrapped them in dry cloths. She placed the hot bricks on either side of Anna and covered her snugly, tucking the blankets about her neck and ordering her to keep her arms under the bedclothes. With the initial dose of quinine, she gave her patient a large glass of hot lemonade and urged her to drink all the water she wanted, hoping to sweat the infection out of her. Despite all the worried physician's precautions, by evening Anna suffered from a sharp pain in her side, rapid respiration, and a marked increase in pulse rate. When the shortness of breath and characteristic cough developed, a grave Suzette diagnosed bronchopneumonia. She resolutely continued her treatment, giving four grains of quinine every four hours.

"You fuss over me too much, *Liebchen*," Anna scolded as Suzette gave her a dose of morphine for the severe chest pain. The hausfrau's blue eyes twinkled mischievously, despite her obvious misery. "You have other people to take care of besides me."

Suzette smiled reassuringly as she listened through the stethoscope for the sound of fluid developing around the lungs. "Nonsense," she said, folding the instrument and shoving it into her apron pocket. She was satisfied there was no sign of pleural effusion. "You are my best patient, Anna. Not one of the others follows my directions worth a darn."

Though Anna smiled broadly, her husband stood at the bedside watching them both with fearful eyes. "*Ja,* you do exactly as Dr. Fräulein says, Mama," he exclaimed. He shook his finger at her in warning. "Don't you dare get out of this bed until she says you can."

In the Grabers' many years of marriage, Jacob's robust wife had seldom been ill. Nothing could have frightened him more than the diagnosis of pneumonia, with its well-known reputation for high mortality.

Suzette was worried as well, for though she was certain that Anna's strong constitution would insure her eventual recovery, the tiny supply of quinine was dwindling rapidly.

One bright ray of sunshine came during the first, critical forty-eight hours of Anna's illness. A letter from Pauline arrived saying that the community of Old Order Mennonites to which the Kaufmans belonged was raising money to purchase medical supplies for the Cheyenne. By the middle of November at the latest, a near-priceless wagonload of drugs and medications would arrive at Lame Deer. The shipment would include anesthetics such as chloroform, sulfate of morphia, cocaine crystals, paregoric, acetanilide, and codeine; antiseptics such as bichloride of mercury, potassium permanganate, and iodine; cathartics and antacids such as calomel, bicarbonate of soda, and milk of magnesia; arnica for treating sprains and bruises; digitalis and belladonna to stimulate the heart and relieve spasms; tonics and stimulants such as cod liver oil, strychnia, and the uterine stimulant ergotine; quinine for influenza and malaria; nitrate of silver and carbolic acid for dressings on burns and wounds; plus other desperately needed items: rolls of bandages and iodoform gauze for surgery, plaster of paris for broken limbs, and silk and catgut violin strings for sutures.

In addition, her younger sister added that the baby girl

was well and thriving. "And so, my darling sister," Pauline had written, "you can rest easy now, assured that you'll soon have all the things you so desperately need to fulfill your mission of mercy among the Indians. But let me hear more about that handsome guide of whom you wrote such a tantalizingly short postscript. Or am I, as Christian says, 'reading too much between the lines'?"

Elated by the news and confident of Anna's recovery once the initial crisis had passed, Suzette could now turn her attention to the frustrating task of getting her Indian patients to follow her medical orders. She'd come to the unhappy realization that if there was no immediate improvement after the first dose of medication, the Cheyenne would simply not bother to take any more. She'd left a bottle of cough elixir for the elderly Chief White Elk, who, finding the alcoholic taste to his liking, drank the entire bottle down at once. So mystified by her remedies were her patients, they'd use whole bottles of liniment, which she'd given them for strained muscles, pouring it over their skin in one swift application in the firm belief that if a little was good, complete relief would surely follow the use of the entire amount.

Nor did War Lance's people turn their backs on their own medicine doctors. For, although the Indians were willing to give her strange-looking pills and nose-tingling concoctions the benefit of the doubt, they never once lost their abiding faith in the proven, age-old wisdom of their ancestors. When it came to a real crisis, they inevitably turned to their traditional healers.

An esteemed medicine woman, Blue Crane Flying gladly shared with a curious Suzette the natural flora that the Cheyenne women had always used to relieve the suffering of painful periods and for female purification. There were plants for a safe pregnancy and birth, and for helping the new mother have enough milk.

Yet Suzette knew also that, despite the confusion and misconceptions surrounding her own practice of medicine, the Indians held her in high regard. It was evident that she could travel over the entire reservation without fear. War Lance's people made it clear that they regarded the *náevehoka* in a class far above all other whites.

"It is your kind, gentle, and loving ways," Blue Crane Flying had explained as she crushed the stems and petals of a bright yellow flower in the bottom of a heavy wooden bowl. She was going to use the powder to make a strong tea that would stop a young woman's menses that had gone on for too long.

They were sitting in Blue Crane Flying's lodge. The nine-year-old Yellow Feather sat between them, a little doll cradled on her lap. Every once in a while she peeped up at Suzette with enormous brown eyes and smiled shyly. She listened in fascination while the two grown-ups talked of healing herbs and plants, eager to help at any task.

Blue Crane Flying handed her daughter the wooden bowl to hold, and rose to pour fresh water into a small kettle. "My people are good judges of character," the thin woman continued with quiet dignity. She looked fondly at the lady doctor with serene, untroubled eyes. "We see in you, Little Red Fox, the best of what is fine and self-less in the healer. My people regard you even higher than the Blackrobes."

Suzette knew she was referring to Jacob and Anna Graber. The Indians called all missionaries by the name given originally to the Jesuits, the first white holy men to come among them.

"Then what should I do?" she asked in frustration. "How can I get my patients to follow my instructions and take the medicines I give them exactly as I've ordered?"

Blue Crane Flying hung the copper pot on a tripod over the fire and turned to her guest. "If our medicine men were to support you," she answered thoughtfully, "the rest of the people would follow." Suddenly her nut brown eyes sparkled. "Perhaps you could give a feast for the medicine doctors and ask for their help. They might listen to you."

Suzette was thrilled with Blue Crane Flying's suggestion. The thought of seeking the cooperation of illiterate shamans didn't bother her in the least. During her internship in the hospital, she'd seen many deaths among people of all religions, creeds, and sects: Quakers and Amish, Episcopalians and Methodists, Catholics, Mohammedans, even Hindus and Buddhists. Watching them prepare themselves to meet their God as they understood Him, she'd gained respect for all points of view, and the spiritual beliefs of her own early upbringing had been drastically liberalized.

So Suzette invited the Tongue River Reservation's medicine men to a grand feast. To her great delight, all twenty of them paraded into Blue Crane Flying's lodge on the designated evening in their finest traditional regalia of feathers, beads, necklaces, armlets, and bells. The shamans, dressed in warm flannel shirts, leggings, and breechclouts, sat in a circle around the fire, leaving the place of honor at the back of the tipi for the *náevehoka*. War Lance Striking and Blue Crane Flying were on either side of her. Each man was painted in his own peculiar way, with his secret medicine bundle tied to a necklet or to the base of his scalp lock, and a special healing rattle made of buffalo skin or a gourd filled with little stones. Several held turkey feather fans which they used to cool a sick person.

Earlier that day Prairie Grass Woman, Blue Crane Flying, and even little Yellow Feather had worked with Suzette to prepare huge kettles of soup and cakes of pemmican made from pulverized beef, tallow, and dried plums. After the meal and the pipe smoking, Suzette, with the help of War Lance, turned the conversation to a discussion of their mutual interest in healing the sick.

"We can work together," she told the shamans earnestly. "If both Indian and white doctors cooperated, more lives would be saved. I am not here to take your

place, for you represent all the old, honorable ways of
your people. War Lance Striking has taught me some of
your spiritual beliefs. While I am only a doctor of the
body, you are doctors of the spirit as well. I can work
with you, if you are willing to help me. When someone
is sick, there is no reason why he cannot come to both of
us for help. I can care for the sick person's body and you
can heal his spirit."

When she'd finished speaking, Standing Antelope, the
head medicine man of Bear Scalp's band, rose with majestic grace. Half of his face was painted deep scarlet, the
other half a shocking white. A small lock of black hair
above his forehead was drawn down over his left eye and
wound with a thin brass wire from which dangled three
large yellow beads.

"I can speak only for myself, Little Red Fox," he said
solemnly, "for no Cheyenne ever tries to tell another
what he must or must not do. But if a sick one comes to
me and I know he needs your great medicine, I will send
for you. And I will see that any treatment you order is
carried through faithfully by the one who is sick."

At his promise of cooperation, Suzette smiled in delight. She knew that Standing Antelope had envied the
many little bottles she carried in her leather case. She
suspected that he longed to learn the secrets of her powerful medicine. Several times he'd pretended to be ill, so
that she'd leave him some of her pills or powders, which
she was certain he later doled out to other sick Indians.
But she had realized that he was faking, for he'd had no
visible symptoms, so she'd left him only harmless potions.

In the end, all the shamans agreed to work with the
white woman doctor for the benefit of the entire tribe.

In the weeks to follow, Suzette enjoyed one of the
happiest times of her life. By the first of November,
Anna had completed her convalescence from pneumonia
and was scurrying busily about the cabin. Suzette and

War Lance, her constant companion, went from camp to camp together as she shared the responsibility for the treatment of the sick with the Cheyenne medicine men. Knowing that the much-needed medical supplies would soon arrive from Pennsylvania, she treated their illnesses, stitched up their cuts, performed a tonsillectomy, and even removed a bullet resulting from an accidental shooting, all without the former sense of panic she'd felt as she'd watched her provision of drugs dwindle to almost nothing. She was received with joy in every village, the women trilling their ear-piercing welcome at her approach.

Her intimate relationship with War Lance was calmly accepted by all of his people. The Cheyenne seemed to believe that, since he, too, was part white, the half-breed and the *náevehoka* were meant by the Great Medicine to find each other. Clearly that was why they'd both been sent to Lame Deer.

Even Prairie Grass Woman felt the bond between the two had been ordained by the Being Above. "Call me 'Grandmother' from now on," she told Suzette, her bright eyes flashing with happy satisfaction. She ignored War Lance's sudden scowl and continued with a chuckle. "As my grandchild's woman, *nixa,* you will no longer be called Little Red Fox by his family. That name will be used by outsiders, but not by the people you belong to."

"Thank you, *niscehem,*" Suzette replied, blinking back the sudden tears. "It is an honor to be your grandchild."

And although her Indian hosts smiled to themselves at the white lady doctor's peculiar need for nighttime privacy, in every camp there was always a young couple who would insist on giving up their small tipi to the visitors and sleeping with relatives. As far as the Cheyenne were concerned, she was War Lance Striking's woman, and that was that.

As he braided her long red hair one evening, in the caring way Cheyenne husbands often did, he told her how proud he was of her.

"The cooperation you've evoked from the shamans is amazing, angel," he said, his long fingers deftly plaiting the unruly waves into one thick braid down her back. When they were alone together, he spoke English, knowing it was far easier for her. "I realized how much you wanted to be the agency doctor," he teased, "but I didn't expect you to join forces with the reservation's medicine men just to get a few patients."

She sat with her back to him, her head bent forward to give him better access to his work. "You underestimated my stubbornness," she laughed. "My father used to claim it was a mile wide and fathoms deep."

He finished tying the end of the coppery braid with a strip of otter fur, gave it a quick, gentle tug, and placed his hands on her shoulders. "If I'd had any idea just how muleheaded you were that first afternoon you hired me as your guide, I'd have taken off for the Wolf Mountains and never come back down."

Tipping her head back, she gazed at him upside down. "I'm the one who's stubborn?" she protested. "Just because I insisted on trying to teach a perverse Indian warrior how to speak proper English when he was bound and determined not to learn it?"

"Mmm," he replied, as he took the opportunity to run his fingertips lightly down the length of her exposed throat. He cupped her breasts with his large hands and brought her back against his solid chest, her head resting comfortably on his shoulder. "What else would you like to teach this woodenheaded dunce? I believe that was what you called me, wasn't it?"

"Let's work on that fancy British accent next," she purred, turning her head to peep up at him suggestively from beneath her lashes. "We can practice by naming parts of the human anatomy. I'll have you talking like a regular American in no time."

He turned her around and lifted her onto his lap. The wolfish grin on his handsome face was positively predatory. "Besides being stubborn, did your father ever tell you that you are shameless?"

He didn't wait for her reply. In the quiet coziness of the borrowed lodge, he taught her in a dozen different lessons how a Cheyenne warrior schooled a headstrong, bold-faced female.

Buried deep in the warmth of a pile of fur robes, they spent the night wrapped in each other's arms. By the fire's light, they took turns reading poetry to each other from Suzette's treasured volume of verse. They whispered and laughed and teased and romped with the light-hearted abandon of young lovers. But Lance never talked about commitments or promises. And he never spoke of tomorrow.

Late in the afternoon, on the thirteenth of November, Bear Scalp came to Suzette's cabin frantically seeking the *náevehoka.* A look of dread on his pockmarked face, he spoke in a troubled, anxious voice. Blue Crane Flying was gravely ill. His brother's woman must come at once and bring her powerful medicine with her. Wasting no time, Suzette changed quickly into her riding outfit, while Lance readied the horses. Then the three of them raced to the Indian village alongside Rosebud Creek.

Inside the lodge, they found War Lance's worried grandmother sitting on a worn buffalo robe next to Blue Crane Flying. The gaunt features of the young woman were bathed in sweat. She lay on a mattress of woven bulrushes covered by a thin blanket that was soaked with perspiration, as were her red woolen blouse and skirt. A small fire was burning in the center of the tipi, and Standing Antelope, the band's medicine doctor, was throwing juniper needles on it and singing an old-time medicine song to the accompaniment of his painted gourd rattle. As the sweet-smelling fumes of the burnt needles filled the tipi, he shook the rattle over the prostrate woman and chanted.

"She is very sick, *nixa,*" Prairie Grass Woman said in

a soft whisper. Suzette could see the cold fear in her black eyes. "It is the white man's shaking sickness, which she first had on the southern reservation. Though it was many moons ago, the chills of the fever shake her once again, just as before. She needs the bitter white powder that makes it go away."

Kneeling down, Suzette placed her hand on the young woman's forehead. Blue Crane Flying shook with chills so hard, her teeth chattered, but she was conscious, for her eyelids fluttered open at the light touch. She looked up at the white woman with dull, weary eyes.

"How do you feel?" Suzette asked.

"I'm ... I'm very tired, my ... my sister," she stuttered hoarsely, as the chills racked her thin frame.

"Grandmother says you've had this illness before."

"Yes. The doctor at Fort Robinson gave me medicine that made the fever and shaking go away. But now it's come back as bad as ever."

Suzette listened to the woman's words with despondency. The "white man's sweating sickness" was the Indian name for malaria, for which there was only one cure. And she'd used every last bit of the needed quinine to fight Anna's pneumonia. If only someone had told her before now that Blue Crane Flying had contracted the deadly disease in the Oklahoma territory!

Just that morning, Suzette had spoken to a cold and unsympathetic Horace Corby about the shipment of medical supplies she expected to arrive any day from Pennsylvania. Pauline had written that it might reach Lame Deer as early as the first of November. Leading her brusquely to the door, Corby had sneered that he couldn't be held responsible for the false promises of the Mennonites.

Heartsick, she took Blue Crane Flying's temperature and pulse rate. Both were dangerously high. She rose and turned to War Lance, who waited nearby with Bear Scalp. "You must go to Fort Custer," she told him, swallowing the painful ache of fear in her throat. "I'll write a note begging Dr. Gilbreath for some more quinine. Bring it back as fast as possible."

He grasped her shoulders and squeezed her in a comforting gesture of reassurance and cool-headed male strength. "We'll leave at once, angel. The soonest we can get back is tomorrow night. Is there anything I can do before I go?"

As she met his gaze, she tried to hide her concern for him. The two brothers would be traveling alone across the Crow Reservation at night without permission from the agents. If anything happened to them, no one in authority on either reservation would be held accountable.

"Just go quickly, War Lance," she replied calmly, placing her hands on his upper arms. He bent to press his cheeks to hers, and she whispered in his ear. "Take care of yourself."

Bear Scalp knelt down on one knee beside the pallet and spoke softly to his wife, who smiled up at him faintly. Then he gently touched her hand and rose. His tortured eyes were filled with apprehension. "Until my wife is well again, the children will stay with Touching Cloud, who has already taken them to her mother's lodge," he told Suzette. "But my grandmother will remain here to help you, *nitam*. And I have asked Standing Antelope to do exactly as you wish." He started for the door of the tipi, then paused and turned. "My woman has never looked so ill before," he said in a low, frightened voice.

"I'll do everything I can to make her comfortable," she assured him, only vaguely aware that Bear Scalp had just addressed her as his sister-in-law. "But we must have the white powder as soon as possible."

The two warriors left the tipi, and Suzette turned back to the sick woman, determined not to let her alarm show. She'd treated other cases of malaria, though not many, but she'd always had the needed quinine. And even then, she'd once lost a patient.

She remained at Blue Crane Flying's side during the

long, agonizing night, helpless to break the continuous high fever. The paroxysms of severe chills and sweating at irregular intervals continued through the next day, with the addition of diarrhea and an enlarged, tender spleen.

Prairie Grass Woman helped Suzette bathe the suffering woman with vinegar water in a vain attempt to bring the fever down. Together they helped her sip small amounts of cool water, lifting her head up gently, for she was too weak to drink by herself. All the while, Standing Antelope chanted songs of healing and fanned the patient with a sacred eagle's wing. The music seemed to have a soothing effect, for Blue Crane Flying frequently dozed off during the singing, only to be awakened again by the racking chills.

By midday, when it was still too soon to hope for the return of the men, Blue Crane Flying called out to Suzette in a weak voice. "I must speak to you alone, my sister."

Suzette met Prairie Grass Woman's gaze and found no surprise in her guarded expression. "I shall go down to the creek for fresh water," the old woman said calmly, and left the lodge.

Standing Antelope, in his turn, politely excused himself, saying he would go up on a nearby hill and smoke a pipe. He would continue his praying there, in the hope of driving away the evil spirits who had brought the sickness to Blue Crane Flying.

When he had gone, Suzette bent over the young woman's still form. For the moment, the chills had eased and she lay motionless in exhaustion. "What is it you wish to say, *nisima?*" Suzette asked softly, addressing her as her younger sister.

Blue Crane Flying gazed up at the white medicine woman. Her face was deathly pale, and the grayish skin was stretched tautly across her high cheekbones. Yet her beautiful brown eyes were clear and lucid. There was a brief respite from the shaking that tortured her, but they both knew it would soon return.

"It is about the little soldier chief," she croaked through her parched throat. "The one whose picture you keep beside your bed."

Compassionately Suzette slipped her arm beneath the young woman's neck and raised the small tin cup to her cracked lips. "You mean Jordan Maclure," Suzette explained as the woman drank a tiny sip. "I was going to marry him. But he was killed in a battle."

"I know," Blue Crane Flying rasped. The water trickled in a fine stream from the corner of her mouth. She was too weary to even swallow. "I questioned my husband's brother about it, and he told me."

She lay still for a few minutes, gathering strength to continue. "I know, too, that your love for the Long Knife has remained in your heart though he has been dead for many years. There is something I must tell you, my sister. Something that only I and the Lance know for certain, though my husband's grandmother suspects."

"Whatever it is," Suzette said in astonishment, "it can wait till you're better." She wondered if the pitifully sick woman was suffering from a delirium caused by the terrible fever. Good Lord, there was no way that Blue Crane Flying could possibly know anything about Jordan.

"I must tell you now, while I still can, before the shaking begins again." She reached out to Suzette with a trembling hand. "The little soldier chief who promised to marry you was my daughter's father."

Chapter 21

"No," Suzette exclaimed. "You're mistaken. Jordan's not Yellow Feather's father. He couldn't be!"

The Indian woman's lambent brown eyes, sunk deep in shadowed hollows, were filled with compassion. "It is the truth, *namhan*," she said, addressing the woman doctor as an older sister in a tone of utter weariness. Shaking her head slightly, she tried to push away the cup held once again to her lips, but she was too weak to do more than lift her hand. Suzette placed the tin of water on the woven mat next to them and waited for her to continue.

"I never intended to tell you. There was no reason. But now I must think of my little daughter, who, like my husband's brother, is a half-blood. She must learn to walk the road of her white soldier father."

Sitting back on her heels, Suzette stared down in horror at Blue Crane Flying. She wanted to deny what the Cheyenne woman was telling her. Her mind screamed that it was just some crazy mistake. To a frightened little Indian girl, all white soldiers with yellow hair and big mustaches would look alike. And nine years ago, Blue Crane Flying would have been far too young for Jordan to ever . . .

But in her heart, Suzette knew the desperately ill woman spoke the truth. Always there had been something about Yellow Feather that reminded Suzette of the

321

past. Jordan hadn't given the child his bright golden curls or his deep blue eyes, but he had bequeathed her his startlingly handsome features, clear-cut and finely chisled. The delicate shape of the head. The wide brow. And more. Little idiosyncrasies of gesture and expression. Traits that identified her as his daughter more clearly than any birth certificate possibly could. It had been there, in front of her all the time, but her pride and intellect had refused to acknowledge what her unconscious feelings had intuitively recognized.

Yellow Feather was Jordan Maclure's daughter. His little girl. The child Suzette should have borne.

"How . . . how did it happen?" she asked, as two tears slowly trickled down her cheeks. She choked on the painful words. "Did he . . . did he force you?" She didn't want to hear the answer, but she knew she had to. Somehow, someway, she had to make sense out of this horrible insanity.

"It was the year before the great battle at the Little Big Horn," Blue Crane Flying croaked in a raspy voice. "The little soldier chief the whites called Henely attacked Medicine Arrow's camp on the Sappa. The Arrow was a great peace chief and the Keeper of the Sacred Arrows. Though the bullets of the Long Knives rained all about him, he walked bravely forward toward the soldier chief, carrying a white cloth of surrender and holding his hand up high in the sign of peace. But he was cut down by the big guns of the buffalo hunters."

"Yes, I know. War Lance told me how the whites took no captives that day, not even the children and babies."

"After the attack on Medicine Arrow's band, my people scattered into small groups and fled north ahead of the whites. It was spring, but still bitterly cold, and the snowy ground revealed our tracks in spite of our attempts to hide them. A few days later, the soldiers came upon my father's band. This time, though every male over twelve was killed, the women and children were taken captive and marched away in the snow. That night, when the young girls were chosen for the lodges of the soldier chiefs, I was sent to Yellow Long Knife, the man you call Jordan Maclure."

"How old were you?" Suzette whispered in horror.

"It was my fourteenth spring and I had not yet known a man. When a bluecoat pulled me from the line of captives, my mother leaped upon him, begging that he take her instead. She knew the evil ways of the *vèho,* who does not honor the *nihpihist,* our women's protective string. The big man clubbed her with the wooden end of his gun, and she fell to the ground. The blood from the gash on her head made a red stain on the snow at my feet. I do not think he understood a word of what she'd been saying."

Exhausted, Blue Crane Flying stopped, too short of breath to continue. Suzette gently lifted her patient's head and held the tin cup to her parched lips. With agonizing effort, the depleted woman sipped the clear water.

Tears flowed unheeded down Suzette's cheeks. "You must rest now, *nisima.* Save your strength to fight the illness."

Moving her head slowly from side to side, Blue Crane Flying gave a harsh, grating cough. "There is more I must say while I can." She met Suzette's gaze, her dark eyes unnaturally bright as the soaring fever gripped her once more. "Yellow Long Knife did not hurt me. When he took me to his bed, he was kind and thoughtful. He brushed away my childish tears, as though aware of my tender age. And the next day, he sent the soldier doctor to heal my mother's wound. He also saw that my little sisters were given shelter and food and clothing. Our band remained camped beside the fort for twenty sleeps, and during that time I stayed with him in his canvas tent. Then my people were allowed to join our relatives, who had already made it to safety in the north. My daughter was born in our winter camp near the Tongue River, during the snows of the Little Racket Moon."

Suzette drew a long, trembling breath. January 1876.

Six months before Jordan was killed at the age of twenty-nine, leaving a heartbroken fiancée grieving and inconsolable back in Lancaster, Pennsylvania. It had all come around, like some giant wheel spun by the gods of fate. For here she was, trying desperately to save the life of the young girl he had so callously used and tossed aside.

She leaned over Blue Crane Flying, and the teardrops fell on the prostrate woman's gaunt face. "Why have you been so good to me, when you knew who I was, and what he'd meant to me?"

"How could I have blamed you, gentle sister? You have brought your sweet medicine to my people. It was you who saved my little son's life." Drawn and pale, the dying woman smiled faintly and lifted a shaky hand to touch Suzette's cheek. "And even though you thought you were still in love with the yellow-haired soldier chief, I knew the Great Spirit Above meant you for my husband's brother. Anyone who saw you together knew that it was only a matter of time before you would become his woman. The Cheyenne are not like the whites, who fall in and out of love just for the fun of it. We love deeply, completely, and for a lifetime."

"War Lance hasn't made any promises about spending the rest of his life with me," Suzette said with a quavery laugh.

Blue Crane Flying's answer was nearly inaudible. "Whether he stays with you or goes far away to his home across the water, he will love you, *namhan,* for the rest of his life."

With an aching heart, Lance stood beside his grief-stricken brother in the camp's open circle. Bear Scalp, his long black hair unbraided and falling loose about his shoulders, was giving away his entire herd of horses to the other members of the Rosebud band. Even the spirited Appaloosa he'd ridden so skillfully in the horse race at Lame Deer was led off, as well as the gentle mustang that had pulled the travois, laden with his dead wife's body, up into the hills for burial.

Lance looked across the grassy meadow to the curved line of tipis. Prairie Grass Woman, her arms and legs slashed and bleeding, was keening a hauntingly sweet, sorrow-filled death chant. Her hair, too, fell unkempt about her, in the Cheyenne sign of mourning. Next to the elderly woman, a shocked and distraught Suzette stood by helplessly, watching the people of Bear Scalp's band take all the household goods from the family's deserted lodge. Weeping women carried out the dishes, cooking kettles, blankets, clothing, robes, backrests, and sleeping mattresses until there was nothing left. When the tipi stood completely empty, it, too, was dismantled and carted off—even the lodge poles—until there was nothing left that had once belonged to Bear Scalp and his deceased wife. The sorrowing family was completely destitute.

Watching the tragic custom, so familiar from his boyhood, War Lance held his father's pipe with reverent fingers. Bear Scalp had given him the treasured calumet, and Lance was poignantly reminded of the day Strong Wolf had died. In those years the food and possessions of a nomadic people were easily replaced. Vast herds of buffalo abounded on the plains, providing the brave hunter many opportunities to acquire again the things necessary for life. That fluid, simple existence was gone forever, but the tradition of turning a grieving family into homeless paupers still remained.

It had all happened so fast. By the time the two brothers had returned from Fort Custer with the medicine sent by Dr. Gilbreath, Blue Crane Flying had already slipped into a coma from which she'd never regained consciousness. The fever continued to soar, with repeated chills and sweating, until the lovely young woman's overburdened heart had finally given out. The precious quinine had come too late. The funeral had taken place almost immediately, in the time-honored Cheyenne manner, and the children had been kept away for fear their mother's ghost would try to take their spirits with her.

When the last of the horses had been given away, War Lance and Bear Scalp walked over to join the two grieving women.

"Where will you sleep tonight, *niscehem?*" Lance asked his tiny grandmother lovingly. He knew that she would be sheltered by relatives, now that she was without a home. "I will take you there, for you look very tired."

Prairie Grass Woman gazed up at him, her eyes clouded with sorrow. "I will live for a while with Standing Antelope's family. Since his two wives are the daughters of my dead sister, they have asked me to stay with them and bring Young Wolf with me."

Just then, Touching Cloud came up with the two children. Running over to the group of adults, Young Wolf threw his chubby arms around his father's massive thigh and cried in heartsick misery.

"My mother, my mother, my mother," he sobbed.

Bear Scalp bent down and lifted his son up into his arms. Yellow Feather looked about in bewilderment, and Lance's heart ached for the pain and confusion in her light brown eyes. He was about to call her to him when Suzette hurried over to the child.

"I will be your new mother, *nàtóna,*" she said, addressing the orphan as if she were her own daughter. Suzette crouched down before the woebegone nine-year-old. "You will come to live with me in my cabin at Lame Deer, and I shall take care of you. You shall be the little girl I always wanted."

Yellow Feather looked at the *náevehoka* with uncertainty. "Do you really want me?" she asked with a pathetic smile.

Suzette held her arms out wide in answer. With a burst of fresh tears, the young girl threw herself into the white woman's embrace and buried her head against the soft, waiting shoulder.

Appalled at Suzette's rash words, Lance moved quickly to her side. "You don't know what you're saying," he corrected quietly. His taut jaw clenched in unqualified displeasure. "My brother's daughter will stay with relatives." He turned to Bear Scalp. "Have the child go with Touching Cloud for now, while I speak to the *náevehoka.*"

The circle of listeners grew silent and wary. Then, at an imploring look from Bear Scalp, the good-hearted Touching Cloud took Yellow Feather compassionately from the white woman's arms and led her away.

Suzette rose, rigid with anger and the humiliation of being so rudely contradicted in front of others. Before she could speak and embarrass herself further, he grabbed her elbow. "We will discuss this alone," he said in a voice loud enough for all to hear. Then he led her swiftly across the grassy field and into the stand of cottonwoods that bordered the creek.

As soon as they'd gained privacy, she yanked her arm out of his grasp and whirled to face him. Her violet eyes sparked with indignation. Her face was white with fury. He didn't wait for the tongue-lashing she'd prepared for him on their way across the meadow.

"What the hell's the matter with you?" he shouted in English before she'd even opened her mouth. "Have you lost your mind? You can't take Yellow Feather to live with you. She's an Indian."

Throwing her shoulders back, Suzette drew herself up to her full height and corrected him with icy calm. "She's *part* Indian. She's also part white. And I intend to raise her as my daughter. It's what her mother wanted."

"What the devil are you talking about?" he said through clenched teeth. He'd known that Yellow Feather was Jordan's child since the time her mother had seen the photograph in Suzette's cabin. Blue Crane Flying had asked him why the *náevehoka* kept the likeness of the little soldier chief beside her sleeping pallet. When Lance questioned his sister-in-law about Maclure, she'd admitted the truth.

"Before she died, Blue Crane Flying asked me to take care of Yellow Feather. She knew that her son would be looked after by his father and his father's relatives, but she was worried about her half-breed daughter."

"Goddammit! Bear Scalp will provide for her," Lance exploded. He moved toward her, and she stepped back cautiously. The automatic reflex made him even angrier. "Do you think my brother would abandon his wife's child just because she's a half-blood? He's Cheyenne, not white, you little fool."

"There's no need to call me names," she lashed back. "Blue Crane Flying knew her husband would take care of Yellow Feather. But she wanted her daughter to learn the customs of her white heritage, just as you followed the white man's road at the death of your father. She asked me to raise Yellow Feather, to see that she received schooling, and maybe someday, if she wished, to learn to be a medicine woman like me. It's what her mother wanted."

"You're not adopting Yellow Feather," he told her with implacable certainty, "regardless of what you and Blue Crane Flying may have decided between you." He wanted to shake her till some common sense penetrated her single-minded stubbornness. She stood facing him resolutely, her chin tilted upward, her lips pursed together in the all-too-familiar stance of pigheaded rebellion.

Lance took a deep breath and forced himself to calm down. Shouting at her would only make her more intransigent. She was already overwrought. The tragic death of her beloved friend, the quinine arriving only hours too late to save her, had taken its toll. She looked white and pinched and extremely fragile. Her coppery hair fell in tangled snarls down her back. Her jacket and pants were wrinkled and soiled from nursing the dying woman. He knew she hadn't slept in over twenty-four hours.

"Think about what you're proposing, Suzette," he said in a quiet, urgent voice. "Yellow Feather would be treated with contempt and disdain by all the whites she encountered. She'd never be accepted, and neither would you, if you adopted her. You'd both end up broken-hearted, alone, and friendless."

"That didn't happen to you," she pointed out with quick-witted perversity. "You made a life for yourself in the white man's world."

"That's different."

"How?" she scoffed.

"I'm a man. That's the difference."

She placed her hands on her slim hips and tilted her head in mockery. "You think just because we're females, we can't withstand a little prejudice? Well, I happen to think we're both made out of stronger stuff. And I'm going to bet my future on it."

"No, you're not, Suzette," he said, furious at her willful obstinacy. "I absolutely forbid it."

"Forbid it?" she gasped, her eyes huge and round in stunned outrage. "By what right do you forbid me anything? You, who's always been so careful to avoid any mention of my future. Who's always taken such heedful precautions to insure there'd be no pregnancy to complicate your precious freedom. Well, go on. Go back to England alone. I don't need you. I've got Jordan's child now, and I'm going to raise her as my own."

The full meaning of her spiteful words slammed against his heart.

She didn't love him.

She'd never loved him.

She was still in love with that goddamned dead soldier.

All she wanted was Maclure's child, no matter if it meant adopting a little Cheyenne half-breed.

"You're not going to destroy Yellow Feather just to live out your fantasies, Suzette," he said with scathing bitterness. "I won't let it happen." He turned to leave, but she followed after him.

"What are you going to do?"

"I'm going to talk to Bear Scalp about it."

"If you do this to me," she cried hysterically, "I'll never forgive you."

Without bothering to reply, Lance strode purposefully back to the village.

A snowstorm came south from Canada on the third Sunday of November, leaving huge drifts in the mountain passes. Although the weather had grown steadily colder, the Montana air was so dry that the temperature could drop as much as twenty degrees unnoticed without the constant use of a thermometer. Snow blocked the divides between the rivers, making travel on horseback nearly impossible.

Lance acquired two harness-broken mustangs that his brother had given to a friend the day of Blue Crane Flying's death. With Jacob's help, he repaired the dilapidated spring wagon and then put runners on it.

Bundled up in a heavy sealskin coat, cap, and gloves, with the added luxury of heated bricks, which had been warmed overnight by the fire and placed under the soles of her snug winter boots, Suzette rode beside Lance in the open sleigh. She hardly felt the cold beneath the warm fur robes that he tucked around her. The joyous sound of the tinkling sleigh bells fastened to the harness straps would have made her smile in delight at any other time. But the dreadful estrangement between them had left her numb and devastated. As she went from camp to camp in his morose, short-tempered company, she'd never felt so miserable.

She'd have given anything to take back the petty words she'd flung at him that terrible day. She hadn't meant them. Her feelings for Lance were far deeper, far more honest, than anything she'd ever felt for Jordan. Good Lord, she wasn't sure she'd even been in love with her dead fiancé. Oh, she'd been infatuated with the dashing cavalry officer, all right, turning him in his absence into a fulfillment of all her girlish fantasies. A romantic fantasy no real man had been able to compete with in nine long years.

Until she'd met War Lance Striking. He was real. And all male. Not a phony, smooth-talking charmer, who'd taken the innocence of a little fourteen-year-old girl while writing love letters of undying devotion to his hometown sweetheart.

Now, at last, she understood what genuine love was all about. Mature love between two adults, who recognized each other's faults and loved in spite of them. At twenty-eight years old, she'd finally grown up. But it was too late. Lance despised her.

After speaking to his brother the day Blue Crane Flying had died and effectively blocking Suzette's proposed adoption of Yellow Feather, Lance had ridden off into the Wolf Mountains. He'd remained there for nearly a week. When he returned to her cabin, ready to resume his responsibilities as the agency doctor's hired scout, he had completely shut her out of his private life. It was as though there'd never been anything intimate between them. He was studiously polite, always careful to see to her safety, and more than willing to transport her to her patients. But there was an impenetrable wall of cold disinterest surrounding him that couldn't be overcome. After several humiliating attempts to do so, she'd given up trying.

Her latest interview with Horace Corby had been equally disastrous.

"I can't understand," she complained to the agent, "why the shipment from the Mennonites hasn't arrived yet. My sister wrote that it would be here by the middle of November, at the absolute latest. Could it possibly have been unloaded and stacked in the agency warehouse at Custer Station by mistake?"

"Apparently your precious sister and her holy friends

didn't come through with the medical supplies as they'd promised," he simpered, a supercilious grin spreading beneath his huge handlebar mustache. He hadn't bothered to stand when she'd entered the room, and now he leaned back insolently in his chair, resting the back of his bald head in his cupped hands. "Either that, or it's been waylaid somewhere on the Great Plains by a snowstorm. Do you think a large shipment like that could be accidentally overlooked? Come now," he goaded, "you don't think I'm that incompetent, do you?"

She bit her tongue, for an honest answer to that question would have resulted in her immediate expulsion from the reservation.

"No," she lied. "I just thought maybe your employees had slipped up somehow. No one can be on top of everything."

Corby's smile faded. His beady green eyes were as cold as a lizard's. She half expected a forked tongue to come flicking out from beneath the ugly black mustache. He brought his arms down and leaned forward to grip the edge of his desk with white-knuckled fingers. "On the Tongue River Reservation, Miss Stanwood, I control everything but the weather. Though it's been hard for you to come to grips with that truth, here at Lame Deer I am the supreme authority. And don't you ever forget it."

She wondered if he was aware that the Cheyenne had complained scathingly to her about him. Every article of merchandise or food that was part of their government allotments came to Lame Deer hauled in the agency wagons from Custer Station. The two agency storehouses, one at the railroad station and one at Lame Deer, were always kept closed tight with heavy spring locks. No Indian was ever allowed inside either building. And according to Major Hairless Head, the monthly allotments had been drastically reduced by the Bureau of Indian Affairs, until they were now only a small part of the original rations promised to the Cheyenne by the Great Father in Washington.

Corby pointed to the door in abrupt dismissal, then called to her as she opened it. "I understand that young, good-lookin' squaw I talked to the day of the horse race died of malaria."

"Yes," she replied, surprised that he'd be interested. "Blue Crane Flying would have lived, if only I'd had some quinine."

"Too bad," he said with a careless shrug. "But a foul-mouthed squaw like that was bound to end up badly."

Speechless at his callous remark, Suzette had slammed the door as she left. Then she'd fled to her cabin and immediately written a letter to her sister.

Although the haunting problem of her dwindling medical provisions had not been resolved, Dr. Gilbreath had come to her rescue once again, and sent a limited amount of supplies over to Lame Deer from Fort Custer. With these medicines, she was able to continue her practice, at least for the time being. She had succeeded in one thing. The idea of working hand in hand with the shamans had proved to be an excellent one. The Cheyenne listened to their medicine men, who encouraged the sick to take the medications exactly as the *náevehoka* prescribed. In turn, she made no attempt to demean or denigrate the tribal doctors.

None of the Indians blamed her for the death of Blue Crane Flying. They were all too familiar with the deadly effects of the white man's sweating sickness. There wasn't one of them who hadn't lost a relative or friend to the disease while they'd been forced to remain with the Southern Cheyenne in Indian Territory.

Thanksgiving came with fresh snow. Suzette and the Grabers celebrated quietly over a roast beef; there probably wasn't a domestic turkey to be had in the entire state of Montana. The day before, Jacob had lifted down his antiquated muzzle-loading carbine from its rack above the cabin door and gone out hunting for any kind of wild fowl he could find. He'd come back empty-handed, his cheeks cherry red and his blue eyes twinkling from the sheer fun of it.

Suzette did most of the cooking and even set a festive table, complete with a centerpiece of pinecones, evergreen branches, and wild rose berries on the white linen tablecloth. The week before, Anna had developed a severe bronchitis that hung on despite all Suzette's best efforts to clear it up. After supper, Jacob piled the hearth high with logs and lit a roaring fire. He drew a whipsawed wooden chair up close and insisted that his wife remain there while he helped Suzette with the dishes.

They were snowed in at Lame Deer for the entire first week of December. Suzette continued to treat Anna's bronchitis, which was slowly getting better, while Jacob worked on his project of compiling an English-Cheyenne dictionary. On Wednesday War Lance stopped by to deliver a haunch of fresh venison and check on their other provisions, but he bluntly refused to take Suzette out in the bad weather, despite her pleading that she ought to call on some of her patients.

"A frozen doctor isn't going to be any help to the sick," he stated curtly, and left the cabin, shutting the door in her astonished face.

Although it hadn't seemed possible, the temperature continued to drop till one night it reached twenty-two degrees below zero. But the sun came out during the day, and at last War Lance agreed to take Suzette on her rounds to the nearby camps. He burned a piece of pitch pine and insisted she blacken the skin beneath her eyes with its sooty ashes, for the dazzle of the sunshine on the glistening snow could easily cause snow blindness. The colder the weather became, the stiller the air and the greater the risk of frostbite.

"If I take you," he said as he bundled her up in the sleigh, till all that was exposed was her face peeking out from under her fur hat, "you're going to follow my orders. I want you to leave those smudges under your eyes as long as there's sunlight. You're to keep your gloved hands inside your muff, and your muff in front of your nose while we're moving. And if I say the weather looks bad and we have to stay in camp till it blows over, we stay put with no arguing."

She glared at him but wisely kept her acid retort to herself.

"Is that understood?" he drilled, coming around to his side of the conveyance and stowing his Winchester rifle in its scabbard by the seat.

"It's understood," she snapped. "Why is it that whenever you're in a foul mood, you speak to me in English?"

Her unexpected question caught him off guard, and he paused in the act of climbing into the sleigh. A smile hovered about his lips as he slid onto the seat beside her and gathered the reins in his gloved hands. "I can swear in English, that's why. There isn't a decent obscenity in the entire Cheyenne language."

"How can an obscenity be decent?" she exclaimed.

"Good question, angel." He gave up trying to scowl and grinned at her instead. "On the other hand," he added with maddening insouciance, "when it comes to talking erotically, the best words are all in Cheyenne."

She turned and stared at him in shocked surprise. His entrancing eyes glowed with irrepressible laughter. It was the first time since their terrible argument at the Rosebud camp that he'd so much as alluded to the physical intimacy they'd shared together. She felt the heat of a flush on her cheeks, and buried her nose in the downy white rabbit fur of her muff, forgetting about the black smudges under her eyes until it was too late. With the sound of a chuckle rumbling deep in his chest, Lance slapped the reins and called to the team.

They took off, skimming over the snow at an exhilarating speed, the musical jingle of the sleigh bells punctuated by the rhythmic beat of the horses' hoofs on the hard-packed snow and the underlying accompaniment of the steel runners cutting over the icy crust. Behind the protection of the white fur muff, Suzette smiled to herself. Perhaps, just perhaps, he didn't despise her after all.

Little by little they established a tentative truce between them, each careful not to say anything that would touch upon the subject of Yellow Feather's adoption. Suzette had by no means given up her intention to keep her promise to the girl's dying mother. By the time Lance returned Suzette safely to her cabin five days later, they were able to talk and laugh with each other, instead of riding side by side in that god-awful silence. But he'd made no attempt on the journey to move beyond an easygoing friendship.

As he lifted her down from the sleigh, he held her in midair above his head for a long minute, looking up to meet her gaze with solemn black eyes. Then he set her on her feet. Freeing her waist, he caught her gloved hands in his.

"Suzette . . ." he began hesitantly.

"Dr. Fräulein," Jacob called from the cabin door. "Come quickly. Mama's sick again."

Chapter 22

Two days after Christmas, Suzette crossed the covered dogtrot from her office and entered the cabin's parlor. She inhaled the wonderful holiday aroma of pungent evergreen boughs, spicy gingerbread, and freshly popped corn as she wiped the snow from her boots on the braided rag rug in front of the door.

"How's my patient today?" she asked with a smile of encouragement. Wrapped in a thick wool shawl, Anna sat beside the fire in the wooden armchair that Jacob had cushioned for her with three gray wolf pelts.

"I'm feeling much better, *Liebchen*. Papa just went to pick up the mail. It was due in from the Birney post office this morning, and he saw the young cowboy who brings it ride by the window a few minutes ago." Anna's blue eyes twinkled in her round face, but her usually rosy cheeks were pale and drawn. "I was sitting here admiring our beautiful tree," she added.

"It is pretty, isn't it? I've always loved the Christmas decorations. Shall I light the candles for you?"

At Anna's nod, Suzette picked up the box of wooden matches near the fireplace and walked over to the fragrant balsam fir. One by one, she lit the tiny candles and then stood back to admire their glow.

"Good gracious, there's no doubt about it," she said with a chuckle of pleasure at the sight. "This has to be the tallest Christmas tree in the whole Montana territory."

Four days after she'd returned from her rounds to the nearby camps, Suzette had opened the door of her office to find Lance holding the enormous fir tree upright with a delighted grin. He'd found it in the nearby mountains and hauled it all the way to Lame Deer, dragging it behind Red Wind over the snow. When he brought it into the parlor, the uppermost branches scraped against the cabin's open-beamed ceiling.

Thrilled, she'd decorated the tree with iced gingerbread boys. She'd left the cones, which stood erect on the springy boughs like shiny brown candles, right on the tree and tied bright red bows at the base of each one. While Jacob strung popcorn for a garland, Anna sat and watched them from her chair, offering her suggestions for adorning their marvelous *Tannenbaum*.

Lance's thoughtful gesture had brightened the otherwise gloomy holiday. For on Christmas morning, Suzette was forced to tell Anna and Jacob the news she hated to break. She'd put off the unwelcome task until she was absolutely positive of her diagnosis. After a bout of pneumonia in October, followed by severe bronchitis the following month, Anna had come down with pleurisy. Though seldom fatal of itself, it was believed to often be the starting point of tuberculosis. Suzette realized that Anna was not going to stay well as long as she remained at Lame Deer. The Montana climate was too severe for her to even regain her previously robust health.

The Grabers had been devastated. They would have to give up their mission on the Tongue River Reservation and return to Oklahoma territory and their work among the Southern Cheyenne. No one would be coming to take their place, at least not right away, for there were presently no other Mennonite missionaries available. Suzette's heart went out to the dejected couple, who'd labored so hard and made such meager inroads in their evangelical work with the Indians. Only a few Cheyenne had come to the services Jacob held in the parlor each Sunday morning. But those who did had grown genuinely fond of the two Blackrobes who spoke their language and showed such a deep and sincere affection for the Cheyenne people.

Even aside from Anna's illness, the holiday would still have been bittersweet. On Christmas afternoon War Lance had brought Suzette a sumptuous bearskin rug. He'd carried it in from the frigid air and tossed it with a flourish on the rough planks in front of the decorated fir tree.

"This is to place on the cold floor beside your bed, Little Red Fox," he said, speaking in Cheyenne, since the Grabers were there also. "So your bare feet will be warm when you get up in the morning."

She met his look of tender amusement, and her heart thrummed. "It's beautiful," she whispered.

"I shot the great black bear when I went into the mountains to hunt for wild horses," he explained. His glance included Anna and Jacob. "It was the week I caught Red Wind and Painted Doll. My grandmother prepared the skin."

"But you didn't have a rifle then," Jacob pointed out. "Did you kill it with a bow and arrow?"

War Lance's hearty laugh boomed out. "I used my brother's gun. If I'd had only a bow and arrow, I'm not so certain I could have brought the bear down before it reached me. It was charging straight at me at the time."

Suzette lifted the luxurious pelt to her face and rubbed her cheek against its softness. It was still cold from exposure to the frosty air. "What a lovely Christmas present, War Lance. Thank you." She met his gaze, trying to read the thoughts hidden behind his guarded expression.

When she had presented him with an embroidered chamois-skin cover for his father's ceremonial pipe, his joy had appeared sincere and heartfelt. Yet each night she'd hoped in vain that he'd return to sleep with her in the lonely brass bed. It soon became clear, however, that though he was willing to renew their old friendly ways, he intended their future relationship to be a platonic one.

He'd forgiven her for what she'd said the day Blue Crane Flying had died. But he hadn't forgotten. Nor had she abandoned her intention of adopting Yellow Feather. An intention he was fully aware of and still adamantly opposed to. Whenever possible, she continued to visit the child, who remained with Touching Cloud at the camp beside the Rosebud, but Lance's fierce scowl and obvious disapproval had kept her from bringing the subject up again with Bear Scalp.

With a sigh, Suzette relinquished the sad memories and patted Anna's arm in silent reassurance. She walked over to the window above the kitchen sink and looked out at the snow-covered quadrangle. Lance was in the agency's stable, checking on their horses and trying to repair the battered wagon-sleigh. She'd hoped to start out again on her rounds that morning, but he'd insisted they wait to see how the weather looked.

Suzette placed her fingertips on the cold glass pane above the kitchen sink and wiped away the misty blur caused by her warm breath. Outside, the sky was gray and overcast. It wasn't likely War Lance would agree to take her anywhere while the weather looked so foreboding.

At that moment, Jacob came into the cabin. "Look what I have for you, Dr. Fräulein," he called cheerfully. "A letter!" He brushed the snow from his boots and waved the envelope high in the air. "If that handwriting isn't your sister's, I'll eat my hat."

She hurried over, suddenly breathless with excitement. It had to be from Paulie! She'd written to her before Thanksgiving, begging to know why the shipment of medical supplies hadn't been sent as she'd promised. Now, at last, Suzette would learn if the Old Order Mennonites in Lancaster had been able to raise the necessary funds she'd counted upon so desperately.

Taking the letter from Jacob's outstretched hand, Suzette smiled at the familiar handwriting. The round, childlike letters embellished with blotches of ink were definitely Pauline's. She plopped down on a kitchen chair, tore open the envelope, and quickly scanned the pages.

> *My Darling Suzie,*
>
> *I'm sure by now the medicines we sent have reached you. I hope you find that everything came through safely. We packed it all with such great care.*
>
> *Mr. Tobias Schrag, a fellow Mennonite and long acquaintance of Christian's, was journeying to Butte to visit a dying brother, who'd left home many years ago. (It was the story of the prodigal all over again.) Anyway, Mr. Schrag rode with the cartons and boxes all the way across the country. He wrote Christian the first week in November to say that he'd stayed right in the mail car with the mail clerk to watch over the precious supplies, for we know that on the frontier such a shipment of drugs, etc., would be nearly priceless. Mr. Schrag wrote to tell us how he helped unload the cartons at the Custer Railroad Station and personally signed the shipment over to the clerk of the Tongue River Reservation, a Mr. Obadiah Nash. Mr. Schrag was delighted to let us know that as the train was pulling out of the station on its way to Billings, he saw the boxes being loaded onto the agency wagon.*
>
> *With that problem so happily resolved, let me tell you all about our precious little Rachel . . .*

Suzette jumped to her feet as the letter fell to the floor unnoticed.

"Oh, my God!" she cried.

It was Corby all along! He'd confiscated her shipment of supplies and then denied it had ever reached Montana. He'd probably sold the drugs in Billings or Miles City to unsuspecting pharmacies. Corby's wretched greed had killed Blue Crane Flying!

Racing to the door, she flung it open and tore out of the cabin.

"Dr. Fräulein," Jacob shouted.

"*Liebchen*, whatever's the matter?" Anna called, and then began to cough.

Jacob hurried to the door, left standing wide open in the freezing air. He peered after Suzette, who was dashing over the snowy ground toward the agency's headquarters, and then turned back to his sick wife. Anna was racked with a cough spasm and grimacing in severe pain. He shut the door and hurried to his spouse.

Outside, Suzette slipped and skidded across the icy quadrangle. She caught the heel of her boot in the hem of her blue dress, faltered, and almost fell. Barely aware of what she was doing, she freed her boot with a frantic jerk. Then she lifted her skirt and its ruffled train and continued her wild race over the snow and ice. She ignored the small group of Indians walking to the trading post who called out a friendly greeting, brushing past them with barely a glance. Down the row of log buildings, her unsuspecting prey came out of the commissary with Obadiah Nash and Lew Rumsey.

"Corby! You bastard!" Suzette screamed at the top of her lungs as she came to a standstill. "*Where are my medical supplies?*"

An ominous hush came over the compound as her shrill words echoed in the still winter air. At the blacksmith's shop, three of Rumsey's ranch hands emerged from its dim interior to look out the narrow doorway. A cluster of idlers in front of the agency headquarters turned to watch the white medicine woman standing in the middle of the street. The post trader peered out his store window, framed on either side by a curious Indian.

Over by the stable, Lance and a group of braves, who'd been deep in discussion about the dwindling rations, looked up. "What's going on?" he asked a nearby Cheyenne woman, who immediately signaled her own ignorance.

Everyone had stopped dead in their tracks. Everyone except Horace Corby. Ignoring the high-pitched shrieks of the female doctor, he continued on his way across the snowy compound. Once his two appalled companions realized he wasn't going to stop, they hurried to catch up with him.

But Suzette was not to be put off by the agent's disdainful treatment. She picked up her skirt and petticoat, and raced after him.

Seeing her renew the chase, Lance started to run across the open area between them. If he hurried, he'd be able to reach Corby before she did. He was knocked off his feet by five burly Cheyenne braves, who hurled themselves on top of him without warning. They ignored his muffled threats and aborted his blows while they silently pinned him in a snowdrift beneath them, afraid, no doubt, that he was about to attack the agent. An attack that would very likely end in his own hanging.

Suzette was barely aware of the people up and down the snowy plaza who stood and watched the scene in horrified fascination. Her mind was completely on the agent. She'd almost caught up with him by the time he reached the door of his headquarters.

"Corby, you filthy scum!" she screeched from the edge of the frozen roadway. "What have you done with my shipment? You've sold it, haven't you?"

The agent turned to Lew Rumsey with a smirk. "I think that skinny redhead's got cabin fever. She's ranting and raving like a lunatic." Not waiting for the astounded rancher's reply, he started for the door.

Suzette hurled herself at him. As though expecting her attack, the agent struck out. He backhanded her with a vicious smack, and the force of the blow knocked her off her feet. With the sound of the crack ringing in her ears, she landed on her back on the frozen ground. From all around, Indians wrapped in striped blankets against the winter's cold moved hurriedly toward their fallen *náevehoka*. Angry words in Cheyenne could be heard up and down the snow-covered plaza.

"Jesus!" Rumsey shouted. He reached down to help her up.

"Holy cow," Obadiah muttered, glancing at his boss from the corner of his eye with a disgusted grimace. "For chris'sakes, she's a woman."

With Rumsey's help, Suzette struggled to her feet. Blood trickled from the corner of her mouth. Undaunted, she met the malevolent glitter of hatred in the agent's pale green eyes. "You'll pay for this, Corby," she said in a breathless, shaky voice. "As God is my witness, you are going to pay for what you've done. I'm not going to let you get away with it."

Before he or anyone else could say a word, she pushed through the crowd of concerned Indians and raced back to her cabin.

Once inside, Suzette whirled to face the big hunting rifle that hung above the door. She reached up, lifted it down from its rack, turned, and continued on to the kitchen area. Frantically she searched through the corner pantry, shoving aside canned goods, spice tins, and jars of homemade plum preserves.

"Where are they?" she muttered to herself, nearly oblivious to Jacob and Anna, who stood staring at her in mystified confusion. "Where are those cartridges?"

The couple hurried to her side. "Let me take this, Dr. Fräulein," Jacob coaxed as he tried to reach for the old muzzle-loader. "Calm down now, *Liebling*, and tell us what's going on."

Wildly Suzette jerked the rifle out of his reach. "No, Jacob," she cried. Her sore chin trembled, and two tears rolled down her cheeks. "I'm going to kill him. I'm going to shoot that murderer like the reptile he is."

"Child!" Anna exclaimed. She clasped her plump hands together and held them to her bosom, her eyes wide with horror. "You don't mean it. Give Papa the gun."

His sheepskin jacket and heavy winter moccasins covered with snow, Lance threw open the cabin door and strode into the parlor. He found the two missionaries trying to wrestle Jacob's antiquated Springfield out of the taller Suzette's determined grasp.

"Suzette," Lance called sternly in English. "Give Jacob his gun."

She turned to face him, still clutching the huge rifle, its forty-inch barrel pointed at the ceiling above their heads. Her eyes were hysterical with pain and grief and an overwhelming anger. A tiny trickle of blood and the bright red blotch on her jaw marked the spot where Corby had struck her.

Lance felt a cold rage go through him at the sight of her injury. Suzette was right. The son of a bitch deserved to die. But she wasn't the one who would have the exquisite pleasure of killing him.

She met Lance's gaze and crumpled, allowing the gun to slip from her fingers. With a swift movement, Jacob snatched it away and placed it in a far corner out of reach.

When Anna had first heard the perfect English words spoken by the Cheyenne brave, she'd covered her mouth with one hand to muffle her startled exclamation. Now she put her arm lovingly around the distraught woman's shoulders and guided her to a nearby kitchen chair.

"It's all right, little *Leibchen*," she soothed, her German accent heavy in her agitation. "Sit down, dear child. It's going to be all right."

"No. No, it's not," Suzette cried. She covered her face with her hands. Her slim shoulders shook with heartrending sobs. "It's never going to be all right. No one can bring Blue Crane Flying back to life. She didn't have to die. It's all his fault."

Lance walked over and crouched down in front of her. He pulled Suzette's hands away from her swollen face and clasped the graceful fingers, wet with tears and her own blood, in his own long ones. "What happened, angel?" he asked quietly, still speaking in her native tongue with the hope that it would calm her.

At the term of endearment, Anna met her husband's blue eyes in shock. But Jacob didn't seem at all surprised. He only put a finger in front of his lips to signal his astonished spouse to remain silent.

Suzette carried Lance's hands to her bruised mouth and kissed his fingers. "He killed her," she sobbed. "That bastard killed Blue Crane Flying."

Lance waited for the hysteria to subside. "How did Corby kill my brother's wife?"

She looked up. The tears sparkled on her russet lashes like clusters of diamonds. A shudder went through her as she attempted to gain control of her shattered emotions. "He . . . he stole my shipment of medicine. He had the quinine all the time, and I could have saved her. I could have saved her."

Gently Lance cupped her battered face in his hands. His words were harsh and filled with an unswerving resolution. "I promise you, Suzette, that Corby will pay for everything he's done."

"What . . . what do you mean?"

Lance rose and stood before her. He could feel the tautness of his jaw as he spoke through clenched teeth. "The moment he touched you, angel, Corby was a dead man."

The silence that followed his words was shattered by a pounding on the cabin's heavy wooden door.

Cautiously Jacob walked across the parlor and opened it. At his gesture of welcome, an Indian brave stepped inside. He was wrapped in a threadbare blanket, and his dark, almond-shaped eyes were shadowed with fear. "I am Bull Hump on Shoulder," he announced in the Cheyenne tongue. "I am a member of Chief White Elk's band." He looked frantically about until he found Suzette, still sitting in the kitchen chair. "I need the *náevehoka* to come with me at once to our camp near the Tongue River. My wife is dying."

Suzette sprang up and hurried over to him. "What's wrong with her?"

"She's been trying to have a baby for three days, Sweet Medicine Woman," he answered. "But the child won't come out."

Suzette turned to War Lance. "How soon can we leave?"

"Going anywhere right now is a bad idea," he said with a scowl. Her answering frown told him she wasn't about to listen to reason, but he continued anyway. "The sky's been getting darker by the minute, and the temperature's dropped steadily all morning. If we go, we could get caught in a snowstorm."

"If we don't go, the woman will die," she replied. "You get the sleigh ready while I go to my office and gather my things." She headed for the door, as though there really weren't any other choice. And for her there wasn't.

When she'd left, Lance turned to Jacob and spoke once again in English. "I'm sure that what you've seen and heard has shocked and confused you both," he said. "But I hope you'll wait until we've returned before you tell anyone else about this. There's a great deal I need to explain first."

Jacob raised his hand in reassurance. "I'm not so surprised as you might think, War Lance. I knew your grandmother while we were in the Oklahoma lands. She often spoke to me of her half-white grandson who went to live with his mother's people. When you showed up out of the blue, it wasn't that hard to put two and two together." He walked over and offered Lance his hand. "You have my word that neither Anna nor I will say anything about what's happened here today."

From his office window, Horace Corby watched the team and sleigh leave the agency with the doctor and her Indian guide. They were accompanied by a buck on horseback.

"I tell ya, we've gotta get rid of that meddlesome bitch," he snarled as he sank down in the chair behind his desk. He picked up a ruler and whacked it against the scarred oak top. "It's her or us."

Lew Rumsey braced his shoulder against the window frame and gazed out at the departing trio. "Don't be a fool, Corby," he replied in disgust. "You managed to get away with killing two special agents by making their deaths look accidental. Killing that white lady doc isn't quite as simple. The bureaucrats in Washington would never rest until they were sure exactly what happened."

"We wouldn't have to make it look like another accident. It could be murder. By her own guide. Rape, and then murder to cover it up. Course, he'd be killed outright by the cowboys who discovered it happening."

Rumsey straightened and shook his head. "I'm against it. Nobody in the Indian Bureau is going to pay any attention to an eccentric spinster physician who writes crazy letters accusing the Tongue River agent of stealing her medicine. But they sure as hell will notice if she's suddenly killed—by her Indian guide or anyone else. This reservation would be swarming with government investigators. Let's just leave well enough alone. We've got a sweet thing going here. Don't ruin it."

"I'm not a fool," Corby snarled as he lunged to his feet.

"Let's just let things cool down before we try anything." Rumsey readjusted his Stetson and met the agent's irate gaze with easygoing assurance. "I'm going on over to the trading post and pick up a few supplies. After that, I'm heading for the ranch. I'll be back in a couple of days, and we'll talk some more about this then. In the meantime, just calm down and relax. No one heard what she screamed at you except a few dumb Indians who can't even understand English."

"By God, I wanted to choke the life outta the slut right then," Corby exclaimed. He followed Rumsey out of the room and walked with him across the headquarter's outer office. At the front door the agent watched his partner cross the snowy plaza and enter the trading post. As soon as Rumsey's lean frame disappeared from sight, Corby turned to his clerk, who sat behind a paper-littered desk. "Nash, run on over to the blacksmith's shop and find Gus Troxel. Tell him I want to see him right now. Tell him I've got a little job for him."

Bull Hump had been right. His young wife was dying. Goose Woman lay on her sleeping pallet drenched in sweat. Her dark eyes mirrored the fear and pain she'd endured for the past three days while several women from her camp had hovered nearby in sympathetic helplessness. Suzette's first instructions were to send the other females to their own lodges. But before they left, she asked them to continue to sing their strong-heart songs for the pregnant woman.

"Sweet Medicine Woman," the exhausted Goose Woman gasped in a weak voice. "Please help me."

Suzette examined her patient to find the baby was in breech presentation. Worse, there was complete uterine inertia. According to the other women, there had been no contractions for the past five hours. The only good sign was the strong fetal heartbeat.

"I'll need hot water," she told Lance. "And you're going to be my assistant." She hurriedly yanked the forceps, scissors, chloroform, bichloride of mercury, sterilized cotton and gauze, and a solution of permanganate of potassium out of her leather satchel. "We're going to deliver this child immediately."

Lance proved his levelheaded strength once again as he administered the chloroform drop by steady drop. With the aid of the forceps, Suzette moved the baby through the narrow passageway until the only barrier that remained was the skin at the outlet. She cut that resistant wall with her scissors and delivered the male child as Lance pressed on the top of the uterus to help ease the baby out.

While Suzette delivered the placenta, he took the baby, a limp, red mass, in his large hands and looked down in awe. Suddenly the baby cried out a tiny wail, his wet arms and legs flailing aimlessly, and a slow grin of amazement spread across the warrior's face.

With a smile at Lance's thunderstruck expression, Suzette turned back to her other patient. The hemorrhaging continued unabated, and she could get no contractions whatsoever.

"What's the matter?" Lance asked in concern when he saw her worried scowl.

"I've got to stop the bleeding."

Hurriedly she administered a hypodermic of ergotine to the failing mother, then checked the life signs. The pulse was barely there, the breathing slow and shallow. The woman was bleeding to death before their eyes.

Desperate, Suzette looked up at Lance, who remained on his knees beside her. "I need some ice. Fast."

Handing the baby to Bull Hump, he grabbed a tomahawk from its place beside the doorway and left the lodge. He was back in minutes with a chunk of ice he'd hacked from the nearby creek. Suzette slipped the ice up to the opening of the uterus, and it contracted immediately. The bleeding slowed, then stopped, and she quickly repaired the episiotomy.

With a sigh of relief, she met Bull Hump's worried gaze with heartfelt compassion. "I think your woman is going to live. But she will need a lot of rest. Now let's see to your baby boy."

Suzette and War Lance stayed with Bull Hump and his family that night. The two visitors slept side by side beneath a thick fur rug. Exhausted emotionally and physically, Suzette curled up in Lance's strong arms and fell asleep at once. She awoke twice during the night to check on her two patients, and found the baby nestled contentedly against his sleeping mother's breast. Both times, Bull Hump on Shoulder was wide-awake. He sat beside the fire, deep in prayer. Suzette knew he was thanking *Maheo* for the safety of his two loved ones. She didn't intrude on his meditation, but returned in silence to the guests' side of the lodge.

Each time she slipped back under the fur robe, Lance enfolded her in his welcoming embrace.

"Everything all right?" he whispered when she'd returned for the second time.

"Yes," she said in a hushed tone. "Go back to sleep." Tucking her head under his chin, she drifted off, in total peace.

When she awoke in the morning, she was still cradled in his arms. He was watching her with solemn eyes.

"What is it?" she asked softly. Across the lodge, Bull Hump snored at last beside his wife and newborn child.

Lance shook his head. "I was merely thinking, angel, that if only you were Indian or I was completely white . . ."

She reached up to touch his cheek. "What difference does it make, if we love each other?"

He smiled and pulled her closer, his large hands sliding across the folds of her skirt to cup her bottom. His quiet words were clipped and edged with irony. "The only person it doesn't make any difference to is you, *zehemehotaz.*"

He bent his head and kissed her. His tongue swept the inside of her mouth, and she met him eagerly, with all the yearning that had built up inside her for the past six lonely weeks. Her eyes misted with tears: He had called her his beloved.

The wail of a hungry baby broke the morning quiet, and the family stirred on the other side of the tipi.

"I think I'd better get up and look after my charges," she told him as she traced the line of his mouth with her fingertip. "But believe me, this discussion isn't over."

Lance let her go with aching reluctance. It would be the last time he held her in his arms. With the Grabers' realization that he spoke English, everything would change. He had promised Jacob an explanation, and as far as possible without involving Suzette, he intended to tell the truth. Finding the proof of Corby's guilt was no longer so important. The agent wouldn't live long enough to be tried in court anyway. But there were others involved in the swindling, and he wanted them to pay for what they'd stolen from the Cheyenne people.

And for Suzette's sake, Lance knew he must leave the reservation as soon as possible.

They were on their way back to Lame Deer by midday. The sky was still dark and threatening, but the storm had held off. Lance would have preferred to remain at Bull Hump's camp, but the need to return to the agency and make one last search for proof of Corby's misappropriation of monies, as well as Lew Rumsey's participation in the duplicity, overrode his concern about the possibility of bad weather.

Suzette was snuggled beside him under the thick fur robes, dozing peacefully. She'd treated all the sick Indians in the camp that morning, beaming with pleasure at the new name the Cheyenne had given her. Sweet Medicine Woman was the highest possible tribute, for their greatest spiritual leader and prophet, who'd given the Cheyenne their rules of government and moral conduct long ago, had been called Sweet Medicine.

The sleigh fairly skimmed over the snow as Lance guided the team across the rolling hills. Suddenly the crack of a rifle rang out, followed by the whine of a bullet that buried itself in the snow just in front of them. Suzette sat up and looked about in confusion.

"Get down," he shouted. He reached over and shoved her under the blankets.

"Is it someone out hunting?" she asked, her voice muffled by the thick robes. "Was it an accident?"

Just then, three riders rode out of a thicket of lodgepole pines and into the open meadow directly across from them. Lance recognized them immediately. "It's hunters, all right," he said. "But that was no accident. They're hunting us."

Chapter 23

With a piercing whistle, Lance slapped the reins, and the nervous horses bolted. The sleigh careened wildly over the packed snow at breakneck speed, flying past stands of bare cottonwoods and mountain ash. Team, sleigh, and occupants sailed over the frozen creek bed and through an open meadow, with their pursuers steadily gaining. Rifle lead zinged around them. The aims of their attackers improved drastically as the distance between them shrank.

Lance turned the horses away from the road to Lame Deer and headed into the Wolf Mountains. His only hope was to find cover. There was no way he could protect Suzette from the lethal hail of bullets out in the open. Once in the rougher terrain, the advantage would be all his. He knew every coulee and draw in the mountains. The low clouds and biting wind were his allies as well. Right now he'd even welcome a snowstorm. He knew how to survive the bitter elements that would prove to be the other men's downfall.

He reached the foot of a snow-covered ridge and hauled back on the reins. "Get out!" he shouted, and leaped down, grabbing his Winchester from its scabbard.

Suzette scrambled out of the sleigh and turned to reach for her medical bag.

"Leave it," he hollered.

She ignored him and tugged on her precious satchel.

He raced around the sleigh, tore it out of her gloved hands, and threw it back behind the seat.

"Goddammit, I said leave it!" He grabbed her arm and pulled her up the steep incline. Her long skirts slowed their progress, and he cursed fluently under his breath.

They scrambled over the boulders, dislodging small rocks as they climbed. Below them, the three cowboys reached the abandoned vehicle. He could hear their crows of delight as they decided they'd cornered their prey.

Lance shoved Suzette unceremoniously from behind when she stopped in paralyzed fright at the sound of their voices.

"Go," he urged. "Go!"

At the top of the ridge was a gently sloping incline forested with lodgepole pines, and the pair fled into the cover of the dense foliage. At last they reached his goal. Carved into the rocky mountainside was a natural fissure just big enough for Suzette to hide in. The face of the low-hanging crevice was covered with juniper shrubs and drifted snow.

"Get in," he said as he shoved the brush aside with the butt of his rifle.

"No! Not without you!" Her violet eyes were huge with fear, her shoulders rigid with an all-too-familiar stubbornness.

"Get in there," he ordered. Unable to waste precious minutes arguing, he grabbed her arm, ready to physically stuff her into the small opening. But his resolution must have communicated itself, for she bent down without another word and crawled into the shelter.

"No matter what you hear," he said, "don't come out of there until I pull you out."

With lightning speed, he replaced the snowy branches. There was no time to cover their sign, but at least she was safe from stray bullets. And he had no intention of letting the bastards get close enough to her to spot the tracks in the disturbed snow.

As he raced back through the tall pines at an oblique angle from Suzette's place of concealment, Lance checked his repeating rifle. Then he found a large tree at the edge of the clearing and halted behind it. He could hear the three men crashing up the ridge. They were making enough noise for a whole herd of stampeding buffalo. The moment the first one came in view over the top of the ledge, Lance aimed and fired.

There wasn't so much as a grunt of pain. The pale-haired cowboy named Bouten flew backward off the edge, his arms flung wide in incredulous surprise. From his position behind the tree trunk, Lance could hear the series of thuds as the body crashed back down the rocky incline, scattering pebbles and brush on the way. He'd struck the man square in the middle of his forehead.

"That's one less son of a bitch," Lance muttered.

"Injun!" Gus Troxel yelled from behind the cover of the ridge. "We ain't after you! It's the woman we want. You jest go on now and git, and we'll leave you alone."

"Ne-náeste!" Lance called, urging them to come after him.

"Shit," he heard Titus Kraus exclaim to his cohort. "He cain't even understand English. How the hell we gonna talk him out of there?"

Lance waited in silence for the answer. Finally the sound of rocks pinging against the ledge wall broke the long silence. The two men were stealthily retreating.

Cautiously Lance eased out from behind the large pine and crawled to the ledge. Kraus and Troxel had already scrambled down the rocky incline and disappeared, but their mounts were still ground-tied next to the team and sleigh. They'd managed to slip into the surrounding trees and brush, intending to circumvent the ridge, climb the steep face of the mountainside, and circle around behind him. It would take a while, but they could do it.

"Damn," Lance cursed softly. He scanned the sides of the nearby slopes, searching for their footprints in the snow and hoping for some sign of movement. Nothing. If

they were smart, they'd separate and come at him from
different directions. He moved back into the cover of the
trees and waited.

At last there was the rapid flutter of wings as a startled
grouse rose from its cover in the brush, and Lance
moved.

In the dark confines of her narrow hiding place, Suzette tried to hear something—anything—above the
pounding of her heart. She lay on her stomach under the
low ceiling, resting her head on her folded arms.

"Dear God," she pleaded over and over, "don't let
anything happen to him."

The minutes passed, and the absolute silence slowly
became unendurable. She fought the claustrophobic feeling of being suffocated beneath tons of collapsing granite. Not knowing what was happening, not even if Lance
was still alive, was more than she could bear.

Suddenly the primordial quiet was shattered by a
blood-chilling war whoop, followed almost simultaneously by a man's agonized death scream. She knew
somehow that the long, drawn-out cry that echoed
against the rock walls surrounding them was made by a
man dying in excruciating pain.

Then the unnatural silence returned.

She heard someone whimpering in terror and realized
it was her. With a choked sob, she clamped her hand
over her mouth to cover the telltale noise. She knew she
couldn't stand much more of the waiting. Nothing could
be worse than this feeling of helplessness as she lay
there, straining to hear the slightest sound. If Lance was
injured, she needed to find him, not cower there alone in
the darkness.

Slowly Suzette edged out from under the rocky crag's
low roof and pushed aside the juniper shrubs that covered
the opening. She peeked out to find that it had started to
snow while she'd huddled in her solitary shelter. The
tracks in front of the crevice had been completely obliter-

ated. There wasn't a sign of life, human or animal. A feeling of mind-numbing desolation engulfed her. Had Lance been killed by that single rifle blast? Had she been left to die alone on the side of a mountain?

She rose to her feet and crept into the stand of tall pines. Afraid to call out, unable to discover any footprints, she started to move faster and faster, until she was running. She had no idea in which direction to go, but raced in blind panic through the forest. The ground was littered with the carcasses of dead pines nearly hidden beneath the snowdrifts, waiting to trip her. Her fur cap was knocked off by a low branch as she scrambled over the silver trunk of a fallen lodgepole, and her loosened hair was caught on the evergreen needles. Gasping in the high elevation, she breathed in the pungent smell of pine as she tore the coppery strands loose and continued to run.

From behind a tree, she heard the snap of a twig.

Or the click of a gun.

Turning in midstride, she looked back over her shoulder. And crashed headlong into a giant. She screamed in terror as Gus Troxel caught her in his arms.

"Well, lookee here." He grinned. His words made little puffs of white mist in the frosty air. His shaggy black eyebrows and mustache were sprinkled with delicate snowflakes. Despite her frantic struggle to break free, he held her securely imprisoned against his damp buffalo-robe coat. He clutched a big buffalo gun in one hand, and its long metal barrel struck her head as she jerked backward. Stunned, Suzette tottered, but Troxel's grasp held her upright. He slammed her against the trunk of a nearby tree, knocking the wind out of her. As he leaned over her, she could smell the fetid odor of his breath and gagged in fear and revulsion.

"Hummph," she gasped. She turned her head aside and tried to control the nausea.

"Where's the Injun?" he demanded. One gloved hand

ruthlessly squeezed her throat. Black dots danced in front of her eyes.

She tried to shake her head. "I don—don—don't know," she stuttered incoherently.

Recognizing she was nearly immobilized with fear, he loosened his grip slightly and glanced cautiously around. "Let's go find him."

He dragged her through the snow, yanking her up brutally when her legs became entangled in the folds of her dress, or the hem of her petticoat snagged on the bark of a tree. Her arms felt as though they were being torn from their sockets, and she bit her lower lip to keep from moaning in pain.

"Injun!" Troxel screamed into the silent wilderness. "I got the woman now. Come on out and we'll parlay."

The falling snow was a dense curtain of white, cutting visibility down to only a few feet in front of them. The silence was terrifying. Lance must have been killed by one of the other cowboys. Otherwise, he would have answered Troxel's call. He would have tried to save her.

"Kraus, where are ya?" her captor hollered, apparently following the same train of thought. She fell again, and the burly man pulled her up by the neck of her sealskin coat and shoved her ahead of him with a vicious kick of his boot on her backside.

She stumbled over the feet of a corpse and fell palms first into the powdery snow. Sobbing out loud, she pushed up on her hands and knees to stare at the dead man's face. It was distorted in horror. And small wonder. He'd been scalped. The front of his heavy coat was flung wide, revealing a brutal incision. He'd been ripped open by a sharp-edged blade from the lower abdomen to the sternum, and parts of the stomach and intestines lay in a bloody, congealed mass on the white ground. It was Kraus. He was already starting to freeze like a side of butchered beef in the swirling snow.

"Holy shit!" Troxel cried. He whirled about, searching the trees around them, his rifle leveled.

The only sound was the blood rushing in Suzette's ears.

"Get up," he snarled at her. He jerked her upright and pulled her backward against his barrel chest. Pressing one brawny arm against her throat, he started to squeeze the life out of her, and she clawed at him frantically.

"*Injun!* I swear to God, I'm gonna kill her right now."

A gray mist encircled her. Her vision blurred and her knees buckled as she started to lose consciousness.

Lance came up behind the burly cowboy on silent, moccasined feet. With his left hand he reached around Troxel's head and jerked it back, his palm and wrist covering the man's eyes. He held the greasy head pinned immobile against his own upper arm and shoulder. Continuing the momentum he'd created, Lance stepped back, and his opponent staggered with him, off balance, blind, and disoriented. Troxel, still clutching the buffalo gun, flailed about wildly as he tried to regain his balance, and Suzette was pitched forward into a snowdrift like a child thrown from a runaway toboggan. With the ten-inch hunting knife in his right hand, Lance slit the grimy, exposed throat with such brutal force that the man was nearly decapitated. Troxel was dead before he even knew what was happening. Lance let him fall to the ground, then bent over and scalped him with cold-blooded precision. The entire kill had taken less than five seconds.

Suzette crawled to her hands and knees in the snow, staring at the grisly sight. Then she sat back on her calves and looked up at War Lance in stunned bewilderment. He tossed the scalp and knife into the snow and moved to her, his sharp features distorted in fury.

"Goddammit, I told you to stay in that cave," he shouted. He yanked her to her feet and shook her, and her tumbled curls flew back and forth with the violence of his anger.

Unable to think of a reasonable excuse, she looked up at him in confusion. "I was only try—trying to help you," she said at last, her teeth chattering in delayed shock. "And there you go, swearing at me in English again. I wish you'd stick to Cheyenne when you're angry." As she spoke, she pounded her doubled fists against the front of his heavy sheepskin jacket. Hot tears stung her eyes, and she glared at him in hurt and rebellion through the lacy snowflakes that drifted around them.

With a sudden, suffocated laugh, he grasped her by the back of the neck and pulled her to him. He held her in his arms, her face smashed against his broad chest. "Jesus, angel, you scared the bloody hell out of me."

The abandoned trapper's cabin was exactly as Lance remembered it, not much more than a dugout cut into the slope of a hill, with a lean-to on one side for livestock. But as the driving snowstorm turned into a blizzard, the ramshackle place took on the appearance of a wintry paradise.

Lance lifted Suzette down from the sleigh, snatched his Winchester and her leather satchel, and guided her to the door. The biting wind pierced their layers of clothing and drove icy needles into their flesh. The howling gusts and blowing snow caught at her sodden skirts, nearly toppling her over like a child's unbalanced toy boat skidding across a frozen pond. He pulled on the latch string, opened the door, and drew her inside.

The gloomy interior was dry, at least. The former owner had lined the ceiling with a canvas wagon sheet. The trapper must have been disgusted with the bits of grass and dirt drifting down from the sod roof. Either that or he'd had a woman living with him. There was a small stone fireplace on the lean-to side so the fire's heat could warm the animals as well.

"Sit down and rest, sweetheart," he told her. He leaned his rifle beside the doorframe and set her medical bag on the dirt floor. There was no need to worry about unwanted company. No one could track them in this blinding gale. "I've got to unhitch the team and get them sheltered."

Suzette nodded and staggered over to a dusty three-legged stool beside the cold hearth. "Yes, go on." She was so weary, she could hardly speak. "I'll be all right in a minute."

When Lance had left, she removed the fur hat that he'd rescued from the snowdrift, stripped off her soaked gloves, and laid the items down on the stone hearth with agonizing slowness. Barely able to move her ice-cold fingers, she tried unsuccessfully to unbutton her heavy coat. Then she gave up and looked around the tiny room, her eyes slowly becoming accustomed to the darkness.

Everything was covered with dust. Layers of it, as though the cabin had remained undisturbed for years. Canned goods stood on open shelves, exactly as the home's previous occupant had left them. A rough whip-sawed table was covered with a grimy oilcloth. There wasn't a window in the place, but a kerosene lantern sat on the floor next to a barrel. And on top of the wooden keg was a box of matches.

She'd just managed to light the wick when Lance returned, carrying an armload of dry logs. Seeing the glow of the flame, he kicked the door shut behind him with a happy bang.

"We're in luck," he said, grinning with satisfaction. "I found firewood shoved back inside a shallow cave dug into the hill behind the lean-to. And a barrel of straw to bed the horses."

He pulled off his leather gloves, gathered up some yellowed papers from under the leg of a battered chest, and soon had a fire crackling in the fireplace. He came over to where she sat on the little stool and crouched down in front of her.

"Now let's take a look at you," he said. His raven eyebrows were a straight line of concern. He unbuttoned her coat and eased it over her shoulders. "It'll warm up in here in no time," he reassured her in a soothing tone. "Dugouts like this are amazingly weatherproof."

She winced as he slid the heavy sleeves down her sore

arms. His worried gaze traveled over the length of her blue wool dress as he lightly ran his long fingers over her shoulders and arms and then down to rest on the curves of her hips. He sat back on his haunches. "Do you hurt anyplace in particular? Or just all over?"

She managed a feeble smile. Leaning toward him, she rested her forehead against his brow and clasped his hands. "Honest, there's nothing wrong with me except a few bumps and bruises. And I'm unbelievably tired. It's not every day I take part in something so . . . primitive."

"I'd have tortured them first, before I scalped them," he said simply, "but there wasn't time."

Shocked, she drew back to meet his serious black eyes. "Because of what they did to you that day on the ranch?"

He chuckled softly and bussed the tip of her nose. His deep voice was gruff. "No, baby. Because of what they planned on doing to you today." He rose, retrieved his gloves, and started for the door. "You stay put. I'm going to bring in our supplies from the sleigh."

By the time Lance returned with their packs and fur robes, Suzette was teetering back and forth in sleepy exhaustion on the hand-hewn stool. He took off his thick sheepskin jacket and hung it on a peg near the fireplace. Smiling at her valiant attempt to stay awake, he spread a bearskin on the floor, swung her up in his arms, and placed her in the middle of it.

"Before you fall sound asleep," he said as he hunkered down beside her, "let's get these wet clothes off you." He undressed her, removing her blue dress and white petticoat, the ruffles soaked with melted snow, her embroidered camisole, and her red flannel drawers. She was too tired to even blush at her nakedness. Then he wrapped her in a buffalo robe that he'd placed near the fire.

"Mmmm, I'm warm already," she murmured drowsily.

"Don't get too comfortable," he warned. He slipped off his wet moccasins and padded around on the hard-packed dirt floor. "I'm going to wake you up in a little while to eat something, just as soon as I get it fixed."

"I'm too tired to eat," she protested. She snuggled down into the luxurious bearskin with a sigh of contentment.

"You have to eat something first, before you settle in for the night," he ordered. "You'll need the food to keep up your body heat."

"Which one of us is the doctor?" she reminded him with a sleepy chuckle.

He looked over his shoulder and flashed her a confident grin of male superiority. "You may be the doctor, but I'm the scout that's in charge of the doctor. Remember?"

While she dozed, Lance fixed hot coffee with melted snow and threw chunks of salt pork from their packs into a kettle of baked beans. He opened a can of tomatoes and heated them in a tin pan he found upside down on the back of a shelf. Then he threw dried apples into a crock of hot water and let them steep. When everything was ready, he woke her up and ruthlessly insisted that she eat, ignoring her mumbled complaints about wanting to be left alone. Only after she'd finished a full portion of everything did he let her slip back down on the fur and fall sound asleep.

Suzette could feel the sun's warmth caress her. Its heating rays moved over her limbs and torso in rhythmic undulations. In the fragrant branches of a nearby blossoming crab apple tree, a warm breeze whispered her name. She was lying on a Pennsylvania hillside. It was a glorious spring afternoon, and for some reason she didn't fully understand, she was stark naked. But goodness, that was perfectly all right, for so was Lance. Though she couldn't see him, she could feel the hard, sinewy length of him pressing against her backside as they lay in the thick grass, his strong arms around her.

Her name was repeated again, and she realized with a

sigh that it wasn't the breeze at all. He was calling her name softly, persistently, his lips close to her ear. Nor was it the sun's rays, but his hands that moved over her unclothed body. Perhaps he wanted her to go swimming with him in the nearby bubbling stream. When he nuzzled the tender spot just behind her ear, she smiled lazily and shook her head. She was really too tired to go splashing about in the water, but the thought was certainly entrancing.

He cupped her breasts with his hands and grazed their pink tips with the pads of his thumbs. She sighed again, stretched, and came slowly awake to find herself in a trapper's cabin in the middle of a Montana blizzard. She was throbbing with desire. Her breath caught high in her chest as Lance reached down and stroked her between her thighs. With a whimper of sexual need, she tried to turn in his arms and kiss him, but he held her in place with her back to him.

They were snugly ensconced beneath the luxurious folds of a buffalo robe, stretched out on their sides in front of a blazing fire, while the wind shrieked across the front of the dugout. Since she must have been asleep for hours, he'd undoubtedly just added new logs and come back to bed. But not to sleep.

She could feel his hot erection pressing against her bare bottom. She tried once more to turn and face him.

"Stay the way you are, angel," he commanded in a husky voice. "That way I can touch your gorgeous body and be inside you, both at the same time."

He lifted one of her legs to allow him entrance and thrust his tumescent manhood deep into her moist, welcoming warmth. She moaned in pleasure as he moved inside her.

"But I can't touch you," she gasped, sparks of fire igniting within her.

He chuckled. "I've been waiting patiently for you to get some rest, little doll. Since I can't wait any longer,

I'm going to make it worth your while to wake up. You just lie here and enjoy it."

It had been over six weeks since he'd lain with her. She was wild with excitement. Again and again he drove deep within her, his thick shaft filling her completely. His expert hands moved over her body, caressing her breasts, abdomen, and thighs, his fingers threading through the russet curls of her mound to stroke the sensitive folds of her womanhood. He rasped explicit sexual phrases in her ear that heightened the unbelievable pleasure. He told her how he'd longed for her, how every time he'd been near her, he'd wanted to strip off her clothes and caress her with his lips and tongue, how he'd yearned for the taste of her.

She surrendered control of her thoughts and feelings to his erotic words and skilled hands and allowed him to take her to a swift, pulsating climax. When he heard her cry of fulfillment, he didn't pull away, but remained buried deep within her as he continued to fondle and rub her, drawing out the climax till she was writhing and sobbing with ecstasy in his powerful embrace. Just when she thought she'd go mad with the pleasure, she felt his body tense and stiffen. He groaned and withdrew before his seed was released.

Once again, Suzette felt the deep disappointment at his premeditated act of caution. "Lance," she panted, trying to turn in his arms. "There's something I want to say."

He held her fast, bent his head, and nipped her bare shoulder. "Not now, angel. We're both too tired. Go back to sleep, and I promise we'll talk in the morning."

When Suzette awoke again, she was still in his embrace, her cheek resting on his upper arm. At her slight movement, he woke, and she turned to kiss him.

The fire in the hearth had burned out, but they were toasty warm under the buffalo robe. His large form radiated wonderful male body heat. She kissed him, stroking his tongue boldly with her own, entangling her bare legs with his.

"Sleep well?" he asked with a throaty chuckle. One strong hand moved down her spine to cup her buttocks and bring her closer. He was already swollen with desire.

"Yes, very well," she answered with a smile. "And I had the most marvelous dream."

"Was I in it?"

She flushed at the memory of their passionate intimacy. "Most definitely." She slid her fingers across his muscled thigh and stroked his rigid manhood with a shy caress. His erect shaft leaped in her hand, as though welcoming her touch.

"Are you always like this?" she teased as she continued to stroke him.

He shook his head and flashed her a wolfish grin, but the thickness of his voice betrayed how deeply her touch affected him. "Only when I'm around you."

He rolled onto his back and closed his eyes, openly enjoying her sensual ministrations. Suzette thrilled at the way he accepted her inexpert caresses with such natural grace and obvious enjoyment. He made their mating seem so normal and right, she forgot to be self-conscious.

"Come here," he murmured. He met her gaze with a look of scorching desire. "Let's put you on top this time." Grasping her hips, he lifted her up and eased her onto his rigid erection.

Suzette gasped at the pagan excitement of straddling him, of being the one in control. She could feel the hard length of him deep inside her, her sensitive folds rubbing against his solid body. She moved in reflexive response and then looked into his black eyes in delighted surprise at the incredible pleasure.

"Go ahead, baby. Ride me," he urged. He reached up and flicked her nipples with his fingertips, and she responded with a low moan.

Bending over him, she placed her palms on his muscled chest. She stroked her tongue over his lips and then entered his mouth. It was impossible to stop moving her hips. The feeling was too wonderful to remain still.

Eyes closed, she sat up and arched her back, presenting her breasts for him to fondle.

"Don't be in a hurry," he coaxed as he lifted the taut globes in his cupped hands. "We're not going anywhere today. Take your time and enjoy every little movement."

Her lids fluttered open and she sought his gaze. Raw sexual hunger burned in the fathomless depths of his dark eyes. Instinctively she knew it would never be like this with anyone but him. Never. Nor would she ever want to be with another man for the rest of her life. Her fingers brushed over his chest, caressing the flat nipples. She stroked his bare skin, tracing over the curves of his well-defined muscles. Biceps, deltoid, trapezius, pectoralis major, obliquus externus. It was a litany of praise as she adored his glorious male body. Good God, he was beautiful.

Suddenly she remembered how she'd told him just that, when she still believed he couldn't understand a word of English. Her eyes widened at the thought, and his deep chuckle told her he knew exactly what she was thinking. She smiled and shook her head at the memory.

"Oooh, I should make you pay for that," she threatened as she lightly clawed her fingernails across his chest.

"Go ahead," he taunted with a grin. "Scratch and bite. I love it when you treat me rough." The underlying laughter in his words told her that against his strength, he counted hers as equal to a gnat's.

She bent and took his lower lip gently in her teeth. In retaliation, he grasped her hips and moved inside her ever so slightly. She gasped in sweet enjoyment.

"I love you so much, Lance," she said, her lips brushing against his as she spoke. She froze in sudden confusion.

She hadn't meant to confess it.

She'd wanted him to tell her of his love first, but it

was too late. She'd already blurted it out like a lovesick schoolgirl. When he only kissed her in reply, her heart ached with the pain of it. She tried to pull away, but he wouldn't let her. Instead, he rolled over and pinned her beneath him, keeping her impaled on his rigid shaft. He grabbed her hands when she attempted to push him away, and imprisoned her wrists on either side of her head. Refusing to allow her the chance to protest, he covered her mouth with his own and forced his tongue inside. He thrust and withdrew his turgid manhood again and again as he slammed into her tense, resisting body and rekindled the inner excitement, till an uncontrollable fire raged within her, sweeping all other thoughts before it. She shook her head, trying to deny what was happening inside her.

"Don't fight it, Suzette," he ordered roughly. "Let it happen."

She clung to him, her lips pressed against his shoulder. She sobbed in frustration as her body gave him exactly what he wanted. Spasms of pleasure rocked her. Her muscles clenched and tightened on his engorged shaft, lifting them both up in a spiraling flight to fulfillment. She felt herself surrender and wrapped her legs around him.

"If you can't give me your love," she begged, "at least, give me your child."

"Oh, Suzette, Suzette," he said in a voice thick with emotion. "You don't know what you're asking."

Chapter 24

$\sim\!\!\sim\!\!\bigotimes\!\!\sim\!\!\sim$

S he looked so small and vulnerable. Her red-gold hair, as thick and unruly as a child's, spread out in tangled waves across the dark bearskin; her face was pale and luminescent in the flickering glow of the lantern. The sight of her fragility stirred an overpowering desire within him to protect her from all of life's sorrows. As she stared up at him from the fur rug, her violet eyes were enormous with pain and an unwarranted sense of humiliation, and his heart ached with the thought that he was the cause of such defenseless misery.

Though he'd withdrawn before his seed could spill into her, just as he'd done each time previously, there was no guarantee that even now she wasn't carrying his child. There were other, better ways to prevent a pregnancy, and as a physician, Suzette knew as well as he that they could have made use of them. But she wanted his child, just as she wanted to spend the rest of her life with him. Her mistaken belief that he wanted neither was evident in the crystalline glitter of her unshed tears.

Lance clenched his jaw and willed himself not to respond to the unguarded hurt he read on those delicate features. It would be far better if she never suspected that he'd fallen in love with her—with a love so binding, so irrevocable, that for the rest of his life, no other woman would ever take her place. When they'd parted and he was once again in England, she'd believe that for him it had been no more than a brief affair. Eventually, as the memory faded, she'd find someone who could fit into her life and bring her the happiness she deserved.

"I couldn't leave you to raise a child alone, sweetheart," he said gently as he stroked his fingertips across her cheekbone. Though he'd moved to lie beside her, he still held her locked beneath one heavy thigh. "Especially not a quarter-breed Indian," he continued when she shook her head. "And for the same reason, marriage between us is out of the question. You've no idea how cruel people can be. No man would ever say or do anything to hurt you and live to tell about it, I can promise you that. I'd carve the bastard's heart out and serve it to him on a platter. But you'd find yourself ostracized from polite female society, and there wouldn't be a damn thing I could do about it. Neither you, nor our daughters if we had any, would be invited to teas or dances or whatever the hell else women set so much store by. I won't be the cause of that kind of lifelong exile."

For Suzette, understanding came at last with his tortured words, and a thrill of joy went through her. *He did love her.* He just wouldn't admit it because of some foolish idea of sacrificing himself for her happiness. What he didn't realize was that without *him,* she'd never be happy. She wasn't going to stand by and see him ruin both of their lives for some lunatic notion that she couldn't handle whatever the world might send her way because she was the wife of a half-breed Cheyenne.

"Is that what it's all about, then?" she demanded. She struggled to sit up, but he held her pinned against the bearskin robe. Impatiently she shoved his leg aside with both hands and leaned over him. "You think because I'm a female, I can't stand up to the prejudice of ignorant fools? Only I have the right to make that decision, Lance, not you."

"You're wrong, angel." He sat up beside her and glowered, his deep baritone like a roll of thunder. "It's my decision, and by God, I won't subject you to the derision of others so that I can take what I want in life. The only thing I'd bring you is unhappiness. If our relationship was public knowledge, you'd be held up to scorn and ridicule. You might even be injured by self-righteous snobs who thought they'd been given the job of enforcing society's unwritten rules."

She gave a soft, unladylike snort of derision and rose from the fur rug. Grabbing her undergarments from the stool by the hearth, she slipped on her camisole and then pulled on the red flannel drawers. "How noble of you to want to save me from such a terrible fate," she mocked in a high-pitched, singsong voice. She lifted her hands in feigned surrender. "I might not be invited to Sunday tea with a bunch of backbiting old biddies. Goodness gracious, how terrifying." Returning to the bearskin, she braced her hands on her hips and bent over him. "You're looking at a woman who fought against all odds to become a doctor. Do you think that was easy? Even in Lancaster, people who'd known me since I was a child treated me as though I were some kind of three-eyed freak when I enrolled at the medical college." She straightened and brushed the tangled curls away from her forehead with restless fingers. With a sigh, she looked away and then back again to meet his scowling gaze. He was staring at her in stubborn resolution, and she knew she hadn't budged him one inch. "You once asked me why I came to the reservation, Lance. I'll tell you why. I spent an entire year trying to open a medical practice in my hometown. Not a single person came to me as a patient. I saw my father die a heartbroken old man watching even his close friends treat his eldest daughter like a pariah. Do you honestly think I can't stand up to a little bigotry dished out by a bunch of gossips after what I fought against and endured for so long in order to become a physician?"

He rose and jerked on his breechclout and Levis. "It wouldn't be just a little bigotry, Suzette. It'd be a whole bloody lifetime of social banishment."

She shrugged with exaggeration and walked over to the line of rope he'd strung across the small cabin. Lifting down her petticoat, she stepped into its ruffled skirt, pulled it up, and fastened the ties. "If I'm willing to endure such exile, as you term it, then it should be my choice. I happen to think that the love between two people is far more important than socializing with narrow-minded idiots who mistakenly consider themselves the pillars of society. You were always the one who hid our relationship from others. I never tried to pretend there was nothing between us. I'm not ashamed of what I feel for you. In fact, I'm ready to announce it to the entire agency: *Dr. Stanwood loves War Lance Striking.*"

He was directly in front of her before she could draw another breath. "You're not going to do that," he bit out savagely. He towered over her in a blatant attempt to intimidate her by his size alone. "I won't allow it."

"And are you going to keep me from loving you, too?" she exclaimed. "Well, you can't. I'll always love you. For the rest of my life. And I think you love me, too, even if you haven't the sense to admit it. When you're back in London, lying awake night after night thinking of how it might have been between us, wondering if you really did the right thing in tossing it all away for some romantic notion of playing the knight in shining armor for a damsel who didn't want to be rescued, remember that I'll be somewhere missing you. Wanting you. Loving you."

His jaw was clenched so tight, he could hardly speak. "You'll get over me."

"Will I?" she cried with a shaky laugh. "I'm the one who grieved for nine years over a man who wasn't good enough to shine your boots, remember? Do you really think I'm going to get over you in the next thirty? If you're going to give me credit for anything, it's got to be for sheer, single-minded tenacity."

He slipped on his flannel shirt and sat down on the

stool to pull on the heavy winter moccasins. "You'll just have to accept my decision on this, Suzette."

"Fine! Just tell me you don't love me," she said, "and I'll abide by your wishes. I need to hear you say it, that's all. Then I'll be able to watch you leave, knowing there wasn't a darn thing I could do to keep you beside me. Go on," she goaded. "Tell me you don't love me."

"Jesus!" he roared as he grabbed his sheepskin jacket off the peg and stomped toward the door. "Do you have to make it so damn hard? Why can't you ever listen to reason, instead of being such a pigheaded little fool?"

"Me, pigheaded? I'm not the one who's afraid to tell the truth. Or to meet life on life's terms. You pretend that it's me who doesn't have the courage, but you're wrong, Lance. It's you who's the coward."

He released his grip on the latch bar and strode back to her. "You don't know what you're saying. I know from personal experience that a woman can't face that kind of cruel treatment."

"Whatever spineless female you knew in the past," she scoffed, her chin held high, her arms folded across her chest, "please, don't compare me to her. I have many faults, but cowardice isn't one of them."

Lance clenched his fists in fury and glared at the slender woman who dared to question his courage to his face. She was wrong. Dead wrong. He had to protect her, even from her own rash actions. He could never marry her. No woman could face the discrimination that would be heaped upon their children. If there were sons, he could train them to be as strong as he. But there was no assurance of having only male offspring. And daughters, like their mother, would be far too vulnerable. He turned with a growl of exasperation and headed back toward the door.

"I'm going out to check on the stock," he said, and lifted the latch bar.

"Good. How soon can we leave?" She hadn't dared to add the word *coward*, but he knew she'd thought it.

"You're going to have to put up with my craven presence for a little while longer," he said to the door in front of him. "We can't go anywhere till this storm dies down." As he lifted the horizontal bar from its slot, he fought the urge to tear the whole damn door off its wooden hinges and hurl it out into the snow.

Behind him, he heard her walk over to the three-legged stool and sit down. It wasn't necessary to turn his head to know she was sitting there broomstick straight with her snippy little nose pointed up in the air.

"Very well," she said. "Just let me know when it's safe to leave. Until then, you needn't be afraid. You have my word, I won't bring the subject up again."

He left the cabin, slamming the door so hard, the entire building shook.

Suzette stared at the deserted portal nearly blinded by tears, while bits of grass and sod sifted down through the rips in the canvas sheet that covered the ceiling, and landed in her tousled hair.

She was going to lose him.

Not because he didn't love her, but because he did. She sensed, with an ache that knifed through her breastbone like a surgeon's incision, that there was nothing she could say that would change his mind. Whoever the girl had been, whatever she'd suffered for his sake, he was convinced that he alone was to blame. And the more he loved Suzette, the more determined he'd be not to bring the same unhappiness down upon her.

Bear Scalp had moved his camp from Rosebud Creek to a small canyon at the base of the Wolf Mountains. Lance and his ill-tempered companion arrived two days after the great blizzard to find the old site deserted. Although the bright sunshine sparkled on the snow, dazzling the eyes with its brilliance, Suzette sat beside him in the sleigh as rigid and cold as an icicle. But her arctic exterior didn't deceive him one bit. Inside, she was fuming. Despite all his attempts to make her see reason, she

refused to admit that he was right. And she was wrong.
At first, he'd tried to explain calmly why they could
never be married. She contradicted everything he said
with ill-conceived reasons why they could. Like all members of her sex, she persisted in seeing the world through
rose-colored glasses, thinking with her heart and not with
her head. The more logical he became, the more she dug
in her heels like an irrational little donkey. Finally he'd
lost patience and started shouting. He'd slammed his fist
against the front wall of the sod dugout and punched a
hole right through it. That was when she'd stopped talking.

Dammit, he'd wanted to spend their last few days together holding her sweet body next to his. He'd hoped to
take back to England the parting memory of her graceful
fingers stroking his naked flesh, of her whispered words
of love in his ear. Instead, she'd maintained a frigid silence for the rest of their enforced stay at the cabin,
speaking only when it was absolutely necessary.

Now, with a stiff-necked Suzette bundled up in furs
beside him, he followed the trail left by the lodgepoles
that had been dragged through the drifting snow. They
found the new village strategically placed, with natural
fortifications on three sides.

"We have been waiting for you, *nis'is*," Bear Scalp
called to him, as Lance drove into the snowy camp circle. Wrapped in a heavy buffalo robe, his brother reached
up and grabbed the nearer horse's bridle. "Agent Corby
and the *vèho* called Rumsey are out looking for you.
Three of the rancher's horses came back riderless two
days ago. Major Hairless Head was certain that you had
something to do with the disappearance of the cowmen."

"I killed them," Lance told his brother without elabo-
ration. He looked around the fortified camp. Mounted on
painted mustangs, men with rifles were guarding its outer
boundaries. "Were you attacked?"

"Not yet. But the whites are very excited. When they
find the bodies of the dead men, they may attack the vil-

lage. The old men chief are afraid the Long Knives will ride over from the fort, so our military societies have moved all of the camps to places where they can be more easily protected. With banks of earth on three sides, we can defend ourselves here no matter which direction the whites come from."

Suzette scrambled down and hurried to Bear Scalp. "Why would the soldiers attack the village? Innocent people would be hurt!" She glanced up in horror at Lance, still seated in the sleigh, and then back to the tall brave beside her. "Those three men tried to murder us. Your brother saved my life."

"The deaths of our defenseless women and children have never stopped the whites before, *nitam,*" Bear Scalp replied. "The one thing we fear the most is that the soldiers will have an excuse to come and destroy us completely. There are many whites who would like to remove our people from this earth."

"I'll go back to the agency at once," Lance told him. "I want to make another attempt to find proof of Corby's cheating. In the meantime, send someone with a message to the big soldier chief at the fort. He knows who I am and why I'm here. If I'm taken by the white men for the killings, Colonel Hatch will be the one in charge, not the agent."

"I will send Touching Cloud's brother," Bear Scalp said. "Many Coups is a brave and resourceful warrior." He hurried away to signal one of the mounted men guarding the village, and Lance started to lift the reins.

"Wait," Suzette cried in alarm. She rushed forward and grabbed his elbow, afraid he would leave without her. Switching from the more difficult Cheyenne to English, her words tumbled out in a rush. "I want to go with you, Lance. If that posse finds you, I can tell them that you killed those cowboys in self-defense. Otherwise, they might not wait for Colonel Hatch or the soldiers. You'd never get a fair hearing without me. They could lynch you right there on the spot."

Lance pried her fingers off his arm and bent toward her. He continued to speak in Cheyenne, as though to emphasize the unbridgeable distance between them, and the finality of his clipped words brooked no disagreement. "You're not coming, angel. If I'm caught by a group of angry white men, they'd never listen to you anyway. But if they suspected you cared about me, they'd turn their rage on you, as well. I won't take a chance on your getting hurt."

"I don't care," she insisted, speaking in Cheyenne once more to demonstrate her own resilience. "I'm the only one who can prove your innocence. Do you think I could stay here in hiding while you risked being hanged? I'm willing to let you go back to England, Lance, to satisfy your fantastic male pride. I'm not going to let you get yourself killed trying to protect me."

Reaching down, he brushed back a lock of hair that had come loose from under her fur hat. "I understand what you're feeling, *zehemehotaz*," he said, his voice husky with emotion. "And believe me, I'm deeply touched. I'll never forget that you were willing to risk your life to protect mine. But I won't let you get involved. It's too dangerous."

He straightened and gathered the reins. "You wait here with my brother. Stay inside the camp circle and you won't be in any danger. And sleep in Touching Cloud's lodge tonight. That way you can visit with Yellow Feather. Colonel Hatch will come as soon as he gets my message."

She looked up at him and held her tongue. She knew from the determination in his black eyes that he'd never allow her to go with him. But he couldn't keep her from following.

He slapped the reins, and the team took off at a brisk trot. As the sleigh disappeared over a snow-covered knoll in a jingle of bells, Prairie Grass Woman came to stand beside her. Suzette met her concerned gaze and smiled blithely. "Your grandson said he would go ahead to the agency headquarters. He told me to borrow a horse from someone and return to my cabin when I was ready."

Prairie Grass Woman stared at her thoughtfully for a long minute, and Suzette was certain Lance's grandmother knew she was lying.

"I heard about the dead white men," the tiny woman said at last. Hugging her striped blanket tighter around her frail shoulders, she turned and looked northward in the direction of Lame Deer. Her wrinkled face was filled with apprehension.

"I've got to go after him, *niscehem*," Suzette pleaded. "I'm the only one who can save him from hanging."

The alert black eyes searched the younger woman's face. "When you first came here, *nixa*, I was very suspicious of you. Why would a beautiful *vèhoka*, even a strange one like you who had such strong medicine, come to the Tongue River Reservation? I sensed about you an anger toward my people I couldn't understand. And then my beloved grandson, whom I hadn't seen in twenty years, appeared before me. It was as though the Great Spirit Above had dropped him from out of the blue sky to the ground in front of my lodge."

Suzette shifted her booted feet in the snow and forced herself to listen politely. To interrupt an elderly loved one was totally unacceptable to Cheyenne etiquette.

Prairie Grass Woman seemed to sense her restlessness and, stepping closer, grasped Suzette's arm. With an insistent tug, she led her across the camp circle. "Not until I saw the two of you together did I understand completely. *Maheo* sent both of you here for several reasons. First, of course, to help the People. My grandson, to remove the evil agent from our lands. And you, to work with the medicine men, earning the trust of the Cheyenne, so they will be willing to use the strange *vèho* cures for the sick and injured. But there is a second, more important reason that the two of you arrived in this land so far from your homes at exactly the same time."

The old woman stopped and looked up at Suzette.

"When my grandson arrived, his eyes were filled with a bitter loneliness. It is not the Cheyenne custom for a man to remain unmarried, so I asked him why he had never taken a wife. He pushed my questions aside with laughing remarks that told me nothing." Prairie Grass Woman raised a hand twisted with age and stroked Suzette's cold cheek. "For the past three months, *nixa*, the bitterness, the loneliness, have left my grandson's eyes. Yes, the Being Above knew exactly what He was doing when He sent you both here. For how else could either of you find the mate He had created, one for the other?"

"But War Lance says we can never marry," Suzette burst out, unable to hide her misery any longer.

The elderly woman smiled, her dark eyes lighting up with merriment. "You followed the iron path all the way out here to our Cheyenne lands. I am certain you can find your way to my grandson's home across the great water."

Suzette took Prairie Grass Woman's hands and enclosed them in her own. Bringing them to her lips, she saw the sparkle of her own teardrops on the gnarled fingers and discovered that she was crying. "Grandmother, though I live to be as old as you are now, I shall never be half so wise. Nor will I ever forget you."

"I will get a horse for you whenever you wish, *nixa*," Prairie Grass Woman said with the unruffled wisdom of the very old. "But I wanted you to wait a little while before leaving. If you came upon my grandson too soon, he'd just bring you right back and tell his brother to keep you in camp."

Suzette caught up with War Lance just a few miles outside of Lame Deer. He'd met Jacob and Anna and had stopped alongside the road to talk with them. When Suzette rode up between the two sleighs, bareback on a little painted mustang, with her wool skirt and petticoat hitched up and her calves in their red drawers exposed to plain view, War Lance didn't look the least surprised.

"It took you long enough," he said in English without a smile. But he wasn't roaring at her, either.

"You knew I was following you?"

"For the past two hours," he answered with maddening acceptance. "Why do you think I was going so slowly? I was afraid you'd get lost and end up in Billings." He nodded toward the other sleigh. "The Grabers were looking for you."

Suzette turned to the missionaries. "I'm sorry if you were worried about me," she apologized. "I didn't mean to frighten you. Lance and I took refuge from the blizzard in an abandoned trapper's cabin."

Jacob smiled his relief. "It wasn't that, Dr. Fräulein. We knew you were with War Lance and would be well taken care of. It's Horace Corby we're worried about. He's got men out looking for both of you. Lance will be hauled off to jail in Miles City, if they don't kill him outright when they find him. You're going to be taken into custody and forcibly removed from the reservation."

"Corby can't do that!" she cried. "I have to stay here and testify on Lance's behalf. The agent can't make me leave."

"Ja, he can, *Liebling,"* Anna said with sympathy. "He wrote to Washington last month accusing you of consorting with the Cheyenne medicine men. He charged you with witchcraft and all sorts of heathen abominations. It was a good excuse to get rid of you. Your contract as agency physician has been revoked by the commissioner of Indian Affairs. Corby showed the letter to us this morning."

"Mama and I are going out to Bear Scalp's camp," Jacob interjected. "We were packed and all ready to start the train journey to Indian Territory once we knew you were safe, Dr. Fräulein. Then the bodies of three cowboys were discovered this morning. For the past two days, Corby's been whipping up the fears of all the white folks for miles around. There are ranchers from as far away as Sheridan scouring the reservation. We hope to prevent any bloodshed by staying right in the village with the Cheyenne and talking to any vigilantes who might threaten them."

"I sent a message to Fort Custer," Lance said. "As soon as Colonel Hatch gets here, things will calm down." He turned to look at Suzette. "In the meantime, I want you to go with Jacob and Anna. You'll be safe with them. No one will try to hurt you while you're under their protection."

"No! If Corby finds me, I'll be on the next train leaving Custer Station. I'm going to tell my side of what happened to those three hoodlums before I leave this reservation." She met his eyes with unswerving determination. "I'm coming with you."

"Go with the Grabers, Suzette."

"Are you blind?" she shouted, heedless of the two startled missionaries or the fact that the little pony had reared up in surprise. "This is me, you blockhead, the lady you helped to deliver a breech birth and save the dying mother four days ago. Not some simpering, pea-brained debutante who thinks the most important thing in life is whether she's been invited to the grand ball of the season. I don't care what the world thinks of me. All I have to do is be true to myself. And I'm sure as heck not letting a half-crazed mob hang you while I can prevent it."

He must have recognized that this time she wouldn't give in. Even if he took her off her horse and placed her bodily in the sleigh with the Grabers, she'd trail after him, on foot if she had to.

"Tie the pony to the back," he said with a jerk of his head, "and get in."

She did as ordered and was up on the seat beside him in minutes. Smothering a grin of triumph, she waved to Jacob and Anna as Lance cracked the buggy whip over the horses' heads.

"When we get to the agency," he said in quelling accents, "you're going to do exactly as I tell you. I'll have your promise on that right now. Otherwise, I'm going to dump you in the nearest snowdrift and let you walk to Lame Deer."

Chapter 25

O badiah Nash was sitting at his desk in the outer office when Lance and Suzette slipped cautiously through the front door of the agency headquarters. They'd half expected the building to be empty. All of Lame Deer had appeared deserted as they'd driven into the silent compound late that afternoon. No doubt every *vèho* was out beating the bushes for the savage redskin who'd murdered and scalped the three cowboys, and every Indian was safely hidden behind a barricade somewhere on the reservation.

The agency's chief record keeper, who'd been wiping his red beak of a nose on an oversize handkerchief, jumped to his feet in alarm the instant he saw them. They were still dressed in their heavy coats, and the snow on their boots melted into puddles on the floor around them. His protuberant eyes huge with fright, he stared stupefied at the water stains spreading across the pine boards. Almost imperceptibly, he reached for the top drawer of his desk.

"Don't," Lance warned. He pointed the long barrel of his Winchester straight at the buttons on the clerk's stained vest.

Nash froze, his eyes bugging out in horror at the terse command spoken in English by a man he'd been convinced couldn't understand a word of it. Obadiah rolled his eyes in piteous supplication to Suzette and then looked back at Lance. He nervously cleared his throat, and the large Adam's apple bobbed up and down on his scrawny neck. With a visibly shaking hand, he reached across the desktop and gingerly shut a large accounts book with the ink-stained tip of an index finger.

Lance was across the room in two long strides. Just as the lanky bookkeeper tried to shove the ledger under a pile of papers, Lance's gloved fist crashed down on top of its closed cover.

"You can't . . ." Nash sputtered indignantly as he jerked his hand quickly away.

Ignoring his protest, Lance picked up the book. "Sit down," he said.

The clerk turned white. "I didn't do nothin'," he whined, his nasal voice cracking in fear. "Honest, I just work here." He turned to Suzette. "Dr. Stanwood," he implored, "you gotta believe me." When there was no response from her either, he slumped down into his chair.

"Get the rope from the back of the sleigh, angel," Lance said. At his words, she turned and flew out the door.

She was back in minutes, and Lance carefully laid his long rifle on the top of the paper-littered desk. After removing his leather gloves, he tied Nash to the spindle-backed chair and stuffed the soiled hankie into his mouth, then lifted the ledger and turned the pages.

"I'll be damned," he cursed softly under his breath.

"What is it?" Suzette asked, tugging off her gloves and trying to peek over his shoulder.

Lance flashed her a lopsided grin. "The answer to the riddle, angel. I knew Corby was rustling part of the beef that was driven onto the reservation twice a month for the government allotments. What I couldn't figure out was how he covered up the stolen cattle in the figures he reported to the Indian Bureau."

"Well? How did he?"

He turned the book so she could read the names listed

down the yellow page in Obadiah's loose-jointed script. Lance pointed to two of them. "Recognize those?"

She shook her head, mystified. "Wild Boar and Owl Crooked Beak? Who are they?"

"My brothers."

"Gracious, I didn't know you had any brothers alive except Bear Scalp."

His answer was as cold as a week-old corpse on a dissecting table. "I don't. Those are my two older half brothers who were killed on the journey north from Indian Territory four years ago. They never even reached the Tongue River, let alone applied for their shares of the government allotments."

Lance turned and studied Nash with narrowed eyes. The clerk looked as if he were about to faint from terror.

"If Corby's been collecting your brother's allotments of beef all this time," she said with sudden comprehension, "then there's probably other false names listed in this book as well. Names of people who are already dead."

"Plus the monies allotted them for purchasing the monthly rations of sugar, coffee, bacon, cloth—you name it. All those extra funds were earmarked and shuffled aside by Nash before they even reached the agency."

"But you looked at the records before," she said. She scowled in puzzlement. "The night I found you in Corby's office, you'd gone through his records and hadn't found a thing."

"And I should've known better," he answered with a grimace of disgust. "The plan was simple enough. They just kept two sets of books. One in Corby's office to show any government investigator who might turn up unexpectedly, and the real ledger kept by the agency's bookkeeper, who, no doubt, carted them home every night for safekeeping."

Suzette glanced once again at the gaunt, chalk-faced man tied to the wooden office chair. It was plain that

Lance had hit on the truth. Obadiah was gagging in fright.

"Under the regulations of the Indian Department," Lance explained to her, "each agent is required to take a census of his charges once a year. He certifies the rolls for the annuity payments, adding the births and subtracting the deaths. When the money is sent to him, he divides the shares among the Indians accordingly. From what I estimated of the stolen beeves, there are probably over three hundred fictitious names on this roll."

"That's right, you phony, English-talkin' Injun."

They whirled to find Corby holding a Sharps carbine leveled squarely at them.

"Shit, it was so damn easy," the stocky agent bragged. He swaggered into the room with the imperious air of a Roman emperor. "With the help of my Crow interpreter, I just collected the extra shares right under the noses of the two unsuspecting white witnesses required by regulations. Since the rolls were perfect on the face of it, it was impossible for those moron accountants in Washington to detect the fraud."

He paused and swept the Sharps's deadly barrel toward the center of the room. "Now, Big Lance, or whatever the hell your friggin' name is, if you'll just ease away from that rifle . . ."

Lance slowly edged into the center of the room, increasing the distance between himself and Suzette by a wide margin.

"All right, Dr. Slut," Corby continued, swinging the gun her way. His bald head, covered by a bearskin cap, jerked toward Nash. "Untie that idiot."

Fear numbing her reflexes, she tore her gaze from the end of the carbine's barrel to meet Lance's eyes. His quiet strength reassured her without words. When he nodded for her to follow Corby's orders, she hurried around the chair and bent over the clerk's tied hands. She struggled to loosen the tight bonds, breaking a fingernail in her clumsiness.

"Don't make the mistake of thinking you can get out of this with your hide intact," Lance warned the agent. "I was sent here to find the proof that you murdered two special agents by Commissioner Price himself. If you kill us, he'll know it was you."

Corby's pale green eyes lit up with malicious glee. "Hell, I'm not going to kill you, buck," he said. His crooked teeth flashed beneath the thick handlebar mustache. "You're going to be lynched by an unruly mob before I can save you. Unfortunately for the lady doc here, you'll have already raped and strangled her with your bare hands before we could apprehend you. Why, you're a bad Injun, plain and simple. Anything else but hangin' would be too good for you."

Lance took an automatic step forward, and the carbine, aimed directly at Suzette's heart, clicked ominously.

"No! Not the woman, you ass," Lew Rumsey shouted from the office doorway. He lunged for the Sharps, attempting to knock the barrel aside. As Corby jerked it away, he pulled the trigger, and the sound of the blast boomed through the room.

Lance hurled himself on the agent. The carbine and fur cap went flying as the two enemies crashed to the floor. Arms locked about each other, they rolled over and over, each man struggling to gain a lethal hold.

Standing behind Obadiah Nash, Suzette had been spattered with the clerk's blood and brains as the bullet entered the front of his cranium and exited the back, just missing her shoulder. Wildly she dove over the dead man, still tied upright in his chair, in a futile attempt to reach the Winchester lying on the desktop. Rumsey was there before her. His fingers curled around the steel barrel, and he yanked the rifle toward him. The butt swung up and cracked Suzette's temple, splitting it open across the hairline. The last thing she saw before pitching forward into the velvety blackness that enveloped her was the look of wretched horror on the rancher's face.

Pinning Corby to the hard floor with his shoulder,

Lance shifted his weight as his opponent sought to push upward with his beefy hand against Lance's jaw. Although a much shorter man, the agent was built with the tough resilience of an old grizzly. Lance slid to one knee, crouched, and brought his hand up to the agent's thick neck. Relentlessly he pushed his thumb against Corby's windpipe.

Already breathless, the thickset Corby gasped for air, sweat dripping across his flushed face. The insane fear in his pale green eyes belied the truth. He was no match for the well-trained athlete pitted against him, and he knew it. His only hope was for mercy. Their gazes locked, and in that split second, Lance gave Corby his answer. There'd be no pity for the bastard who'd callously allowed Blue Crane Flying to die, or backhanded Suzette so savagely.

Lance moved to his feet, dragging Corby to his knees in front of him. From behind the stocky man's back, Lance gripped his right forearm tightly against his enemy's throat. The agent grunted and wheezed, trying in panic to wrench and claw himself free. Impeded by the weight of his heavy bearskin coat, he choked, straining for air. Eyes distended in horror, Corby's thick face grew purple as the precious supply of oxygen was slowly closed off.

Muscles straining as he searched for leverage, Lance curved his free hand over the top of the bald head. His long fingers hooked Corby's smooth skull, digging into the sockets just above the eyelids. With the cold expertise of a trained assassin, Lance stepped forward, pushing his knee into his opponent's back. Corby's spine arched backward under the pressure of the excruciating pain, locked and immovable in the lethal hold. Giving a violent jerk, Lance cracked his adversary's spine with methodical precision. For a brief second, Corby hung lifeless in his executioner's embrace. Then Lance shifted his weight, nudged the corpse forward with his knee, and sent it flying, face first, on the pine boards.

Lance turned with lightning reflex to the second assailant. Rumsey waited beside the desk, his face distorted with guilt and remorse, holding the Winchester aimed at Lance. Behind the rancher, Suzette lay in a crumpled heap on the floor, covered with blood, an open wound on her head.

"Jesus, I'm sorry," Rumsey said in a bewildered voice, his craggy, weathered face furrowed with regret. He darted a quick glance at the unconscious figure huddled on the pine boards and then crept sideways around Lance toward the door. "I never meant this to happen. You gotta believe it. Christ, she grabbed for the gun. I wouldn't have hurt the woman. Not for a few lousy bucks."

Blood-chilling anguish ripped through Lance.

Nooo!

Ignoring the rifle pointed at him, he raced to her motionless form. His heart lurched to a halt inside his chest as he knelt beside her and lifted her limp body into his arms. Encased in the sealskin sleeves of her coat, her arms dangled loosely at her sides, her graceful fingers trailed in the pools of blood on the floorboards. The front of her winter coat was soaked with blood.

She was as still and peaceful as death.

Blood oozed from the wound on her head, partially hidden by her hair, and when he gently touched her angelic white face, his fingers were coated with it, all sticky and red. He reached beneath her skirt with one hand and frantically yanked on the ruffle of her petticoat, ripping it full circle along the seam. Then he held the wadded cloth to her head in a heart-searing attempt to staunch the bleeding.

At that moment, Colonel Hatch, Lieutenant Roe, and a half dozen troopers rushed into the room, their sidearms drawn. Rumsey immediately threw the rifle to the floor at the officers' feet and raised his hands in surrender.

Hatch, with a signal to his men to apprehend the prisoner, tossed back the cape of his greatcoat and holstered his pistol. He glanced at the agent's dead body sprawled in graceless defeat on the pine floor, then over to the gory corpse, with the top of its head blown away, still seated in the wooden chair behind the clerk's desk. In the midst of the carnage, Lance Harden knelt on the blood-stained floor, holding a woman's body in his arms.

"Dr. Stanwood," Lieutenant Roe cried in horror, and hurried across the room. Removing his hat, the blond officer crouched down on one knee and reached over, as though to take her from the man who held her.

"Get out," Lance gritted in a vicious undertone. When Roe hesitated, the half-breed continued, without ever taking his eyes from her pale face. "If you so much as try to touch her, soldier, I'll kill you."

"Do as he says, Lieutenant," Colonel Hatch called from the doorway. He looked around at the horrified cavalrymen, most of whom had put away their weapons and stood watching the pathetic tableaux before them in awkward silence. "Let's clear this room, soldiers. Now. We can take care of the bodies later."

When the office was emptied of the troopers and their prisoner, Hatch followed them to the door to issue further orders, then walked over to the man who knelt on the hard wooden floor, holding the lifeless woman in his arms. Harden's head was bent over her coppery curls, his black hair adorned with a cluster of primitive ornaments tied to his braided scalp lock. At the base of his bronze throat was a choker of smooth white shells. There wasn't a hint of the cultured diplomat—that brilliant, British-educated special agent the colonel had first met at Fort Custer four months ago—hidden beneath the heavy sheepskin jacket and blue Levis.

"I've sent for Dr. Gilbreath," Hatch said simply. "And the Mennonite missionary." He turned about in a small, futile circle. Clearing the huskiness of grief from his throat, he looked up at the ceiling and shook his head in a pathetic gesture of helplessness. "God, Harden, I'm sorry."

In shock, Lance stared in agony at her bloody face. Certain from the gaping bullet wound on her head and the awful amount of blood that covered the front of her coat that she was dying, Lance cradled her pitiful form against his chest and told her the things he could never have spoken otherwise. The finality of death had freed him from all need to shield her from the outside world. Held in the arms of the man who loved her more than life itself, she was safe, at last, from all cruelty, from all censure of their hopeless love.

"My beautiful, beautiful angel," he whispered into her deaf ear. "I love you so much. Don't leave me on this wretched earth without you. Don't disappear from my life like some fantastic dream of paradise. I can't face those endless years ahead, knowing I refused you, when all I had to do was reach out and take the love you offered."

Suzette concentrated on the hushed words that drifted toward her through the darkness. Struggling to regain consciousness, she tried to open her eyes, but her lids were too heavy to lift. Her head ached unbearably.

Despite the pain, she realized that Lance was talking to her, saying everything she'd always longed to hear. Joy, warm and bright and hope-filled, soared higher and higher inside her. She was like a child on a swing pumping madly toward the sun, only to be pulled back to earth each time by the inescapable law of gravity. Longing to reach out and touch him, she discovered that her arms were hanging uselessly at her sides. Or was she merely dreaming? She tried to remember what had happened, but the effort to think was too exhausting.

His warm tears spilled onto her cheeks. He held her as though he'd never let her go, rocking her back and forth, his moist face pressed against her wet, sticky one.

"I should have listened to you, sweetheart," he mourned. "You've courage enough to face anything. Even marriage to a crazy, stiff-necked, muleheaded half-breed like me."

Good Lord, it was about time he admitted it.

"But what about our daughters?" she murmured. She wasn't going to let him slip off the hook now, when all she had to do was reel him in. She may have been hit on the head, but she hadn't lost the good sense she was born with. In a supreme exercise of mind over matter, she lifted her lashes, and their softness brushed against his lean cheek.

He moved back to look at her, astonishment at her question in his black eyes. His deep voice shook with emotion. "You're the only woman, angel, who could give me daughters brave enough to face the world and thumb their little noses at it."

Her words were faint. "Then you'd marry me?"

"Yes," he said with unutterable tenderness.

"Right now?"

He nodded, tears blurring his eyes. "We've sent for Jacob Graber, darling. He can perform the ceremony as soon as he gets here."

She turned her head slightly and looked up at Colonel Hatch, who stood towering above them. "You heard him?" she asked.

Hatch swallowed noisily. "I did."

"Then I have a confession to make," she admitted.

Lance strangled a sob, knowing there was nothing she could have possibly done serious enough to require absolution before she met her Maker. "What is it, voice of my heart?"

"I'm not dying, *zehemehotaz,*" she replied. A tiny smile curled the corners of her lips. "I wasn't even shot. I'm just covered with Nash's blood. I was knocked out by the butt of the rifle when Rumsey grabbed it."

His heart stood still.

But it didn't matter. For he'd also forgotten how to breathe.

Frenziedly his gaze roved over her, searching for the truth. He explored the wound with cautious, trembling fingers. He unbuttoned her coat and eased it open carefully. Aside from the gash on her temple, which even now had begun to congeal, she was miraculously unharmed.

"You'd better have someone bring in my medical bag from the sleigh," she told him with matter-of-fact aplomb. Her eyes stared up at him with the boldness of certain victory. Those expressive violet orbs were sparkling with elation. "I'm going to need a little cleaning and bandaging before the marriage ceremony begins."

It started as a low rumble deep in his chest. Then boomed out, filling the room with great whoops of laughter, till she was bouncing on his chest with the reverberations of his happiness.

"You wicked, wicked little angel," he murmured as he bent over her once again, this time seeking her lips with his own. "My God, how I love you."

Epilogue

May 1891
Alexandria, Virginia

Monique Harden was perched atop a huge traveling trunk, her shiny patent leather sandals dangling well above the Kurdistan carpet that covered the floor of the sumptuous bedroom suite. Beside the little girl sat her elegantly dressed and meticulously coifed grandparent. Their two heads, one a mass of unruly auburn curls, the other silvery gray, were bent in fascination over a picture book.

The child, who'd been listening in rapt attention, suddenly interrupted the storytelling with all the officious solemnity of a British barrister. "She's going to fall in a hole, *niscehem.* She'll be sorry if she chases that white rabbit."

Her grandmother burst into laughter as she hugged Monique closer, and the joyful sound echoed like the musical tinkle of sleigh bells in the large room. For the past eight weeks, Lily Harden had delighted in renewing her acquaintance with her two granddaughters and meeting her young grandson for the very first time. It had been four years since she'd visited her son and his family in London, and Christopher hadn't been born till the following year. Lily squeezed the petite girl lovingly. "Yes, *nixa,* poor Alice is bound to land headfirst into

394

trouble. You know what they say: Curiosity killed the cat."

Monique rolled her blue eyes in studious contemplation, attempting to conjure up the brutal picture.

With the bittersweet realization that her family's two-month holiday had come to an end, Suzette paused at the bedroom doorway and watched the entrancing scene. The visit with Lance's mother in her stately Georgian mansion had flown by all too fast, as had the time on the farm in Lancaster with Pauline and Christian and their brood of five. Suzette had waltzed with Lance at a charity ball in Philadelphia, given to benefit the Women's and Children's Hospital, where she'd once interned. In Washington, D.C., she'd watched with pride from the gallery of the Senate as her husband addressed the Congress in a heart-stirring appeal for the just treatment of all American Indians.

Now Lance and Suzette, with their three children, would be leaving Alexandria the following day. They'd travel to New York by train, and from there would sail to Rome, spending two weeks in Paris on the way. Her husband had been appointed minister to Italy, and he'd soon be resuming the diplomatic responsibilities he had laid aside during his leave. A friend had already leased the Palazzo del Drago on the Quattro Fontane for the Harden family, and Lance had assured his wife that one of her nearest neighbors in Rome would be the king of Italy himself. With a sigh mixed equally with regret and anticipation, Suzette entered the bedroom suite, and the cozy pair on the trunk looked up at her approach.

"*Niscehem* is reading the book she gave me," Monique called to her mother. "There's a queen in Wonderland just like the queen in England. Will there be a queen where we're going?"

Pausing to set down the stack of her husband's shirts on the marble top of an ornate side table, Suzette smiled at her daughter with pride and love. The child's natural curiosity was as unbounded as her father's.

"Yes, dear heart. And a king, as well. Your father and I will meet them when we get to Rome. I promise to tell you all about them."

"Do you suppose she'll be as short and fat as the English queen?"

"Fee! Fie! Foe! Fum! Who's short and fat like an Englishman?" boomed a fearsome voice that sounded remarkably like the fabled giant who lived at the top of Jack's beanstalk. Lance entered the room with his small son riding piggyback on his shoulders and his eldest daughter dancing along at his side. Suzette's husband grinned at his family in perverted glee, as though certain he'd fooled them into believing a wicked colossus was out in the hallway just waiting to eat them up. The two younger children favored their father with ear-piercing giggles, only serving to feed his outlandish histronics still further.

"Queen Victoria's fat and short," offered the teenage girl beside him, trying unsuccessfully to keep from giggling as well. Her enormous brown eyes gleamed in merriment. "At receptions in St. James's Palace, the queen stands on a stool with the hem of her dress hanging down to the floor, trying to make herself look taller and slimmer. But everyone knows what a little butterball she really is."

"Want to see fat queen," Christopher demanded from his view at the top. The chubby three-year-old wrapped his arms tighter around his father's neck and rested his dimpled chin on the broad shoulder. The little boy had inherited Lance's raven eyes and hair, and their startlingly similar looks were now emphasized by their nearness.

Suzette tried to scowl in maternal disapproval, but the laughter bubbling up inside her refused to be smothered. "Now, Martine," she scolded halfheartedly, "you mustn't say such scandalous things about a ruling monarch out loud."

"But there's only our family in the room, *nàkohe*," the

dark-haired girl answered with a captivating smile. *"Nihoe* has always told us to ask questions at home because that's the best way to learn things."

"Mmmm, no doubt your father is right. You certainly have asked plenty of questions. You've mastered the English tongue, studied French, and speak Italian better than I do—all in a few short years."

Suzette walked over and slipped her arm around her adopted daughter's tiny waist. At fifteen, Yellow Feather was a lovely, vivacious young woman. She'd chosen her *vèho* name in honor of Suzette's father.

Peeking up at Lance from the corner of her eye, Martine grinned in pleasure at the sincere praise. "But I still think in Cheyenne, just like *nihoe,"* she bragged irrepressibly.

"Cheyenne like *nihoe,"* Christopher parroted with enthusiasm.

Lance swung the boy down. "Say hello to your grandmother, little warrior," he instructed with a pat on the child's rump, and Christopher raced across the room.

Martine followed the youngster to stand beside Lily. In her hands she carried a thin, gilt-edged volume. "Thank you for the book of poetry, *niscehem,"* she said. "I haven't started to read it yet. I want to wait till we're on the ship."

"Poetry?" Lance asked his oldest daughter as he moved to stand beside Suzette. He flashed his wife a mischievous grin. "I used to read a little poetry myself once upon a time."

Martine offered the book to her father. "It's by the Romantic poets of Great Britain," she explained. "Byron, Shelley, and Keats. Have you read any of their poems, *nihoe?"*

A smile hovering suspiciously around the corners of his mouth, Lance took the book with the air of a scholar and turned the pages. "As a matter of fact, *nàtóna,* Keats happens to be a personal favorite of mine."

Suzette's head snapped up at his audacious remark,

and she found her husband's ebony eyes leering at her wolfishly over the top of the book.

"I have a few more going-away presents for you children," Lily announced as she rose from her spot on the trunk and lifted Christopher up into her arms. "Right now might just be the time to give them to you." Carrying the littlest Harden, she led her two granddaughters out into the hall like a Pied Piper. She had the nerve to wink dramatically at her son and daughter-in-law as she left their bedroom.

Suzette could hear the three children quizzing Lily unmercifully as the noisy party descended the wide, curving staircase. She turned to her husband, who was watching her with a gaze of tender amusement. He laid the open volume of Romantic verse next to the pile of folded shirts, destined for the large trunk in the center of the room, and drew her into his strong arms.

"Well, angel, are you ready to take Rome by storm?" he teased with a devastating grin. "After conquering the stiff-lipped British aristocracy, bewitching those hot-blooded Italian nobles should be child's play."

Smiling to herself in blissful contentment, she wrapped her arms about his lean frame and laid her head against the starched front of his white shirt. His fears of bigotry and prejudice had proved to be unfounded, outside of a few instances started by churlish louts and ended by her assertive, strong-willed, and courageous husband. Six years before, Lance Harden's new bride had been accepted into the highest echelons of British society.

When he'd told her in Montana that his family was well-to-do, he'd been far too modest. She'd found the Hardens on both sides of the Atlantic enormously wealthy and politically powerful, with the added coup that his great-uncle had inherited a title at the death of a cousin, who'd passed to his reward without issue. To her astonishment, she reached England with her husband and adopted daughter to learn she was related by marriage to a duke. Added to that was Lance's diplomatic rank, which gave them an entrée anywhere.

To no surprise of her own, she'd also discovered that Lance was held in high esteem by his large group of personal friends. True, in the magnificent London ballrooms there were some faint whispers behind painted silk fans about his former mistresses—all exquisitely beautiful and voluptuously endowed, if the gossip could be believed—but she soon recognized that the jaded married women of the ton were simply covetous of Suzette's astonishingly handsome husband. She refused to give them the satisfaction of even listening to their jealous, wagging tongues. She'd spent six whirlwind years in which she'd juggled her roles as the wife of a highly admired American diplomat, a respected visiting physician on the staff of St. George Hospital in Knightsbridge, and eventually, a mother of three.

At his wife's heartfelt sigh of happiness, Lance kissed the top of her coppery curls, remembering the day he'd first met her. He'd been certain she'd disappear like some heavenly vision, should he attempt to woo her. He'd been even more positive that, if he dared to keep her beside him, she'd suffer lifelong social banishment. He'd been wrong on both counts. In Britain the wives of his closest friends had welcomed Suzette into their circle with open arms. Scarce wonder, for she possessed an intelligence that bordered on genius, an unquenchable zest for life, and a sparkling and witty sense of humor.

He'd been wrong about a lot of things, he'd discovered. The day of Monique's baptism, to which all the high-ranking officials of the British government, including the entire Foreign Office, had been invited, a white-haired and frail Lord Bancroft had quietly approached Lance after the ceremony.

"I'd like to apologize, sir," he said. Pensively the older man looked over at a radiant Suzette, her arms enfolding their precious bundle, and then met Lance's astonished gaze once again. "That should have been my granddaughter baptized today, Mr. Harden. I want you to know how badly I feel that it wasn't.

"All during her childhood, my daughter suffered periods of nervous excitability followed by bouts of severe melancholia. Cecily didn't seem to be able to handle the everyday stresses and strains of life. When I convinced her of the hopelessness of a marriage with you, I thought I was protecting her. Instead, my stupid, bungling interference cost me the life of my only child. I hope and pray that you will find it in your heart, sir, to forgive me for the pain I caused you." Bancroft reached out and solemnly offered his hand.

Lance grasped it immediately. "There's nothing to forgive, Lord Bancroft. My Cheyenne grandmother believed that my wife had been sent to me by the Great Spirit Above. I'm sure that Cecily is abiding in the presence of that All-Wise Being even now."

The older man had beamed through tear-filled eyes. "Perhaps my daughter was the one who suggested to the Almighty the very plan your wise grandmother explained to you. Anyway, I'd like to think so."

With her arms wrapped about her unusually quiet husband's waist, Suzette tipped back her head and met his faraway gaze. "Not only am I ready to go to Italy with you," she informed him huskily, "I'd travel to Timbuktu and back again, if that was where you were going."

He brushed her forehead with his lips, then turned her slightly so they could both see the pages of verse he'd left open on the table beside them. "Do you remember the day you explained those lines to me?"

"Indeed."

"At the time, I thought you were reading my mind. For despite all my efforts to the contrary, I couldn't help falling in love with you. Yet I was certain you'd disappear from my life, like some vision of paradise, the moment I reached out to take you for my own." He rested his forehead against her brow. His deep voice was filled with wonder. "To think I almost returned to London never having told you that I loved you. Never having asked you to marry me."

Suzette cupped his face in her hands, the pads of her thumbs tracing the line of his upper lip. She smiled when he kissed them and pulled her closer. "Do you really think I'd have let you go off without me? Goodness gracious, *nàhyam,* your grandmother told me what to do."

Lance looked down at her quizzically, as though wondering what Prairie Grass Woman, who'd passed away three years before, could have said to the beautiful *náevehoka* who'd fallen in love with her grandson. "She did?"

"Had you left me out there on the Tongue River Reservation, my darling husband, I would have followed you all the way to the American legation in London. I'd have buzzed around your head like a hornet." She tapped his high cheekbone, aquiline nose, and stubborn chin with the tip of one manicured fingernail. *"Zzt, zzt, zzt."* With three more gentle taps, she struck his high forehead. "And hammered at you like a redheaded woodpecker. *Tek, tek, tek.* I wouldn't have left you alone for a minute, War Lance Striking, until I'd maneuvered you into such a compromising position, you'd have had to marry me just to save your good name, not to mention your diplomatic career."

Lance's black eyes sparkled with delight. "And here I believed that I was the one who'd made the decision for us to wed. I foolishly thought I'd trapped you in my maze like some clever hunter. And you were the spellbinding enchantress all along." He bent to brush her lips with his own in blatant enticement. "While I was unaware of what was happening, you ensnared my soul in yours and filled my empty heart with love."

Suzette slipped her arms around her husband's neck. "And trapped in my embrace, and in my soul, is exactly where you're going to stay."

Author's Note

~~~~~~~~~~~~

Readers familiar with the history of the Mennonite
Church on the Tongue River Reservation will know
that the first Mennonite missionary to arrive was Rev.
Rodolphe Petter in 1899. Upon his arrival, Dr. Petter, a
trained linguist born in Switzerland, amazed the Northern
Cheyenne by speaking their language fluently. He and his
wife had worked among the Southern Cheyenne at the
mission in Cantonment, Oklahoma, for many years,
where he had developed a practical alphabet and a gram-
mar for their language. Petter's *English-Cheyenne Dictionary* remains the primary work on the language, and I
have used his spelling and diacrital markings almost exclusively.

Although Reverend Petter apparently wanted to remain
in Montana at that time, he was unable to do so due to
his wife's poor health. He did return, however, after the
death of his first wife from tuberculosis. Petter and his
second wife served at the mission in Lame Deer for the
remainder of their lives, and a Cheyenne Mennonite
community continues to worship at the Petter Memorial
Church in Lame Deer.

So forgive me for exercising the privilege of an author
of historical romance and altering the calendar to suit my
romantical fancies.

Avon Romances—
the best in exceptional authors and unforgettable novels!

THE EAGLE AND THE DOVE Jane Feather
76168-8/$4.50 US/$5.50 Can

STORM DANCERS Allison Hayes
76215-3/$4.50 US/$5.50 Can

LORD OF DESIRE Nicole Jordan
76621-3/$4.50 US/$5.50 Can

PIRATE IN MY ARMS Danelle Harmon
76675-2/$4.50 US/$5.50 Can

DEFIANT IMPOSTOR Miriam Minger
76312-5/$4.50 US/$5.50 Can

MIDNIGHT RAIDER Shelly Thacker
76293-5/$4.50 US/$5.50 Can

MOON DANCER Judith E. French
76105-X/$4.50 US/$5.50 Can

PROMISE ME FOREVER Cara Miles
76451-2/$4.50 US/$5.50 Can

Coming Soon

THE HAWK AND THE HEATHER Robin Leigh
76319-2/$4.50 US/$5.50 Can

ANGEL OF FIRE Tanya Anne Crosby
76773-2/$4.50 US/$5.50 Can

Buy these books at your local bookstore or use this coupon for ordering:
....
Mail to: Avon Books, Dept BP, Box 767, Rte 2, Dresden, TN 38225   B
Please send me the book(s) I have checked above.
I I My check or money order—no cash or CODs please—for $_____ is enclosed
(please add $1.50 to cover postage and handling for each book ordered—Canadian
residents add 7% GST).
I I Charge my VISA/MC Acct#_____ Exp Date _____
Phone No _____ Minimum credit card order is $6.00 (please add postage
and handling charge of $2.00 plus 50 cents per title after the first two books to a maximum
of six dollars—Canadian residents add 7% GST). For faster service, call 1-800-762-0779.
Residents of Tennessee, please call 1-800-633-1607. Prices and numbers are subject to
change without notice. Please allow six to eight weeks for delivery.

Name_____

Address _____

City _____ State/Zip _____

ROM 0392

America Loves Lindsey!

The Timeless Romances
of #1 Bestselling Author
Johanna Lindsey

PRISONER OF MY DESIRE 75627-7/$5.99 US/$6.99 Can
Spirited Rowena Belleme *must* produce an heir, and the magnificent Warrick deChaville is the perfect choice to sire her child—though it means imprisoning the handsome knight.

ONCE A PRINCESS 75625-0/$5.95 US/$6.95 Can
From a far off land, a bold and brazen prince came to America to claim his promised bride. But the spirited vixen spurned his affections while inflaming his royal blood with passion's fire.

GENTLE ROGUE 75302-2/$4.95 US/$5.95 Can
On the high seas, the irrepressible rake Captain James Malory is bested by a high-spirited beauty whose love of freedom and adventure rivaled his own.

WARRIOR'S WOMAN 75301-4/$4.95 US/$5.95 Can
In the year 2139, Tedra De Arr, a fearless beautiful Amazon unwittingly flies into the arms of the one man she can never hope to vanquish: the bronzed barbarian Challen Ly-San-Ter.

SAVAGE THUNDER 75300-6/$4.95 US/$5.95 Can
Feisty, flame-haired aristocrat Jocelyn Fleming's world collides with that of Colt Thunder, an impossibly handsome rebel of the American West. Together they ignite an unstoppable firestorm of frontier passion.

Buy these books at your local bookstore or use this coupon for ordering:

Mail to: Avon Books, Dept BP, Box 767, Rte 2, Dresden, TN 38225   B
Please send me the book(s) I have checked above.
☐ My check or money order—no cash or CODs please—for $_____ is enclosed
(please add $1.50 to cover postage and handling for each book ordered—Canadian residents add 7% GST).
☐ Charge my VISA/MC Acct#_____ Exp Date _____
Phone No _____ Minimum credit card order is $6.00 (please add postage and handling charge of $2.00 plus 50 cents per title after the first two books to a maximum of six dollars—Canadian residents add 7% GST). For faster service, call 1-800-762-0779. Residents of Tennessee, please call 1-800-633-1607. Prices and numbers are subject to change without notice. Please allow six to eight weeks for delivery.

Name_____

Address _____

City _____ State/Zip _____

JLA 1291

The Passion and Romance
of Bestselling Author

Laura Kinsale

THE SHADOW AND THE STAR
76131-9/$4.99 US/$5.99 Can

Wealthy, powerful and majestically handsome Samuel Gerard, master of the ancient martial arts, has sworn to love chastely...but burns with the fires of unfulfilled passion. Lovely and innocent Leda Etoile is drawn to this "shadow warrior" by a fevered yearning she could never deny.

Be Sure to Read

THE HIDDEN HEART   75008-2/$4.99 US/$5.99 Can
MIDSUMMER MOON   75398-7/$3.95 US/$4.95 Can
THE PRINCE OF MIDNIGHT
76130-0/$4.95 US/$5.95 Can
SEIZE THE FIRE   75399-5/$4.50 US/$5.50 Can
UNCERTAIN MAGIC   75140-2/$4.95 US/$5.95 Can

Buy these books at your local bookstore or use this coupon for ordering:

Mail to: Avon Books, Dept BP, Box 767, Rte 2, Dresden, TN 38225   B
Please send me the book(s) I have checked above.
  My check or money order—no cash or CODs please—for $_____ is enclosed
(please add $1.50 to cover postage and handling for each book ordered—Canadian
residents add 7% GST).
  Charge my VISA/MC Acct#_____ Exp Date_____
Phone No_____ Minimum credit card order is $6.00 (please add postage
and handling charge of $2.00 plus 50 cents per title after the first two books to a maximum
of six dollars—Canadian residents add 7% GST). For faster service, call 1-800-762-0779.
Residents of Tennessee, please call 1-800-633-1607. Prices and numbers are subject to
change without notice. Please allow six to eight weeks for delivery.

Name _____

Address _____

City _____ State/Zip _____

                                                        KNS 1191

If you enjoyed this book, take advantage of this special offer. Subscribe now and get a

FREE
Historical
Romance

No Obligation (a $4.50 value)

Each month the editors of True Value select the four *very best* novels from America's leading publishers of romantic fiction. Preview them in your home *Free* for 10 days. With the first four books you receive, we'll send you a FREE book as our introductory gift. No Obligation!

If for any reason you decide not to keep them, just return them and owe nothing. If you like them as much as we think you will, you'll pay just $4.00 each and save at *least* $.50 each off the cover price. (Your savings are *guaranteed* to be at least $2.00 each month.) There is NO postage and handling – or other hidden charges. There are no minimum number of books to buy and you may cancel at any time.

Send in the Coupon Below

To get your FREE historical romance fill out the coupon below and mail it today. As soon as we receive it we'll send you your FREE Book along with your first month's selections.

- -

Mail To: **True Value Home Subscription Services, Inc., P.O. Box 5235 120 Brighton Road, Clifton, New Jersey 07015-5235**

YES! I want to start previewing the very best historical romances being published today. Send me my FREE book along with the first month's selections. I understand that I may look them over FREE for 10 days. If I'm not absolutely delighted I may return them and owe nothing. Otherwise I will pay the low price of just $4.00 each: a total $16.00 (at least an $18.00 value) and save at least $2.00. Then each month I will receive four brand new novels to preview as soon as they are published for the same low price. I can always return a shipment and I may cancel this subscription at any time with no obligation to buy even a single book. In any event the FREE book is mine to keep regardless.

Name _____

Street Address _____ Apt. No. _____

City _____ State _____ Zip _____

Telephone _____

Signature _____
(if under 18 parent or guardian must sign)

Terms and prices subject to change. Orders subject to acceptance by True Value Home Subscription Services, Inc.

76581-0